All for a Song

All for a Song

A NOVEL

ALLISON
PITTMAN

Tyndale House Publishers, Inc.

CAROL STREAM, ILLINOIS

Visit Tyndale online at www.tyndale.com.

Visit Allison Pittman's website at www.allisonpittman.com.

TYNDALE and Tyndale's quill logo are registered trademarks of Tyndale House Publishers, Inc.

All for a Song

Designed by Ron Kaufmann

Edited by Kathryn S. Olson

Published in association with William K. Jensen Literary Agency, 119 Bampton Court, Eugene, Oregon 97404.

Unless otherwise indicated, all Scripture quotations are taken from the *Holy Bible*, King James Version.

Scripture quotations marked NLT are taken from the *Holy Bible*, New Living Translation, copyright © 1996, 2004, 2007 by Tyndale House Foundation. Used by permission of Tyndale House Publishers, Inc., Carol Stream, Illinois 60188. All rights reserved.

All for a Song is a work of fiction. Where real people, events, establishments, organizations, or locales appear, they are used fictitiously. All other elements of the novel are drawn from the author's imagination.

Library of Congress Cataloging-in-Publication Data

Pittman, Allison.
   All for a song / Allison Pittman.
     p. cm.
   ISBN 978-1-4143-6680-7 (sc)
   I. Title.
   PS3616.I885A79 2013
   813'.6—dc23   2012028214

Printed in the United States of America

19   18   17   16   15   14   13
7   6   5   4   3   2   1

For my family—
extended in number,
abundant in faith,
gifted with grace

ACKNOWLEDGMENTS

*So I decided there is nothing better than to enjoy food
and drink and to find satisfaction in work. Then I
realized that these pleasures are from the hand of God.
For who can eat or enjoy anything apart from him?*

ECCLESIASTES 2:24-25 (NLT)

What a world of stories opened when my agent, Bill Jensen, asked, "Have you ever heard of Aimee Semple McPherson?" Thank you for introducing me to this passionate woman of God, and thank you for always being an ear and a shoulder and a champion.

I feel so blessed to be a part of the Tyndale family—thank you for your support and your patience and for trusting me with your family name.

And as for my little family at home . . . you all have had to make a lot of sacrifices so that I could step through the door God opened for me. I am thankful every day for the life we share together. We see God's mercy played out minute by minute, and I marvel at his perfection in meeting all of our needs.

BREATH OF ANGELS NURSING HOME
OCTOBER 13, 2010—11:56 P.M.

Ma always called it cheating to stay up past midnight.

"Tomorrow don't come with the dawn," she'd said. "When that big hand sweeps across the top, it's past midnight. End of one day, start of the next. It's like stealing two for the price of the one God gave you."

In the dark, of course, she can't see the sweeping hands. But she hears them. Steady, rhythmic ticks coming from the same round-faced clock that once graced the big stone mantel in her parents' home. One of the only possessions she has from that place. In just a few minutes, she'll close her eyes and transport herself back there, but for now, she directs stubborn, sleepy attention to the harsh, glaring red numbers on the table next to her pillow.

11:57.

Three more minutes until this day passes into the next.

It's part of her rhythm, dozing through the evening only to wake up in time to witness the changing of the day. Or at least the first few minutes of it. Cheating not God, but death, living a little longer than anybody imagined possible. As a child, it had been a challenge, sneaking out of bed to gaze at the clock face by the waning light of the fire. These days, it's less of a game, given how few days must be left.

11:58.

A tune enters her head, filling in the spaces between the ticking of the

1

clock. The fingers of her right hand, thin and curled in upon themselves, move in listless strumming of silent strings as her left hand contorts to create chords on the neck of an invisible guitar.

I know not why God's wondrous grace to me he hath made known . . .

She hears a million voices joining in, her own, clear and strong, above them. Somewhere at the edge of hearing, a less familiar sound pierces the darkness. Tuneless, wordless. The only kind she's made since that blinding light took her voice away.

A soft knock on the door—a mere formality, really. She turns her head.

"Miss Lynnie? Everything okay in here?"

She hates that her singing could somehow be mistaken for a cry for help. So she stops and nods, bringing her fingers to stillness at her sides. She looks back at the clock.

11:59.

She hasn't missed it.

"You ought to be asleep by now."

Now soft shoes bring the even softer body of Patricia Betten, RN, to the bedside. She hears every swish of the woman's barrel-like thighs.

"Let me tuck you in, make you a little more comfortable."

She surrenders to Nurse Betten's ministrations, keeping her arms still as those pudgy, purposeful hands smooth the thin sheet and blanket. Yet another blanket is dropped over her feet, anchoring her to the bed with its warmth.

"There, there," the nurse prattles on, obviously quite pleased with her efforts. "Rest up. You've got a big day tomorrow."

12:01.

Nurse Betten's wrong.

The big day's today.

↭§ CHAPTER ONE §↩

LATE. Late. Late.

She could feel both moss and mud caught up between her toes as she ran across the soft carpet of the forest floor. With one hand she clutched her cardboard-covered journal to her heart. The other gripped the neck of the guitar slung across her back. Every few steps, the strings would brush against her swiftly moving hip and elicit an odd, disjointed chord.

It was too dark for shadows, meaning Ma would have supper on the table. Maybe even eaten and taken off again. Bad enough Dorothy Lynn hadn't been home in time to help with the fixing, but to be late to the eating—well, there was no excuse.

The dark outline of her family home stood off in the distance, soft light coming through the windows. And then through the front door, when the familiar silhouette of her mother came forth in shapely shadow.

Dorothy Lynn slowed her steps. Ma always said a lady shouldn't run unless a bear was on her tail. Now, to Dorothy Lynn's surprise, Ma actually came down off the porch and, with quick, striding steps, met her at the edge of the stone footpath that ran from the main road to their front door.

"Dorothy Lynn Dunbar, I promise you are goin' to make me into an old woman."

Even in this new darkness, Dorothy Lynn could tell that her mother was far from old—at least by all outward appearances. Her face was smooth like cream, and her hair, the color of butterscotch, absent even a single strand of gray. She wore it coiled into a swirling bun that nestled in a soft pouf.

"I'm so sorry—"

"Not that you've ever been a great deal of use in such things, but even an extra hand to peel potatoes would be nice."

"So, is he here?"

"Been here for nearly an hour. He's been entertained, looking through some of your pa's books, but he's here to have supper with you, not your mother."

"Wouldn't surprise me if he was just here for the books. They served Pa well all his years behind the pulpit."

Three wide steps led to her home's front porch. Ma hesitated at the first step and dropped her voice to a whisper. "From the way he talks about you, your pa's books are the last thing on his mind." Ma's face was bathed in light from the eight-pane glass window, her smile as sly as any fox.

Dorothy Lynn brought her face nearly nose-to-nose with her mother's. "I think you're crazy. Could be he thinks I'm just a silly girl."

"A silly, pretty girl. Or one who *would be* pretty, if her hair weren't scattered out wild as wheat stalks after a windstorm. If I didn't know better, I'd say he'd be askin' Pa for your hand most any day. Guess he'll have to settle for askin' me."

Dorothy Lynn clutched her pages tighter, willing herself to match Ma's excitement. "Well, I'd think if he was going to ask anyone, it'd be me."

Ma looked instantly intrigued. "Has he?"

Dorothy Lynn lured her closer. "There's hardly any time between the kissing."

Shocked but clearly amused, Ma turned and resumed her ascension, her old-fashioned skirts swaying with authority. At the top, she looked back over her shoulder and said, "Leave that," indicating the guitar.

Without question, Dorothy Lynn wriggled out from the strap and placed the guitar gently on the swing, knowing she'd bring it in before the night was through. Then, as her mother held the screen-covered door wide, she walked inside to take the first step on the smooth, varnished floor.

"So, has our wood sprite returned?"

Brent Logan, looking entirely too comfortable in Pa's leather chair, glanced up from the thick green tome open on his lap. *A Commentary on the Letters of Paul.* Pa's favorite.

"She has." Ma's voice was at least ten degrees cooler than the temperature outside.

Brent stood, and the minute he did so, all thoughts of Pa sidestepped behind the commanding presence of a man who seemed perfectly at ease in another's home. He had broad shoulders and thick, strong arms, testifying to a life of good, honest labor. He might have been taken for a local farm boy, but there was a softness to him too. His hair—free of any slick pomade—tufted just above his brows, which at this minute arched in amusement at her disheveled appearance. Were her mother not standing here, Dorothy Lynn knew she would be wrapped in those strong arms—swept up, maybe—and he'd kiss away each smudge. The thought of it made her blush in a way she never would if they were alone.

"Sorry I kept supper waiting," she said, rather proud of the flirtatious air she was able to give her words, despite her ragged appearance.

Ma caught her arm, turning her none too gently in the direction of her room. "Why don't you go wash up, honey-cub, while I get supper on the table?"

Any womanly charm Dorothy Lynn might have been able to muster came crashing down around her at her mother's singsong tone and that detestable nickname.

"Honestly, Ma," she said, rolling her eyes straight to Brent, who had the grace to avert his gaze. Instead, he'd wandered over to the fireplace to look at the pictures on the mantel. The largest, in the center, was her brother, Donny, looking more like a boy playing dress-up than a man in uniform, ready to go to war. On each side of Donny were wedding photos: Ma and Pa's, in which Ma—standing—was only a head or so taller than Pa, who sat tall in a straight-backed chair, and her sister Darlene's, which featured the same wedding dress worn by the bride, whose new husband stood by her side.

Those in the photographs were long gone. Darlene's husband was an automobile salesman in St. Louis, and though the battles had ended, Donny had yet to come home after the Great War. *The world is to big,* he'd once written in purposeful, albeit misspelled, block letters on the back of a New York City postcard. *I aim to see what I can.*

On the far end of the mantel, Dorothy Lynn's high school graduation photo showed her in half profile, gazing into an unknown future.

Brent took her picture off the mantel. "This was last year?"

"Two years ago," Dorothy Lynn said.

"Do you have any idea what you were thinking about?"

"Not really." But she did. The photographer had told her to

look just beyond his shoulder and to imagine her future—all the adventures life would hold for a young woman born into this new century—and she'd thought about that single road leading out of Heron's Nest, the one that took her brother and sister off to such exciting lives. Every time she looked at that photograph, she saw that road—except tonight, when she saw her future cradled in Brent Logan's hands.

"It's beautiful," he said, and though he was looking straight at the picture, Dorothy Lynn felt his words wash right over her, straight through the dirt and grime.

"Give me five minutes," she said, eager to be some semblance of that beautiful girl again.

❧

Despite the lateness of the hour, Ma showed no inclination of bringing the evening to an end, and Brent seemed even less eager to leave. The night had turned too cool to sit on the front porch, so the threesome gathered in the front room, where Dorothy Lynn placed a tray laden with dessert and coffee on the table in the center. No sooner had Brent taken a seat on the sofa than Ma stretched and let out an enormous yawn.

"Why, look at the time. Is it nearly nine o'clock already?" She handed a large serving of cobbler to Brent and one half the size to Dorothy Lynn. "Honest folks ought to be in bed by this hour."

"I don't see how time can have any kind of a hold on a person's character," Dorothy Lynn said.

"I think your mother's saying that there's a natural rhythm to life and days."

"That's right," Ma said, shooting him an unabashedly maternal gaze. "The good Lord has them numbered and allotted, and we ought to rest easy within the hours he gives. I never knew your pa to be up five minutes past ten."

At the mention of Paul Dunbar, every touch of a fork took on a deafening clamor.

"Three months ago today," Ma said, marking the anniversary of the day Pa left this world after a short battle with a vicious cancer. She returned her plate to the tray and stood.

"You're not having any, Ma?"

"Why, I don't know that I could keep my eyes open long enough to eat a bite. Not that I eat with my eyes." She laughed—rather nervously. When Dorothy Lynn took her hand, she squeezed it. "No, I think I need to trundle myself off to bed. But don't let this old lady interfere with your evening. You young folks go on and enjoy yourselves."

Ma's voice had climbed into a falsetto rarely heard outside of the Sunday choir, and while any other person might think she was trying to escape into her grief, Dorothy Lynn knew her mother better.

"She misses your father."

"True, but she has other issues on her mind, like creating an excuse to leave the two of us alone."

"Subtle."

"Like a club to the side of your head."

"Well, then . . ." Brent grinned with enough devilish appeal to shock his congregation and patted the empty sofa cushion next to him. "Seems wrong to let an opportunity like this go to waste."

"This is not an *opportunity*, Reverend Logan." She remained perched on the arm of the sofa—not quite out of his reach—and used her fork to toy with the sugary mass on her plate.

"It's delicious." He was down to one remaining bite.

"I know. I've eaten it all my life."

8

"Are you as good a cook as your ma?"

She speared a thin slice of soft, spicy apple and nibbled it before answering. "Nowhere near. But that's because Ma don't hardly let me near the stove."

"You never wanted to learn?"

"I know plenty." She held her hand out for his empty plate, dropped it along with hers on the tray, and headed for the kitchen.

He followed, as she knew he would.

Ma had left the basin full of soapy water. Dorothy Lynn scraped the uneaten portions into Ma's blue glass baking dish, then handed the empty plates to Brent, who, having rolled up his sleeves, began washing. Dorothy Lynn leaned back against the table, sipped the flavorful black coffee, and watched.

Theirs had been a proper courtship, fitting for a new, young minister and his predecessor's daughter. He'd come to Heron's Nest at the prompting of one of his professors—a lifelong friend of Pastor Dunbar who knew of the older man's illness long before any of the congregation did. Soon after Brent's arrival, he and Dorothy Lynn were sitting together at church suppers, walking the path between the church and her home, and taking long Sunday drives in his battered Ford. It was, he said, the only chance he had to drive, given the twisting, narrow roads of Heron's Nest, but she'd learned the true purpose of such outings when he parked the car in a shady grove ten miles outside of town. Nothing sinful—just some harmless necking—but enough to have set every small-town tongue on fire with gossip had anybody thought to follow them.

Now, watching him in her kitchen, some of those same feelings stirred within her, like so many blossoms set loose in a spring breeze. And yet there was an anchoring deep within, like a root growing straight through her body into the kitchen floor. She'd never known any home other than this, never seen any man in this room other than her father and her brother. Suddenly, here was Brent, looking completely at ease, like he'd been here all along. Like he'd be here forever. And the thought of both felt inexplicably frightening.

"I don't think I ever saw my pa do dishes." She hoped the introduction of her father would push away some of the thoughts that would have undoubtedly brought about his displeasure.

"He must not have lived many years as a bachelor."

"Guess not."

She drained her coffee and handed him the empty cup as the clock in the front room let out a single quarter-hour chime.

"It's late." Brent dried his hands with the tea towel draped over a thin rod beneath the sink.

"Just think, if I hadn't been so late for supper, you'd already be safe and snug in your own home."

"Well then, I'm glad. Gives us more time together."

He was leaning against the countertop with both hands in his pockets. A lock of hair had dropped below one eye. She stared down at the familiar blue-and-white-checked cloth that covered the kitchen table and worked her finger around one of the squares. "Had some extra time with my ma, too."

"I did."

The ticking of the clock carried clear into the kitchen, the silence between them thick as pudding. She felt his eyes on her but kept her own downcast, even when she knew he'd come around the table—close enough that she could feel his sleeve brush against her arm.

She looked up. "What did you talk about?" As if she didn't know, as if Ma hadn't been corralling the two of them toward each other since the first Sunday Reverend Brent Logan came before the church board last winter.

He smiled. "Ecclesiastes. I'm drafting a sermon series. Wisdom for These Wicked Times."

"Do you really think these times are wicked?"

"No more than they ever have been, I guess." He'd come closer. Had the little lamp burned like the sun, she'd be consumed in his shadow. "But your ma has some pretty clear ideas about how to avoid the pit of certain temptations."

"Does she? Well then, I'm surprised she left us here alone."

"And I, for once, am glad she did."

He hooked his finger under her chin and tilted her face for a kiss. "You know I care for you."

"I know you do."

He kissed her, long and deep—such a thing to happen right there in her mother's kitchen. The strength of it wobbled her, and she reached down to the table to steady herself. Her hand brushed against the cobbler dish as she tasted the spiced sweetness on his lips.

"I probably shouldn't take such liberties," Brent said, drawing away.

"Then you prob'ly should be headin' home."

Before either could have a change of heart, she took his hand. "We'd best go out through the kitchen door, lest Ma get a splinter in her ear from listenin' so close. I'll walk with you to the path."

He looked down. "You don't have your shoes on."

His grin broke the tension, and she lifted one foot, arranging her toes in a way that, to her, seemed provocative. "Are you scandalized?"

"Merely impressed."

He led the way, holding the door open to the damp spring

night and touching the small of her back as she walked past. Once they were off the narrow set of steps, she felt her hand encased in his. The warmth of it centered her. Together they walked around to the front of the house, her steps instinctively taking them to the worn stone path that connected their home to the main road.

"Cold?" he asked.

"A bit." She tucked herself closer to him.

"Can I ask you a question?"

There was little walking left to do, and he seemed to be slowing their pace to allow for conversation.

"Of course."

"Where were you today? What kept you so late into the evening? I mean, when you came home, you looked positively—"

"Wild?"

"For lack of a better word, I guess."

She looked up past him, to the velvet sky dotted with diamond stars. The tips of the trees looked like a bric-a-brac border.

"There's a grove in yonder." She pointed vaguely up the road. "Like a fairy clearin' in the middle of the forest. Been goin' since I was a little girl. And when I have myself a mostly empty day—" she shrugged—"I go."

"And summon the fairies?"

"No." She traced her toe along a ragged edge of stone. "I write."

"Stories?"

Nothing in his face or voice mocked her, and if whatever she felt for him was ever going to turn to pure love, it would begin at this moment.

"Not so much. More like poems, I guess. Or even prayers. Whatever the Lord brings to my mind. And sometimes I have my guitar—"

"Guitar?"

They were at the end of the path, fully stopped. Dorothy Lynn tossed a wistful glance toward the darkened porch.

"Ma hates it. Says it's not fit for a lady. It was my brother's. He left it to me when he went off to the war, so I play it. At first just to help me feel closer to him. These days, I guess, just for me. And then sometimes what I write, well, it gets to be a song."

She waited for him to protest. Or laugh. Or, worse, give her the equivalent of a pat on the head and proclaim her hobby as something delightful.

"I'd love to hear one of your songs sometime."

Dorothy Lynn let out her breath. "No one's ever asked that of me before. Fact is, I never told nobody. Sometimes in the evenin' I used to play for the family, just singin' hymns and all. But never my own songs. I don't think Pa would have taken to such vanity."

"I'm not your pa. But I wish he were here. I'd like to talk to him. As it is, I've gone to the Lord, praying for guidance, for him to show me—" He broke off and took a step back, holding Dorothy Lynn at arm's length. "Dorothy Lynn Dunbar, I've loved you since the moment I laid eyes on you. Do you remember that day?"

Even after nearly a year, she remembered it perfectly.

"You and Pa were workin' on the baptistery—"

"And you brought us a bucket lunch from home. You were wearing a white dress with a pink sash."

She remembered how Ma had practically pushed her out the door to run the errand. Always there had been this inextricable link between them—Brent under Pa's guidance, Brent the object of Ma's insistence.

"Sometimes I worry that I'll get this all mixed up," she said, "you comin' along so soon after Pa took sick. Havin' you here at night, in his chair, readin' his books. It warms me, but—"

He interrupted her with what started as a quick kiss, probably just to stop her from her rambling, but she drew him close before he could pull away. There in the night he became a man different from any she had known as he lifted her clear off her feet, weightless as the mist.

❧ CHAPTER TWO ❧

THE ENGAGEMENT was not made official until the third Sunday in May, when Brent, having patiently waited through the litany of prayer requests, announced that not only had he found a home in Heron's Nest First Christian Church, but he'd also found a bride in its midst. If gossip were to be believed, nobody was truly surprised, and they erupted into applause—something more frowned upon than not. Brent walked out from behind the pulpit and stood at the top of the aisle—the groom awaiting his bride. At Ma's subtle insistence, Dorothy Lynn joined him there, looking out into the sea of faces as familiar as her very own. Afterwards, Dorothy Lynn took her place in the front-row family pew where she'd spent nearly every Sunday of her entire life. Ma sat to her left, but the rest of the bench loomed empty, just as it had for years. For a moment, it seemed very little had changed.

Brent took his place in a high-backed chair, like a prince on a throne. Not a king, for the Heron's Nest congregation would recognize no man other than Jesus as king. As he sat, the church's eldest deacon and music leader, Rusty Keyes, came to the pulpit.

"Now if you'll join me in the reading of the psalm."

This was something Pa had started in his declining health, asking Deacon Keyes to read a psalm to make up for his own inability to preach the entire hour. Near the end, the deacon often bloviated, progressing from mere reading to something more akin to preaching. Since his ascension, Brent sometimes had to stand and clear his throat as a gentle signal that the prince was ready to take the pulpit.

As the room filled with the whispers of turning Bible pages, Dorothy Lynn felt the weight of a gaze. Brent was looking straight at her in a way that would leave any member of the congregation without a doubt of their dark-parlor antics over the past few weeks. Heat rose along the back of her neck, trapped under the weight of her hair coiled and pinned at the nape.

Ma cleared her throat and nudged her daughter's arm. Dutifully, Dorothy Lynn lifted her Bible to her lap. "Where are we?"

Ma pointed a silent finger to the top of the page of her own well-worn Bible, and with just one more glance at the prince, Dorothy Lynn quickly turned to hers.

"The Lord is the portion of mine inheritance and of my cup: thou maintainest my lot." Deacon Keyes half read, half sang the words. "The lines are fallen unto me in pleasant places; yea, I have a goodly heritage."

This morning the lines of Dorothy Lynn's lot seemed very clear. They stretched no farther than this pew, the pulpit, and the man in the high-backed chair who was to be her husband. She looked up to see Brent Logan offering yet another opportunity for a passing glance. It might be fine for the pastor to be engaged to the former pastor's daughter—after so much courting and going to her home for suppers and taking the occasional walk and such—but making lovey eyes during Deacon Keyes's reading was downright disrespectful.

She lifted her brows, sending a clear warning.

In response, Brent straightened in his chair and drew his spectacles out of his breast pocket, settling them on his face even as he settled into the Scripture.

Pleasant places.

The phrase rattled around in Dorothy Lynn's head, taking up too much space to allow any commentary to peek in.

Pleasant places. Familiar faces.

She brought her hand to her mouth, ostensibly to stifle some cough or yawn or sneeze, and mouthed the words silently, relishing the warm pop of air against her fingers.

"O church, let our hearts be glad," Deacon Keyes intoned from the pulpit.

Dorothy Lynn barely had the presence of mind to chime in with a soft amen with the rest of the congregation. She rummaged in her handbag, finally producing a stub of pencil, and found a scrap of paper within the pages of her Bible—a detailed flyer about the previous summer's Fourth of July celebration. The information on the front was useless, but the back was covered margin to margin with scribbled lines and verses. She found one empty corner and prayed for enough time to record her words before they disappeared from her mind.

My world is full of pleasant places,
Surrounded by familiar faces,
Yet sometimes I yearn for life beyond these lines.
The Lord has given me this cup,
And I'll trust him to fill it up
With the—

By now the scratching of the pencil was audible. Enough to attract Ma's attention, anyway. A victim of a sidelong glare, Dorothy Lynn folded the paper in a guilty palm and slipped it into her dress pocket. Deacon Keyes hadn't noticed; he waved his hands and kept his eyes above the heads of the congregants, delivering his lines with the pomp of a great orator. But Brent openly stared, his head cocked to one side, a curious grin granting her forgiveness for such distraction.

❧

At the end of the hour, after Brent had made his final, thoughtful point and the congregation relinquished the last note of "Jesus Is All the World to Me," the church was emptied, save for mother and daughter Dunbar, Brent, and the deacon charged with sweeping the floors. Ma had left a pot of ham and beans simmering on the stove and was laying out the rest of the Sunday menu to Brent, whose attention seemed equally divided between Mrs. Dunbar's daughter and biscuits.

"You all are free to start without me," Dorothy Lynn said. "I'll telephone Darlene."

Ma frowned and checked the watch pinned to her blouse. "Are you sure? It seems early."

"Maybe I'll be first in line." Dorothy Lynn dug around in her handbag and then her pockets, where the folded, unfinished poem called to her. "Or I'll wait if I have to. But I don't seem to have a dime."

"Here." Before she'd finished speaking, Brent had extended his hand with the shiny, oddly tiny coin resting in the middle of it.

"Thank you." She allowed his fingers to close around hers briefly in taking it. "I'll tell my sister you're paying for the call, so she'll have to be nice."

"And tell her to be sure she's drinking enough milk. Three glasses a day; that's what I did." Ma's voice was raised nearly to a holler to impart this wisdom to her disappearing daughter. The sweeping deacon reprimanded the entire group with a "Hush!" so severe Dorothy Lynn giggled all the way down the church steps.

With so many people already home from their time of worship, the streets of Heron's Nest were deserted. Not that they were ever bustling. For that matter, it was a stretch to say that Heron's Nest had streets in any conventional sense. The roads sprawled and curved and intersected one another in ways that made the town more nest-like than not. Some were even paved to better accommodate the automobiles that made their way through town every now and again. But it was obvious to anybody that the town was not the end result of any settlers' preconceptions. There had once been just a lumber mill. Then came a dry goods store, then a church, then a blacksmith, then a laundry, and on and on with dwellings of various sizes sprinkled in between. The roads were nothing more than formalized paths stretching namelessly from door to door.

Dorothy Lynn walked along such a path, humming a new tune just under her breath. Her shoes were unfashionably brown and sturdy, but they made a pleasant rhythm with her unhurried steps. Already the fresh, crisp air had revived her from the heaviness of conviction, and her mind played with the phrase "pleasant places," winding it around the images of her hometown. A candy shop with pink awnings covering the window, the younger children's school with the bright-blue door and tire swings on the trees surrounding it. The narrow, tin-roofed structure that people knew to be a saloon but were too polite to say so.

She ignored the rounded curve of the road and cut through the barber's yard to arrive at her destination—Jessup's Countertop Shop. Already there were five people queued up at the locked door. Still, Dorothy Lynn picked up her step and trotted to take her place in line.

While the town of Heron's Nest had a strict ordinance prohibiting any kind of commercial sales on the Lord's Day, an unwritten exception was made for Sunday afternoons at Jessup's. This was not a typical store. No goods lined the shelves, because there were no shelves. It was one long, narrow room with a gleaming oak countertop lining one wall and five narrow booths lining the other. Behind each booth's folding door was a single chair and a telephone. This, then, was the heart of the shop. Jessup had been the first man in Heron's Nest to have a telephone line, and though other aspiring citizens had put in their own since then, most continued to take advantage of Jessup's original generosity. One phone call, one nickel. Twice that for long distance, which most calls were. After all, why call a person when you could stand on any given porch and holler for their attention? During the week, telephone customers could also purchase a cold Coca-Cola from the icebox in the far corner or a candy bar from one of the baskets along the counter. But on Sundays the icebox remained closed, and piles of Hershey's chocolate bars remained untouched as honorable citizens waited to give far-flung loved ones their weekly conversation.

Jessup, still dressed in his Sunday suit, smiled through the window of his shop as he opened the door. He was a tall man and thin, with a long, narrow nose that ended in a bulbous lump just above his stubbled lip. Smiling, he greeted each customer with a warm "Afternoon," while standing a respectable distance from the jar on the countertop.

"Hello, Jessup." Dorothy Lynn dropped in her dime and settled back against the counter with her elbows up on the varnished wood.

"You gonna call that sister of yours?"

"Yes, sir, if she don't call me here first. It's her turn, but you never know."

"Not that I begrudge the business, but seems to me your pa should have put a telephone out at your own place, bein' the preacher and all."

"That's just it." Dorothy Lynn leaned forward and lowered her voice to guard her words from the few people gathered behind her. "Bad enough we get people on our doorstep day and night. Can you imagine if anyone could just pick up the phone and call? Pa always said he'd have to wear his waders to get through the gossip, how people are."

Jessup touched the end of his nose and winked. "Ain't easy bein' a keeper of secrets. That machine in there makes spreadin' stories easy as hot butter on bread. Not that I'm ever listenin'."

Dorothy Lynn winked too. "Of course not. By the way, I know my brother has the number here, should he ever need to call. You'd tell me if he did?"

"Child, I'd keep the line open and run for you myself."

"Thanks."

In a move so sneaky she almost missed it, Jessup slid a Clark Bar across the counter and whispered, "For the walk home."

She smiled a thanks so as not to call attention to the gift and turned her eyes toward the row of closed louvered doors. Intermittent conversation seeped through, punctuated with laughter and a few incredulous shouts. When a door finally opened, Mrs. Philbin—a middle-aged, pear-shaped woman—came out. No doubt she had spent the last ten minutes speaking with her worthless son who'd just been arrested for running moonshine in Virginia, as she kept her eyes downcast in a failing effort to hide her tears. From the corner of her eye, Dorothy Lynn noticed that Mrs. Philbin got a candy bar too.

Once inside, she pulled the door shut, sat on the narrow bench, and waited for her eyes to adjust to the dim light provided only by the two-foot space between the top of the door and the ceiling. Lifting the earpiece, she tapped the receiver and said, "Long distance, please. St. Louis," to the familiar voice of Mrs. Tully, one of Heron's Nest's three switchboard operators.

"Long distance. St. Louis," Mrs. Tully repeated. "How are you doin', Miss Dorothy Lynn?"

"Just fine." But before she could say more, the line clicked, then hummed, and another woman's voice came on.

"Number, please?"

"St. Louis, four-two-one-five."

"Four-two-one-five, connecting."

Another click, another hum, then a ring, and a young woman's voice with the inevitable sound of screaming children in the background.

"Darlene!"

What followed was a muffled sound as Roy, Darlene's slight, eager husband, received his orders to round up the boys and take them to the kitchen before Darlene's attention fully returned.

"It's early," Darlene said against a new background of only slightly fuzzy silence.

"It's past one."

"We usually talk at two. We haven't sat down to dinner here yet."

Dorothy Lynn held the candy bar to her mouth, gripped the wrapper in her teeth, and tore it open. "I couldn't wait to tell you." She spat out the scrap of wrapper. "We announced the engagement this morning."

"To the handsome young minister? He proposed three weeks ago." Darlene, as always, seemed up for a scandal.

Dorothy Lynn rolled her eyes as she took the first bite of the crispy, chocolate-covered candy. Were this any day other than a busy Sunday, Mrs. Tully would no doubt be lingering on the line.

"We wanted—I wanted—to be sure, before we made it official. First to each other, then to our families, then the church."

"And you're sure?"

"Of course."

"*Of course.*" Darlene's mimicry sounded accusatory. "Why didn't you spend the afternoon with your beau and let Ma call?" She could tell Darlene was battling between suspicion and concern.

"I wanted to talk to you."

"Why? It can't be a problem with the man himself. He's handsome as anything and tall and well-mannered. Just like Pa in every way."

Dorothy Lynn had only the blank, dark wall of the telephone booth to stare at, but she could clearly picture her older sister, plump in her third pregnancy, sitting at the ornate telephone table nestled in the nook under her stairs. Right then, she knew, both sisters were leaning in, drawing closer to the flared tube that carried their voices, as if doing so could bring them closer to each other. She took another bite of the Clark Bar and spoke through her chewing.

"Getting married to him means I'm never going to leave this town."

"Where were you planning to go?"

"I don't know. Nowhere, I guess. I just thought . . . You got to move up to St. Louis, and who knows where Donny is. He's probably been all over the world by now. And me? I get to move into that old, run-down parsonage behind the church."

"Donny's seeing the world because his britches are too big

to come home. And I'm in St. Louis because my husband is here. That's my place. I had no idea you were struck with such wanderlust."

"I'm not." For reassurance, Dorothy Lynn sat up straight and gave her head a vigorous shake. "I'm sure it's nothing more than my first case of pre-wedding jitters."

Just then the comfortable, low buzz on the line played host to a faint click, and Dorothy Lynn knew the line had been opened to a third ear.

"Enough about all this," she effused. "Ma told me to ask if you're drinking enough milk."

"Tell her I'm becoming a cow myself."

"And the boys? They still growin'?"

"RJ can climb up to the cookie jar all by himself, and Darren has peeled the wallpaper off one half of the playroom."

"And to think, there's one more on the way. And Roy? How's business?"

"Couldn't be better. He's thinkin' he'll be hiring another sales-man. Hey, maybe if that *other situation* doesn't come through, you can move up here and sell cars."

They said their good-byes, and Dorothy Lynn returned the earpiece to its cradle. The last bit of the Clark Bar was more than an average bite, but she stuffed it all in and crumpled the wrapper in her hand. A local farmer in his Sunday overalls shuffled past her, eyes down, and closed the louvered door. Jessup maintained his place at the counter and tipped an invisible hat as she left, her cheeks full of candy.

CHAPTER THREE

THE MINUTE SHE STEPPED away from what was known as "town," Dorothy Lynn slipped her shoes off in favor of the cool earth beneath her feet. She hooked the two straps over one finger, where they dangled as listless as her steps. The other hand held the unfinished verse of the poem she'd written during the church service. Boundaries and lines, fences and lots. Portions. Enough.

Tall trees encroached on the path toward home, swallowing up the town behind her. She knew the path by heart, of course, and memories called to her mind what her eyes couldn't see. The large stone around the next bend. The tree that was split in half when lightning struck it last spring. When the birth of his second child had forced Pa to move from the single-bedroom parsonage, the parishioners had tried to get him to build a house in town, but he clung to what privacy his family could have.

My lot is a tiny clearing, nestled in the pine.

For Ma, it was enough, though she'd once lived in North Carolina, where she'd actually seen a horizon where water touched the sky.

If my portion were an ocean, would I be satisfied?

Her brother certainly hadn't been. He'd crossed oceans on

ships and had even drunk wine on the streets of Paris, France. Heron's Nest would never be enough for him. The way he sounded in his infrequent letters, no place yet was worthy to be his lot. For him, the world was an endless portion of adventure. His last postcard—Christmas, before Pa died—was from Seattle. How could it be that the Lord could be so generous with Donny, dole out his life with an open hand, and squeeze her and her inheritance in one tight fist?

She was humming to herself, mind locked on the question, when Brent stepped into her path—something she realized only when she bumped into him.

"You looked like you were a million miles away," he said once she'd steadied herself.

"Nope. Just here." She tapped the side of her head. "Thinkin' about the sermon."

"It was a good one, if I dare say so myself."

"You dare."

He sounded uncharacteristically nervous. She noted the large basket in his hand.

"Your mother packed us a picnic. I thought, if it's all right with you, we could have some time together. Alone."

"Didn't we have time alone last night? Ma might get suspicious."

"It . . . um . . . was your mother's idea."

Her feet seemed rooted to the ground at that moment, though she felt the urge to fly. As a compromise, she took the free arm Brent offered and charged him to lead on.

"Actually," he said, "I was hoping you would lead me."

"To?"

"To the place you told me about. Your fairy ring."

He said it with such intimacy, such *ownership*—not of the

place, but of her, and the arm linked through hers both held her and compelled her to lead him.

"And I thought," he said, as if picking up a thread of conversation, "you could bring your guitar."

"My guitar?"

Speaking the same word right after him, Dorothy Lynn noticed the difference in their speech—almost a reversal of syllables. He must have noticed it too, because he smiled, leaned into her, and said, "Yes, your *git*-tar," in such a way as to join them together in the word.

"It's at the house," she said, giggling.

"No." He handed the basket to her and, with a mischievous air, ran ahead and stepped off the path, where he reached behind an impressive pine and produced her guitar, holding it triumphantly by the neck.

Dorothy Lynn's toes curled into the moist earth. "You set it on the ground?"

He looked stricken. "Just for a few minutes. I wanted to surprise you."

She reached and took it from him, trading the basket. "It'll warp." She ran her hand along the familiar curve of the wood. "That can ruin the sound."

"It wasn't long, I promise. I held it the whole time I waited for you. I didn't set it down until I heard you coming."

As far as she knew, the only other person who had ever even touched her guitar was Donny, and she felt a surge of protection not only for it, but for her music. Her path. Her portion. "I told you I never shared my songs with anybody."

He resumed walking, and she fell into step beside him.

"I noticed you were writing during the sermon."

"Not the sermon; the psalm. There's a difference."

He granted her that. "And I heard you humming as you came up the path. Is it a song?"

"Not yet. I have to think on it."

By the time they reached what Dorothy Lynn had come to know as *her* clearing, their conversation was equal parts laughter and words, with moments of breathlessness in between.

"If Pa had known you were such a jokester, Brent Logan, he'd never have let you set one foot behind his pulpit."

"I wish I could have heard him in his prime."

"He was so good. So powerful, like his very words were keepin' us held to our seats. I used to love it when he'd let me come up and recite a verse of Scripture, seein' all those faces. Kind of turned my stomach. . . ." Her voice trailed off, remembering.

"It's not an easy thing to do. But your father had a gift, and I like to think I have a calling. I can only hope God will equip me to be worthy of that legacy."

Dorothy Lynn leapt to restore his confidence. "Oh, Pa might have only heard you preach a few times—and he was mighty sick at that—but I heard him tell Ma more than once that he thought you were a fine preacher."

"I take that as the highest compliment."

"You ought to, since I think he concerned himself more with handin' over his flock than handin' over his daughter." Then she swung her arms wide. "We're here."

They'd stepped into a nearly perfect circle of soft, green grass under an expanse of cloudless blue sky. Large, rounded stones sat in groups of three or four, as if arranged for a formal parlor rather than a simple clearing in the Ozark Mountains.

"It does seem magical," he said, twisting his head to take it all in.

"This is my lot," Dorothy Lynn whispered. "Take your shoes off."

"Are you saying it's holy?"

"No, just inviting. God made the grass the softest carpet here. Seems a shame not to take every advantage of it."

He did. After taking the folded blanket from the top of the basket and sending it wafting to the ground, he sat right down and removed his shoes, socks, and garters and rolled the cuffs of his pants up for good measure.

Dorothy Lynn sat next to him. "Nice feet, but I don't think they'd hold up for the walk home."

"I don't mind telling you that my own mother would have been mortified at the thought that I was about to eat lunch barefoot."

"Why, Reverend Logan," she said, feigning shock, "do you intend to eat with your feet?"

"Well, I'm hungry enough."

With that, they dug in, each with a cup of Ma's ham and beans—no less flavorful for having cooled—and biscuits. There was a jar of cold tea, which they passed back and forth between them in an intimate gesture.

She grew drowsy and comfortable and warm with her belly full of Ma's familiar cooking and her ears full of Brent's deep voice. After a time, his words slowed, then stopped altogether. She propped herself up on one elbow and watched him—from a respectable foot away—lying flat on his back, arms beneath his head. His chest, so broad it seemed set to bust his buttons, rose and fell with sleep, and his face was a mask of contentment as the first faint snore passed through parted lips.

This was not a man to covet anything—right at home and content wherever his lot. Her parlor, her kitchen, her church, her lot, her life.

Slowly, she rose to her feet and moved to where she'd set her guitar on one of the tall, smooth rocks. Just as she'd done a hundred times before, she settled the curved body against her thigh and bent low over the neck. Eyes closed, something like a prayer came through, but nothing in words she'd ever recall. Her fingers found the strings and danced across them, aimlessly at first, until they found the tune that had been whispering and waiting all morning. It ran from beginning to end, finding life and breath where she strummed and pressed, and when Dorothy Lynn reached the point where she knew it had defined itself, she added her own voice. Then she opened her eyes, and though she looked out at the solid screen of blue-green needles, she saw the folded bit of paper on which she'd managed to scratch a few words. And she sang.

There is a clearing in the forest
Fine as any palace parlor.
Walls papered with the pine trees,
Lush green grass carpets the floor.
Here is my portion, here's my cup.
Here the good Lord fills me up
To overflowin'. . . .

She strummed some more, both to see if those words had found a home and to wait for the next phrasing to form itself.

"Beautiful." Brent's voice cut through the music, but she did not stop. She did, however, look up to see him still reclining, hands behind his head and a huge smile on his face.

"It's not finished. Sometimes words won't come."

"Did you mean what you said?"

Still she played. "About what?"

"About here being where the Lord fills you up."

She stopped and held the strings silent against the wood. "This place. It's like I can't think anywhere but here. And the Lord speaks to me so clearly, makes me want to speak right back to him."

"Like King David."

She smiled and softly strummed again. "Is this my lyre?"

"I reckon," he said, mimicking her accent again.

"I don't think nobody will be singing my songs a thousand years from now."

"Why not?"

"'Cause so far only one other soul has ever even heard one. Or part of one. Pa always said it ain't fittin'."

He sat up, drew his knees to him, and locked his arms around them. "I could listen to you sing every day."

"No, you can't." She played a flourishing chord, silenced it, and made a teasing face. "Because this here is *my* fairy ring, and you can only come here when I invite you."

"I don't mean here." Something in his voice drew her close, though the guitar kept her anchored to her rock. "I mean in our—" He stopped himself. "I mean in the home I'll build with you. And in our church, when you're my wife and it's truly for me to say."

Never had she imagined such a promise, but it compelled her to ask for another.

"Anything," he said, the sincerity in his eyes leaving no room for doubt.

"You have to let me get away sometimes. To myself, up here alone."

"On one condition."

She waited, silent.

"If you go off, you'll always come back."

"I might run late sometimes."

He stood and walked toward her, took the guitar from her arms, and brought her to stand. With her bare feet on the smooth stone, she stood nose-to-nose with him, and all of God's creation disappeared from view. Nothing but his eyes, clear and blue like bits of sky. She touched her hands to his broad shoulders, then held them to his face. His skin was smooth and warm, not unlike the rock beneath her, and when she kissed him, his lips brushed hers soft as a breeze.

This, she knew, would be enough.

❦

Later, in the quiet of the night, Dorothy Lynn sat next to Brent again, folded into the crook of his arm, her feet tucked up beneath her as he coaxed a gentle motion out of the ancient, creaking front porch swing.

"No turning back." She felt his words rumbling through his chest. "The banns have been read, so to speak."

"What do you mean, 'banns'?"

"It's an old marriage tradition. It's never been practiced in this country, but in England, a couple has to announce their intention to get married at least a month before the wedding. That gives people enough time to declare an impediment. To raise an objection, if they have any."

"We had a weddin' here once, and when Pa asked if there was anyone gathered who knew why the two shouldn't get married, a woman stood up in the back of the church and declared that the groom had been in her bed just the week before."

He pulled away and looked down at her. "You're making that up."

32

Dorothy Lynn crossed her heart. "And I'm thinkin' that you might be the only person in town who doesn't know the story, or who I'm talkin' about."

"Tell me."

"Never. You face them every week, knowin' them as the fine Christian couple they are. It would be sinful for me to tarnish their reputation in your eyes. Don't you tempt me into gossip."

"You're already knee-deep in gossip."

"It ain't gossip without a name. It's just a parable."

"And just what is the spiritual truth to be gleaned from this 'parable'?"

"What would you say it is?"

He'd stopped the motion of the swing but started it up again. "That depends on which woman is now part of that fine Christian couple. If he married the bride at the altar, the truth of the story is that the person we are willing to commit our lives to takes precedence over any lustful temptation."

"And if he chose the other?"

"Then I suppose we need to see that, in some cases, the heart can follow the body, and it can be a graver mistake to pledge to love and honor somebody you simply don't love at all. It makes the whole marriage a lie."

"So you're sayin' both are true, equally?"

"I suppose. So, who did he choose, this busy groom?"

Dorothy Lynn rose up to her knees beside him, turned, and took his face in her hands. "It's not fair to say he *chose*, exactly. But I tell you, he married the woman he loved."

Then she kissed him, willing to let her lips rest on the surface of his but putting forth no protest when his arms drew her close. She did not pull away until Ma's voice, carrying clear from the kitchen, asked the world at large if someone could lift down the good baking dish from the top shelf.

"A hint?"

"Hurry back," Dorothy Lynn said, peeling herself away.

When he came back, she'd restored her pulse and her hair and her dress to an unmussed state.

"So, tell me," Dorothy Lynn said, stretching herself so there'd be no room for him on the swing, lest they fall into coveting the activities good Christian morals disallowed, "what kind of objections do them people in England expect to hear?"

He looked at her quizzically.

"The banns."

"Ah." He humored her and walked to the edge of the porch, as if ready to deliver a history lesson to the critters waiting out in the dark. "All kinds of things. It could be that either the bride or groom is already legally married to somebody else in another village, or that one is not a true believer of the faith. Or maybe they're cousins, more closely related than the law allows."

"Well, I don't think we'll be havin' any of them problems." She slouched in the swing until her toe reached the porch, then set herself swinging. "You're a preacher and I'm a preacher's daughter. And I know for a fact our family don't have any relations north of St. Louis. So unless you got a wife hidin' out in Illinois waitin' for you . . ."

He turned and leaned against the railing. "The Lord brought me here. To this church and to you."

"And you plan to stay? Here? Forever?"

"As long as the church will have me."

She pondered this but dared not ask what would happen if she ever wanted a glimpse of life outside the twisted paths of Heron's Nest. To live for a time away from the scrutiny of friends and neighbors and family—all of whom had been witness to every day she'd lived since her first. As long as the church would have him, so would it have her.

"So nobody can object?" She surprised herself at speaking aloud.

"Only me. Or you."

"Then you can start on for home, Brent Logan. I think we're safe."

"Before I go," he said, not looking like he had any intention to do so, "shall we plan on a June wedding?"

She laughed out loud. Perhaps the congregation wouldn't keep him around forever after all. "June is next week, sir."

"I'm aware."

"Can you imagine the waggin' tongues if we get married a week after announcin' an engagement?" She moved away from the square of light coming from inside the house.

"People know we've been seeing each other for months."

"That don't help matters. If you're goin' to be leadin' this flock, you best learn how they think."

"July, then?"

"That's not much better. Ma will want to make a fuss, and that hardly gives any time at all to get a dress made."

"August?"

"Too hot. And Darlene will be too close to her time, so she might not be able to come."

A change came over his spirit, like he was succumbing to a slow-spreading wound. "Perhaps, then, I'll leave it to you to set the date."

Dorothy Lynn glanced inside and saw her mother making a pretense of working on some sort of needlework. A tea towel, most likely. She'd been doing a lot of that since Brent Logan began his earnest pursuit. If she concentrated, she could imagine the tip of Pa's shoe as he was stretched out in his chair reading *The Saturday Evening Post*. It had been his special respite every Sunday night. How many Sunday nights had the two of them spent in just this way? Ma with some quiet, necessary chore and Pa immersed in the rare nonbiblical text? The children had always known that Sunday nights were quiet nights. Having grown up, Dorothy Lynn realized that her parents didn't even use this time to talk to each other.

Surely, though, there'd been a time when they sat on a porch swing, chatting into the night. She tried to imagine her pa, making one excuse after another not to leave Ma standing in the doorway, or Ma, breathless after a kiss.

Her own breath, by now, was slow. Steady.

"October," she said, hopping off the swing and making her way toward him.

"October?"

"First Saturday. Or, better yet, the fourteenth, my birthday. Darlene's baby will be here, and I might even hear from my brother by then. Plus, it's so lovely here in the fall."

He started to take her in his arms but, in a move that looked for all the world like fear, drew away instead. "You think that will give you enough time?"

"To plan a wedding?"

"To reconcile whatever it is that makes you want to postpone our wedding for four months."

"Oh, Brent." She wedged herself into his embrace, pressed against him until she felt his heart. "The world turns slow here, but time goes fast. Blink and it'll be tomorrow."

"I don't want tomorrow. I want October."

"Then, my darling, blink twice."

> *I communed with mine own heart, saying, Lo, I am come*
> *to great estate, and have gotten more wisdom than all*
> *they that have been before me in Jerusalem: yea, my*
> *heart had great experience of wisdom and knowledge.*

ECCLESIASTES 1:16

BREATH OF ANGELS
OCTOBER 14, 2010—8:28 A.M.

Most days Lynnie likes to be wheeled down to the main room for breakfast. Not that the food is any different there. Cream of Wheat is Cream of Wheat— the same as she's been eating since she was a little girl. But the main room has one of those big televisions, and watching the *Today* show on it is like having Matt Lauer life-size right in the room. Oh, how she loves that man. She's watched that television show every day of its existence, clear back to when they had that monkey, but it didn't become a part of her life until Matt Lauer took his place behind the desk.

Today being her birthday, Nurse Betten comes in with one of those shiny silver balloons and a tray covered with a silver dome. She's not alone, as a choir's worth of nurses and aides and volunteers come with her. It's the largest gathering that has ever been in Lynnie's room, and it appears there are one or two heads that don't quite make it through the door.

On Nurse Betten's cue, they sing, "Happy birthday, Miss Lynn-nnee" and clap their sanitized hands when Lynnie summons the breath to blow out the three candles burning in a bran muffin.

"Sorry wo oouldn't fit tho other hundred and four on there," Nurse Betten

37

says, but she does point out where a bubbly *107* has been written with black marker on the balloon.

Apparently some bit of Lynnie's pleasure at their attention and ingenuity shines through her eyes, because Nurse Betten leans forward and places a soft, broad hand on her shoulder, a touch Lynnie feels clear through her bone. "It's gonna be a great day for you, Miss Lynnie."

One by one, the crowd disperses as pagers beep in pockets and names are called over the static-filled PA speakers. In the end, only one remains, a young girl folded up in the corner chair, gnawing a black-painted thumbnail.

Lynnie stares. *Who are you?*

The girl sits with her body facing the door, her head twisted to watch the clock high on the wall. A full minute goes by. The bran muffin remains untouched, Lynnie's eyes stay fixed, and the girl's long, thin neck never moves. The black-painted thumb is given a temporary reprieve.

Who are you?

Then an almost-imperceptible move. More like a twitch. Like she is about to turn her head before, with absolute resolution, the thumb is brought back to be punished for whatever crimes it may have committed.

You're too old for that.

Upon continued inspection, Lynnie realizes the girl is actually older than she first thought. Not a girl at all, no more so than Lynnie had been at about the same age. Eighteen, she guesses. Or maybe nineteen. It is so hard to tell these days, with the rap videos and laundry commercials getting everybody's ages all mixed up. She's seen those programs, even on *Today*, how kids are getting so violent, committing crimes once thought reserved for psychopaths and monsters.

But Lynnie is not without recourse. She presses her own thin, gnarled finger to the call button beside her bed. Minutes later, a voice cracks, "Yes?" on the other end. Lynnie maintains her silent surveillance of the girl, who jumps at the intrusion. She turns just long enough to give a quick flash of her face. Thin it is, and foxlike, with high, narrow cheekbones and narrow eyes that almost disappear behind thick, black outline. Kohl, they used to call it in the old days.

She seems ready to resume her clock staring when the callback squawks, "Sorry. We'll send someone right away."

That's when the girl bolts up from the seat only to run straight into the wall of Nurse Betten in the doorway.

"What'd you need, Miss Lyn—" Then, looking at the girl, she places her hands on her hips. "And just who are you?"

The girl doesn't hesitate. "Charlotte Hill." Her voice is as small as she is, and husky, as if it has carried her for miles and miles.

"And just what are you doing here, Miss Charlotte Hill?"

"They told me to come here."

"Who told you to come here?"

Charlotte Hill shrugs, but Nurse Betten reinforces her stance, having none of it.

The girl starts to chew her thumb again but lets it down. "The judge."

"The judge? This your community service?"

Some hesitation. "Yeah."

"Who are you supposed to report to?"

A shrug. "I just came in here cuz I saw there was a buncha people."

Nurse Betten looks at the clock on the wall, then at her watch as if to confirm the time, and sighs. "I was supposed to be off ten minutes ago. You need to go to the front desk, downstairs in the lobby, and have a talk with Mrs. Buford."

"That's where I went first, and nobody was there. Someone said come back at nine. So I came up here."

"Is it nine o'clock?"

"Almost," Charlotte says. She seems to have aged five years and gained one hundred and fifty pounds over the course of this exchange, as Nurse Betten takes the slightest step backward.

"Hm. Must be board meetin' time. All right then, Miss Charlotte Hill." She turns the girl around. "Have you introduced yourself?"

Charlotte looks straight into Lynnie's eyes for about half a second, then twists her head to look up at Nurse Betten.

"Can she hear me?"

Nurse Betten chuckles. "Oh yes, ma'am. She can hear you just fine. Understands everything that's going on. She just can't talk." She lowers her voice and brings Charlotte close to her, bending to whisper in the girl's multiple-pierced ear. "Strokes do that sometimes—pick and choose what they gonna take away. She's had three; beat them all."

Go on, tell her the rest.

"First one, just minor, she lost use of one of her hands. But the second? That one nearly took her." She looks at Lynnie, as if just realizing she's in the room. "You don't mind if I tell all this, do you?"

Lynnie waves her on with the hand God didn't take.

"Well, the second one, they lost her for a while."

"What do you mean, *lost* her?"

"She *died*." Nurse Betten mouths the last word.

"No way."

"The way she told it, she saw the light, walked right into it, saw everyone she loved waiting right there for her."

Ma, Pa, Darlene . . .

"And came right back."

"Awesome."

As if she could possibly know.

"Then that's all she could talk about. How she felt so at peace, how she couldn't wait to go back and be free of all this pain. She'd say things like, 'Please, Lord Jesus, take me today.' Didn't you, Miss Lynnie?"

Nurse Betten makes it sound like some kind of joke. How can she know the longing that pierced Lynnie's heart with every breath? Or the urgency she'd felt? She even tried to get on the *Today* show, but they hadn't returned her letters. She'd had a chance, once, to inform the world, and then . . .

"So when the third stroke came, naturally nobody thought she'd come out of it. But she did."

Most of me.

"Except her voice?" Charlotte sounds disappointed.

"It's a shame, too. I hear she used to sing every Sunday in her church

40

choir. And now—you don't mind me saying so, do you, Miss Lynnie? Her face, somewhat. She don't really smile much. You gotta watch her real close in her eyes."

Charlotte does just that, though keeping her distance.

"So," Nurse Betten says, patting the girl's shoulder, "since you have to wait around for a while, why don't you help out here? See if she needs any help with her breakfast."

"Okay," Charlotte says, slowly extricating herself from Nurse Betten's touch.

"That okay with you, Miss Lynnie?" Nurse Betten pauses for exactly three seconds before clapping her soft hands together three times. "Then I am off. You have yourself a great day today. Don't get yourself into any trouble."

Fat chance of that.

Lynnie looks at the TV.

"Want me to turn that on for you?" Charlotte finds the remote control and, after just a brief study, the power button. "Tell me when," she says, flicking through the channels.

Lynnie reaches out, surprised to see how clawlike her hand looks next to the girl's, and snatches the remote away.

"Sorry." The word is dragged through four syllables.

Soon enough she finds channel 5, NBC, the *Today* show. More than thirty minutes gone, meaning she's missed the big stories. And Matt Lauer isn't even there. She drops the remote control beside her on the bed and reaches for her breakfast tray.

Charlotte rolls it closer. "Want me to cut up that muffin for you?" Seconds later, her fingers—including that same thumb that had spent so much time in the girl's mouth—are tearing the bran muffin asunder, breaking it into bite-size pieces. "Can I try it?" She pinches a bite and brings it up to sniff, holding it just below the thin gold ring that goes through her nose, before popping it in her mouth. "It's dry."

Worst muffins in the world here.

Charlotte continues to eat, nibbling bits from her snaggled fingers. In between bites, she removes the silver dome from Lynnie's tray and peels back the plastic wrap, releasing steam from the bowl of hot cereal. "You take sugar in it?"

Lynnie tries to shake her head.

"I could never eat it that way. Just plain. My grandma makes it with brown sugar and milk." With moist crumbs still clinging to her fingers, Charlotte has unraveled the spoon from its napkin and, with something close to daintiness, dredges it through the Cream of Wheat. She holds it, suspended, just below Lynnie's chin. "Open up."

I'm not a baby, you snot.

Indeed, left to her own devices, Lynnie would be quite capable of performing all the tasks Charlotte has taken upon herself, though she's been forced to forgo sugar since those little packets became so difficult to open. Still, she opens her mouth for the familiar, bland bite.

Just as she swallows, a familiar face comes on the TV. Willard Scott, the garrulous weatherman who manages at once to be both ancient and ageless, stands with the White House lawn as a backdrop. "Happy Birthday to You" plays in the background, and then the picture of a spinning jam jar fills the screen. She knocks Charlotte's hand out of the way and leans forward. Somehow, the girl has enough wits to turn up the volume.

Every year since the first stroke, Lynnie has entered her name for the honor of being recognized for living an entire century. Or more. They used to be a rare breed, these people who lived past one hundred. But lately, Willard Scott and the Smucker's jam jar have been saluting so many men and women that it makes turning one hundred seem as common as taking a bath. Last year she even allowed Nurse Betten to e-mail the information. But never has that jar spun around to show her name, her face.

"Norm Cheswick," Mr. Scott announces, "lives in Brooklyn, New York. One hundred years old, and still a Dodgers fan."

Who cares, old fool!

And then some old woman who owes her longevity to her Saturday night beer.

But after that . . .

She might not recognize herself if not for her name written so prominently within the checkered label of the jar. They must have sent in a picture from her birthday three years ago, because she is sitting in front of an enormous slice of cake. Her mouth is open just the slightest bit, and the skin around it is slack and spotted, like it's melting from the flames of the birthday candles.

"Well, there you are," Charlotte says, just as Mr. Scott says her name. If Lynnie could be granted just one more word—*just one more chance to speak, dear Jesus*—it would be to tell Miss Charlotte Hill to shut up.

"This young lady is one hundred and seven years old. Can you believe that? And looking just as lovely as a sweet spring chicken."

Oh, Willard. Not everybody gets that kind of commentary.

"Says she spent her youth singing in the church choir. And that she's seen the light and can't wait to go back."

And that is it. Her moment over. The jar spins on to reveal a one-hundred-and-one-year-old who still walks his two poodles around the block every day.

"Sing in the church choir?" Charlotte drops the spoon back in the cooling Cream of Wheat and tears off another piece of muffin. "That's nuts."

Lynnie picks up the spoon and runs it slowly around the edge of the bowl.

"Can I tell you a secret?" Declaring the meal over, the girl moves the tray to the stand near the door and comes back to sit herself right next to Lynnie on the bed. "I lied. Earlier? I mean, I have been arrested before. And had to serve some community service. But not here, not now."

She bends down to whisper, even though they are clearly alone. Her breath smells like cinnamon.

"I came up here on my own because, unlike Mr. TV there, I know you didn't just sing in a choir. I know exactly who you are."

❧ CHAPTER FOUR ❧

DARLENE AND HER HUSBAND, Roy, lived in a modest home on the outskirts of St. Louis, though Darlene seemed determined to elevate its status. The house was painted a shade of soft powdery blue, trimmed in a deep lacquered red. Flower beds lined the cobblestone walkway to the front porch. There, two wrought-iron benches flanked a gilded screen door where Dorothy Lynn stood, listening to the sounds of screaming on the other side. The actual words were muffled, but the scene was clear—the boys had gotten into one mischief or another, and thus were the victims of Darlene's vocal admonishment.

Dorothy Lynn took what she knew would be the last peaceful breath for a while. She dropped her bag on the porch and pressed the bell but kept the guitar in its sack slung over her aching shoulder. It had been a long five-block walk from the bus stop. She cocked her head toward the door and listened as the rumpus died down. Moments later, Darlene appeared behind the filigree and swung the door wide.

"Come in, come in! You should have telephoned from the station, or I could have told Roy to bring you home."

"Little walk never hurt no one," Dorothy Lynn said. "And just look at you! Ma would say you look positively radiant."

"That's because Ma's a liar," Darlene said, ushering her into the front parlor. It was papered in a bold combination of stripes and florals—two of the seven different patterns of wallpaper to be found throughout the house.

"Won't be too much longer," Dorothy Lynn said. The last time she'd seen her sister had been at their father's funeral, and then the baby had been more of a suggestive lump—boosted by the leftover softness of its older brothers. Now Darlene carried it like a sidecar.

"Can't be soon enough. Here, let me look at you, Miss Bride-to-Be."

Dorothy Lynn braced herself for Darlene's barely masked indulgent pity.

"I can't believe you still haven't cut your hair, Dot."

"Ma says a woman's hair is her crowning beauty. Well, not Ma, but the Bible, I guess."

"Ma should recognize that we're well into the twentieth century. She herself could look much more chic. And that dress?" She clucked her tongue. "At least you're wearing shoes."

Dorothy Lynn shrank under her sister's scrutiny. Even eight months gone in ninety-degree heat, and Darlene still looked like something from a fashion plate. Her dress was some sort of sea-green foamy material that draped across her rounded stomach, banded by a silk ribbon just at her hip. Her hair was the same dark-caramel color as Dorothy Lynn's, though it shone in a bobbed cap of rippling waves just below her pierced, bejeweled ears.

Suddenly, the weight of Dorothy Lynn's dull, brown braids felt oppressive on the back of her neck, and the plain, sack-like fit of her dress had more to do with the natural fall of the fabric than the fashion of the day.

"Things aren't as fancy in Heron's Nest," Dorothy Lynn said, though even she admitted there was no excusing her scuffed brown shoes.

"Well, thank the Lord you saw fit to come here for your wedding dress, I say." Darlene cupped her red-tipped fingers around her mouth and, in a voice more suited for her mountainous home than her city dwelling, hollered for her boys to come fetch Auntie Dot's bags.

A clattering of steps followed as Darlene's sons, RJ and Darren, ran down the stairs, screaming, "Auntie Dot! Auntie Dot!" They tumbled over each other when it came to the final steps, then erupted into fisticuffs in a competition to see who would have the privilege of carrying the bags. They were six and four years old but tussled with each other as if they'd been fighting since the womb.

"Careful with this," Dorothy Lynn said, taking the guitar from her shoulder. "Hold it up. Don't let it bump along the ground."

RJ, the older of the two, took on the responsibility with a solemn nod.

"Why on earth did you bring that thing?" Darlene asked.

"It needs new strings. And rather than orderin' from the Sears and Roebuck, I thought I'd find a music store here in town, let them string it for me." Part of that was a lie, though. She simply couldn't bear the thought of being away from it for the weeklong visit their mother intended.

Darlene linked her arm through Dorothy Lynn's and began leading her down the hall. "I doubt very much you'll have time for that. The wedding's what—seven weeks away? I just got the Butterick in the mail yesterday, and . . ."

She kept on and on about the dress pattern, but Dorothy Lynn heard none of it. Her eyes went to the ceiling, where the telltale sounds of her strings indicated that the boy, indeed, was dragging her guitar on the ground. In fact, he'd bumped it all the way up the stairs.

"Are you listening to a word I say?"

"Sorry," Dorothy Lynn said, feeling like too much of a child herself to be here for a wedding gown.

Darlene sighed. "I know, I know; those boys . . . But mind that you aren't too critical, because God has a way of paying you back. Now, I said I have a snack and some lemonade waiting in the kitchen, but you'll probably want to wash up first."

Her voice hinted at a grand surprise, which turned out to be a brand-new water closet at the end of the hall.

"We just got it put in last week. Such a blessing not to have to run up and down the stairs. But look who I'm telling. Poor thing, you still have to run clear across the yard, don't you?"

"So did you all your life. Don't see that it hurt anything."

"Ah, but it is so nice to have all that behind me."

"Especially since you have *that* behind," Dorothy Lynn said, pointing at Darlene's ample seat. The comment may have been cruel, but somehow she didn't feel a spot of guilt, especially when her sister giggled right along.

Darlene went in with Dorothy Lynn just long enough to pull the chain that turned on the light and point out which hand towels should and shouldn't be used. Left alone, Dorothy Lynn ran her hands under the cool water pouring from the spigot, cupped them, and splashed her face. To think, her sister did this every day—twisted a handle and watched water flow. Hot and cold, according to the two handles. Patting her face dry, Dorothy Lynn gave a sidelong glance at the glistening commode and sighed.

In the kitchen, Darlene had prepared a tall glass pitcher of lemonade and a plate of cheese sandwiches.

"Now," Darlene said, smoothing the dress pattern on the table, "we might have to do some alterations, here with the sleeve. It might be chilly in October."

Dorothy Lynn leaned forward, chewing her sandwich and studying the line drawing of the woman modeling the dress. Her figure was as two-dimensional as the drawing—flat-chested and narrow-hipped—much like Dorothy Lynn's own. The artist's pencil had given her a cap of close-cropped curls. One arm extended gracefully, showing off the flutter of the sleeve; the other was bent, bringing a narrow finger to touch her dark, puckered lips, as if hushing herself.

"In an ivory sateen," Darlene said, running her finger over the image as if feeling the fabric. "That would give it a nice weight against the chill. And see how the sash gathers here and ties at the hip? I thought maybe a rose-colored lace, and get silk shoes dyed to match."

"That all sounds a bit fancy for a simple wedding. I don't see why I don't just wear Ma's dress."

"Because nobody rides in covered wagons anymore."

"It was good enough for you."

"I didn't have a choice," Darlene said, expressing a regret she'd managed to keep hidden all these years. "We didn't have any money, and the styles weren't so terribly different. But we've won a *war* since then. You deserve a new dress."

"Seems a waste to spend so much on something I'll never wear again."

"Oh, but of course you could wear it again. Change out the sash and the shoes. It would be perfect for any kind of smart party."

"We don't have smart parties in Heron's Nest," Dorothy Lynn said. "Things haven't changed so awful much since you left."

"Maybe you won't be in Heron's Nest forever. Your man's from a big city, right? Could be you'll end up right back there someday."

"You don't know Brent. He thinks he's found paradise itself."

"That's because you're his little bird."

Dorothy Lynn blushed. "Well, I've been happy enough there up to today. No need to think things'll change much."

Just then a whoop heralded the arrival of the boys, one chasing the other, wielding two pistols and screaming, "Bang! Bang!" as he fired bullet after bullet into his brother's back. They circled the table three times, each snatching a sandwich on the final pass.

"Those aren't for you!" Darlene leapt from her chair and gave chase, though the sandwiches had been ferreted away in the boys' mouths.

In their absence, Dorothy Lynn browsed through one of the pattern books scattered on the table. Ma had said not to worry about the money, that they'd been putting aside a little for her ever since Darlene's wedding.

"I just don't know if I can see myself in it," she said to the empty kitchen. The ride up from Heron's Nest and even these few minutes in Darlene's house made it impossible to ignore just how quickly the world was growing up without her. Who besides Brent, her mother, and every other soul she'd known all her life would see her in this dress? The day before the wedding would be just the same as the day after—and all the following. Seemed an awful lot of trouble for a bit of fabric.

When Darlene came back in, she had a triumphant smile on her face and two half-eaten sandwiches in her hand.

"Savages," she said, but her eyes conveyed a glint of humor.

The boys followed behind, significantly subdued, and climbed up to the table. Without speaking a word, Darlene placed the remnants of the recovered sandwiches on a plate in front of each boy. Slowly, as if their very appetites had been stripped away, they nibbled in silence.

Darlene plopped herself back in her chair, only mildly breathless. "You'll see, when you're a parent. It's never too late to demand obedience."

❦

Later, those words echoed in Dorothy Lynn's mind as she stood obediently, arms extended, while her sister wrapped a measuring tape around her bust and waist and hips, clucking at the minute difference between the numbers.

"You've got a flapper's figure."

"Doesn't sound like much of a compliment."

"Maybe because I'm jealous. I see them all over town here, looking so stylish, and here I look like a basket of melons in a dress."

Dorothy Lynn made a thoughtful sound and slouched, contorting her body in the way she'd seen women do on the covers of magazines. She brought an imaginary cigarette to her lips. "We don't have any flappers in Heron's Nest. I could be the first."

"I don't think your fiancé would take to such a thing." Darlene never had much of an imagination. She jabbed Dorothy Lynn's thigh. "Stand up straight. I have to measure for the length."

Since pregnancy hindered Darlene's movements, Dorothy Lynn slipped off her shoes and climbed up on a chair. Simply being here—*up* here—made everything else seem so far away. She looked down at the top of her sister's head, only half-listening to the one-sided debate over the hemline. Not once did Darlene

51

look up to ask her anything. She must have assumed Dorothy Lynn had no opinion. After all, she'd lived her whole life in the simple frocks Ma pieced together or the ready-made dresses from Sears and Roebuck that came in plain brown packages in the daily post. How could she have an opinion about something that was no more than a series of confusing-looking solid and dotted lines and diagrams spread out over the kitchen table? She had no idea what sateen was, or that lace came in the color of roses, or that she would be called upon to walk not only in shoes, but in shoes with heels.

Most of all, though, she had no opinion because it all seemed so far away. Seven weeks was forever; Heron's Nest, a world away. She closed her eyes and tried to picture Brent—not as he would look at the head of the aisle as she made her way toward him, but as he looked when he was sitting at her family's kitchen table. Or on their front porch. Or in his designated chair at the front of the church. Or when he kissed her. Or when—

"Dorothy Lynn!"

Darlene's voice cut through the fog, and she opened her eyes.

"Girl, you've gone white as a sheet. Are you feelin' all right?"

"I'm fine." But she wasn't. A cold clamminess formed a second skin over every inch of her, yet she could feel a band of burning where Darlene once again held the tape around her hips.

"So?" her sister asked, expectantly.

"So . . . what, again?"

Darlene let forth an exasperated sigh. "So, do you want to create more of a bustle effect at the back? If so, we might consider using organdy or dotted swiss instead of the sateen."

The words sounded like the gibberish of an unknown tongue.

"Whatever you think is best, I guess."

"Bustle it is. Now, organdy or dotted swiss?"

"It doesn't matter."

"Well *of course* it matters. Because otherwise, the sash . . ."

Dorothy Lynn couldn't breathe. Darlene's babble wrapped around her like a tape, constricting her lungs, her throat. It squeezed, measuring her smaller and smaller. She wanted to rise up on her toes, look for a pocket of air, but Darlene flicked a red-tipped fingernail against her ankle, forcing her down to her flat, bare feet.

That's when her knees buckled.

At the edges of the haze, she heard her sister talking, blaming the long bus ride, the heat, hunger, and the excitement of the day as Darlene caught her in her arms and brought her gently to rest on the cool linoleum floor. A clatter of sound, and two giant little boys loomed over her, one pointing a stubby gun and pow-powing her dead. If she'd had the power, she would have lifted her arms, caught the boy, and taken him in an embrace of gratitude.

Anything to be out of this misery.

❧

Dorothy Lynn spent the rest of the afternoon on one of the two narrow beds in the boys' room. The boys themselves made occasional visits, once to offer a glass of water, and other times to bring her a grubby fistful of soda crackers or a copy of *The Delineator*.

"Mama says maybe you'll find something you'd like better in there." By the way he squinched up his face and held the magazine with two fingers, it was clear he had nothing but disdain for the fashions within.

"Thank you." Dorothy Lynn took the magazine and sent him away. Though it was an issue from just the previous month, the pages were soft and worn. Several had turned-down corners, and when she opened to them, she saw notes written in her sister's pristine, feminine hand.

> *Bare shoulders? In H. N. church?*
> *Silk flowers sewn at the gathering?*
> *Ask Ma about gloves.*
> *Driving coat for honeymoon.*

She tried to see the pages through Darlene's eyes, to feel the same excitement evidenced by her sister's scribblings, but nothing came of the effort. Ma had played her part in bringing her the groom, and here Darlene was circling, ready to swoop in with the gown. Both had seemed content to win Dorothy Lynn's approval for their choices. To her surprise, a tear fell on the page, blurring the description of a winsome hat. She hadn't even known she was crying.

There was a soft knock at the door and, at her answer, it opened to reveal the narrow shoulders, long neck, and impeccably groomed head of her brother-in-law, Roy. He'd shed his suit jacket and unbuttoned his vest, but he still looked the part of a successful businessman, even as he loosened his tie.

"Hear you gave my wife a scare earlier this afternoon." His voice was deeper than one would assume upon looking at him. Darlene had mentioned that he was doing some radio announcements for his car dealership on Saturday mornings.

"I didn't mean to," Dorothy Lynn said, hastily wiping away a stray tear. Something about Roy always made her feel shy. He was slick and polished, and she'd never understood how he found his way into her family.

"It's that crazy book," he said with mock exasperation. "Dar cried every time she looked at it. What is it about you women and weddings?"

Dorothy Lynn shrugged. "It's a mystery."

"Tell you what, why don't you stay up here and rest. I'm granting you official reprieve from supper downstairs."

"Oh, I don't want to hurt Darlene's feelings."

"She's doing some of her special 'company cooking,' which means it's a recipe from a magazine that has nothing to do with how real people eat."

She giggled. "It can't be that bad."

"Cold beet soup."

The inside of her mouth went sour. "Maybe it can."

Roy started to shut the door before saying one more thing. "You're a sweet kid, Dot. Darlene's happy for you, really. It's just the baby that has her so emotional."

"I know." She wasn't even sure, exactly, what aspect of Darlene's behavior he was trying to excuse. She only knew that the back of her throat felt salty with tears, and her smile was on the verge of collapse.

"I'll tell her you're sleeping?"

The idea seemed wildly indulgent, her sleeping while a pregnant woman bustled about to make a company supper, but whatever gathering fear had gripped her as she stood on the kitchen chair earlier in the afternoon seemed determined to keep her pinned to this cot. "Thanks." She clutched the magazine as tightly as she held her tears. Once he'd shut the door, she released both.

Women and weddings. Of course.

This wedding was to be nothing like the last one. Darlene had worn their mother's dress; Dorothy Lynn's was only an idea—a sketch on newsprint, not meant for her at all. On Darlene's big day, half of the Heron's Nest church was bursting with the groom's family, who'd made the trip from St. Louis, and they'd mingled with the natives for a festive afternoon of music and dancing and tables full of food. Brent's parents were both dead. He'd have no relations coming to witness the joining of their lives. Their reception would be nothing more than a Saturday version of a run-of-the-mill after-church fellowship, giving more an excuse not to attend. Darlene had walked the aisle with their father, who had then stepped to the front of the church to perform the ceremony. Donny had been standing as a witness next to a nervous, fidgeting Roy. Neither would be there for Dorothy Lynn. Rusty Keyes would officiate, but there was no one to give her away.

Not that she'd be taken anywhere.

The tears started anew.

"Oh, Lord . . ." She wiped her face with the back of her hand, swung herself out of bed, and began to pace the room. "Forgive this foolishness."

It would be easier if she didn't love him, but it took only the thought of Brent, his strength and his warmth, to stop her in her steps. She wrapped herself in her own arms, feeling his embrace, and felt her breath once again become even and smooth.

It was Ma who first suggested they ask Darlene—chic, fashionable Darlene—to make her wedding dress. It was Brent who recognized her longing to tuck her private life to herself and get away.

"Go see your sister," he'd said one oppressive Sunday afternoon as they lay head-to-head in the forest clearing. It had become a regular custom to walk there, to get away from the prying eyes of the town and the prattling plans of her mother. "Spend some time with her, just in case she can't make it to the wedding."

"You're not worried that *I* won't make it to the wedding?"

"Should I be? Do you think you might forget?"

She'd rolled herself over, propped herself on her elbows, and looked straight down into his eyes.

"Of course not. It's my birthday. A girl never forgets her birthday. Maybe I'll have two cakes."

A piercing pain snatched her from her reverie. She lifted her bare foot to reveal a small toy soldier wielding a tiny rifle in defense. Mindless of the ruckus it might be creating downstairs, she hopped back to the bed, where she sat down to rub the throbbing instep. As she did, she realized her tears were gone, having disappeared in the midst of her memory. Pity had disguised itself as fear.

Raising her eyes to the ceiling from which model fighter planes flew in constant battle, she thanked God for the distraction.

Wincing with pain, she gingerly put a bit of weight on the veteran foot and reached for her guitar, propped against the iron footboard. She cradled it in her lap and strummed it lightly, cringing at the sound. A bouncing five-hour bus ride followed by the handling of two boisterous boys had done nothing for its tuning. She rummaged in her bag for her tuning pipe and played an A, tightening the string until the guitar and the pipe were married in tune before going to the next.

Oh, Lord, be the captor of my tears. She strummed, trying to match the chords to her prayer. *Oh, Lord, be the conqueror of my fears.*

She reached down for the magazine, flipped through, found a page near the back devoted to infants' christening gowns, and ripped it out. Then, with a grubby stub of pencil fished from underneath the bed, she scribbled in the white spaces surrounding the chubby, well-dressed infants.

Downstairs, the boys were complaining loudly about their

dinner, and it seemed no adult at the table had the power to soothe them. Her stomach rumbled behind the guitar, but the idea of joining them at the table seemed as repulsive as the menu.

Lord, be the conqueror of my fears.

She tilted her head and narrowed her eyes until the world became nothing but her words and her music. As she held still, a familiar song worked its way into both her fingers and her voice.

What have I to dread? What have I to fear?
Leaning on the everlasting arms . . .

Dorothy Lynn closed her eyes and gave in to the chorus, "Leaning . . ." only to hear a second voice in an echoing alto join hers. They'd sung together before—with Ma joining them—on rare Sunday evenings at Heron's Nest First Christian Church. She kept singing, without missing a note, but turned her head to where her sister's unmistakable form had entered the darkening room.

"Beautiful as ever," Darlene said.

"Sounds better when you're singing with me." She played on.

"Oh, I don't know about that." Darlene walked in, carrying a plate covered with a linen napkin. She was wearing an apron over her dress. "Don't worry—no beet soup." She cleared away an army of tiny tin soldiers on the desk between the beds.

"I think I killed a deserter," Dorothy Lynn said. "Or he killed me."

"Sorry. With children you have to learn to look down when you walk—not that I can see my feet." She spoke with lightness, but when she turned around, Dorothy Lynn noticed for the first time a hint of pure exhaustion on her sister's face. She might have been quick to blame the light for the cast of her complexion, but the way she brought her hands around to brace her back announced fatigue beyond measure. She plopped herself on the opposite bed and kicked the shoes off her swollen feet before taking a large gulp of what was left of the water the boys had brought up earlier. "You know, when you play, you sound just like Donny."

Dorothy Lynn played a few more chords, bringing the song to a conclusion. "I can barely remember."

"You were young, always out in the woods, scribblin' in that notebook."

Dorothy Lynn smiled at the laziness that had returned to her sister's speech. "I'll bet Pa would've let him play in church. And lead the singin', too."

"He never let you? Play, I mean. Of course you couldn't lead."

"Just for the children—spring and summer Sunday school, outside in the yard. Brent's the same, but he says once we're married and he can have proper say, he'll let me sing on Sunday mornings. I wish Pa could've heard me." She truly hadn't intended the last statement to carry so much resentment.

"It's a woman's place, Dot. Where her father says, then her husband."

"Our father told you to stay put in Heron's Nest."

"But then I fell in love with a traveling salesman from St. Louis."

"Were you scared?"

Darlene moved over to sit beside her. Dorothy Lynn set the guitar on the floor and leaned into her sister's comforting embrace.

"Is that what happened earlier?" Darlene asked. "You felt scared? There's nothing to be frightened of, Dot. Mother says Brent is a wonderful man, and I know he'll take good care of you."

"That's not it." Everything Dorothy Lynn longed to say sat in a jumbled pile in the pit of her stomach.

"Is it . . ." Darlene hesitated. "Is it the wedding night? Because—"

"No!" Dorothy Lynn interrupted, sparing her sister the embarrassment. She and Brent had shared enough kisses and passionate embraces to leave her more eager than anxious to experience more.

Darlene pulled away. "Then what is it? You do love him, don't you?"

"Yes." It was the first time anybody had asked her that question. "It just seems, sometimes, like it's happening too fast."

"Seven weeks is plenty of time—"

"All of it. Pa gets sick, and one night Ma brings the new pastor to dinner, and it seems the next we're engaged. And now . . . it's all decided for me. Where I'm going to live and who I'm going to be, without ever having a minute to live a life of my own."

"Pre-wedding jitters, that's all."

Of course. Hadn't she come to the same conclusion just moments ago? And here she was again, not knowing whether her fears or her faith would win out.

"I know just the thing to cheer you up. Why don't we leave Roy to take care of the boys, and you and I can go to the pictures?"

"You know Ma don't like us goin' to the movies."

"And we might not go if she was here. But she's not. And if she ever asks what we've done to entertain ourselves, we'll say we went for a walk. Which we will—to the theater."

"I don't think Brent likes them either."

"Well, you don't have to obey him . . . yet."

Dorothy Lynn felt a spark of intrigue at the thought of a rebellion, even one this small.

"C'mon, Dot. The theater's air-conditioned. And it'll give us a chance to talk more along the way."

"All right," she said, as if talked into a great sacrifice.

"Wonderful!" Darlene got up from the bed only when Dorothy Lynn herself had stood and was able to pull her up. "And don't worry. I'll loan you one of my dresses so you'll have something decent to wear."

✑ CHAPTER FIVE ❧

THEY LEFT JUST AFTER eight o'clock, after it had turned full dark. Darlene had applied fresh powder and lipstick, but it was Dorothy Lynn who felt truly transformed. Darlene had brushed and brushed Dorothy Lynn's hair, smoothing it at the crown and pinning it in loose coils all around the nape of her neck. She wore a dress of pale-green cotton jersey that felt as cool and light as water against her skin—and a hat that looked somewhat like a mixing bowl turned upside down on her head. And for her feet, the most delicate pair of shoes she'd ever worn, made of soft leather the color of oatmeal, with two thin straps crisscrossed over the top of each foot.

"Well, look at you." Darlene spoke in a reverent half whisper.

"I can't believe how comfortable the shoes are," Dorothy Lynn said. She'd fully expected to break her neck coming down the stairs.

Roy was in the front room battling an oscillating fan to read his evening paper. He barely acknowledged Darlene's good-bye, much less the kiss she blew to him.

"He don't mind?" Dorothy Lynn asked as she opened the front door.

"Goodness, no. He hates the movies, unless it's Buster Keaton."

It was a short walk to the nearest streetcar. Darlene dropped two nickels in before Dorothy Lynn could open her purse.

There was an empty seat three rows back, and Dorothy Lynn slid in first, eager to be near the open window to catch the breeze and watch the city fly by. "I think I would like the city."

"I think it would break Ma's heart if you moved away. No wonder she's so thrilled about you marrying the preacher."

"That's the way it feels," she said, softly enough that her words were carried on the wind.

The car dropped them off three blocks away from the theater, and from the way the crowd reacted, everybody on board was going to the pictures. They moved in one mass, with the sisters caught up in the wave at first, but Darlene was in no shape to keep up, and soon they'd fallen behind.

"We've plenty of time," Darlene reassured.

"Oh, I'm not worried a mite." In fact, she was glad to have the chance to take in the sights. The entire population of Heron's Nest would fit in this single stretch of street—ten times over. Her mind raced to take in all the faces bathed in the light coming from the flashing signs atop all the buildings.

"I wanted to show you something." Darlene sounded slightly winded, so Dorothy Lynn slowed her steps as her sister retrieved a postcard from her purse. "I just got it last week."

"From Donny?"

"Yes. I didn't say anything earlier because you seemed upset. And I guess he hasn't written to Ma, or you'd have mentioned it."

They stopped under a streetlight.

"Where's it from?"

"California. Culver City. It's where they make the movies."

"What happened to Seattle?"

Darlene shrugged. "Beats me. What happened to New York, or Memphis, or any of those places?"

The image on the front of the card didn't look like anything special. A wide boulevard against a bright-pink sky. Dorothy Lynn flipped to the back to read the inevitably short message.

Making seenery for movies. Good stedy work and beutiful girls. Never hot. Never cold. Tell Ma not to worry, I found heaven.

Don

She read it three times over, looking for more. "Still can't spell," she said, bathing her comment in affection.

"School never was a strength."

"When's the last time he telephoned?"

Darlene thought. "Almost a year. Before we knew Pa was as sick as he was."

"And there's no way to contact him, I guess." She handed the postcard back to Darlene, who snapped it away.

"No. But as soon as I got this, I sent a letter to general delivery telling him about the wedding. And the baby. Who knows?"

"What about Pa? You didn't tell him?"

"Bad news is better in person."

An explosion of light caught Dorothy Lynn's eye, and she looked up to see red, yellow, and orange rays bursting from a neon star. The words *New Grand Central* shone in green above a set of double doors. She was making her way to join the people pouring into them when Darlene stopped her.

"Where are you going?"

"Isn't this the theater?"

65

"Oh, that's the old one. We have a new one that just opened up last year." She pointed down the street to the corner, where a sign big enough to dwarf the Grand Central's spelled *Missouri* in enormous, white-lit, descending block letters.

"So what's happening in here?"

The sisters stepped back to read the marquee above the door. "Who's Sister Aimee?"

Darlene wrinkled her nose. "Oh, her. Aimee Semple McPherson. She's a preacher."

"*She's* a preacher?" The very idea lodged in Dorothy Lynn's mind like a foot in an ill-fitting shoe.

"Roy thinks she's insane, but I've never given her much thought at all. She came through town a few years ago, driving a car with a sign about Jesus coming soon. Striking the fear of God in people."

"Really?" The first notes of a familiar hymn, performed by what sounded like a full orchestra, drifted through the open door. "Can we go in and listen?"

Darlene grabbed her arm and compelled her toward the looming Missouri. "Not when we're half a block away from Rudolph Valentino." Her voice dropped to something warm and throaty. "Come, my sister. *The Young Rajah* awaits."

Giggling like girls, they locked arms and made their way down the street, indulging in breathless banter about the dreamy eyes of the movie's star. They stopped briefly at a street vendor's cart and purchased two chocolate bars and a small sack of licorice pieces, which Darlene stashed in her purse.

Once they reached the doors of the Missouri Theater, Dorothy Lynn was grateful for her sister's insistence. Not only did she have the opportunity to see the face of Rudolph Valentino displayed on a poster large enough to dominate the massive doorway, she also felt a blast of cold air the minute she walked inside.

"Oh my," she said, wishing she could go outside and walk in again.

"They call it Pike's Peak," Darlene said, handing over the stub of a ticket. "Isn't it marvelous?"

"It's like nothin' I've ever seen—or felt—before."

Her feet were sinking into the carpet like it was a soft, lush mud. Massive columns held up a rounded ceiling; gaping fireplaces sat cool and dark and empty in the recesses. Tall trees and leafy green plants grew under an artist's sky while young couples canoodled on round red velvet sofas.

Dorothy Lynn was sure her eyes were about as round as walnuts as she tried to take it all in.

"Just wait," Darlene said.

Another set of massive double doors, and what was left of Dorothy Lynn's breath was stolen by the icy fingers of refrigerated air.

A sea of seats.

True, she'd never actually seen a sea, but no other word would do. Thousands of them, one rolling row after another flowing down a gentle slope. The seats toward the front were dotted with people; their soft murmuring underscored the strains of the tuning orchestra. From here they seemed a world away, and before she knew it, so did Darlene. Dorothy Lynn concentrated on walking downhill in heels, ignoring for the time being the lush surroundings, focusing on her sister's rounded figure under the swaying green skirt.

Minutes later she was enveloped in black velvet, the cushion beneath her more comfortable than any chair her behind had ever known. The lush fabric caressed the backs of her bare arms, and she wondered if Brent would ever consider letting her furnish their future home in theater seats.

"I'd come here every night if I could," Darlene said. "I've sat through some of the most awful films just to get away from those boys and the heat."

"I can imagine." Dorothy Lynn could feel the sheen of sweat on the back of her neck being lifted and cooled, and she took off her hat, sighing with pleasure at the icy touch to her brow.

"Put that back on. Do you want everyone to see what a bumpkin you are?"

Dorothy Lynn felt too happy to be hurt by the words. "I don't care what they think. Besides, nobody's lookin' at me anyway."

"Well, they might." Still, Darlene took off her hat too, and fluffed her fingers through her flattened curls.

For the next few minutes they chatted—bits of news from Heron's Nest about people Darlene had long since forgotten and amusing people in St. Louis that Dorothy Lynn had never met. Intermittently, they contorted themselves in their seats to allow someone or another to pass by.

The noise grew with the crowd, and when Darlene excused herself to visit the powder room, Dorothy Lynn allowed her eyes to wander. The sea of seats had crested with waves of faces. They turned to one another in conversation or faced stoically forward, eyes trained on the empty, looming screen. Nobody looked at her. Maybe if she stood up and shouted, or engaged in some crazy antic, she might have garnered some attention, but simply sitting there quietly, she might not even be there at all. Never in all her hours of solitude in her clearing in the woods back home had she felt so alone. There among the trees of his creation, she could feel the eyes of God holding her like an embrace, his breath in the cool breeze, his voice in the silence.

Sitting here, encased in black velvet, shivering in artificial air, she felt about as far away from that place as she'd ever been.

Words built walls around her, and she couldn't imagine offering the simplest greeting to the young woman just two seats away. And yet there was no fear, no discomfort. Just fascination coupled with a bit of envy. Part of her felt guilty, as if she were betraying a first love. But this was nothing more than a peek into another world, a brief respite from mundane familiarity.

Somewhere, three chimes rang out. She twisted to look for her sister's return and offered a wide smile to the middle-aged woman sitting directly behind her. To her relief, the woman returned the gesture and asked if Dorothy Lynn was looking forward to the movie.

"Very much," she said. Before she could say more, Darlene returned.

The lights went low and the orchestra, after a beat of silence, came together in a single enthralling note. Dorothy Lynn and Darlene settled back in their seats and quietly unwrapped their chocolate.

And then she was lost. She nibbled her candy in the light of Valentino's smoldering dark eyes, following the story of the young Indian prince taken away from his family to be raised in a wealthy American family. She followed the heart of the young woman enticed away from her betrothed and got chilled when the hero experienced disturbing psychic visions of his future.

When the closing image disappeared into darkness with the final strains of music, she joined the audience in wild applause. It seemed the best way to get her heart to start beating again.

"I just can't imagine walkin' back out into the world after somethin' like that," Dorothy Lynn said. She and Darlene remained rooted in their seats while the rest of the crowd began to exit around them.

"Nothing like a bit of fantasy to make you appreciate your reality."

Darlene was attempting to get out of her seat but obviously needed a hand, so Dorothy Lynn stood and offered her arm. As they exited, everybody around them was talking about the movie—its handsome star, unsettling plot. Young men nudged their girls, promising that they were some sort of secret prince too. The isolation she'd felt before the movie disappeared as she became part of a common conversation that lasted up the long aisle and through the plush lobby. The minute they stepped through the massive doors, however, any sense of camaraderie dissipated in the blast of warm summer night air.

"The cars run until eleven," Darlene said, "so we have some time. Want ice cream? Or maybe chow mein?"

Dorothy Lynn groaned and grabbed her stomach. "Not a chance. The chocolate and licorice was enough for me."

Darlene pouted. "Fine. I should be getting home to Roy anyway."

"Does he make you swoon the way Valentino does?"

Darlene patted her pregnant belly. "I'll take Roy over Rudy any day."

Dorothy Lynn held her tongue, hoping her sister wouldn't return the question. Not that her answer would be any different—it just seemed indecent to admit to such feelings without the benefit of marriage.

When they once again passed by the New Grand Central Theater, shouts coming from the crowd inside piqued her curiosity.

"Dar—let's go inside."

"Are you kidding?" She let out a long, jaw-stretching yawn. "It's late."

"It wasn't too late for chow mein. C'mon, just for a minute?"

Darlene looked up and down the street, almost furtively, as if any of the hundreds of people milling about would give their actions a passing thought. "All right. For a minute."

Though the lobby of the New Grand Central was humble in contrast to the luxurious Missouri, it had its own elegant charm. The minute they stepped inside, a dark-suited gentleman with a sweaty brow strode directly toward them, extending his hand. "Good evening, sisters. There's still plenty of time to hear a blessing from the Lord."

Darlene clutched her purse closer, but Dorothy Lynn allowed her hand to be taken by his moist grip. "Shall we go on in?"

He swept his arms in a wide, welcoming gesture. "Absolutely. And may God bless you."

Walking into the auditorium, it was immediately clear that this theater did not boast the Pike's Peak air-conditioning of its cousin down the street. The air was thick and hot, not only because of the late summer's night, but due to the hundreds of people packed into the seats. Although not all of them were actually *in* their seats. Here and there, clumps of people were standing, arms raised and waving like a line of laundry in a gale. Where the crowd watching the movie had comported itself in cool, reserved silence save for the calm, rippling applause, the people in here were worked up into some sort of frenzy.

And at the front of it all, a vision Dorothy Lynn would never have imagined could exist.

She was tall. Or at least she *seemed* tall—from their vantage point at the back of the theater, it was hard to tell. But somehow the woman on the stage looked like she would tower over anyone who crossed her path. Her hair, cut in a stylish bob, was a cap of pale gold atop the pure white column of her dress. And though

Dorothy Lynn knew nothing of the fabric, she felt sure the dress was sateen. No other word could possibly describe its milk-like shine.

"That's her," Darlene said, as if pointing out the local disgrace.

"What's her name again?"

"Aimee Semple McPherson. Sister Aimee, they call her."

"They, who?"

"They, everybody. She's in all the papers."

Sister Aimee stood behind the microphone. Arms outstretched, she shouted, "Are you ready?"

A wave of noise erupted, following Sister Aimee as she strode from one side of the stage to the other. Dorothy Lynn felt a tug on her body with every step, coming to rest only when the woman was behind the microphone once more to repeat, "I'll say it again. Are you ready?"

An even bigger response this time, which hardly seemed possible. This time half the audience jumped to their feet. Some fell into the arms of others, weeping; others shouted and whooped in what must have been spiritual approval. Men tossed their hats into the air. At least three women fainted.

Something in Dorothy Lynn's core was dying to respond, even if she wasn't sure exactly what she was ready for.

"We need to tell them!" Sister Aimee paced all around the microphone, stopping only to speak. "From the highest mountaintop to the deepest valley! And in the depths of our lost cities."

She spoke with an unfamiliar accent and in a cadence Dorothy Lynn had never heard coming from a woman. Simultaneously thin and strong—like a wire.

"Jesus!"

One word, one name, and the wire pulled tight. The crowd echoed, "Jesus! Jesus!" Dorothy Lynn's throat filled with the sound, *Jesus!* But there at the back, standing at the elbow of her disapproving sister, she dared not even give in to a whisper.

"Are you ready for Jesus?"

A single shout splintered into a thousand voices, and Sister Aimee grew taller.

"Are you ready for Jesus?"

Oh, how they were ready.

"Are you ready to meet your Savior? Are you ready to be his bride?"

"Come on," Darlene said, grabbing her arm. "Our father would kill us twice if he saw us in here."

Had she not been compelled by her sister's strong grip, nothing would have moved Dorothy Lynn from that spot—unless it was to join those people who had spilled into the aisle, making a slow, steady pilgrimage to the stage.

Walking back into the lobby did nothing to break the spell. Her mind echoed with the question.

Are you ready?

There was some measure of relief in escaping the heat of the crowd, and Darlene moved astonishingly fast for a woman in her condition, both of which made Dorothy Lynn breathless, her mind transfixed on the echoes coming from behind the door. She trusted her body to follow her sister's steps and was startled when she found herself stopping short, her nose plowing into Darlene's soft shoulder.

She looked up to see what had brought a halt to their hasty escape and immediately understood.

The man looked like he belonged in the other theater—not in the audience watching the movie, but on the screen. He was only half a head taller than the sisters, with a slim body that perfectly fit its wrinkle-free linen suit. His dark hair rippled in a single slick wave, and his dark eyes sparkled like jet beads in firelight.

"Ladies." His hands were clasped behind his back, making not one move to hinder them, yet neither sister attempted to take a step around him. "I trust all is well?" His voice had a certain hoarseness to it, as if he'd spent the first part of the day shouting into a windstorm.

"No, it's not." Darlene positioned herself between Dorothy Lynn and the man, a measure of protection the younger sister somewhat resented.

"I know it can be an overwhelming thing," he said, opening his arms in a wide, comforting gesture, "when you think you are hearing the very voice of God—"

"We didn't hear the voice of God," Darlene said, dismissive and bossy.

He smiled. Dorothy Lynn had never seen teeth so even and white.

"You came in here for a reason. Seeking something, aren't you?"

"No," Darlene said. "Just a mild curiosity. Come on, Dot." She reinforced her grip and trotted them past, and whether it was poor maneuvering on her part or deliberate on his, Dorothy Lynn's bare arm brushed the sleeve of his suit, and she turned her head to find him staring right at her.

"I'm sorry," she said. "My sister's condition. She's real tired."

He put his hands in his pants pockets and rocked back on his heels. "Don't be afraid to listen to your own heart, sister. We'll be here tomorrow night."

❧ CHAPTER SIX ❧

THEY STOOD IN A VALLEY surrounded by mountains of fabric under the direction of Mrs. Lorick, the proprietress of the store. For more than an hour, they had been pulling bolts from the shelves, setting free rippling brooks of material to run along the cutting counter. Darlene and Mrs. Lorick seemed to think that the fate of the marriage itself rested in the drape and length of the wedding gown.

Dorothy Lynn might have been ignorant about fabrics before, but she could by now identify a crepe de chine in her sleep, blindfolded, with both hands tethered by bric-a-brac. Never had she imagined that there were so many shades of white: ivory, eggshell, ecru. But all the conversation and planning washed over her, much as the waves of fabric wafted over her ever-slumping shoulder. She felt no connection to any of it. Every interwoven thread called to mind the image of Sister Aimee, a towering voice on the stage bringing an audience of a thousand to their feet for Jesus. His bride.

And try as she might to flick the thought away, she couldn't forget the impeccable white linen suit, or the man who wore it.

"Oh, she's thinkin' about her future mister," Mrs. Lorick said.

She was a soft, plump woman with eyes the size of quarters swimming behind thick eyeglasses. Besides the measuring tape draped across her shoulders, a pair of sewing shears the length of her forearm hung in a jewel-encrusted holster at her waist, and she wore a lavender-colored pincushion like a corsage on her wrist. "You just tell me all about him, love, and then we'll know exactly how to proceed."

Then, in an unexpected move, Mrs. Lorick came to stand right in front of her, putting one chubby hand over Dorothy Lynn's heart and the other over her own, saying, "Speak of him."

Having a clear line of vision over the woman's head, Dorothy Lynn cast a desperate glance at her sister, but the look of serene acceptance promised no hope of rescue.

"She did the same thing when I needed a gown for the Chamber of Commerce New Year's Eve ball," Darlene whispered, "and it was fabulous."

"The ball or the gown?"

"Both."

"Speak of him," Mrs. Lorick insisted again.

Not knowing the length to which the woman might use her shears to encourage obedience, Dorothy Lynn licked her lips and spoke. "He—his name is Brent, Brent Logan. He's tall. . . ."

Mrs. Lorick encouraged more.

"He's twenty-five years old and a pastor. At my father's church. He went to college for it in Chicago. So he's very smart. He wears glasses when he reads. And he has a deep voice. . . ."

Mrs. Lorick pressed the heel of her hand into Dorothy Lynn's rib, backing her up into the cutting counter for support.

"Deeper," she said, her voice almost trancelike.

In the back of her mind, Dorothy Lynn heard the quivering violins from the movie the night before, as they had played during the young rajah's psychic visions. The thought of it made her giggle.

"Ah," Mrs. Lorick sighed. "He makes you laugh."

Dorothy Lynn scoured her brain trying to single out a time Brent had made her laugh, and while she couldn't recall any particular joke, she answered that yes, he did, sometimes. Often.

"And he makes you feel safe?"

She thought of his broad shoulders, his strong arms that could wrap around her twice over. "Yes."

"And you love him."

She could feel the warmth of his shirt beneath her cheek during those moments they stole away together. Perhaps there was something to Mrs. Lorick's touch, because she suddenly felt very warm, a flush rising to her cheeks at the thought of Brent's embrace. The pounding of her heart bounced off the woman's palm as it doubled its pace.

"I do."

"And when you are ready to go to him, to walk down the aisle to be joined to him, this man who makes you feel so safe and loved, this man whom you love, this man you are prepared to have at your side for the rest of your life, wouldn't you love to be wearing a headpiece trimmed with artificial-pearl-beaded lace?"

The question did nothing to jar Dorothy Lynn from her trance. "Yes," she said. Of course she would.

"I thought so." Mrs. Lorick removed her hand and turned to Darlene. "That's a dollar fifty a yard."

That got Dorothy Lynn's attention. "Oh, that's too much."

"Veils are rather old-fashioned," Darlene said in a rare moment of support.

"Perfect for an old-fashioned girl marrying a man of God," Mrs. Lorick countered.

"No," Dorothy Lynn insisted. "I'd marry Brent in this if I had to."

Here Darlene and Mrs. Lorick joined forces, clucking their tongues and shaking their heads, even though she was wearing the same fashionable green dress she'd borrowed the night before.

An hour later, they left with a large canvas sack filled with the rolled lengths of fabric, lace, and trimmings that would be transformed into a wedding dress. It was nearly noon, and the heat radiating up from the sidewalk felt like an assault.

"Let's get home," Darlene said. "The boys will be ready for lunch, and I'm sure Mrs. Mevreck next door will be ready to send them home."

"You said we could go to the music store," Dorothy Lynn protested, knowing she sounded childish. But she'd hauled her guitar on their errand run because of her sister's promise.

"Tomorrow." Darlene spoke with the experience of a seasoned negotiator. "Aren't you eager to get started on the dress?"

"Of course I am. But—" knowing her sister's unintentional selfishness, she chose another tack—"wouldn't you like to have some time to sit under the fan and prop your feet up? Ask Mrs. Mevreck to make lunch while I get this over with, and then when I get home I won't be so distracted."

She tried to use the same hypnotic pace and tone that had worked so well for Mrs. Lorick and was rewarded when Darlene's face turned to something peaceful, like she could feel the breeze already.

"That sounds nice. Do you know where you're going?"

"Just two blocks up. Roy wrote it all down for me this morning before he left."

"And you know which car to take home?"

The idea of being alone in the city should have terrified her;

instead, she felt herself swell with pride and anticipation. "Yes." She thought so, anyway.

Darlene fished in her jeweled purse and produced a few coins for carfare.

"I have money," Dorothy Lynn protested, the thought of taking from her sister infringing on her fledgling freedom.

"Just this once. If you want to get some chop suey for lunch. You should try it at least once before you go back home."

"But I wanted to try it with you."

Darlene patted her mounding stomach. "Not these days. Stuff makes me swell up like a dirigible."

They exchanged a kiss good-bye, and the next thing she knew, her sister had disappeared around the corner, though she'd disappeared in the crowded sidewalk long before that. Dorothy Lynn turned in the opposite direction and looked at the slip of paper where Roy had written the directions and address of the music store. It would be a walk, but she knew she would enjoy it.

Never had she imagined so many automobiles could try to occupy a single road, but here they were, four abreast in the street, horns honking to get other drivers' attention, echoed by shouts and pumping fists when the horns were ignored.

And people walked so fast! Men in suits wove in and out of girlfriends strolling arm in arm, leisurely taking in the displays in the myriad of store windows. Those on foot traveled twice as fast as those in cars, and if Pa were here, he'd advise those frustrated drivers to abandon their cars and walk like the good Lord intended.

When it came time to cross the street, Dorothy Lynn held up at the corner and waited until some semblance of a crowd had formed around her—not only to create a buffer from the oncoming traffic, but to give her an idea of when it was safe to venture into the street. More than once her guitar was jostled against her, though she tried to hold it as protectively as possible.

Soon she was back on Grand Avenue, where she could see the massive *Missouri* lettering, no less impressive in the daylight. The thought of its cool air almost tempted her in that direction; after all, she had more than enough money to take in a matinee. Judging from the line of people at the door, she wasn't alone in her thinking. But her destination—the Strawn Brothers Music Store—was, according to her notes, just around the corner and two doors down. With renewed spirit, she strode right past the looming Valentino poster and followed the curve of the sidewalk.

It was a modest storefront by any measure. A window lined in green velvet held a display of several stringed instruments, with a trio of violins at its center. There was no hint of a neon sign here, only simple painted letters on the glass. According to the printed sign in the corner, they repaired all instruments, sold all accessories, and gave lessons on violin, cello, and viola.

A bell rang when she opened the door, and within seconds a stocky man with a bushy moustache popped up from behind the counter. She presumed him to be one of the Strawn brothers.

"Good afternoon, miss. How can we help you today?" His accent was thick, making him pronounce *good* like *goot*, and he pronounced *we* like *vee*. Dorothy Lynn wondered just how many dozens of accents one would hear by simply stopping in at all the shops in downtown St. Louis.

This particular shop may have had a humble exterior, but inside, the walls were stained a rich mahogany meant to showcase the instruments displayed on hooks at all levels.

"I need to restring my guitar," she said, painfully aware of the lowly sack cinched just above its head.

"That there?" Strawn pointed a stubby finger, making her feel worse.

"Yes." Dorothy Lynn untied the rope, letting the burlap fall to the floor, then lifted the instrument by the neck and placed it on the counter. "It's havin' trouble holding its tune. Needs new strings."

Strawn took a pair of spectacles from his vest pocket and turned the instrument over and over.

"Martin. 1912. Fine specimen."

"It was my brother's."

"You play?"

Dorothy Lynn nodded before realizing the man was too absorbed in the guitar to see. "A little."

He strummed a few notes, wincing. "And you love this?"

"I do. At first it made me feel close to my brother, but now . . . well, it's become like a part of me. I suppose that sounds silly."

"Not silly at all. You want silly?" His tufted eyebrows inclined toward the burlap-sack puddle on the floor. "*That* is silly. It is miracle this has not become worthless kindling, carted around in such a way. You need a case."

Dorothy Lynn hung her head, wondering what he would say if he could see her running through the forest without even the burlap sack. "I guess I never thought about that."

"Well, you should." His voice was stern, and she felt a sudden pang for her father. Then, just as Pa would, he softened and said he would look in his storeroom to see if he had an extra one.

"Thank you," she said, clutching her handbag tighter. She'd come to St. Louis with three dollars and still had most of that, but a guitar case wouldn't be worth sacrificing her bus fare home.

Strawn seemed to understand. He made a *psh, psh* sound through his moustache.

"I would be happy to clear out the space for such an instrument. You go. Come back in one hour."

He turned on his heel without another word and walked through the door at the back of the shop. One hour? What was she to do for one hour? She'd imagined that she might be allowed to restring the instrument herself—something Donny would never have allowed. Still, she could tell the guitar was in fine hands, and the idea of an hour to herself with the entire city at her disposal was an unexpected treat. The bell above the door rang again as she exited, and the sounds of the street exploded in contrast to the quietness of the shop. She looked up one side of the street and down the other. Drugstores, shoe shops, bookstores, and stationers. There were signs for bakeries and watch repairs and one boutique that seemed to sell nothing but women's stockings.

Briefly, she considered what Brent would have to say about such a place. For the life of her, she couldn't picture him here, surrounded by what he would call the excess of humanity. True, he had come from a big city himself—Chicago—but he never talked about his hometown with any hint of either fondness or disdain. Only that he was meant to live a quiet country life, even if he hadn't been born to such.

"Sometimes," he'd said, "you need a good dose of what you don't want before you can know what you truly do."

She breathed deep, finding it oddly thrilling to sense no hint of nature in the air. The acrid smell of automobile fumes might not be pleasant, but as she took her first few steps toward the corner, better odors found their way to her. And then one, foreign and exotic, overpowered the others, enticing two senses at once. She found herself looking through a window with bold red letters slashing through her reflection.

Golden Bowl Chinese Restaurant.

This must be the place Darlene had wanted to visit last night after the movie. Savory, unfamiliar scents enveloped her like a cloud, their warmth enticing and welcome even in the heat of the afternoon.

Here, then, her taste of adventure.

She grasped the door and walked inside only to stand, blinking, as her eyes adjusted to the relative darkness. Slowly, the room revealed itself. Red, everywhere. The walls, the table coverings, the tassels hanging from the delicate chandelier in the middle of the ceiling. Even with a whole life lived near a kitchen, nothing sparked a memory. Her stomach gurgled both in anticipation and nerves. She'd only been in a restaurant of any kind a handful of times, and never alone.

As the room came into full focus, though, she realized she was not alone. At all. In fact, as her eyes scanned the tables, there didn't seem to be a single empty seat.

An ageless Chinese man appeared at her elbow.

"You have seat here." He gestured toward the window with a menu featuring a somber-faced younger image of himself set within an ornate red frame.

Dorothy Lynn could just barely understand the words through his accent. How odd it was to hear so many different accents in one day.

"I'd like to eat," she said, holding one hand in the shape of a bowl at her chin while scooping invisible food with the other.

"Yes, yes, miss." He gestured again, pointing toward a row of chairs lined up against the window. "Sit by window, please. Few minutes."

She looked over her shoulder, confused. Did he intend to serve her there? People all around were eating long, steaming noodles. Was she to be forced to eat without a table?

"Perhaps you'd care to join me?"

The voice was familiar, distinctive, and she felt it touch the back of her neck long after he'd stopped speaking. She turned around, and there he was—the man who'd tried to stop them from leaving the church service last night. No suit coat today, just a white shirt, with the sleeves rolled to his elbows, and suspenders, but his hair was meticulously combed and slick.

"Oh, hello." Dorothy Lynn knew the blush to her cheeks must be bringing her face to roughly the same shade as the table coverings, as she was wearing the exact same outfit as the night before. Perhaps that's how he'd recognized her.

"Please."

Before she could think, he'd taken her arm, steered her through the narrow passageway between the tables and pulled out a chair at a small table in a dark corner. In one fluid motion, he was sitting across from her.

"You'll have to forgive my bad manners," he said, after asking the ever-attentive waiter to bring a second glass of water. "A gentleman should always introduce himself before rescuing the damsel." He reached his hand across the table. "My name is Roland Lundi."

She took his hand in the spirit it was offered—shaking it like a man would, in good humor with a firm grip. "Dorothy Lynn Dunbar."

"Nice to meet you, Dorothy Lynn Dunbar. I trust you and your sister made it home safely last night?"

He remembered. "We did."

The waiter arrived with a glass of water, which he placed in front of her, giving a slight bow before leaving. She took a sip, not to calm her nerves, but because she had nothing else to say. Truth was, she didn't feel nervous at all.

Roland Lundi leaned back in his seat, his demeanor as cool as the water in the glass. "I sincerely hope I did not make the two of you feel uncomfortable as you were leaving. In our ministry we see so many people touched by the Holy Spirit, but they are affected in different ways. Some run to Sister Aimee; others run away."

"Well, I wasn't runnin' away, and I don't know who Sister Aimee is. I was just goin' home." Even in the midst of her reply, she knew she sounded rude, and she would have apologized if he had not laughed.

"You don't know what a relief it is to hear something spoken with such honest clarity."

Dorothy Lynn smiled along, assuming the remark to be a compliment. Anything Roland Lundi said would probably sound like a compliment. His words were not so much accented as smooth, the consonants buried in the stream, but she noticed again a certain hoarseness to his voice, a soft quality that begged the listener to lean forward and listen closer. So she did.

"In a ministry such as ours, it seems everybody either wants to run us out of town or try to win some sort of spiritual favor."

"I don't think I understand exactly what you mean."

"They believe, sometimes, that our prayers are stronger than their own. Or they assume they are entitled to some cut of the provisions God has made for us. They look for intercession and healing, without regard to the fact that such things must be Spirit-led."

"Well, Mr. Lundi, I don't want anything." Which wasn't exactly true, and her conscience nipped. "Although, I'll say, I did find Sister Aimee to be a fascinatin' sight to behold. Like an angel, almost. But then, to think, she's just a woman same as me—"

Something changed in his countenance, and she wondered if referencing herself as a woman might be seen as a vulgarity.

"Well, maybe not like me. Guess I'm more of a girl."

He laughed. "These days, it seems your sex is working hard to blur the line between the two."

"I don't care about blurring any line. I just want to be what God made me."

"Which is exactly why I need to spend this afternoon with you. It's the closest thing I've had to a holiday in a very long time."

She reached for her water again. *This afternoon,* he'd said. Where she'd only planned on the hour. And for the first time since she'd walked into the restaurant, she wondered if even that was a good idea. What would her sister think if she were to change her mind, come by, and see her through the window? For that matter, what would Brent say? Suddenly it all smacked of illicitness. Her eyes darted to the door, yet she didn't move.

Roland picked up the menu. "So, what would you recommend?"

Now it was her time to laugh—soft and self-conscious. "I'm new to this."

"Really?" He set the menu down and leaned forward. "To this restaurant? Or to Chinese cuisine in general?"

"To both, I guess."

"If it weren't for restaurants, I'd starve."

Such a sad sentence from such a handsome man.

"Your wife doesn't cook?"

His eyes held her every bit as much as did his hand when they first sat down. "I'm working to bring the message of Jesus Christ to the entire country. That doesn't leave me any time for a wife."

She wanted to say she understood, but she didn't. "My father was a minister. We never felt neglected."

"Let me guess." His speech changed to an exaggerated drawl. Not mocking, but bordering on affection. "A tiny white clapboard building with a steeple and a big ol' bell somewheres out in the woods?"

Dorothy Lynn giggled—something she rarely did. In the back of her mind, Darlene accused her of flirting, but before the guilt could fully take hold, the waiter had returned.

"We'll both have the beef chow mein," Roland said. Then, to her, "If that sounds good to you."

She nodded. The interruption afforded a moment for her to come to her senses, and the minute the waiter said, "Very good," and bowed away, she cleared her throat and sat up with a straighter resolve. "I'm going to be a preacher's wife. The man who took over the pulpit when Pa died, he and I are engaged. We're gettin' married in October. That's why I'm here, in St. Louis. My sister's makin' the dress." It all poured out of her like a confession. "I'm not one of those girls."

His brow rose quizzically.

"I mean, a girl who would just go out to lunch with a strange man. Or any man. Or even . . . lunch."

His amusement grew with her frustration, and for the first time it seemed he was actually laughing *at* her.

"I'm sorry," she faltered, finally. "I don't mean to insult you."

"I've been called worse than a 'strange man,'" he said, "and I didn't intend for my invitation to imply anything about your character. I simply saw you, remembered you, and thought it might be nice not to eat another meal alone. But if I'm making you uncomfortable . . ."

He began to scoot his chair away from the table, and a new guilt washed over her.

"Don't leave." Her words stopped him midstand. "You

were very kind to ask me to join you. I wouldn't have known what to do."

The warm smile returned as he settled back into his chair, and the food arrived soon after. Dorothy Lynn looked down at the bowl brimming with strips of meat and vegetables—some she didn't even recognize—in a lake of noodles. Steam rose from the dish, and she inhaled her first taste, leaving her mouth watering for more. She looked over to see that Roland had bowed his head to pray, and she followed suit, asking not only for a blessing on the food before her and the hands that prepared it, but also forgiveness for her unintentional sin.

When she opened her eyes, Roland had taken up the pair of narrow sticks that had been laid beside his bowl and used them to bring up a heaping mouthful. Not finding a fork, she picked up her own sticks and attempted to do the same, only to find he'd made the procedure look deceptively easy. Less than a full bite of food made it into her mouth, but that taste was enough to whet her appetite.

"Here," he said, his brown eyes twinkling with humor. "Watch me. You need to balance them, see? First this stick on your third finger, and then the second . . ."

Dorothy Lynn tried to match his grip, and she felt successful until it was time to actually grasp the food. She fell into laughter even as the pile of noodles and peppers fell back into the bowl. "I'm hopeless."

"Nothing's ever hopeless. Try again."

This time, when he reached for her hand, he purposefully took her fingers, positioning them to hold the chopsticks properly. Like never before, she was aware of the roughened texture of her skin and nails, and she curled her fingers in an attempt to hide them away.

"It's all right," he said, so softly that she barely heard him. "This is one skill worth learning. When it all comes together, you'll be so happy."

Somehow it happened, and though it meant a messy trail of sauce on her chin, she managed to fill her mouth with beef, peppers, and noodles all at once.

Roland applauded her achievement, and people from the surrounding tables joined in. Dorothy Lynn managed not to laugh until she'd swallowed the entire bite, but then she brought a napkin to her face and twisted in her chair to offer an appreciative wave to her audience.

"What do you think?"

"I think it's the best thing I ever ate," she said, eagerly working her chopsticks for the next bite.

"It's good, but nothing like what you'd get in California. San Francisco, especially."

The image of her brother's postcard flitted through her mind, threatening to steal the pure joy of this moment. "Don't think I'll be goin' to California any time soon."

"Fiancé not an adventurer?"

"Not sure *I* am, but I'd like to hear about it."

And so, as they ate, Roland talked. His travels with Sister Aimee had taken him all over the country, but he spoke most fondly of California. The excitement and uncharted opportunities. As she listened, she could imagine why Donny would want to stay there, if it was half as wonderful as it all sounded. Midway through the meal, she'd become quite proficient with her chopsticks, eventually able to snag a single thin slice of onion between the tips. Though he was in the middle of a rambunctious tale, he paused midsentence to acknowledge the accomplishment.

"You're a quick study."

She beamed under his praise and looked down into her empty bowl.

"Still hungry?"

"Oh no," she protested, but he raised a finger and moments later the stealthy waiter reappeared with two plates, each bearing a slice of dense, sticky cake. She followed Roland's example and picked it up, taking nibbling bites and licking her fingers. By the time it was gone she felt ready to burst.

Their waiter made another discreet appearance, at which time Roland reached into his pocket and produced a folded bill, which he pressed into the Chinese man's hand. Dorothy Lynn's heart raced. A dollar! She'd no idea her meal would be anywhere near that expensive, and with some trepidation she opened her pocketbook. As she did, though, the waiter thanked Roland, saying it had been a great honor, and disappeared.

"Thank you, but you didn't need to pay for mine," she said through a queer mixture of resentment and relief.

He chuckled as he stood. "I suspect a lot of men would appreciate such an attitude."

She thanked him again as he held the door open to the sidewalk, where she had to stand for just a moment to orient herself.

"You came from that direction." Roland pointed up the street behind her. "I saw you through the window."

"Yes." The revelation that he'd seen her before she walked into the restaurant left her a bit too unsettled to thank him yet again. Maybe that step across the threshold was like a step into a snare. She swallowed, still tasting the salt of foreign food. Somehow she'd allowed herself to be trapped into this spot—unfamiliar inside and out. A voice deep within her said, *Go home,* but home was miles away. She'd need a streetcar to get to Darlene's house, a bus to get to Heron's Nest. She had only her feet, and they were in danger of melting in this spot. But then she remembered—home was just half a block away, waiting for her in the music store.

She thanked him a final time and had taken only a few steps when there he was again, right beside her.

"I don't think it's a good idea for you to be out alone in the city."

"I'll be fine," she said, but even as she did, she hoped he wouldn't agree. Although the newness of him rumbled with the noodles in her stomach, his presence also brought an unexpected comfort. Her protest proved unconvincing as he simply dropped his hands into his pockets and fell into a slow step beside her.

They didn't speak at all as they walked, making an oddly comforting pocket of silence in the midst of the city's noise. When they came upon the Strawn Brothers Music Store, Dorothy Lynn said, "I'm goin' in here," at which point Roland—after a quick, curious, twisting smile—opened the door for her and followed her in.

Mr. Strawn emerged from the back room before the front door had closed behind them, carrying her guitar stiffly like it was a treasure to be presented.

"I would say good as new," he said proudly, "but good guitar is like good wine: better and better with age."

Dorothy Lynn took the instrument, gingerly by the neck at first, then instinctively brought it against her body, her fingers hovering over the strings.

"You play?" Roland asked, sounding truly impressed.

"A little," Dorothy Lynn said.

"You should play now," Strawn said. "See how it feels." He gestured toward a chair, and Dorothy Lynn sat down and curled herself around the guitar. She began strumming a few chords—nothing like a song—and cocked her head at the new sound.

"Is in tune," Strawn said. "Play."

Her mind drifted back, stopping and sifting through every song she knew, but none would make the journey to the strings. Only the tune born in this city, the one she'd been humming since the night before, seemed ready for this moment, playing itself through her as she hummed along.

"Is nice, right?" Strawn said.

Dorothy Lynn glanced up both to acknowledge and agree, flashing a quick smile at Roland, who seemed equally impressed.

"I don't recognize the song," Roland said.

"It's mine."

"You wrote it?"

"Not yet. It's still just in my head."

"The lyrics?"

"They're waitin' too."

"I'd like to hear them."

No stranger had ever requested to hear one of her songs. While Brent had expressed interest in them, she could never separate his appreciation from his affection. For the most part, her songs came to life in isolation, never offered to anybody until the words were safely in her journal and the notes perfectly settled in the strings. To sing this one felt like pushing a baby bird from its nest before the mama had a chance to teach it to fly. Before the feathers, even. "It's not ready."

"Please," Roland insisted. "I've never heard a half-written song."

She looked back down, concentrating her gaze on where the hem of her borrowed dress spilled out beneath the curve of the wood, and started again. The song remained wordless through what would become the first verse, but when the chorus found its way, her voice filled the shop.

Jesus is coming!
Are you ready
to meet your Savior in the sky?
He, on his white horse,
will come a-riding
to gather the faithful to his side.

When Dorothy Lynn looked up, Roland was smiling again—a smile unlike any she'd ever seen before on anyone. Not affection, but admiration, and she wished she had a dozen songs to sing.

"Is nice, right?" Strawn said again, though he was clearly more impressed with the sound of the guitar than anything.

"Very nice," Roland said, never taking his eyes off Dorothy Lynn.

"Is seventy-five cents for the strings. And I have case for you too."

Roland was once again reaching into his pocket and pulling out a clip of folded bills.

Dorothy Lynn jumped up from her chair to stop him, saying, "You can't."

"You've never heard of the expression 'Sing for your supper'?"

"You already bought me lunch."

Mr. Strawn unceremoniously held his hand out to Roland. "Let a gentleman be a gentleman. You modern girls will spoil everything." He took the dollar bill and headed to the back room.

"Perhaps," Roland said once they were alone, "I could take you to supper sometime."

"I told you," Dorothy Lynn said, grateful for the guitar that anchored her in place, "I have a fiancé back home."

"In Pigeonville, I know. I just meant—the song. I'd like to hear it when it's done. More than that, I'd like Aimee to hear it."

Immediately the palms of her hands went slick with sweat. "Sister Aimee? Why?"

"Come back tonight."

"I can't."

"We'll be here all week. Just promise me you'll come back."

Her fingers tightened around the neck and she repeated, "Why?"

"Because I think you may be exactly what we need."

There is no remembrance of former things; neither shall there be any remembrance of things that are to come with those that shall come after.

ECCLESIASTES 1:11

BREATH OF ANGELS
9:05 A.M.

Three raps on the door, and it opens.

Charlotte has been sitting quietly beside her, contentedly watching the last part of the *Today* show. It's a cooking segment with that terrible Martha Stewart. Darlene would have loved her, had she lived long enough.

At the sound of the knock, Charlotte jumps off the edge of the bed like a shot and immediately brings her thumb to her mouth for a new round of chewing.

Stop that. It makes you look like an idiot.

As if she hears, Charlotte obeys.

Kaleena Patrice, a nursing aide at Breath of Angels, walks in, pushing an empty wheelchair.

"You the CSV?"

Kaleena may only be an aide, but she speaks with an undeniable authority, due mostly to her accent. Jamaican, Lynnie would guess. It makes every word she says sound like it has been born after much consideration. When she asks if Charlotte is the CSV, she's not really asking at all. It's a confirmation, just in case Charlotte herself has forgotten why she's here.

Wide-eyed, Charlotte nods and forcibly keeps her thumb at her side.

"They told me to send you downstairs to check in at the front desk."

95

"Can I come back later?"

"Oh, I think we'll be able to find you plenty to do."

"I mean in here. With her."

Kaleena plants her hand on her waist and looks Charlotte up and down. Lynnie studies Kaleena's face, knowing this will be the moment she herself will decide just how she feels about Charlotte Hill. A curt nod, and Kaleena approves. If only Charlotte knew what an honor that is.

"Give us about thirty minutes. I'm going to help Miss Dorothy take a shower. That work?"

Again, not an option.

Charlotte nods, but she doesn't move.

"Shoo, now." Kaleena gives a dismissive waggle of her fingers, and after a final, backward glance, Charlotte's high-top tennis shoes float her silently out the door, escorted by Kaleena's warm smile.

"Now," she says, "good morning, Miss Dorothy." Only Kaleena calls her by that name, and she pronounces it with the accent on the wrong syllable—Dor-*thee*.

Kaleena's skin is the color of dark-brewed tea, with large cinnamon freckles scattered across her broad nose and cheeks. Lynnie had freckles herself when she was a girl; Ma used to say that the sun brought them out to play. But they'd worn away with her childhood—something that had been a great relief at the time, though she wonders if they wouldn't have made her more interesting. Kaleena wears her hair in a thousand tiny braids that are sometimes swirled and sculpted into an intricate design. Today, though, she wears them the way Lynnie likes best—long and loose, in singular, thick strands. She abandons the wheelchair to come to the side of the bed, where the bouquet of balloons floats, and reaches out to pluck at one of the strings.

"And happy birthday."

There's none of the false cheer like she'll hear from the rest of the staff today. Some of the staff can wish a happy birthday with the same air of celebration used for a long-awaited bowel movement. With Kaleena, it's a statement of fact.

Lynnie's hands are listless in her lap, and as she does at every visit, Kaleena settles on the side of the bed, takes them in her warm, strong ones, and asks if they can pray together.

Yes.

"Father in heaven," Kaleena begins, "we praise you today for Miss Dorothy's life."

Birthday or not, she opens every prayer with the same praise. Right after the last stroke, the one that finally took her speech, Lynnie would sit in silent spiritual disagreement. Who would be thankful for this life? Had there been any mode of travel between her mind and her mouth, she would have burst right in and said so. Instead, when Kaleena prattled on about the blessings of a new day, Lynnie had prayed, *Lord Jesus, take me home.*

Always yearning for more, just not here.

But every time she opened her eyes—still here, her prayer overshadowed by the honeyed words of Kaleena Patrice.

Now she listens, letting those words wash over her.

"We praise you, Father, on this day that marks the day she came into this world, for the life she has lived, and we commit to you all that remains of her journey. May today be full of good things, as you are good. May today be free of pain, as you are the great healer. We give you this day, and all those to come, until we are swept up to your holy presence."

Amen.

"Now," Kaleena says, standing, "let's get you prettied up. Word has it we'll have quite a few visitors today. Do you want to walk? Or take a ride?"

Kaleena's the only aide who ever asks. Most just come in and automatically lend a strong arm and shoulder to assist her into the chair. The bathroom door is just across the room, no more than ten steps on the smooth floor, but they are slow, creeping steps these days, and the workers always have so much to do. Kaleena, however, never seems to be in a hurry. Lynnie darts her eyes away from the chair.

"Walk it is, then. One, two, three," and the women are arm in arm. The floor is cool and smooth beneath her bare feet, and Kaleena's body is strong beside her. They walk like sisters, one chatting on with the gossip of the day, the other absorbing every word.

"Can you imagine it? After this year, no more Oprah. What's the world going to do at four o'clock every day?"

Never watched her.

"Oh, I know she's not your favorite, Miss Dorothy, but there's a whole world of women who live by what she says. I think God Almighty will have something to say about that, all those silly women who turn to her. Me, I only watch sometimes."

Lynnie summons a huff, and Kaleena laughs. "Oh, I know you got to have some words of wisdom all locked up in there, miss. Live on this earth a hundred and seven years, I can only imagine what you have to tell the rest of us."

Nobody'd listen.

"That's the joy of being here, working with all you wise old souls. And it *is* the soul, what is deep inside, that keeps you here from day to day. The Bible says to be absent from the body is to be present with the Lord. But you know all about that, don't you, miss? God must still have great plans for you, great lady, or he would have kept you that day."

Kaleena talks on, a series of questions and replies as if another voice answers her. Lynnie walks beside her, feeding the conversation if not contributing. When they get to the bathroom, Kaleena opens the small door to the step-in shower and stills her words. She eases the thin cotton gown over Lynnie's shoulders, lets it drop to the ground, and holds the older woman's arm steady as she steps over the threshold.

There is no room for modesty at Breath of Angels, especially for those residents on the third floor, where even these excursions become more and more rare. Lynnie sits on the wide, textured bench. Kaleena reaches above her for the detachable shower head, aiming the soft spray toward the wall until she has found the perfect temperature. All the while, she hums a familiar tune. Soon the warm water is running down Lynnie's skin, the sound and the feel of it intertwining with the song. Both touch her. Instinctively, she closes her eyes and leans her head back.

"You want to wash your hair today?"

She doesn't move.

"Okay, then."

There's a soap dispenser attached to the wall, and she hears the familiar sound of the lever. It's filled with amber-colored shampoo, the kind used for washing babies' hair. As Kaleena's strong hand coaxes the lather, Lynnie's heart fills with the scent. She knows Breath of Angels uses the baby shampoo because old hair is delicate hair—thin and sparse. But the smell of it conjures up memories of a clean, slick baby, splashing in sinks and tubs and buckets. It's a gift better than a picture.

Now it's running in spent bubbles down her spine, and a new scent emerges. Lavender—a favorite. She opens her eyes and extends her hands to hold the soft, round sponge while Kaleena covers it with the liquid soap.

"Got something new for you today. This has soap and lotion all in one—keeps your skin soft."

Lynnie washes her own body, as much as she can, though there's nothing to wash away. No dirt from the forest floor or sticky perspiration from a day's hard work. Just clean skin getting cleaner.

Kaleena's singing. "Face to face with Christ, my Savior. Face to face— what will it be?"

She doesn't sing it the way Lynnie learned it. There's a richness to Kaleena's voice, and she sneaks up on every note, filling the spaces between with runs, chasing around corners from one to the next.

"When with rapture I behold him, Jesus Christ, who died for me."

Tears flow freely down Lynnie's face, and she hands the soapy sponge up to Kaleena to let her rub it softly across her back.

Face to face—what will it be? She knows what it will be. She knows it will be bright and glorious. She knows that old men are restored to youthful vigor; she saw her father in a form she'd never known in life. She knows bodies are whole, as she'd seen her precious young soldier full of vitality and strength. She knows it's an electric rush of the souls of people who knew and loved the Savior she knows and loves.

And the babies.

Try as she might, she cannot recall the babies. They carry the names she never spoke aloud, and an undeniable *belonging* to her. But despite letting her remember the others, God has chosen to hide their forms from her. It is a mercy, really, for if she truly remembered, she'd never be able to bear another moment on this earth. She'd lived far too many years apart from them already.

The sound was that of the ocean waves, endless praise, and above it a familiar, smoky voice telling her, "Hitherto shalt thou come, but no further." Then the tide of light took her, brought her back to the shore of living. She knew she'd be a messenger. *All is well, but all are waiting.*

"You ready, aren't you, Miss Dorothy?"

God, help me. I am.

"You just keep your eyes lookin' for him, don't you?"

Kaleena has rinsed away all traces of the lotiony soap, and with a decisive push the water is off, and a thick, warm towel is placed over Lynnie's shoulders.

"That's why God took your voice, or you'd be tellin' us all you seen when it's not our time yet to know."

The half door opens and Kaleena is inside, helping her stand, slowly patting her dry and wrapping her hair in another, smaller towel. "No walking back to the bed. Floor's too slick."

With Kaleena's help, Lynnie steps out of the shower, uses the toilet, and stands while a fresh, clean housedress is snapped down the front. Once she's settled in the wheelchair, thick socks are stretched over her feet.

"All right, Miss Dorothy." And the time is nearly at an end. Humming again, Kaleena unwraps the towel from the top of Lynnie's head and gently tufts the damp hair with her fingers. Thin as it is, it will soon be a cap of soft curls, the deep chestnut color faded, but miraculously not gone to gray.

Then, working briskly as if to make up for the time lost in gentle bathing, Kaleena is a whirlwind of activity, not only opening the blinds that let in the midmorning sunshine, but also drawing back the curtain of the window that looks out into the hallway where Charlotte Hill is waiting, leaning against the opposite wall.

"Well, lookee there. I believe you have yourself quite a fan." Kaleena opens the door and beckons the girl inside. "So, you gonna spend today with my Miss Dorothy?"

"Yeah—I mean, yes, ma'am."

"Well, let me tell you how it's gonna be. She has people coming to visit in the Family Celebrations Room just off the dining hall downstairs. You know where that is?"

"Yes, ma'am."

"She don't have time for much of a rest before lunch, but maybe a nice walk around the grounds." A hand on her shoulder. "Would you like that, Miss Dorothy? It's a lovely day."

Yes, ma'am.

"But bring her back in half an hour so she can rest up before lunch. You got that?"

"Yes, ma'am. I mean, I have a phone."

Kaleena sighs. "All right, then. You realize Miss Dorothy is a precious, precious woman, don't you?"

"Yes, ma'am. I do."

Out of the corner of her eye, she sees a hand—tattered nails bearing scraps of dark, chipped polish—coming to a tentative rest on her other shoulder.

"All right, then," Kaleena says. "I know we're not supposed to ask, but what'd you do to get your community service? You didn't hurt no one, did you?"

"No, ma'am."

"You didn't steal nothin'?"

"No, ma'am."

"Then what?"

"I got in trouble once, for singing in a park."

Lynnie twitches her head, wanting to turn around.

"And they gave you community service for that?"

"Not exactly."

Then Charlotte does the thing that most irritates her about people. She lowers her voice to a whisper, as if the inability to speak has also taken away her ability to hear. If anything, it's a pain because it causes her to stretch her neck in an uncomfortable fashion, just to catch everything.

"You see," she says, so close to inaudible that Lynnie wonders if she's hearing her correctly after all, "I'm not exactly a CSV. I'm something more like family."

⋘ CHAPTER SEVEN ⋙

DOROTHY LYNN DID NOT RETURN to the theater that night, nor did she intend to the next day. Darlene kept her in a perpetual swaddling of fabric—measuring, draping, pinning. Liberated from their mother's attention, RJ and Darren raced through the house at will, playing bank robbers and cowboys and soldiers—whatever gave license to chase and shoot and die horrible, gargling deaths on the kitchen floor.

"This one better be a girl," Darlene said, standing back to study Dorothy Lynn's hemline with a critical eye. "I'd like to know what life is like with a princess."

"The more time I spend with your children," Dorothy Lynn said, thankful to be standing on a chair, outside of collision range, "the less I want my own."

"Oh, that'll all change once you and your husband start loving on each other."

The whole idea was frightening. Not the loving, but the boisterous results.

"Were we ever that loud?"

"Sister, we were in God's country. Ma just sent us out into

the forest. We might have gotten eaten by bears, and she wouldn't have known until one of us didn't show up for supper."

"That's true."

She supposed that's where Donny got his wandering spirit, and where she would have too, had she ever been given the opportunity to follow it. Yesterday had been adventure enough. She'd played a few chords on the guitar, hoping to impress Darlene's family with the improved sound, but between the boys' restlessness, Darlene's indifference, and Roy's distraction, she realized her best audience had been the two men in the music store. Given that Darlene's sense of adventure didn't extend beyond the new wainscoting in the dining room, she opted not to tell her about lunch with Roland Lundi. Some things, she figured, deserved to be guarded in a heart.

"You're thinking about him now, aren't you?"

"Don't be silly."

"Why would it be silly for you to be thinking about your fiancé while being fitted for the dress you're going to marry him in?"

"If you must know, I was thinking about what it would be like if I didn't get married at all. If I could be like Donny and just go where the wind took me."

"'The wind whirleth about continually,'" Darlene said in a rare spate of biblical quotation, "and it never took anyone anyplace good."

"How do you know? You could say that the wind brought you here."

"Finest Automobiles brought me here, on the arm of my husband. Honestly, Dot, you're beginning to worry me with all of this talk."

"It's just talk."

The sound of the ringing telephone came as a welcome interruption. Throughout the house the boys were screaming, "Telephone! Telephone!" Darlene took the straight pins from between her lips and jabbed them into the little pillow-like cushion tied to her wrist.

"Like I can't hear it," she mumbled before leaving Dorothy Lynn alone with her adulterous thoughts. Not of Mr. Lundi—handsome though he was—but of what he represented. Seeing the world, proclaiming Jesus. Dorothy Lynn never had the desire to follow in her father's footsteps. Such a thing would never have been offered as an option. But to see a woman on stage, speaking the Word of God more powerfully than she'd ever known a man to do, stirred something within her. And then, to have somebody actually ask to hear a song? Brent, of course, had listened to several of her poetic, melodic musings, but he had to. He loved her. Mr. Lundi didn't.

And so she coveted, more than she ever thought possible.

Sometimes I yearn for more.

Of all her verses, that was one she'd never shared with anyone. And here she'd come so close to spilling to Darlene.

Lord, guard my heart and my tongue.

And her temper, as RJ came running into the kitchen, nearly barreling into her.

"Aunt Dot! Telephone for you. Mama says it's your fancy."

"My *fiancé*," she corrected as she climbed carefully down from the chair, mindful of the pins that stuck her in every possible place.

Darlene was sitting at the telephone table in the alcove under the stairs, leaning on her elbows, shouting into the candlestick phone.

"We're having a fabulous time! The dress is coming along

nicely, but we're a bit behind! She disappeared for half the day yesterday!"

Pins or not, Dorothy Lynn strode across the hall and closed her fist around the phone, attempting to yank it away, but Darlene's grip was stronger.

"Not a clue. Said she had to get her guitar fixed or something, but I was beginning to worry she'd run off with one of our city boys!" She punctuated her words with a broad wink and strengthened her grip.

"Give it!" Dorothy Lynn hissed.

Darlene turned toward the wall, hunching her body around the phone. "She's chopped off all her hair, and we can't get her to stop smoking cigarettes. And if you'd seen her dancing—"

Disregarding both her sister's delicate condition and her own precarious one, Dorothy Lynn draped herself across Darlene's wide, soft body, reached around, and finally wrenched the phone away.

"Don't believe a word of it!" She was breathless, laughing and talking all at once while trying to untangle the two of them from the phone's cord. RJ and Darren had clomped in to witness the fun and were jumping up and down, cheering their mother on.

Breathing heavily, Darlene ushered the boys toward the kitchen with the promise of a snack; Dorothy Lynn tucked herself into the alcove, saying, "Hello, darling," once she knew she was alone.

"Tell me you've been behaving yourself." She could hear the trust and smile in his voice, even though he was so far away.

"Of course I have. Darlene is such a brat."

"I knew it would be trouble letting you go up there alone."

He was joking, of course, and she should have laughed, but a sharp pain that had nothing to do with the pins in the garment jabbed at the base of her spine. A flirtatious girl might giggle and tell him not to be silly, but she had never been a flirt, and he had never been silly. The prolonged silence went on long enough that she finally heard a faint "Hello?" on the other end, as if they were starting a brand-new conversation.

"I'm still here," she said softly, then again when he hadn't heard.

"So tell me about your adventures in the big city." There was no hint of accusation or even suspicion in his voice, and she had only a mere second to decide whether he deserved to have either. She closed her eyes, seeing nothing but Roland Lundi across the table, and knew, if nothing else, she couldn't start there. So she told him about the movie and the lights and the streetcars and the eccentric Mrs. Lorick in the fabric shop.

"She said I loved you enough to need a veil, but I said I couldn't afford to love you that much."

"It doesn't matter what you wear. I'd marry you if you came down the aisle in a feed sack."

"I wish you'd tell Darlene that. She's going to make me crazy."

"Put her back on; then put yourself on the first bus home." Though he was clearly joking, she could not ignore the timbre of desire in his voice, and it sparked clear through her skin.

"Tempting," she said, and meant it, "but it is going to be a beautiful dress once it's finished."

Darlene hollered from the kitchen, "Don't say any more! It's bad luck."

Dorothy Lynn relayed that bit of information and continued. "Then I got new strings on my guitar. You should hear it. Sounds like a whole new instrument."

"I can't wait."

"Really?"

"If I can hear your guitar, then you can't be far away."

She brought the mouthpiece closer, wishing she could kiss him right then and there. Instead, she whispered, "And I wrote a new song."

"I didn't know you could write away from the woods."

"I didn't know I could either." Her head had been filled with it all of last night and today, the chorus coming full circle, lyrics knitting themselves as tight as thoughts. She wanted to tell Brent all about it, maybe even sing a few lines over the phone, but her mind brought her back to the Strawn Brothers Music Store, and a newly formed loyalty kept her tongue quite still.

"Anything else?" Brent asked, and the line crackled in anticipation of an answer.

"Just one thing." *A woman evangelist on the stage, dressed in white, with blonde, bobbed hair and an audience of a thousand on their feet.* "I went to a Chinese restaurant for lunch and had chow mein."

"You went by yourself?"

A man who looks like Rudolph Valentino; a man who listened to my song; a man who wants to see me again, and he just might because he's haunting my thoughts. She swallowed. "Yep. I walked in all by myself."

The lie tasted bitter on her tongue, and she wondered if he could taste it too.

"And how did you like it?"

"Too salty." Even now she felt like choking.

Brent chuckled. "Look, Jessup's giving me the eye—got another person waiting for the phone. Any word for me to take to your mother?"

She thought about the postcard from Donny in California. Ma voiced his name in prayer every night, even though she sometimes had a hard time saying it without tears during the day. No such card had come to her, or Dorothy Lynn would have seen it. They would have wrapped themselves around it in the lamplight after supper.

"Just tell her I love her, and that her girls are having a real good time."

"I will."

There was a pause in which she silently poured out all she'd left unspoken. No, not just unspoken words, but lies. Three of them—Sister Aimee, Roland, Donny. She brought her hand to her heart as if to hold them there, harmless.

"I love you, Brent Logan."

"I love you, Dorothy Lynn Dunbar."

Then another silence, another chance, and the line went dead.

Dorothy Lynn placed the earpiece back in its cradle and stared into the empty black void of the phone.

"Chow mein?" Darlene had returned, hands braced at the small of her back, foot tapping. "You didn't mention that."

"Didn't I?" Dorothy Lynn stood, doing her best to smooth the rumpled fabric.

"Where did you go? How would you even know what to eat?"

"I might not live in the big city, but I didn't just crawl out from under a rock. We're from the same hometown, remember? I guess I can shake the dirt off me same as you." Shocked at her own tirade, Dorothy Lynn brushed past her sister on her way to the kitchen, but she couldn't stay more than a step ahead.

"I thought you were awful quiet when you came home yesterday."

"I'm a quiet girl."

"Lucky you were talking to your fiancé on the telephone, so he couldn't see what I see."

They were back at the table, where Darlene shooed RJ and Darren away with their cookies. Dorothy Lynn picked one from the plate and attempted a nonchalant nibble. "And just what do you see?"

Darlene leaned close. "You're hiding something."

"Not tellin' isn't the same as hidin'."

"So? Spill."

"Can I take this off first?" She couldn't stand another second of holding still beneath the pinned fabric.

Darlene frowned but agreed.

The confession started the moment they began to tug the dress off—while her face was hidden in the white crepe de chine tunnel. By the time Dorothy Lynn was once again dressed in her own comfortable clothes, every detail had been shared, from the meeting in the restaurant to the parting in the music store. Whether from shame or defiance, her cheeks burned from the telling, and her voice trembled with the conclusion. "And then I came home."

"So you went on a date?" Darlene said, lowering herself into a chair. "And he's asked you for another."

"It was not a *date*," Dorothy Lynn said, not entirely sure how to define what her sister implied. "And he wants to hear my song."

Darlene snickered. "You're a pretty young girl. Trust me, he's not interested in your music."

"Well, then, he wouldn't be the first." She pouted, knowing full well she looked and sounded like a child, but it drew no pity from her sister.

"Never mind that," Darlene said. "I can understand falling

into a dish of noodles with a handsome man. Not that I condone it, mind you, but I understand. It's that Sister Aimee business. She's an abomination, Dot. Roy says so, and Pa would too, if he were alive. And it's worth a bet that your fellow wouldn't think too highly of her either. But then, you wouldn't know, because you failed to tell him about that little moment of our evening too, didn't you?"

"How can you say that? Mr. Lundi told me they've seen thousands and thousands of people come to know Jesus. All over the country. Pa didn't preach to a thousand people over his entire lifetime. Nor will Brent, I daresay. And you said yourself that Roy doesn't go to church but twice a month, maybe. Who is he to say she's an abomination?"

"She's a *she*. That's enough. It's not a place for a woman, up like that."

"You've never even heard what she has to say."

"Neither have you."

They were nearly shouting, and a burst of unfamiliar anger brought Dorothy Lynn to her feet. "You're the one always callin' *me* old-fashioned. You and your electric sweeper and smart parties—all that makeup on your face."

"There's no sin in any of that."

She softened. "Of course not. But you have to admit, there's sin all around in this modern world. That movie we saw—the fortune teller, everybody on screen drinkin' and carryin' on. And all around us women with their cigarettes, and some of them kissin' and pettin' right there in the lobby. Why isn't *that* the abomination?"

Darlene sighed. "I think it'll be a good thing when you get back home."

"What is that supposed to mean?"

"It means I don't think you're quite ready for life in the modern world."

She didn't know how to respond. In a way, her sister was right. Much of what she'd seen and experienced the past few days was new—how could she have been prepared? Looking back, though, she couldn't remember a spot of trepidation. Discomfort, yes, and caution, and maybe even a hint of regret in retrospect. But not fear, and certainly not failure.

Here she was almost nineteen years old, and everybody she knew seemed to think she had nothing to offer. Resentment took its first churning bite as Dorothy Lynn saw herself through her sister's eyes. A backward bumpkin. Ma only wanted her to be safe and married and close to home. Brent—sweet, wonderful Brent—only wanted her close to him. That, she knew, should be enough. And it was . . . or had been. Until yesterday, when an utter stranger made her feel something new: strong.

"Now, don't be sad," Darlene said, hoisting herself to her feet. "You've got a lovely life ahead of you in Heron's Nest. Like you're following in our mother's footsteps."

"More like I'm livin' her life."

"And it's not such a bad life, is it?"

"No, I suppose not." She sounded more convinced than she felt, as if she were outside watching herself in a moment of revelation. She'd shared every moment of her life with Ma, living within those boundary lines that God had so clearly fashioned. Darlene had her family and Donny had the world, but what could Dorothy Lynn claim as truly, uniquely her own? Certainly not Brent. As a minister's wife, she would forever be sharing her husband with any church member who had the slightest need. How often had she heard Pa slip out of the house in the middle of the night to sit at the bedside of a dying man?

When she looked back on her childhood, she looked into her future. This very moment stood in marked isolation. A hinge. A turning point. Her own little portion. And the appetite to taste it grew within.

Darlene patted Dorothy Lynn's arm and focused on carefully folding the unfinished dress. "Think I'll wait to start sewing tomorrow. I'd just have time to get started, and it'd be time to fix dinner. That all right with you, Dot?"

But the last of her words were lost as Dorothy Lynn walked up the kitchen stairs to the boys' room, where her newly strung guitar stood in the corner, surrounded by a toy mile of train tracks. She picked it up, along with her purse, and quietly walked down the carpeted front steps and out the front door.

Her cup awaited.

❧ CHAPTER EIGHT ❧

SHE HAD NO IDEA where to go but to the theater, and her first step into the gaping, silent lobby made her feel like the embodiment of the fool Darlene thought her to be. The only light came through the open door, and the only sound from the buzzing of an electric sweeper in the hand of a tall, tired man who seemed unwilling to lift his eyes from its repetitive path.

She tried repeating "Excuse me?" at varying volumes, but if he did hear her above the machine's din, he gave no indication. Waving her arm to catch his eye proved equally fruitless, and it wasn't until she moved directly into the sweeper's path that he even looked up, and then not until the machine had tapped the toe of her sturdy brown shoe.

"Whaddya want?" Not only did he not turn off the machine; he continued to maneuver it in a narrow arc around her feet.

"I'm looking for Mr. Lundi. Roland Lundi?" The fact that she had to shout made her sound bolder than she felt, and for that she was grateful.

"Back office." He ran the sweeper to the left, indicating the direction she should take, and she obeyed.

The building only got darker the deeper she walked. Muffled

voices guided her through the gray, and a strip of light beckoned. When she got to the door, she leaned her ear against it. Strange how, after a single conversation in a crowded restaurant, the sound of his voice could be so immediately recognizable. She knocked softly once, and again with three bold raps.

"Who is it?" The question was tinged with clear impatience, but she fought the instinct to back away.

"Dorothy Lynn Dunbar."

A pause, then, "Who?"

She could leave. One quick turn and she'd be swallowed in the dark hallway. A few more and her steps would be muffled by the sweeper. Once outside, she'd be enveloped by the crowd, carried to the streetcar that would take her back to Darlene's house in time for supper.

She cleared her throat. "Dorothy Lynn Dunbar. We . . . You . . . Yesterday—"

The door swung open, and there he was. Not nearly as slick as the other times she'd seen him. Strands of dark hair were strewn across his forehead, his shirt rumpled beneath his suspenders. Those Valentino-dark eyes, though, twinkled in recognition. In an instant he was transformed, like a starched sheet fresh from under the iron. His shirt might not be smooth, but the rest of him was.

"I knew we'd see you again." He opened the door wider. "Come in and meet Sister Aimee."

The moment felt royal. In a transformation opposite of Roland Lundi's, Dorothy Lynn's body turned to water from the rushing in her ears to the feeling of ice pooling in her spine.

"Oh, I don't think so," she protested. "I just came to see you."

"Well, *I* am in *here*, so it seems we must come to an agreement."

During her visit, Dorothy Lynn had often heard Roy on the

telephone working through a sales deal, and she'd spent her life in a church pew listening to first her father, and lately Brent, pleading and persuading people to follow Jesus. Roland Lundi's speech was an enticing hybrid of the two. Persuasive, yes, but tempered with detachment, as if the listener would have no one to blame for the dire consequences of ignoring his instruction.

"If you think it's all right." Part of her was already edging toward agreement.

"I think it's imperative." He ushered her in.

Even in this close, windowless room, Aimee Semple McPherson commanded every bit of the attention that she did on the stage. She was again dressed in white, though now it was a simple cotton jersey, and her hair looked darker than it had under the bright stage light. On stage she had loomed, unapproachable, above any who would dare to come near. Here, she could be any other woman in the world. Dorothy Lynn extended her hand, and Sister Aimee took it in a grip strong enough for any man's approval. She held the firm grip so long that Dorothy Lynn began to wonder whether she'd ever be able to play the guitar again.

"She's cute." Sister Aimee spoke above Dorothy Lynn's head, directing her comment to Roland.

"Cute's just the beginning. Small-town, wholesome, married to a preacher."

"Seems young to be married."

"We're not married yet," Dorothy Lynn interjected, "and I'm almost nineteen." Nobody seemed to be listening.

"And?" Sister Aimee said.

"Think about it. She's what we're fighting for. The remnant of the good girls. She's your message, and she can be your messenger."

Sister Aimee scowled at that. "I don't need a messenger, Mr.

Lundi. I *am* a messenger. What do you think we've been working for all these years?"

"She sings."

"Lots of people sing. You ever hear of a phonograph?"

His smile was patient, indulgent. "She sings what you preach, Sister. Tell her."

It took a moment for Dorothy Lynn to realize he was talking to her, and she overcame her muteness long enough to say, "Tell her what, exactly?"

Roland prompted. "Two nights ago, at the theater, you came in . . ."

"Oh yes." And she continued her tale from there, glossing over Rudy Valentino in favor of relating what she felt that night, in just a matter of moments, at the back of the auditorium during Sister Aimee's service. "I've been in church all my life, ma'am, and I never saw anything like that before. Nor felt it. People so excited about hearing the Word of God. It was so exciting—and scary, too, I'd say."

"Scary how?" It was the first time the woman had addressed her directly.

"The idea of Jesus comin' back. And the call to be ready. So much passion, I guess. That's not common in my church."

"It's not common to preach the return of our Savior?"

"Not like that."

"And your preacher husband. Does he not keep his parishioners in a state of readiness?"

"He's not my husband, and he's only been preaching there for a while. Before him, it was my father."

Sister Aimee stared at her, unblinking at the apparent irrelevance of the facts.

"We're ready," Dorothy Lynn said, "I guess."

"The soul can't 'guess' at its readiness. Resurrected in the air at his return, or in the moment of our final breath, there can be no question. Imagine the young groom, waiting at the altar for his bride, and she, unsure of her walking. Will that decision not determine the fate of her life on earth? Either the joys of communal marriage, or the societal damnation of a life alone?"

Sister Aimee spoke with all the passion and cadence of the woman on the stage, and the confines of the room might have made Dorothy Lynn shrink away from the volume. Instead, she felt herself caught up in the image, to the point of anticipating the next word. And though she was barraged with questions, there was neither the expectation nor the opportunity to reply. But inside, her mind swelled with unwritten songs, and she held them like a breath.

"So tell me, young woman, if Jesus Christ came back to reclaim his church today, would he gather you?"

"Yes," Dorothy Lynn said, without hesitation. "And I've always known that. Well, since I was a little girl, anyway. I guess sometimes you can know somethin' without really thinking about it? But when I saw you, I started thinking. And when I think, I write, and so . . ."

"And so," Roland picked up, "it's your message in her song."

"It is God's message," Sister Aimee said. Her hands were clasped beneath her chin, her eyes upturned. "He has merely called me to be his mouthpiece. Called me to speak it to a world in such desperate need of repentance and salvation."

"Of course," Roland said, and for the first time he seemed to be choosing his words with care. "And we've made great strides. You, Sister Aimee, are the voice for God's message. But Dorothy Lynn, here—I think she could be the voice for all those women falling into sin. Look at her—old-fashioned but not dowdy.

Innocent, pure. Women will see the girl they want to be; men will see the girl they want to marry."

Dorothy Lynn cleared her throat, if for no other reason than to remind him that she was still in the room.

Sister Aimee cracked a knowing smile. "And I am neither of those?"

He sidestepped the question like a dancer. "You said it yourself. You are the mouthpiece of the Lord Almighty. She is your audience. Imagine if we bring your audience on stage, let them see themselves already absorbed by God's truth. What will that be?"

On stage. Audience. Dorothy Lynn realized what they were discussing, and she shook her head in protest. She didn't sing in front of audiences. Women didn't lead congregations in song. That was for men like Deacon Keyes, with their booming voices and command of verse, not a girl like her with a borrowed guitar and songs nobody'd ever heard before.

"You seem so insistent, Lundi." Sister Aimee's eyes narrowed and darted between him and Dorothy Lynn. "Are you sure there aren't *other* issues involved?"

No depth of innocence could obscure the meaning behind Sister Aimee's question. Dorothy Lynn wanted to melt clean through the floor, but instead she looked to Mr. Lundi for rescue.

"Aimee, she's a kid."

His response offered salvation to her reputation but a sting to her pride. He hadn't treated her like a kid yesterday. She wanted to say as much but worried her protest would only strengthen suspicion.

Roland turned to her. "Play, won't you? That song from the other day."

It hadn't taken long to recognize the chain of command, so

Dorothy Lynn looked to Sister Aimee before making a move. In response, she sat down. "Please," she said expectantly. "Play."

"All right," Dorothy Lynn said.

There was a low-backed sofa behind her, and she laid the guitar case upon it. The click of the metal latches made this seem like a weighty task, but the welcome sight of her guitar nestled in blue velvet set her heart at ease. She lifted it out, and Roland whisked the case away so she could sit on the sofa. She was prepared for the usual lengthy ritual of adjusting the instrument, but new strings and a proper case had preserved its tuning. She closed her eyes.

Lord, I really don't know why I'm here in the presence of this woman, but I feel I've followed you. I thank you for this song and for whatever it might do for your Kingdom.

And then she played. And sang.

Jesus is coming!
Are you ready
to meet your Savior in the sky?

The verses stepped up to take Dorothy Lynn's part in the earlier conversation with Sister Aimee. Of course she was ready. Who could sing what the heart held in question? Hard to believe that, just yesterday, this song didn't exist. It flowed through her now as complete as if people had been singing it for generations, like truth forged through the fire of time.

When she opened her eyes after the final words, Roland's arms were folded across his chest, and he looked at her with parental approval and pride. "What did I tell you?"

"Not so much," Sister Aimee said. "You ever sing in front of a crowd before?"

Dorothy Lynn thought about the children gathered on the lawn outside the church. "Small ones, yes."

"Let me guess. Children's Sunday school class?"

It seemed like nothing, coming out of that powerful mouth.

"Hence your sweet and unspoiled." Roland stood beside her, and she felt his hands on her shoulders, as if he was trying to hold her in place.

Sister Aimee turned back to the lighted mirror, picked up a silver hairbrush, and began brushing with a series of short, purposeful strokes. Nobody spoke for a full minute until she paused, holding the brush aloft. "Bring her on at six. I want the orchestra seated and ready in case she's a flop."

"That's my girl." His grip tightened on Dorothy Lynn's shoulders, but it was unclear just which of the two he considered *his* girl. He released her and, with a gentle pat, urged her to stand up. The next thing she knew, he was taking the guitar from her arms and laying it back in the case. As she maneuvered out of his way, she caught a glimpse of herself in the mirror. The three of them, actually—one glamorous woman of the stage, one simple, familiar girl, and the man who brought them together.

"One more thing." Sister Aimee spoke to both of them in the mirror. "There's no money in it. Not even a dip from the plate. We're on a mission here; got it?"

"She's got it." Roland held the guitar case in one hand and hooked the other through Dorothy Lynn's elbow. "Now we'll go work out some of the details."

She was led out into the hallway like one being led from a dream. She'd been nothing more than an observer of other people's conversation, and the entire scene blurred behind her, out of context. At least here, without Sister Aimee, she could assert herself. Being no more enlightened than when she walked in, she dug in her heels before taking another step. "Where are you taking me?"

"Backstage. We've only got a couple of hours to show you the ropes."

Backstage? Ropes? Questions a kid would ask. "That's not why I came here. You said you wanted to hear my song is all."

"And why did you think I wanted to hear it? Just to while away a few minutes of the afternoon?"

"I didn't think about *why.*"

"Well then, you tell me. Why did you come all this way to play it?"

"Not for her," she said. "I wanted to play it for you."

"Aw, kid . . ." He looked on her with pity, like she was the stray puppy who had followed him home. "Sorry if I gave you the wrong impression. I'm sure you're a sweet girl, but I'm old enough to be your—uncle, maybe."

"It's not that." If the hallway hadn't been so dark, her blush might have made the protest less than convincing. "No one's ever told me to finish a song before."

"Really?" He'd dropped her arm and was fishing in his pocket, finally producing a slim metal case. In a second, his face was awash in light as he struck a match and touched the flame to a cigarette dangling from the corner of his lips. "Not even that fiancé of yours?"

"He listens."

"But does he seek?"

"What do you mean?"

"Does he understand? Does he keep an unfinished tune rattling around in his brain for days, going crazy, like when you're trying to remember a name? Because that's what I've been doing since yesterday."

Her nose twitched at the smoke, but that had nothing to do with the tears pricking her eyes. She'd never heard anyone speak with such understanding of what it meant to create music. To think, she and this stranger had been living with such like minds for the past day and night. The conversation had taken a dangerous turn.

She offered up a weak defense. "He loves me, and he says my music will have a place in our lives."

"And what is that place?"

"In my heart, and in our home. And maybe in our church, when it's *our* church. But right now it's his."

"The church belongs to the Lord, and we serve as we're called."

"Well, I don't know that I've been called to do this."

Roland drew on his cigarette and the tip glowed red. "Frankly, neither do I. But where's the harm in finding out?"

Her stomach churned, but whether it was with fear, excitement, or the smoke streaming from both the cigarette and his lips, she couldn't say. She only knew that, with one small act, she'd stepped into a whole new set of boundaries.

"Is there a telephone? I have to tell my sister I won't be home for dinner."

❧ CHAPTER NINE ❧

IT HAD TAKEN THREE ATTEMPTS to explain to Darlene exactly why her younger sister wouldn't be home for dinner, and when the idea finally did register in all its shocking detail, the screech that came across the line could be heard throughout the room, as evidenced by the cringing reaction of the backstage crew.

"I'm coming right down there," Darlene had said once she was again capable of speech, "and bringing you home."

"Bringing the boys with you?" They'd gone on one quick foray taking RJ and Darren on a streetcar—an ordeal Dorothy Lynn never wished to experience again.

"If I have to. But you can bet the minute Roy gets home I'll be there. Better yet, I'll send *him*. Better yet, we'll take the boys to Mrs. Mevreck, and we'll *both* show up. Take you kicking and screaming if we have to."

Odd, but Dorothy Lynn hadn't cultivated any real desire to perform onstage until her loving sister threatened to take the opportunity away.

"Please, Dar. I'll never have a chance to do anything like this again."

"You never *should* have the chance. What would Brent say? Or Pa? Have you thought about that?"

"I have." And she'd ignored it.

Now, with her stomach a mass of crawling caterpillars, Dorothy Lynn wondered if she should have listened to their invented counsel.

A tall, four-legged stool stood alone on the stage with nothing but the rich red velvet curtain behind it. Dorothy Lynn wore a new dress brought to her from a shop around the corner. Nothing jazzy, as she'd initially feared, but a modest pumpkin-colored frock with a square neck and long sleeves. Her hair had been brushed and wrapped around a wide-barreled iron, the curls gathered into one ribbon and draped over her shoulder.

From the wings she could see the crowd arriving, slowly filling the seats. Already, with only two rows filled, there were more people in the audience than in the entire First Christian Church in Heron's Nest, and her throat constricted.

"Look at them." Roland's voice tickled the back of her neck. "All souls gathered to worship the Lord. Some who've never before sought his face."

"It's terrifying," Dorothy Lynn said. More than the sea of faces, she feared the two that hadn't arrived—yet.

"Come," Roland said, tugging her arm. "Sister Aimee is leading us in prayer."

He led her back through the maze of passageways to the same room where they'd been that afternoon. Now it was crammed with people, men and women alike, and at its center, Sister Aimee. She was no taller than anybody else, and Dorothy Lynn could barely make out the spot of blonde at the core of the crowd, but there was definitely a sense that all present were gathered around her. Roland pushed her forward, pressed her in, and shut the door.

Then, at the center of the room, two long, white-sleeved arms rose up, and silence fell.

"Holy Father, God—" the voice from the stage was back— "tonight, holy Father, we dedicate our words to you. We dedicate our lives to you. We dedicate the breath we take to you."

Sounds of agreement echoed each phrase; Dorothy Lynn whispered, "Yes, Father."

"We go into battle clothed in your righteousness. We carry your sword of truth. In your name we will speak."

"Yes, Sister." She joined the crowd.

"In your name we will heal."

"Yes, Sister." Louder this time.

"To a world that is dying, that is turning its back on you. Men and women desperate for healing. To lives drowning in sin we offer salvation in your name."

The words of the prayer were nearly lost in the ocean of agreement, and what had been fear turned to fire. Dorothy Lynn felt a burning within her, spreading to the tips of her fingers, itching to touch the strings of her guitar. And while part of her could have stayed and basked in the glory of this moment, her feet begged to carry her to the stage, her throat to the song.

Sister Aimee continued to pray, her words rushing together and together until they transcended language. Dorothy Lynn's ears awoke to the spiritual tongue, and to the realization that they'd been hearing it for some time. Exactly when the transition happened, she couldn't say; her spirit had been understanding long before her mind became aware.

And it wasn't just Sister Aimee.

All around her, men and women burst forth in syllables, illogical and unfamiliar combinations of consonants, spinning a cocoon of prayer.

She opened her eyes, thinking somehow that to do so would aid her understanding. Perhaps the true message would appear in thin air, like the thought bubble of a cartoon, or flash before her eyes like the dialogue cards in the movies. Her confusion must have been evident, because Roland came up beside her and leaned close to her ear.

"Heavenly Father, we praise you."

Instantly, she trusted his interpretation.

"Heavenly Father, we do battle for you."

She moved her lips in silent participation.

"Savior Jesus, we glorify your name. We gather souls in your name. We heal in your name."

In your name, in your name, in your name.

"Amen."

Amen. And sweet release.

She spun around, straight into Roland, who, given the close confines of the room, seemed predestined to take her in his arms. The smell of smoke lingering on his starched white shirt mingled with the slow-burning ember within her. She looked up into his smoldering brown eyes.

"I'm ready."

❦

She felt three heartbeats with every step, certain the combined pounding of her pulse and her feet would cut through the noise of the crowd. But they were turned in conversation with each other, leaving her essentially alone.

"Just us," she said, speaking to the guitar cradled in her arms. Initially it had been slung over her back, but Roland had declared that "unwomanly," and there had followed an argument about whether she should hold it at all, or whether it should be perched on a stand, waiting for her. In the end, Dorothy Lynn prevailed, knowing she'd never make it out on stage without it. God would be with her, yes, but she needed an old friend, too.

Two microphones waited. One was positioned in front of her mouth to capture her singing; the other, shorter, to pick up the guitar. Earlier, she and Roland and a technician had adjusted everything perfectly. She'd even played a few chords and heard the amplification of her music echo through the empty theater. Glad, at least, to have had that first shock behind her.

She took her seat, as Roland had instructed, and nestled the guitar on her lap. If anybody in the audience knew or cared, they gave no notice. She looked across to where Roland waited in the wings, his smile a lifeline.

Play, he mouthed, strumming an invisible guitar.

Her song rang in her head, her fingers curled in memory around the neck. Nobody heard the first chord, or the second, or the third, so she played through them again. She couldn't sing, not yet. Not without knowing that someone was listening. Something, though, prompted her to speak. She leaned forward, her lips as close to the microphone as the technician had allowed.

"Are you ready?"

To hear her voice, spread thin across the audience, brought on a sense of both shock and power, even though nobody turned an ear. And why should they? Who was she? Tears gathered in her throat, threatening to wash away both her voice and every bit of confidence that brought her to this place. She closed her eyes.

In your name.

This one phrase she prayed over and over, until she was nearly knocked off the stool when his holy name exploded around her.

"Jesus."

His name. Her voice. And when she opened her eyes, more than a dozen were looking back at her.

"Jesus," she repeated, not louder, but with purpose. More eyes. They were watching her the way they'd been watching Sister Aimee the other night—some were, anyway. And what did she have to say? Everything she knew was in her song. Once again, she strummed the opening chords and said, "Jesus."

More turned around, and they answered back.

"Jesus."

She stole words from Sister Aimee. "Jesus is coming. Are you ready?"

A response—scattered amens from those she'd captured, along with a whooping "Yes!"

So she repeated those three chords, those six words, until as far as she could see, faces were turned in her direction. She closed her eyes one last time, picturing a circle of Sunday school children under a tree, and sang.

Jesus is coming!
Are you ready
to meet your Savior in the sky?
He, on his white horse, gath'rin' unto him.
We are his church. We are his bride.

Her hands created music on their own; words poured from her mouth. Her mind returned to the place it was before she began singing—a constant, simple stream of prayer. Each syllable an answer. When she came to the end of the song, there seemed to be nothing to do but to begin again, and this time when she reached the chorus, five hundred voices joined in.

She glanced over at Roland, who stood with his arms folded,

looking like the cat who licked the cream. With the slightest lift of his finger, she knew to play it one more time. In truth, she could have played all night, because her own strength had been taken over from the very first note. Finally, though, it was time to bring the song to a close, and the swell of applause that followed felt nothing like the praise in their singing. She imagined a rush of wind generated from the clapping of their hands, and it could have swept her away like the wings of a million angels.

Immediately her fingers poised to play a new song, one she knew she and the audience shared in a collective consciousness.

Jesus is coming to earth again;
What if it were today?

To her joy, most of the audience joined her by the second line, and by the time she brought them to the chorus, "Glory, glory!" they joined in with such thundering accord she lost her own voice within theirs. She felt ten feet tall yet invisible as she led them through the third verse.

Somehow she knew this congregation would follow her into yet another song, and another. They might have come to hear Sister Aimee preach, but in this moment, they were hers. It was a power she'd never dreamed of, and as she furiously strummed the strings behind the final note, she understood why her father had sheltered her from it, why he'd relegated her to the children's Sunday school beneath the trees. There was danger here, the darkness of pride.

Holding her hands still, she dropped her head and found silence in the midst of praise. "Thank you, Jesus," she said. *In your name.*

Her voice, amplified by the microphone, shot through the

theater. She said it again, and the audience responded with a rallying cry.

She had to leave. If she didn't, she knew she never would. She stood and prepared to exit the stage, hoping her legs would withstand the journey. But Roland was at her side, his arm around her shoulder, leaning into the microphone.

"Ladies and gentlemen." He had to repeat the address before any kind of silence could be found. "Ladies and gentlemen, let me introduce you to St. Louis's own Dorothy Lynn Dunbar."

She tugged at his sleeve and whispered, "Heron's Nest."

He made a *hush* sound out of the corner of his mouth and continued. "In these times, how refreshing it is to see a young woman unspoiled by the trappings of this world. Modest, pure, a shining example of the womanhood of a simpler time. Singing from her heart to yours."

He gave her the smallest of squeezes, and the audience erupted into new applause.

"Can you tell us, Miss Dunbar, how you came to be here this evening?"

They'd rehearsed this, too, while her hair was being coaxed into these cascading curls.

She leaned toward the microphone. "I heard Sister Aimee speak the other night." Her voice sounded faint again, like a child's. "And the Lord spoke to me. And he gave me a song to sing."

All true, but she couldn't shake the deceitfulness of the way she was telling it.

"And sing you did, darling." He pulled her close and planted a fatherly kiss on her forehead, making her feel as insignificant as her voice. "Now, say good night."

This they had not rehearsed, but she complied, saying

nothing but offering a wave with the same hand that, just moments before, had strummed the audience under her power.

She walked off feeling stupid, accompanied by Roland's glowing introduction of Aimee Semple McPherson. *"The evangelistic voice of our day. A woman anointed by God. The prophet with a message to all who would follow Jesus."*

By the time Dorothy Lynn was back in the shadows of the wings, her own skin was wrapped around her, and it was as if she'd never taken the stage at all. She found her guitar case where she'd left it, open and waiting. Kneeling, she placed the guitar within the velvet, closed the lid, and fastened the latches. She laid her hands flat on the lid. If only she, too, could be so easily locked away. Certainly, somewhere there was some space she could crawl into and hide. But here again was Roland, taking her hand and hauling her to her feet.

This time the kiss he gave was not so fatherly, but tight-lipped and lingering, straight on her surprised mouth, and over before she could think to pull away.

"You were wonderful," he said, holding her. "Do you know how wonderful you are? Of course you don't. Otherwise you wouldn't be so wonderful. How did I know?" He took her face in his hands and leaned in close. "What did I see in that face?"

"Stop," she said, though his touch and his words fanned the embers of what she'd felt on stage. "All I did was sing a song."

"Oh no, my angel." Roland took her hands. "You held them. Right here." He kissed her fingers. "And you delivered them straight to Aimee. I knew all we needed was the perfect sweet, young girl."

She curled her fingers and tried to pull away. "I thought you cared about my song."

"Of course I did. And, darling, they loved it. They loved *you*."

"I'm not your *darling*." She wrenched her hands away, picked up her case, and began to weave her way through the dark backstage maze, begging the pardon of the dozen or so people she bumped into. Sister Aimee's voice became nothing more than distant, droning noise.

What had she been thinking? What business did Dorothy Lynn Dunbar from Heron's Nest have taking to the stage? Made such a fool—

"Dorothy!"

He'd followed her, and he grabbed her arm, twisting her to him as the guitar became entangled in a mass of ropes, much to the chagrin of the stagehand set to the task of straightening the mess out.

"Dames back here," the stagehand muttered, keeping a stub of cigar firmly gripped in the corner of his mouth. "Save the drama for the stage."

By the time he scuttled off, Dorothy Lynn felt calmer, if not more secure. She faced Roland, holding her guitar case between them like a shield. "Don't touch me."

"I'm sorry, sweetheart. Forgive me. I get carried away."

She gripped the case tighter, unconvinced.

"Why are you so upset? You sang so beautifully. You captured their hearts."

"It's silly."

"I doubt that. You don't seem like a silly girl."

"You don't know what kind of girl I am. You don't know me at all."

"Don't I?" He reached into the breast pocket of his suit and produced a cigarette. The same stagehand who had untangled Dorothy Lynn from the ropes appeared with a match, then ambled away again. "Let me take a crack at it. You're a sweet girl from the sticks. Sat in the little church every Sunday watching your daddy preach nice, sweet sermons. One thou-shalt-not after another."

"I told you all of that," she said. *But not about the sermons.*

"But that wasn't enough for you, was it? You've got your own voice, don't you?"

"I don't—"

"You aren't satisfied with that life."

"Yes, I am."

"You shouldn't be. You could be more. Have more."

"I don't want more."

"Of course you do. Or you wouldn't be here."

Her mind reached back to that long-ago scrap of paper where she'd written that very thing. The actual paper was still tucked away in her Bible back home. Somehow she'd never been able to bring herself to throw it away. It was like that with all her verses, no matter how complete or worthy. She kept them all, never knowing which one would grow into its own truth.

"Your father never let you sing, did he?" Roland said. "And neither does this fiancé." He picked a fleck of tobacco from his tongue. "And how ridiculous is it, to have a fiancé? Nobody gets engaged anymore."

"I do."

"Then you're a fool."

Surrounded by the heavy blackness of everything that hides behind a stage, he looked like temptation itself. The tip of his cigarette glowed red, then went dark. His lips twisted in an enticing grin, and his eyes sparkled in onyx triumph.

And yet it was not fear that held her feet to the floor. "I like to be truthful."

"You haven't been deceitful."

"Not to you, maybe, or even to them, but to myself. That—" she gestured out toward the stage—"isn't me."

"But you like how it felt." It wasn't a question, because he knew. So she didn't answer. "Stay or go as you like, but don't be angry because a stranger knows you better than people who've loved you all your life."

"I have to get out of here," she said. Perhaps she didn't like to be truthful after all.

"Let's go back to the dressing room. Maybe a cup of tea?"

"No, home. I've been gone all day. I'm sure they'll be worried."

"You can't go home. We want you back out there for the altar call."

"You never told me that."

"We weren't sure how well you would be received." He seemed to be choosing his words carefully. "But the audience loved you. And—" he pointed directly at her, cigarette clamped between his fingers—"as you like to be so truthful, you loved it too."

"We all have to go home sometime, Mr. Lundi," she said. "And if I don't go now, I'm afraid I'll never want to again."

He said nothing, but dropped his cigarette to the floor and ground it with a twist of an expensive-looking leather shoe. Then he reached into his pocket and produced a bundle of folded bills.

"Sister Aimee said I wasn't to get paid."

"I'm not paying you," he said. "What's your sister's address?"

Reluctantly, she mumbled the house number and street, after which Roland peeled two bills off the top. "It's cab fare. Go to the ticket office and ask the gentleman there to hail one down for you. You shouldn't be out alone on the streetcars at night."

He pressed the money into her hand, and she looked at it.

Two dollars. She might not be a city girl, but even she knew that amount far exceeded the cost of a ride home. "It's too much."

"Very well," he said, and to her surprise, he took a dollar back and stuffed it in his pocket. "Good luck to you, Miss Dunbar. Tell the driver to keep the change."

❦ CHAPTER TEN ❦

AS INSTRUCTED, Dorothy Lynn handed the dollar bill over the seat to the eager hand of the cabbie.

"You sure, lady?" he said when it was clear that his tip exceeded the fare. "Gee, thanks."

"It's not my money," she said, and was out of the car before he could open the door for her.

It was close to nine o'clock. She stood in the glow of the streetlight long after the black smoke of the cab's exhaust had dissipated into the night air. The windows shone with welcoming lamplight, and no shouts or thumps could be heard through the open windows. *The boys must be in bed.*

Her head had remained perfectly empty throughout the ride home. No echo of song or hint of new poetry had invaded her thoughts. In fact, no *thoughts* had invaded her thoughts. She had no plan of what she would say at the inevitable confrontation, and her final words with Roland remained trapped in the stale backstage air. From the theater to here, the cabbie had carried on a one-sided conversation about how Rogers Hornsby was destined to lead the Cardinals to the World Series.

She might have stood out on that sidewalk forever if the front door itself hadn't opened, bringing Roy out onto the porch.

"That you, Dorothy Lynn?" He held a thick slice of white bread in one hand and brought the other up to his eyes, as if looking out across a great distance. "Has our prodigal returned?"

She smiled, something she didn't envision happening upon her return, and began the slow approach to the house. "She has."

"In a cab?"

"Isn't that what we prodigals do? Squander our money?"

"As long as it wasn't mine," he said, holding the door open wider in welcome.

Upon closer inspection, Dorothy Lynn could see that his hair, usually pomaded to perfection, was mussed, his shirt equally disheveled with its tail hanging out the back of his pants. He looked tired but happy, and the bread reminded her that she was starving. "I suppose I missed dinner."

He took a bite. "It was an artichoke nightmare. Might want to fry yourself an egg."

She nodded and went past him through the door. She was certain that Darlene had spent the evening filling his head with fears and accusations—premonitions and pleadings to go rescue her sister from the sinister goings-on at the theater. Yet he'd welcomed her home; she needed only make it up the steps to her borrowed room, shut the door, and let this entire day pass into the stuff of dreams and memories.

But by the third step, that was not to be.

"How dare you, Dorothy Lynn Dunbar."

She didn't need to turn around to know that Darlene waited at the bottom of the steps, hands on her ample hips. In fact, she could hear the foot tapping on the floor. "I'm tired, Sis. We can talk in the morning."

"I want to talk now."

"Then do so," Dorothy Lynn said, continuing her plod up the stairs, "just not to me. I'm going to bed."

Now Darlene was behind her saying, "Fine, we can talk in there, but you won't get a snack."

At the landing Dorothy Lynn turned around. "You cannot tell me when I'll sleep and when I'll talk. I'm a woman, perfectly capable of making decisions on my own. Other people understand that about me. Why can't you?"

"Because I'm your big sister, that's why."

"And I love you." To prove it, she leaned forward, giving Darlene a soft kiss on the cheek.

Her sister frowned. "You smell like cigarette smoke."

"I know."

"And that's a new dress. Where's your old one?" Simultaneous shock and horror took possession of Darlene's face, stretching its features to comical proportions. "Did he—did that man—" she dropped her voice to a hiss—"take advantage of you?"

"Yes, he did," Dorothy Lynn said, enjoying her flash of cruelty. "But not in the way that you think. Please, I'm tired. Can't we talk in the morning?"

"Do you promise to tell me everything?" Darlene's expression had been restored to one of mere suspicion.

"Everything."

She went into the room and shut the door behind her. Enough light came through the window, even with the shade pulled down, for her to prepare for bed without bothering to light the lamp. She leaned the guitar against the cluttered desk and stepped out of her shoes. Wishing she had her sister's help, she worked halfway down the row of pearly buttons at the back of the dress, shrugging out of it the minute she'd unfastened enough to do so. The dress landed in a puddle at her feet, and she unsnapped the garters. Sitting on the edge of the bed, she rolled her stockings down and tossed them on the floor. Somewhere, amidst the books and soldiers and overturned rocking horse, she had a nightgown.

Narrow and thin as it was, though, the mattress felt wonderful as she stretched out on it. The best it had ever felt. After all, it was a bed for a child, and in that she found comfort. That, and the sound of hundreds of voices raised in her song trapped within her pillow.

❦

The smell of coffee lured her. Eyes still full of sleep, she found her housecoat hanging on the hook on the back of the door, wrapped it around her, and headed for the kitchen.

"Well, look who's up," Darlene said, though she didn't seem surprised. She wore a dressing gown, though Dorothy Lynn strongly suspected it belonged to Roy, given the blue-and-black pinstripes and wide lapels. For a feminine touch, Darlene had wrapped a thick, blue silk ribbon around her head, securing it with a bow just behind her ear. Her soft, bobbed curls puffed all around it.

Dorothy Lynn had no sooner said "Coffee?" than a steaming cup was on the table, filled to the point of sloshing into the saucer. She leaned forward and took a scorching sip off the top. It was good, better than Ma's, and she said so.

"It's Hills Brothers." Darlene, busily scrambling something delicious in a skillet, used her elbow to point to the can. "You know Ma won't buy it."

She glanced at the can sitting on the countertop. The image of the exotic man wearing a turban, long robe, and slippers as, midstep, he sipped from a cup, embodied their mother's reluctance.

Dorothy Lynn sighed and took another sip. "She's missing out on the whole world."

"From what I remember of Scripture, seems that's what a good Christian woman is supposed to do."

"And if I remember, the Bible also says only harlots cut their hair."

Darlene presented her with a plate of eggs and pulled two pieces of toast from a countertop contraption. "So tell me, Dot, should I take you to the barbershop today and have yours cut?"

The accusation couldn't have been more obvious, and it took all of Dorothy Lynn's control to sink her teeth into the crispy toast and suppress an equally hateful reply, and she was glad she did, because her sister's apology came right on its heels.

"I'm sorry. Of course if anything horrible had happened, I'm sure you would have told me."

"Why would you even think I was capable of such a thing?"

"Well, he is so handsome. And girls these days—"

"*Girls*, Darlene. Not your sister. Do you know what he wanted?"

"What?" Darlene sat across from her at the table with her own coffee, thirsty for a story.

"He wanted my innocence. He wanted to put this perfect, virginal girl on the stage, singing a sweet song, so that people like you and Roy who think Sister Aimee is some sort of abomination would feel nice and safe."

"That's beautiful."

Dorothy Lynn stabbed her eggs. "It is not beautiful. It's loathsome."

"How can you say that?"

"You wouldn't understand."

"Why not?"

"You and Ma and Pa—even Brent—none of you understand what it means when I write a song. Where it comes from. You think it's silly, or quaint. Brent said he'd have no problem allowing me to keep writing once we got married. *Allowing* me! Like it's a right of his to take away. And then, it finally seems that someone is interested—someone with power—and it turns out he only cared about the length of my hair and my unspoiled nature. He would have used a trained monkey if he thought that would get the people's attention."

"He wanted *you*."

"Maybe." She pushed the food around on her plate.

"So, how awful was it?"

"How awful was what?"

"Singing, in front of a crowd. You were so upset last night, but I didn't want to pry. . . ."

"Yes, you did."

"That's when I thought it was about something juicy."

They laughed, putting Dorothy Lynn's mind momentarily at ease. She took a bite of breakfast and studied her sister. Without her usual rouged cheeks and lip color, Darlene's face had a soft, porcelain appearance, made full by the weight gain of her pregnancy. In fact, if not for that, she would look almost like a baby doll, except for the lacquered nails gripping her coffee cup.

"Oh, Sis," she said, steeling herself for the opening of the wound. "It was awful."

Darlene *tsked* into her coffee. "Stage fright?"

"The opposite." Between bites, she told of the rousing prayer with Sister Aimee before the evening began, her own prayer alone on the stage, and the moment she heard herself—as if from the catwalk—singing the song that had before then existed only in her head. She tried to capture the sound of the crowd, singing and praising, and the beautiful, comfortable, natural feeling when she sang a more familiar hymn. "And then," she concluded, "I didn't want to leave. I've never felt such, such . . . *power*. And it was terrifying."

"Do you see? How it corrupts? Innocent little thing like yourself. Keep at it and you'd be just like that woman."

Dorothy Lynn didn't dare tell her that, for a split second, at least, that was exactly what she'd wanted. "They'd never let that happen. Well, not Mr. Lundi, anyway. He made sure that the audience knew I wasn't nothin' but some sweet country girl who wrote a tune for Sister Aimee. Felt like I was back at the schoolhouse on recitation day."

"Well, at least it's over."

She thought for a moment. "Yes."

"And we can get back to making your wedding dress?"

"Yes," she said, gulping the last—now tepid—sip of coffee.

"Then go get dressed while I clean up this kitchen. Mrs. Mevreck said she'd keep the boys until noon."

Flush with the relief of confession, Dorothy Lynn raced up the stairs. In the upstairs bathroom, she splashed water on her face and cleaned her teeth. After running her brush under the tap, she pulled it through her hair, plaited it in two long braids, and wrapped them around her head, pinning them in place.

Back in the room, she was stripped to her underwear when there was a knock and there Darlene stood with the almost-dress draped over her arm. "Now, yesterday, before our *interruption*, I almost had this pinned."

"No reason we can't pick up where we left off."

"I set the machine up in the front room," Darlene said, motioning for Dorothy Lynn to follow.

"I'm not dressed yet."

"We'll get you dressed in this downstairs. It's fine—there's no one here but us."

Wearing only her camisole and underpants, Dorothy Lynn hunkered down and tiptoed behind her sister. Never in her life had she been out and about in a house wearing only underclothes, and she felt especially terrified and daring.

"Relax," Darlene said. "We're all girls here."

They went into the front parlor, where Darlene had mercifully had the foresight to draw the curtains. Though midmorning, the room was a pond of gray, cool light; Dorothy Lynn pulled her arms closer to her, shivering.

"When are the boys due back?"

"Not for two more hours." Darlene made no attempt to hide her relief. "RJ will start school next year, so things'll be easier."

At her sister's prompting, Dorothy Lynn held her arms out stiffly, stepped into the dress, and stood perfectly still as it was brought up gingerly over her shoulders.

"We want a nice, clean line," Darlene said, walking a slow circle around her. "Close enough to show your figure but loose enough for dancing."

"Oh, there won't be dancin'." She couldn't imagine Brent allowing such a thing.

"That's a shame."

"Besides, Pa's not here to dance with, so . . ."

"Oh, Dot. I'm so sorry. That was insensitive of me. But I did talk to Roy the other night, and he said that—if we don't hear from Donny—he'd be happy to walk you down the aisle."

Dorothy Lynn's eyes darted over to the photograph displayed

on the mantel. It was Roy and Darlene on their wedding day—she, nearly unrecognizable in her slender serenity, and he full of protective pride. "I barely remember your weddin'."

"You were young."

"What I do remember is how Ma cried that night. After you'd driven away. And Pa pattin' her and sayin' it would be all right. That we'd see you again come summer. But she just said it would never be the same."

"It's not."

She could feel the fabric cinching close to her as Darlene closed it up the back.

"I don't suppose she'll cry after my wedding."

"Of course she will."

"She won't have nothin' to cry about. Brent already says he wants us to have dinner with her whenever we can so she won't be alone. And it's not but a ten-minute walk from our door to his."

"It won't be the same. You'll be his wife. He'll be your priority."

"I suppose." But it had already become a common thing, the three of them puttering around. "I don't know why we're bothering with this."

"With what?"

"*This*. The dress, the wedding. You're the only family to be there, and that's dependin' on the baby. We're not headin' off to any kind of new life or anything. I'm just changing beds."

Darlene swatted her bottom. "Don't be vulgar."

They said nothing for a while until Darlene took the pincushion from her wrist and declared the fitting done. She took Dorothy Lynn's hand and helped her down from the stool, saying, "Let's try it out."

"What do you mean?"

Humming, Darlene crossed the room to the gramophone and began flipping through the discs piled on the table beside it. When she found what she was looking for, she turned the crank—an amusing sight from behind. As the first strains of a familiar tune filled the room, she turned with her arms open wide. "Shall we?"

A woman's thin voice poured from the speaker.

I once had a gown, it was almost new,
Oh, the daintiest thing, it was sweet Alice blue. . . .

Darlene was so rarely silly, Dorothy Lynn couldn't pass up the opportunity. Carefully, she took her sister's hand and stepped into an embrace, ready to let Darlene lead. They giggled, bobbing their heads until the top of the next count, then launched into dancing.

"You dance divinely," Darlene said, making her voice husky and masculine.

"Why, thank you," Dorothy Lynn warbled. They waltzed a near-perfect box around the room, occasionally bumping into an end table or sofa.

And they sang.

In my sweet little Alice blue gown,
When I first wandered down into town,
I was so proud inside,
And I felt every eye,
And in every shop window, I primped passing by.

More than once, to avoid tripping, Dorothy Lynn stepped in closer, and she brushed against her sister's protruding belly.

"She's dancing too!" Darlene exclaimed, and they laughed louder.

It was Dorothy Lynn who first heard the knock at the door.

"Probably another vacuum cleaner salesman," Darlene said as she lifted the needle off the record. "Roy says I should indulge them, but who has the time?"

She stepped into the entryway, leaving Dorothy Lynn to immediately regret not having been released from the dress before being abandoned. She could never take it off on her own.

The voices were muffled, but it certainly wasn't a vacuum salesman at the door. Darlene spoke in low, agitated tones, but not low enough. *You need to go away. Just leave her alone.*

Roland, and she knew his charms—more persuasive than any salesman could hope to be.

"What does he want?" Dorothy Lynn called, but if she hoped her sister would serve as a buffer, she was mistaken. Suddenly, Roland Lundi was in the front room. His suit, pale gray, blended with the light.

"Dorothy." Then he stopped and cocked his head, noticing what she was wearing.

"It's my wedding dress."

"Is it?" He took a bold step forward and examined it closer, curious.

"It's inside out. We're making it. My sister—she's making it."

"I hope I haven't brought you bad luck by looking at it."

"That's only for the groom," Darlene said without a hint of humor or kindness. "And you're not the groom."

"Of course not," he said with a smile that would make any other woman regret the notion. Then, back to Dorothy Lynn, "Could I speak with you alone for a moment?"

"No, you cannot," Darlene said.

"Very well," he said, unfazed, "we can speak here. Would you sit down?"

"I can't," Dorothy Lynn said. "Pins."

But Darlene could, and she dropped herself heavily in a brocade chair, clearly ready to listen to every word.

"We're leaving town tomorrow."

She had nothing to say.

"And I am here to humbly request that you come with us."

She wasn't aware that she'd been holding her breath, but it wrapped itself around any possible response.

Darlene, however, was plagued by no such silence. "My sweet Moses," she said, a phrase common back home, but one Dorothy Lynn was sure Darlene never uttered among her St. Louis friends. "You must be out of your mind."

"I'm not," he said, not taking his eyes off Dorothy Lynn. "You don't know—we didn't know—how you could affect the audience. Last night, at the altar call, more than fifty souls came to seek Jesus as their Savior."

"That's wonderful," she said, not doubting for a moment the genuine emotion holding him in its grip.

"They saw themselves in you—"

"Stop—"

"And at the end of the night, as they were leaving, people asked after you. Where you were. When they could see you again."

She brought her hands up to cover her ears. "Don't tell me that. I don't want to hear it. You deceived them. You said I was from here. They're never going to see me again."

"He doesn't care what they think," Darlene said, folding her hands across her belly. "Ask him how much money they took in. That's what this is really all about."

"All right," Roland said, not wavering. "I'll tell you. We took in twice what we did any other night here."

"I had nothing to do with that."

"Maybe not, and trust me when I tell you that Sister Aimee isn't thrilled at the possibility that you made any difference at all, but our stakes are too high to ignore the possibility."

"What stakes?"

"We're building a church, out in Los Angeles, California. Bigger than anything anybody has ever seen."

"What does that have to do with me?"

"We've got two more stops—Kansas City and Denver. Then on to Los Angeles."

"Winning souls and taking money," Darlene said.

"Hush," Dorothy Lynn said, suddenly protective. "She's not like that. You don't know how powerful she is."

"With this church, millions will hear her preach. And that's not an exaggeration. Millions, Dorothy. Los Angeles is a growing, vibrant city, destined to be a godless one. There'll be nothing like it anywhere in the world. It's Aimee's vision, the Angelus Temple. But it takes money, sacrifice. We need people who believe in the gospel, who are willing to be part of Christ's church."

"I have a church," she said. And a home, and a husband waiting for her. All rolled together.

"Just come with me to Kansas City. Just there. Only a few days, and we'll put you on a train home, to here or Pigeon Tree—"

"Heron's Nest," she corrected.

"Wherever you want to go."

She could tell he wanted to touch her; his fingers flexed as if he gripped her, but the fact that she was wearing a wedding dress or the pins that held it together or the pregnant sister in the corner kept him from making any such overture.

151

"I don't want to go anywhere."

He stepped closer, lowering his voice, as if that would shut Darlene out of the room. "Would you rather go back to your circle of Sunday school children under the tree?"

"Are their souls any less worthy?"

"Of course not," he said, and she felt dangerously soothed. "But they'll have you forever. We've only got a short period of time. A moment, and it's gone."

"Couldn't you just find some other girl in Kansas City?"

He laughed—no, chuckled. Deep and warm and with absolute affection. "We could, I suppose. But what are the chances of finding one as magical as you?"

"Magical?"

"Oh, no." Darlene worked to get out of her chair. "She might have a soft spot for such talk, but I can spot a line. I'm married to a car salesman; I know flattery when I hear it."

"With all due respect, ma'am," Roland said, relegating her to matronly status with a single word, "Dorothy is a grown woman. She can speak her own mind."

A familiar sound came from the kitchen—the clattering of four active feet punctuated by the slamming of a door and the inevitable call of "Mama!" Mrs. Mevreck must have reached the limits of her patience.

"I'll go see to them," Darlene said, looking at Roland side-eyed with renewed suspicion. "It's almost time for lunch."

After she left the room, Roland said, "I take it I won't be invited to stay?"

"She's very protective," Dorothy Lynn said.

Emboldened by Darlene's absence, he reached out, lightly running the backs of his fingers along the sleeve of the dress. "Do you know what it means to be the bride of Christ?"

"Of course I do." She tensed her arm, drawing herself away from his touch.

"Scriptures tell us that we will be clothed in our acts of righteousness. Think about it: living this life, continuously adding to our eternal garment. Fifty souls were saved last night, largely because of your unselfish act. How many more could come to know Jesus if you would just obey your calling?"

She stepped away. "Your desire is not my calling."

"No, but can you deny the music God has put in your heart? Could you not feel his pleasure surging through you as you sang last night?"

How could she tell him that whatever pleasure she'd felt was tainted by her own pride? "It was a lark, Mr. Lundi. Nothing more."

He looked to be on the bridge of acceptance, his hat halfway to his head. "So, no Kansas City?"

"No."

He used his hat to gesture toward the photograph on the mantel. "So that's going to be you in a few weeks?"

"Yes," she said, only there would be no father, no brother, and she would be wearing this very dress turned right-side out.

He must have picked up on her thought before it was fully formed, because his hat was mere inches away from his head when he brought it back down. "Didn't you say your brother was in California?"

Her mind raced back to their lunch at the Golden Bowl Chinese Restaurant where she'd told him so much—too much—about her wandering brother. Perhaps he'd picked up on the thread of envy she'd kept so closely stitched to her heart. He seemed poised to pull on it, unravel the truth, or worse, wrap it around her yearning to bring her brother home.

"He's in Culver City."

"I'm sure you're looking forward to seeing him again." Once more, his hat was up, hovering mere inches above his head. "I take it he'll be at the wedding?"

How could he know? Not about Donny, but about the hold he could have by using her brother as the rope to rescue them both? "Is it far?"

"From here?"

"Culver City. Is it far from Los Angeles?"

"The two are practically in each other's backyard."

"Would you have any way to find him, do you think? Donny Dunbar—it's an unusual name. And I know he's workin' as a carpenter on movie sets. How many could there be?"

"I'm a busy man, Miss Dunbar." The hat was firmly on his head. "As your sister might say, souls to save; money to raise."

"I've never been anywhere, Mr. Lundi. You can understand how terrifyin' this very idea is for me." Now she knew exactly what it felt like to close a deal. Carefully crafted sincerity, tinged with early triumph.

"You won't be alone," he said, picking up the thread of their unspoken agreement. "We're like a family, all of us. Your travel, your meals—maybe even a few new dresses. The kind that don't come with pins. All for God's glory. And then home by—how long until the wedding?"

"Six weeks."

He snapped his fingers. "Plenty of time. You have my word."

"And you'll help me find Donny?"

"You have my word on that, too."

"I need to think," she mused aloud. "And to telephone Brent and my mother. And talk to Darlene."

"Let them bury themselves," he said, heading to the front door. "Our train leaves at eight."

Is there any thing whereof it may be said, See, this is new?
it hath been already of old time, which was before us.

ECCLESIASTES 1:10

BREATH OF ANGELS
10:20 A.M.

Breath of Angels has three distinct worlds. There's the world filled with card games and dominoes and concerts performed by local high school choirs. The residents there move slowly but surely from room to room through quiet, carpeted halls. They congregate with each other in the lobby, bring family members to lunch in the dining hall, and sometimes even step away for a trip to a local museum or shopping mall. Lynnie had been one of them, her calendar full of penciled events, twenty-minute conversations at the mailbox, swim aerobics three times a week. Even after the first stroke, when she'd been forced to use the walker and keep a battery-operated call button around her neck at all times.

Even then, she knew she'd move on. They all did—either move on or die. The day you couldn't get yourself out of bed, out of the shower, onto the toilet. Every night, late at night, a soundless Angel in soft-soled shoes patrolled the halls of the Breath of Angels apartments, placing a yellow Post-it note on each door. The residents knew to be out of bed and to remove that little square before 10 a.m. That was the sign that all was well. That's how they knew you were alive and ready to function for the day. Otherwise, you moved on.

Moments before the third, and so far final, stroke, Lynnie had just put a

155

bowl of instant oatmeal in the microwave and was making slow progress to open her door and remove the note. Clearly, she remembers thanking God for another day. In fact, she'd write as much on the note and stick it on her refrigerator, which had become a sea of yellow.

August 12, 2001. *Thank you, Lord, for another day.*

August 13, 2001. *Thank you, Lord, for another day.*

One piled atop another, curling at the corners.

When she woke up in her new room after moving on, she wondered what had become of the notes. Everything else she owned had been neatly boxed away.

Now she is at the mercy of Charlotte Hill, piloting the wheelchair.

They lurch around a corner, so close Lynnie can clearly see the dimples in the paint as her footrest scrapes along the wall.

"Sorry about that," Charlotte says.

Had she the power of speech, Lynnie might say something soothing, intended to assuage the girl's anxiety, despite her own terror. Instead, she's locked in her silence, clenching her jaw, fingers curled on the armrest of the chair, as if she has the strength to hold herself in.

One more corner, and they're in an unfamiliar lobby. The furniture is pristine—a rose-colored sofa flanked by an end table and lamp. A low coffee table in front of it boasts a color-coordinated bouquet of obviously silk flowers and a perfect fan of magazines. Clearly, nobody sits here. Nobody waits here. Perhaps they will be the first, she and Charlotte, and Lynnie tries to picture the girl settling on the sofa, the stiff, cheap cushions scraping beneath her jeans. The awkward space seems custom-made for conversation with an invalid.

But Charlotte's not stopping at the couch. She's headed straight for the massive glass doors at the front of the room. At least, Lynnie hopes Charlotte recognizes the barrier of glass between them and the picturesque autumnal vision on the other side. Their momentum hasn't decreased in the least.

Then, with a force worthy of a carnival ride, she is spinning, the world a serene, pastel blur, and she's looking at a long, low, unmanned reception desk.

"Your family sent doughnuts in honor of your birthday," Charlotte says. "I figure the staff'll be in the break room for a good twenty minutes unless somebody rings the bell."

She says it with a mix of triumph and conspiracy, and then Lynnie knows. Charlotte Hill is taking her out. As in, *outside.* The girl pokes into her line of vision long enough to press the oversize silver button that activates the automatic door. Seconds later, she's backing across the threshold.

And Lynnie breathes fresh air—something she's rarely afforded the pleasure to do since she's "moved on."

Birthday or not, she would have known it was mid-October. The humidity of summer has released its grip, and the air holds a burning crispness like a candle has just been snuffed.

Lynnie holds her face up to the sun, its warmth touching her like a welcome caress. Her mother used to say that the sunshine brought her freckles out to play. She brings her hand up to her own face and touches the thin, cool skin, too fragile to bear the weight of such spots.

Charlotte maneuvers the chair with a confident stroll over the winding concrete slabs that snake along the grounds.

"It's beautiful out here, isn't it?" she says, and then launches into a song she's far too young to know. "'Sunshine on my shoulders makes me happy. . . .'"

Lynnie was already an old woman when she first put that album on the turntable in the den. Still, this girl sings with a low, throaty voice, perfectly suited to the turning leaves, and soon tears gather in the corners of her eyes and spill down one by one, feeling cool in the slow-strolling breeze.

"I wanted to have a chance to be alone with you," Charlotte says in place of the second verse, which is a shame because it's always been Lynnie's favorite. "Before everybody else comes because, you know, they don't exactly know me."

Lynnie does her best to crane her neck—*Who is this girl?*—hoping a piercing glare might ask the question for her, but she manages only a glimpse to the left, where a bright-eyed squirrel stares at the nonthreatening parade of two passing before it.

Leaves crunch as they walk and wheel. Charlotte hums the John Denver tune, and Lynnie knows it will cycle endlessly through her head for the rest of the day. In fact, she calls up a few notes herself and almost moves them past the corner of her throat where all sounds seem to stop. Suddenly, Charlotte's face is right next to hers, so close she can smell the scent of the girl's neck. She's never known anybody who smelled like pears before. "Do you like that song?"

Lynnie nods.

"I do too. Music today is useless. Dad says nobody's written a decent song since 1976. Except for Dolly Parton. I watched a *Behind the Music* special about her. She kept the rights to all of her songs. She'll be making millions even after she dies. Isn't that smart of her?"

It's one of the rare times when Lynnie is glad to be free from the burden of speech.

"But you know something about that, don't you?"

They've come to a place where the walkway blossomed out to a wide, round slab with a trio of benches gathered in ever-present shade. Charlotte wheels her in, sets the brakes, and comes to the front, shrugging a well-stuffed backpack off her shoulders and plopping it on the bench before sitting down beside it.

She leans forward, her elbows on her knees, and takes Lynnie's hands in hers. "Do you even know? About your song? What's happening?"

Lynnie shakes her head with all the vigor she can muster.

"Typical." Charlotte hauls her backpack onto her lap and holds it there, bouncing her knees. "I really was arrested once, you know."

Lynnie has no doubt.

"But that's not why I'm here."

No doubt there, either.

"Do you know what I was arrested for?"

Perhaps Charlotte has forgotten she's already told this story to Kaleena back in the room. Or more likely, she assumes Lynnie has forgotten, not realizing there's hardly a day from the previous century that Lynnie cannot recall with almost-certain detail. It feels wonderful to have a new voice talking to her—not yelling overly cheerful platitudes, but simply talking, as if Lynnie could somehow equally engage.

Unless, of course, Charlotte hadn't told Kaleena the truth. Maybe she was arrested for shooting helpless old ladies. A knot of panic suppresses a silent scream when Charlotte digs into her bag and begins rummaging around, though it unravels with a band of silent chastisement when the girl produces not a gun or a knife, but some sort of flat-screened gadget.

"It's an iPad," she says, as if that explains anything. "The newest thing."

She hums quietly as she taps her fingertip on the screen. First here, then there, then she swipes and swipes, bringing her finger and thumb together, then producing a sort of soft, flicking motion.

"Here." She moves along the bench until she's sitting on the edge, hold-ing the screen under Lynnie's nose. "Can you see?"

Lynnie looks at the image; it's like a photograph in a frame. In the foreground is a hand-lettered cardboard sign that says *Let Jesus Feed You*. Charlotte sits next to it, dressed as she is now, in tattered jeans and a snug, short-sleeved shirt, but in the picture she's wearing a knit cap like a bulb tugged over her dark hair, and she has a guitar nestled in her lap. It's a beau-tiful instrument, deep red with what looks like birds etched to take flight from beneath the strings. Lynnie's own fingers itch to strum it, and she unclenches her grip from the armrest of the wheelchair and brings it, trembling, toward the image. At her touch, the small Charlotte on the screen comes to life, looks straight out, and says, "Are you ready?" Her voice, though tiny, carries the weight of a private joke.

"My friend J. D. did the video for me," the real Charlotte is saying, tilting the screen away from Lynnie's startled fingers. She taps it, until gradually the volume is increased and the first few chords emerge.

"I can't believe this," Charlotte whispers, and Lynnie notices that the girl's face has gone pale, and a tremble has taken possession of Charlotte's hands.

Believe what?

"I can't believe I'm sitting here with you. About to share this with you." She takes a deep breath, and her hands steady.

Surprisingly clear and strong, music emerges from the screen. It's immediately familiar, and Lynnie feels a chill at the base of her spine. It spreads up and up, flashing out across her shoulder. She wants to reach out her own trembling hand, to make it stop, at least long enough so she can catch the breath that seems to be knitting itself around the cold within her, but she remains immobile, unable to take her eyes off the small screen.

And then, the small Charlotte of the iPad sings.

Jesus is coming!
Are you ready
to meet your Savior in the sky?

The phrasing is slightly different, as Charlotte's singing voice possesses a sandy quality that scoops each note from a place of warmth. But it is, undoubtedly, the same song Lynnie sang in the Strawn Brothers Music Store a lifetime ago.

Her head fills with questions. *How?* And *who?* She poses them with a simple turning of her head from the girl to the screen and back.

"I call it evangelizing. The city calls it busking. But whatever. I didn't have a permit, so I got a citation. It was either pay a fine or do community service. I did my hours in a nursing home back home, and that gave me the idea to come here."

She turns to Lynnie with a huge smile—the first she's seen from the girl all day. It beautifully complements the delicate silver loop pierced through her lower lip.

"Isn't God amazing? Because I didn't know—honestly didn't know you were here. I didn't know anything about you. I just loved that song from the minute I bought the CD, and then everything started fitting together and . . . wait." Charlotte tilts her head, as if gathering up all of Lynnie's questions. "You don't know any of this, do you?"

Throughout, Lynnie's song has been playing like a reanimated specter between them, but it comes to a sudden halt as Charlotte taps the screen one, two, three times. Now the image is of another young woman with long, dark-blonde braids.

"She was on *American Idol* a few seasons back. Didn't win, but she released an album of gospel bluegrass, a bunch of old—" she sent an apologetic glance—"sorry, *classic* songs. And this one . . ." Charlotte taps the screen again, and for the second time in more than half a century, Lynnie's song fills the air, this time sung with a fresh-from-the-farm twang wrapped in guitar, fiddle, and the trill of a mandolin.

It is pure and sweet and perfect, and its creator's lips open and close in silent mismatched timing with the lyrics. Charlotte's voice joins in, creating dulcet harmony, and Lynnie imagines the three women are a trio, not unlike the Andrews Sisters, who had been such a favorite of Ma's before she died.

"It won a Country Music Award last spring," Charlotte says quietly during an instrumental bridge in which the fiddle's bow weaves the melody through the strings of the guitar. "You probably don't know that, either. I was watching the show, and I saw your name on the screen credited as the writer. And I thought, *I know that name. . . .*"

They are looking at each other again, the girl's eyes full of trepidation and mischief. As the pretty blonde sings the final chorus in the background, Lynnie is determined to hold Charlotte's gaze—her only means to answer for herself the question that's been nagging her since the first hours of the morning. She knows this girl. Knows her and yet doesn't. She's a forgotten third verse, the *la-la-la* of momentarily lost lyrics. The hair, the clothes, the piercings—all bearing testimony to what the world has come to during Lynnie's century of life.

But the eyes.

Strip away the liner, ignore what is clearly a smattering of tiny purple stars bursting from the brow, and look at the eyes. Those are the eyes of Lynnie's earliest memories.

"So I asked Grandpa."

Grandpa. Her breath comes faster and faster as she calculates. *Donny's son? Or grandson, even.*

"And he gave me a box with some things. Mostly pictures and newspaper clippings. Stuff like that. So I scanned it." She takes the screen away again and begins tapping, muttering something about its being a modern-day scrapbook. "There you are."

There she is, indeed. The one they'd put in the corner of the posters outside the theater. Her hair is styled in long, lush curls rivaling those of Mary Pickford. And like the actress, she's dressed to look more like a child than the nearly-nineteen-year-old woman she'd been at the time, with a knee-length pleated skirt and square-collared blouse. That was Roland's idea, of course.

Charlotte swipes her finger, and a new image appears, this one less precise, with the unmistakable tint of aged newspaper. The caption reads, *Sister Aimee prays with a select group of followers just minutes before taking the stage.*

Though the image is little more than a dark blur of bowed heads, Lynnie feels like she could name each of them. These were not "followers," as the caption would have the reader believe, but staff, workmen, and even what the world would one day call "groupies." Hangers-on who followed the evangelist from city to city, creating their own means of worship.

Lynnie is in that crowd too, though no photographer would have known to include her name in the caption, even if the picture was snapped just moments before she herself took the stage. She is there, right at Sister Aimee's side, the woman's long, white sleeve raised in a tower of prayer above her head. And next to her is Roland Lundi. Her shoulder grows warm, recalling the weight of his touch.

Charlotte interrupts Lynnie's thoughts with a touch of her own. "Now this," she says, "is something very special. The film was in terrible shape when we found it, but my friend J. D. is a film student, and he found some guys to restore it. I don't think the rest of the family even knows this exists."

Another swipe and the screen goes dark for just a moment before a pale, silvery, uncertain image appears at its center. The cameraman must have been stationed in the middle of the audience, though on some sort of raised platform, because the very bottom of the frame ripples with dark waves of audience. A black curtain—though in its color-life it was certainly a deep blood-red—stretches across a stage, empty save for a single microphone and a wooden chair. Then, from stage left, Roland Lundi with those swift, confident strides.

To see him again after so many years—Lynnie's heart seems poised to take its well-deserved final beat. She leans forward in her chair, as if doing so could bring her closer. Heat rises to her cheeks, and with it the blush of youth, she supposes. Oh, how he'd make her blush, and how quickly she'd bring her young, unmottled hands to her cheeks to hide his effects.

But she's an old woman now, and she knows for a fact he's dead. She'd heard his voice that day, welcome and familiar, telling her to go back. This far, and no more.

Charlotte's giggle only illuminates the sadness Lynnie feels at the thought.

"Quite a charmer, wasn't he?"

If you only knew.

"There's no sound, of course."

No sound is needed. Lynnie can hear his voice like it's coming from the trees. Soft and deep, roughened by smoke. Introducing the last vestige of pure American womanhood, untouched by vice, unsullied by scandal. Ready to lift her voice in song and lead them in an anthem of utmost urgency.

The tiny Roland raises his arm in the direction from which he'd entered, and the real, live "Dorothy Lynn Dunbar!" wants to leap from her seat at the sight of herself.

"I think this is in Kansas City?"

She confirms with a brief nod.

A sudden gust of wind skitters leaves across the walkway, but in its stead Lynnie hears the roar of a welcoming audience, for by then she'd advanced far beyond mere polite applause. Though there is no recording to confirm her memories, she knows the exact moment the crowd disciplined itself into hushed silence—within seconds of her cradling her guitar on her knee. Tiny white hands form the first chords; the same, gnarled and cold, do likewise.

"You've never seen this before?" Charlotte whispers.

Never.

"But you lived it."

It consumed me.

How could she not have known she was so very, very small? The enormous curtain loomed above her; the orchestra pit gaped at her feet. What twisted fable made her believe she wielded any sort of power? She'd been a girl with a guitar. Nothing more. "Beautiful in its simplicity," Roland had said. "Mesmerizing," he'd called her. "A real-life siren."

Lynnie doesn't need to close her eyes to transport her mind back to that very moment. In fact, she dare not, lest she open them to find herself back on the stage, forced to live through it all again.

"The quality isn't perfect," Charlotte says, and as she does, the image on the screen flickers. Little Dorothy Lynn Dunbar's hands move at a pace far too slow to carry the rhythm of the song, then accelerate into a rough, jerking motion. Such was the product of unskilled camerawork. That's why only the best got to film Sister Aimee, while the opening act was given over to anybody who could turn a crank.

And then, before giving Lynnie the chance to relive the satisfaction of taking a humble bow, the image snaps to black.

"That's it," Charlotte says. "As far as I know, that's the only film that exists. So, what do you think?"

She looks into Lynnie's eyes as if doing so hard enough will ferret out an answer, even though the woman herself cannot bring it into a singular thought, let alone gesture, let alone word. She lifts her eyes, thanking God for his mercy in rendering her speechless. She could never explain the twisted cord of excitement and shame that knotted within these memories.

An angry shout from what seems like miles away breaks their concentration.

"Hey there!" Even though Lynnie has never heard it at this volume, she knows it's Kaleena's voice. "What are you two still doing out here?"

"Just wanted to take in some fresh air!" Charlotte shouts back. "Is that a problem?"

"Well, get her back in soon." Kaleena's voice has softened somewhat. "She's got family coming in."

"We will," Charlotte says, and that seems to end the conversation. She leans in close to whisper, "Family," with a conspiratorial wink.

Nearly a century's worth of stories—marriages and births and deaths—rest in that word, and Lynnie longs to stay under this tree until she's heard every last one, or at least as many as Charlotte Hill is prepared to share with this magical gizmo that holds a wealth of lifetimes within its corners.

"Okay," Charlotte says, "time for one more picture."

She taps the screen again, but then, to Lynnie's disappointment, folds it up in a slim black case. Instead, she goes back into her satchel and brings out a small, framed photograph.

"I looked at this picture every day of my life." She can hear tears in Charlotte's voice. "When I lived at home, anyway. It's been in our family forever, but nobody ever talked about who it was. Who *you* were. . . ."

But Lynnie isn't listening anymore. She's grateful the picture is in a sturdy, permanent, familiar frame. No touch will make it go away. It won't be swiped into nothingness.

A storm gathers at the back of her throat, a churning mass of tears and shouts and a lifetime of words unspoken long before she'd lost the ability to speak.

Lynnie and Donny—their youth awash in the bright California sun.

✤ CHAPTER ELEVEN ✤

SHE'D GROWN ACCUSTOMED to sleeping on a train. The first night she'd tossed and turned—as much as one could, given the narrow confines of a sleeping berth. Truth be told, it wasn't the rocking motion of the car or the rhythmic click-clack of the miles disappearing beneath the wheels that had kept her awake as she stared into the darkness. She hadn't slept because she hadn't been able to escape the final conversation she'd had with Brent from the safety of Darlene's alcove.

"It's a chance for me to find my brother," she'd shouted into the phone, hoping the volume of her voice would convey the urgency she felt.

"Come home," he'd said, his voice no less powerful for its softness. "When we've married, I'll take you to California myself. A honeymoon, if you like. Next summer."

"I want him *at* my wedding."

"Fine, then. Stay put. I'll join you in a few days and we can go out together. Postpone the wedding, if we have to, until we find him."

His words felt like a snare, waiting to catch her in the truth she kept just below the surface.

"It's not just Donny."

"I know." His voice was thick with understanding, and what she thought to be a trap was, in fact, a soft, safe place.

She felt a tiny grain of confession at the back of her throat, planted there by the gentleness of his invitation, nurtured by his love. In less than a minute she'd told him everything—Sister Aimee, the Chinese restaurant, the song, the stage. The grain sprouted and grew, twisting in its rendering of Roland Lundi—older, squatter, and more rumpled than he was in life. All of it leading to a question. Her request for his permission.

"So, our girl is running off to join the circus?"

She could hear his fight for control and tried to match his wit. "Some might say so."

"And this seems right to you? Have you prayed about it?"

She had, of course, during the brief hours between Roland's visit and this phone call, but none of her prayers felt as pure and powerful as what she'd experienced in Sister Aimee's dressing room.

"I'm going to spend the rest of my life obeying you, Brent. I promise you that."

"But not until *after* the wedding?"

Dorothy Lynn closed her eyes and tucked herself closer to the wall. "Please understand. I've never—not once—made a single decision in my life completely on my own."

"Not even when you agreed to marry me?"

"I don't know."

It was she who broke the long, crackling silence that followed. "It was Ma that brought you home, and I think I knew that very first dinner what she wanted to happen. And I love you, Brent. I do. But I want a few weeks of my life to myself."

"A regular modern girl." The bitterness in his voice was uncharacteristic and frightening.

"Please don't."

"What happens if, after living this bit for yourself, you decide you don't want to spend the rest of your life obeying this man your mother thrust upon you?"

"That won't happen."

"How do you know?"

"Because I love you. And I don't want to live the rest of my life resentful of what I could have had. One month, darling. One month and I'll be back home. With you, if you'll have me."

"Make it six weeks."

"What?"

"I don't want you calling to tell me you need more time. Here is your time. My gift to you."

"Six weeks from tonight is our wedding date."

He chuckled. "Actually, it's two days before. Have you forgotten already?"

"No, I'm—just silly. That's all." Her face burned with shame. "And please, don't say anything to Ma. I'll write to her and explain everything."

"One more thing," he said, his voice dropped so low she pressed the phone closer to her ear. "I'm asking you not to call me again."

"Brent—"

"The next time I hear your voice, I want to see your face. To have you wholly and completely mine."

"Always and forever, my darling," she said. "I promise."

That was a month ago. Two cities, and endless miles of track.

Tonight it was not the final conversation with Brent that kept her awake, but the final cup of coffee after a very late dinner following the night's service. She could feel it jangling her very nerves, not to mention making her uncomfortable in other ways, too. As quietly as she could, she rolled up the canvas curtain meant to give her both protection and privacy and dangled her legs over the side. Below, Agnes, the woman responsible for her and Sister Aimee's wardrobes, snoozed behind her own canvas, emitting the light, squeaking snore that had become almost as familiar as the train itself.

Dorothy Lynn dropped to her feet, quiet as a cat, and made her way down the aisle. The women's lavatory was two cars down, through the dining car, all of which she maneuvered expertly, even in the darkness.

It was a strange feeling to be up and around alone. In fact, it was a strange feeling to be alone at all. The hectic schedule of Sister Aimee's appearances afforded no time for solitude, except for Sister Aimee, of course. She traveled in the most luxurious accommodations the Pullman company provided, where she spent their traveling time preparing for the next stop, the next sermon. Dorothy Lynn longed for such enforced privacy. While the schedule of performances had allowed her to perfect not only her signature song but countless other hymns, she hadn't written a single new lyric or note since leaving St. Louis. There was simply no place to go. Nights spent in town meant sharing a room with Agnes, who, when she was not snoring, talked like a woman starved of conversation.

In fact, that was why Dorothy Lynn had been forced from her berth in the middle of the night. Agnes had kept her enthralled with stories of Sister Aimee, speaking in hushed tones while the two finished the carafe of coffee left by the polite, dark-skinned porter.

"She's divorced, you know," Agnes had said, her whisper dropping to an almost-imperceptible volume at the word *divorced*. "And heartbroken about it, I can tell you. She went down three dress sizes at least while it was being finalized. All I could do to keep her from looking like a bag of bones."

"That's awful," Dorothy Lynn had said, and would have gladly stayed up half the night to hear more awful things, but Sister Aimee herself had come into the car, breezing through in her familiar white gown, sweeping them all off to bed like a company of overtired children. Nothing could have been more inappropriate at the time than requesting a trip to the lavatory.

Now, though, her business done, she braced herself for a final, nervous passing from one car to the next and was shuffling barefoot through the dining car when a sudden blaze of light stopped her in her steps.

She clutched her wrapper to her throat in lieu of a scream. "Goodness, Mr. Lundi! You scared me half to death."

"My apologies," he said, touching the tip of the newly lit match to his cigarette. "I couldn't bear the thought of you walking straight past me again." He gestured with his empty hand. "Join me?"

"It's late," she said, resting her hand on the back of a seat to balance herself.

"And you're obviously no more sleepy than I am. Please."

No other place or time on earth would have made his invitation appropriate, but she'd learned during her weeks with Sister Aimee that traveling excused an abundance of behaviors. She slid into the seat opposite Roland, perching on the edge in readiness for a quick escape.

"Relax," Roland said, settling back. "If I was going to bite you, I would've done it by now."

"I'm not worried about your bite. In fact, I'm not even scared of your bark anymore."

He chuckled before taking a draw on the cigarette, lighting the space between them with its red glow. "Look who's getting cheeky."

"Jittery. Too much coffee."

For the first time she noticed the glass on the table, filled nearly to the top with milk. Roland picked it up and took a sip, leaving a rim on his lip, which he wiped away with the cuff of his pajama sleeve. Despite the clacks of the train, she could hear the brush of the cotton against the growth of whiskers.

"Warm," he said, indicating the milk. "Stomach troubles. Doctor's orders. Says I should drink a quart of the stuff a day."

"I'd think he'd tell you to stop breathin' in all that fire. Can't be good for you."

"We're all entitled to one vice, aren't we?"

"That's not what I was ever taught."

"I'd wager there's a host of things in this world you were never taught."

She smiled and relaxed her posture. "And I'm a better person for it, don't you think? Otherwise, how would you have the sweet, unspoiled girl you parade out on stage every night?"

Roland took a long drag, squinting across the table as if distance separated them as much as darkness. "What are we going to do with you in California?"

"What do you mean?"

"We're getting out of the heartland. People out there, they don't care about girls like you. They want the movie stars and flappers. We bring you out onstage, they'll chew you up like a stack of crackers."

"I'm not going onstage in California. That wasn't part of our deal."

"I know, I know. The brother. I was just thinking out loud."

"Well, stop," she said, feeling bolder, "before you get me into any more trouble."

"Troubles, sweetheart?" He reached out and took her chin

in his hand, his touch warm from the glass. "Tell your uncle Roly."

It took only a slight movement to dislodge his touch, which she did with more humor than offense.

"I should have called before we left Denver. My sister, that is. To let her know we were finally on our way. What time should we arrive?"

"Bedtime tomorrow."

"And so, the next day? We can go look for Donny?"

"Soon and soon, sweetheart."

"I don't have time for 'soon and soon,' Mr. Lundi."

"You're young. Your world is full of time. Now, me, on the other hand . . ."

His thought disappeared in a cloud of smoke, and he took a long drink of milk. When he set it down again, he seemed poised for a change in subject. "Do you know how I met Sister Aimee?"

"No," Dorothy Lynn said, though she had the distinct feeling Roland would speak into the void if she weren't there to listen.

"I was working as a night clerk at a hotel in Baltimore. Ten o'clock at night and she comes in, saying she needs ten rooms for herself and her *people*. I ask her for how long, and she says she doesn't know. For as long as the Lord says to stay. She's preaching a revival and won't go until the souls of the city are safe from Satan."

"How long did she stay?"

"Nearly a month. And what a mess, never knowing from night to night if she was leaving the next day or staying for another week. I thought to myself, *That's no way to run an act.*"

"But it isn't an 'act,' is it? She has to listen for the voice of the Lord."

"Soon as I had a night off, I went out to see her. Like nothing

I'd ever seen before. Sometimes she'd go on for hours—until one o'clock in the morning. People might fall asleep in their seats, but they wouldn't leave."

Dorothy Lynn watched him fall under her spell even as he spoke.

"Up to then, the only thing I knew about Jesus Christ was that my old man used to yell it before telling me to get out of his way. Would have thought it was my own name the way he'd holler. Never knew he was anybody real."

Roland rarely spoke about his faith. In fact, this was the first deliberate conversation she'd had with him since the afternoon in Darlene's parlor. Maybe it was the topic, or the lateness of the hour, or the combination of milk and cigarettes—something for a child and a man—that brought about the roughness of his edges. His normally slick, careful speech became clipped at the syllables, and when he paused, he looked out the window to the blackness beyond.

"So I got baptized. Me and about a hundred other people. One after the other, all of us in these white robes. I felt this change. I'd heard her saying, night after night, 'Mr. Lundi, you need Jesus in your life.' And that's just how I felt, like he was *in* my life. Like a whole new person was looking out my eyes."

"Then thank God she came to Baltimore," Dorothy Lynn said. "And that she stayed. Where would you be if she hadn't listened to the Lord's calling?"

"I've learned a lot about God since hitching up with this crew. Didn't know anything about him before, but this I learned: God makes plans, right? Logic and order—not just always off the cuff, you know?"

He'd reached the end of his cigarette and stubbed it out on the floor. Apparently, he'd had the foresight to wear slippers.

"I told her she needed someone to smooth all that out. Making plans, I mean. Someone to manage her traveling. Most of all, I wanted out of that town. If I stayed there, I was gonna turn into the same old man that my father was."

"Certainly not—not after your salvation?"

"I got scared, thinking it was all wrapped up in her. She said no at first, but I wore her down."

"So not even the great Aimee Semple McPherson can resist your charms?"

"I would have tagged along anyway. But I made a place for myself, I think."

"You do a wonderful job. It's obvious how much she relies on you. We all do."

"We've been through a lot together, Sister Aimee and I. Seen a lot of lives change, most of all our own. Her husband couldn't take life on the road, and my wife—she never even gave it a shot."

He said it with such banality that she might have missed the impact, but his final guzzling of the milk—most likely merely tepid now—gave Dorothy Lynn the opportunity to sort out the idea.

"You're married?"

"Not anymore. This isn't the life for a marriage to survive. You did a good thing, leaving the preacher to fend for himself in the woods."

He must have known his upper lip was tipped with milk, though he made no move to wipe it off. It gave him the appearance of smirking. Moments before, she might have had to fight an impulse to wipe it away. It was all she could do not to reach across the table and smack him.

"I haven't left him. We're goin' to be married in—" she calculated—"less than a month."

"Plans change."

"Mine don't."

"Don't they? Do you remember the last time you saw him?"

"Of course I do." He'd sat with her outside of Jessup's, waiting for the bus. The mysterious package he carried turned out to be two Clark Bars, a Coca-Cola, and the latest *McCall's* magazine. The moment the bus was visible in the distance, he'd taken her around the corner and kissed her until her strength was reduced to that of a newborn calf.

"Would you have ever thought, in that moment, that you'd be here?"

"I didn't know that *here* existed."

"But once you did . . . ?" He sat back, hands open, point made.

"I only agreed so you would help me find my brother."

"Ah, yes. The brother. We'll get to him. I'm nothing if not a man of my word. Until then, you be truthful with me. You love this."

He said it as a statement, not a question, and she could only hope her denial rang more true to his ears than it did to her own.

"What do you not enjoy?" he insisted, leaning forward to insinuate himself into a tiny sliver of moonlight that had recently appeared. "Traveling? You've seen more of this country than every other person back in your hometown combined. Or evangelizing? How many people have you witnessed coming to Jesus Christ? Or maybe the singing?" He left no chance for her to answer, making each question as pointless as the one before. "I've seen your face when you're onstage. It's beautiful. Not just that you're a beautiful girl, but something *happens*. There's a calling to your music. Everybody sees that but you."

"No," she said, though here in the dark confines of this

empty railroad car she felt the same pull on both her body and her spirit that she felt every time she took the stage. "If it were truly a calling, I'd have more. More music, more songs. I haven't written a single one since . . . since the last one. I need to go home. I need to *be* home."

"Don't worry," Roland said, slipping another cigarette from his thin, silver case. "That'll happen soon enough. All you know is what you've seen on the road. Movie theaters and community centers. You just wait until we get to Los Angeles. Wait until you see the temple. Then you'll know what *home* is."

❧ CHAPTER TWELVE ❧

IF EVERY BUILDING looked like La Grande Station, Dorothy Lynn might have thought she'd arrived in some exotic country rather than Los Angeles, California. As the train took on its familiar slow, chugging cadence, she stared out the window at a wide, round dome that looked to be shining gold in the fierce sunset. And then, to see massive palm trees—like she'd only ever seen in her *Children's Illustrated Stories of the Bible*—rising above the turrets, she caught her breath, thankful they'd arrived before dark.

"Home at last," Agnes said. She'd been fidgeting in the seat across from Dorothy Lynn for the past hour, smoothing her dress and taking her hat on and off, mussing her hair each time. "I hope my Kenny recognizes me. I feel like I've gained ten pounds since the last time I was home."

"You look fine," Dorothy Lynn said. It hadn't occurred to her that, upon their arrival in Los Angeles, most of her traveling companions would get off the train and go to their actual homes. In the back of her mind they were a permanently nomadic group, traveling from one town to the next, staying at the nicest of cheap hotels and sleeping on trains in between. She clutched her purse, painfully aware of the exact amount of eleven dollars and eighty-two cents within it, what was left of the two dollars she'd been paid for each of her appearances on Sister Aimee's stage.

"Do you have someplace to go?" Agnes asked, craning in her seat to look beyond Dorothy Lynn. "I mean, is someone meeting you?"

"I'm going to see my brother," Dorothy Lynn said. It was what she'd been telling everyone. *See* sounded so much more hopeful than *find*.

"Oh, that's good. That you have someplace to go, I mean. I'd invite you to come home with me, but Kenny and I only have one bedroom . . ."

"I'm fine," Dorothy Lynn said, giving the older woman a reassuring pat. Come to think of it, Agnes might not be quite thirty, but she carried herself with a matronly air that made her seem much older. "I'm sure Mr. Lundi will help me find a room, at least for tonight."

Agnes sniffed. "I'll just bet he will, and you be careful there. Now that we're home, he'll be able to get out of Sister Aimee's sight. He has a bit of a reputation, you know."

"So do I. The wholesome, good girl, remember? Plus, I'll be meeting up with my big brother who fought in Europe. I think I'll be in safe hands."

"Still—" Agnes reached into her bag and pulled out a scrap of pattern paper and a thin, blue pencil—"here's my address. You need anything, you just show up."

"Thank you." Dorothy Lynn felt tears welling. She looked at the numbers, wondering how she'd ever find such a street.

All around them people stood as the train came to its final, shuddering stop. Dorothy Lynn had never been one to hurry off the train, not wanting to get caught in the mash of bodies heading for one exit, only to stand around on the platform waiting for the porter to deliver the bags. Normally Agnes waited with her, making them nearly the last to leave, but tonight the prospect of the waiting Kenny must have been too much for her, and she jumped up to join the fray, disappearing down the aisle, swept away by the excited chatter of their fellow passengers.

Dorothy Lynn leaned her head against the window. From this close, the view looked like that of any other station—bricks and crowds and magazine racks—but she knew outside of it she'd face a city like she'd never seen before. Donny was out there, close somewhere, and the thought of seeing him knotted her stomach in a way she hadn't anticipated. A long line of phone booths beckoned, and she wondered whether she should call home. Or, since Jessup disliked chasing down phone call recipients after dark, she could contact Darlene, let her know she'd arrived safely. After all, she'd mailed her sister a postcard from nearly every stop. Surely a telephone call wouldn't be unwelcome?

Just as she pondered this, a scene unlike any she'd seen at any other station took to the stage on the platform below. Sister Aimee, looking elegant as usual, glided across the platform on the arm of Roland Lundi, who looked much more dapper than the unshaven, milk-swigging man Dorothy Lynn had spoken to the night before. He wore an immaculate blue wool suit—a sharp contrast to Sister Aimee's signature white. A more focused inspection, however, revealed Sister Aimee's garment to be nothing less than a pristine white fur. Dorothy Lynn stood and lowered her window to see if the temperature this evening warranted such a covering, and while her outstretched hand felt cool, it was nothing to justify that magnificent coat.

Then Roland lifted his arm in a summoning fashion, and with a flick of his wrist, a gaggle of men came forward wielding notepads and cameras, shouting and snapping photos in the murky light.

"Sister Aimee! Welcome home!"

"Sister Aimee! Is this the end of your travels?"

"Sister Aimee! Is the church on schedule to open?"

The woman stood in the midst of the light, a close, knowing smile on her face as she slowly turned her head from one reporter to the next before taking one step away from Roland, who managed to quiet everyone with a single lifted hand.

"Thank you for the warm reception." He spoke loudly enough to capture the attention of those standing beyond the assembled press. "Sister Aimee is tired, as you can well imagine after several months' travel. We will be issuing a press release shortly."

He took her arm again and marched her straight through the crowd to where an older woman—distinctive in her fur and jewels—waited with arms outstretched. Sister Aimee bent to embrace her.

"Must be her mother," Dorothy Lynn muttered, her lips pressed nearly to the glass. Until this moment, Sister Aimee had seemed, in her presence and her power, to be a woman untouched by others. Roland, too, kissed the old woman's cheek, doffed his hat to both, and symbolically handed them over to a much larger man in a chauffeur's cap.

By now Dorothy Lynn was the only person left in the car, so she gathered her purse and made her way down the aisle to where a short flight of steps waited to help her descend safely to the platform, where her suitcase and guitar waited alongside the trunk she'd acquired for all the additions to her wardrobe.

Roland appeared at her side. "I'll get those for you."

Before she could say anything in reply or argument, his

hands were full of her belongings as he strode in the direction of the exiting crowd.

"Wait!" she said, holding her hat to her head as she practically ran to catch up. "What about my trunk? Where are you goin'?"

"I assumed you didn't want to sleep in the station," he said, not breaking his stride in the least, "though there are those who might attest to the comfort of the benches. I've made arrangements for your trunk. Now, come on."

People pressed on every side, preventing further conversation. Fearful she might lose him to the crowd, Dorothy Lynn clamped her mouth shut and focused all her attention on the narrow shoulder of his well-cut suit poking out from behind her beloved guitar.

It wasn't until they emerged on the street that she took in her first full breath of California. She'd never had any sort of an interest in science, but the very idea that the air in this place was made up of the same components as the air back home seemed utterly ridiculous. Never before had she smelled salt, though as she lifted her head, closed her eyes, and inhaled, she instinctively identified the essence of ocean. For a moment, Roland Lundi and her guitar were forgotten as her lungs filled with cool, pleasantly tart air.

"Nothing like it." Roland's voice came through her darkness, narrating her thoughts. "Open your eyes."

She did, and was rewarded with the sight of a broad boulevard lined with fashionable automobiles and people dressed like they were on their way to some event of great importance.

"This is the future," he said, and Dorothy Lynn could hear hints of the rough Baltimore boy he'd introduced last night. "Anybody who doesn't think so is a sucker. The whole world is coming to California."

"Then I shouldn't feel so alone?" She hoped she sounded more playful than she felt.

"Sweetheart, you have me and you have Jesus. You're never alone."

He led her to a snazzy-looking red car parked at the curb. Already, his luggage—a stately looking set of green—waited in the open trunk. He tossed her bag on top of it, treating the guitar with more particular care, and opened the front door with the formality of a footman.

"What is this?"

"This," he said, "is a Marmon."

"How did it get here?" she asked, feeling inexplicably giddy.

"We have people," he replied, as if that should answer all remaining questions. "Get in."

What choice did she have?

The car was unlike any she'd ever seen before. The white leather upholstery embraced her at every contour; the inside panels were inlaid with polished wood and brass. The engine had been left running, though it sounded more like the purr of a large, powerful cat. The smells of strong varnish, leather, and sea air mingled into an exciting scent, igniting a gnawing hunger that had earlier been hidden behind queasy anticipation.

"Dinner first," Roland said, landing in the driver's seat beside her. "Then we'll get you settled in."

He maneuvered the car into a sea of traffic, an exhilarating experience for Dorothy Lynn. Men and women alike cast appreciative glances from both the sidewalk and their own automobiles, some even leaning out the windows of the electric streetcars that shared the street.

She must have looked like quite the bumpkin, twisting her head left and right, gawking at her surroundings. The buildings weren't any grander than those in St. Louis or Kansas City, but they seemed newer, somehow. Like they'd been built specifically for this century. They rose as many as ten stories high—some probably more, but she could only crane her neck so far. To the left as they drove, a wide gate made way to a world of green behind it.

"That's Pershing Square," Roland said at her inquiry. "One square block of nature. Being in there, all of this disappears."

"I can't imagine wantin' this to disappear."

"That's my girl. Welcome to the future."

A few minutes later, he pulled the car over in front of a series of glass doors covered by a deep-red awning. The Alexandria Hotel.

Roland hopped out of the car and said, "Evening, Jackson," to the aging bellhop who'd met them at the curb. "You can take my bags up to my room. Leave the others at the desk."

"Very good, sir," Jackson said. He opened the car door for Dorothy Lynn and offered a white-gloved hand to assist her.

A glance straight up into the sky showed that the hour had moved from dusk to dark. She stood on the sidewalk, held in place by the flashing shower of lights coming from all directions until she felt Roland's arm slip through hers.

"Dinner? They serve a fabulous steak here. Then we'll get you to your room."

"A room? I can't stay here—not with you. . . ."

He took a step away from the hotel, bringing her along, and with the tip of his finger touched to her chin, forced her gaze upward again.

"Do you see? Hundreds and hundreds of windows. Each window a room, and that's just on this side. Don't worry, sweetheart; it's in the best interest of both of us to keep you far away. I just happen to have the connections here to set you up for cheap. And by cheap, I mean free. So don't knock it."

"Of course," she said. "I only wish we had some sort of a chaperone. I'd hate for people to think there was anything improper—"

"A word about life today. Nobody thinks anything is improper. So it's up to us to guide our behavior. See, I have every intention of conducting myself as a gentleman, and I'd like to assume you will be conducting yourself as a lady. Can we count on each other for that?"

"We can." For good measure, she unlocked her arm from his before following him inside.

Perhaps it was the harp music, the golden light, the glittering floor, or the combination of them all, but Dorothy Lynn's first reaction to seeing the lobby of the Alexandria Hotel could be captured in one word—*heaven*. Massive marble columns lined the walls, with rich, ornate tapestries hung between. Everything was beautiful—the carpet, the ceiling, the people. Men in tuxedos and women in exquisite, sequined gowns.

"This can't be right," Dorothy Lynn muttered. Even if it weren't wrinkled and limp from a day's travel, her modest dress would seem out of place in the midst of this luxury. In fact, nothing she owned or ever hoped to own would make her fit to be a part of this crowd. She clutched at Roland's arm again. "Why are we here?"

He gave her hand a reassuring pat. "I live here."

"You *live* here?" She trained her eyes on the ground, hoping to maintain some dignity by not looking at anybody directly. "How does somebody live in a place like this?"

"Sweetheart, I've worked in the hotel business enough to know that, if you can swing it, it's the best living there is. We keep two rooms reserved here for guests of Sister Aimee. When actual guests are in town, my accommodations are much less luxurious."

"And it's all right with her if I stay in the other room?"

"This is one of the many, many responsibilities I handle so she can keep her mind focused on higher things."

"So she wouldn't know."

"Not until she needs to. I'll go to the desk and make the arrangements." He led her to one of the leather-upholstered chairs dotting the lobby, depositing her without a hint of chivalry. "Stay here. Be good, then food."

She clutched his sleeve. "Don't leave me here. Please? Look at these people, then look at me. I can't stay here."

As she spoke, a tall woman, thin to an almost skeletal proportion, glided past. She wore a dress made entirely of overlapping black feathers and a headband of thick, black silk. She was flanked by two handsome gentlemen in black tuxedos who shared her obvious distaste for the rumpled girl in the lobby.

"Must be some big happening at the Palm Court," Roland said, staring the trio down with his own superiority. "People make a couple of movies and act like they own the city. They forget that a few years ago they were nobodies just like you and me."

"You're hardly a nobody, Mr. Lundi."

"I'm the nobody behind the somebody. And there's not much lower to go than that."

"Still, I'm not comfortable here."

"Five minutes, sweetheart. Then, if you'd rather, you can go straight up to your room. I can have your dinner sent up."

Relief rushed through her at the thought of escape. "You can do that?"

"It denies me the pleasure of a dinner companion, but life's nothing without sacrifice."

Nobody in this place looked like they'd ever sacrificed a thing.

Dorothy Lynn remained perched on the edge of her seat, afraid someone might take her for an actual vagrant if she were to fall back into its comfort. She tried to make some sense of the conversations happening around her—contracts and shooting schedules and producers and studios. Movies. Hollywood. One of these people might know her brother. Well, not *know* him, exactly. But they might have seen him. Or looked past him, the way they made such an effort to look past her. How ridiculous would it be to walk up to one and say, "Excuse me. Do you know a young man named Donny Dunbar? I believe he might be a carpenter on your set?"

If nothing else, she could reward herself with a tiny ribbon of confirmation. Roland Lundi said he had connections. He knew people. Apparently, the people he knew congregated on the first floor of his home regularly. She'd seen him stop and shake two hands already.

Attempting a casual air, Dorothy Lynn allowed her eyes to wander throughout the room, coming to light eventually on a row of rich, dark-paneled phone booths flanked by impressive marble columns. Roland had completely disappeared from view.

Five minutes.

She straightened and stood, straightening still more once she'd gotten to her feet, and strode purposefully to the first of the empty booths. Maybe she wasn't as swanky as all of these people, but she had a nickel just as good as any of theirs to make a phone call.

Keeping her eyes trained on her abandoned seat, she listened to the series of clicks as she was connected to long distance, St. Louis, and finally her sister's voice after several long rings.

"Darlene?"

"Dot! Where are you?"

"Los Angeles. We made it here—all in one piece. Have you been getting my postcards?"

"I suppose so." She sounded distracted. "I've been a bit busy here."

"There's one more coming from Denver. Can you believe it? Two days ago I was in Denver. We were on the train all night."

"Hm." Not even the miles and miles of telephone wire could hide her sister's disapproval.

"Darlene? Is everything all right? You sound . . . tired."

"Well, it's an exhausting thing having a baby."

It took a moment for the weight of her words to sink in. "You had the baby? How wonderful!"

"A little girl—Margaret. Nine days ago." Darlene's voice became instantly lighter. "Our hearts are full."

"So's your family," Dorothy Lynn said, unable to imagine adding another soul to that busy house.

"But don't worry. I got your dress finished first and shipped it home to Ma."

She wanted to say, *Who cares about the dress?* But she knew Darlene did, and deeply. "Now I have good news to share with Donny when I see him. Besides the wedding, I mean."

"Have you had a chance to look for him yet?"

"Of course not, silly. We only just got here. You should see it. It's a hotel, the Alexandria, I think? Yes. And the people here—I think some of them are actual movie stars, but you'd know better about that than I do. And there's a ballroom called the Palm Court."

"Oh, Dot." This time, the speaking of her name dripped with awe and envy. "That's where some of the most important

Hollywood people go. I've seen their pictures in the magazines and everything. That's where you are at this very moment?"

"Yes." Suddenly she felt more nervous than ever. "And I'm going to get a room all to myself. Mr. Lundi has it all arranged."

"You be careful about what that Mr. Lundi arranges."

Before Dorothy Lynn could reply, she heard Darlene's muffled command to RJ and Darren to, for the last time, get upstairs and get in bed before she sent their father up there to give them the whipping of their lives. Thankfully, by the time she returned to the conversation, Roland Lundi was forgotten, and a more painful topic introduced.

"Ma is sick with worry over all of this, by the way."

"She won't care once she sees the baby."

"Well, she's not going to see her until after. Margaret's just too little for that bus ride. I hope you understand."

"Of course," Dorothy Lynn said, not wanting to burden Darlene with her disappointment. "What have you told her?"

"Just what we talked about. That I had a postcard from Donny and you went to find him, to bring him back for the wedding."

"All true, by the way."

"True, but not *all*. You should have called me earlier, Dot. You shouldn't have waited."

Darlene's voice had dropped low as a grave, and a ball of fear rolled over on itself in Dorothy Lynn's stomach.

"What do you mean?"

"She said Brent hasn't said a word about the wedding. Not since you left. The announcement's still hanging in the church, but people in town are talking, saying you've run off with another man. They're feeling sorry for her having two children disappear without a word."

"Don't tell her." She was met with a long, unnerving pause. "Do you hear me? Not a word about Sister Aimee."

"You would rather she believe that you took it upon yourself to up and go to California alone?"

"Yes. Brent knows the truth, and that's enough."

"Oh, Sister. You can't start off your marriage with the two of you sharing a lie."

"It's not a lie. Why should I give Ma one more thing to worry about?"

"Should she be worried?"

"Of course not," Dorothy Lynn said. "I'll tell him everything when I get home. Ma, too. But for now . . . can't you understand? Don't you have little pockets in your life that are all your own? That Roy doesn't know about?"

"I do not."

"Even your charge account at May's?"

"The two hardly compare," Darlene was quick to say, but Dorothy Lynn could sense that she'd struck a nerve.

"It's all going to be fine," she soothed.

"I still think you're being reckless."

"Maybe I am, but if you'd ever taken the time to really listen to Sister Aimee, you'd understand. This is a chance for me to be a part of something so powerful. I've never heard the Word of God the way she speaks it. And not because she's a woman, but because she's just so *full*."

"So Brent doesn't need to be jealous of the handsome Mr. Lundi, but the amazing Mrs. McPherson?"

"Brent doesn't need to be jealous of anyone." As she spoke, she saw the handsome Mr. Lundi himself beckoning her from the center of the room. Each sister ended the telephone call with a promise to the other: Darlene to tell their mother that all was well, and Dorothy Lynn to ensure that all remained so.

"Your lovely sister?" Roland asked the minute she joined him.

"None other."

"And how is she?"

"Worried."

He said nothing but steered her through the crowd that had become a web of silk and perfume and smoke. They emerged on the other side, where a young man stood attentively at a gilded elevator door.

"Evening, Mr. Lundi. Welcome back."

"Evening, Howard. Big shindig happening tonight, eh?"

Howard shrugged. "One tycoon has a birthday, and the sheiks come out of the woodwork."

The arrow above the door made its arch. A bell rang, and young Howard excused himself to slide open the gate and stand at the ready. Three women emerged, each wearing a dress more revealing than the next. Intrigued by the expression on Howard's face, Dorothy Lynn followed his gaze, shocked to see that one of the young women had her entire back exposed, framed in rippling pink chiffon anchored at sharp, protruding shoulder blades.

"Winky-dink," Howard said appreciatively, momentarily forgetting that Roland and Dorothy Lynn were waiting. The tips of his ears turned bright red, and he stepped to the side with near-military precision.

The operator inside the elevator wasn't nearly as young or talkative as Howard. Roland said, "Fourth floor," and with the slightest acknowledgment, the compartment shook and they were on their way. Mere seconds later, the operator announced, "Four," and silently asked them to leave.

"Hold here, please," Roland said as they exited.

The hallway was carpeted in a lush, thick weave that absorbed each footfall. Dorothy Lynn fought to appear calm, not wanting Roland to mistake her nerves for fear, as fear might be insulting to his integrity. He walked at a respectful distance beside her, not talking, not touching. For the first time she noticed the key adorned with a silver medallion; when they arrived at room 403, she stepped aside as he opened the door.

"Your room," he said, taking her hand and placing the key in her palm. "Your bags should arrive shortly, and I took the liberty of ordering up your supper."

She glanced over his shoulder at the amber-lit room, not knowing what to say.

He gave a playful tap to the tip of her nose. "Then straight to bed. And sleep as late as you please. Meet me tomorrow in the lobby at noon."

He spun on his heel and was halfway down the hall before she thought to call out, "What's tomorrow?"

He turned and removed his hat, managing to walk backward and bow at the same time. "Ah, sweetheart. I ask myself that every day."

❦ CHAPTER THIRTEEN ❦

IN HER DREAM, Brent walked among the trees, stepping in and out of them like a silent, stately sprite. She heard music all around—hers, she assumed. Deep and rich, she stood within it, able to feel the very notes touch her skin. More than touch her, they held her. Catgut cords lashed around her ankles, anchoring her to the moist, cool earth. Somehow, she knew she need only call out to Brent and he would save her; his strong arm would reach through the fog of notes and pull her to the safety of the trees. But she kept silent, merely watching until little by little the music faded, the forest became light, and she opened her eyes.

The sheets were drawn up to her nose, and she could smell the hint of lavender that had so thrilled her last night when, clean from a hot bath and sated from the enormous steak that had magically appeared at her door, she'd fallen, exhausted, between them. She stretched her legs before scooting over to the cool, unmussed empty half to better see the time on the softly ticking bedside clock.

Ten fifteen.

In any other circumstances—in any other *world*—she would have jumped out of bed, horrified at the hedonism. But for all she knew, the revelers of last night's party were strewn through-out the rooms around her. Today, she was accountable to only one person—Roland—and she hadn't the first clue as to where to find him. Noon in the lobby, he'd said. Why, she could close her eyes and go back to sleep, and she might have if not for the soft knock on her door.

"Just a moment," she said, her voice rough after so many hours of silence in sleep.

She hadn't bothered with a housecoat last night, seeing as she had the entire room to herself, but she'd draped it across the foot of the bed. She wrestled with it now, pulling her arms through as she untangled her feet from the sheets. Once at the door, she rose to the tips of her toes to peek through the tiny hole. Fully expecting to see Roland, she rocked back to her heels at the sight of a gentleman in the familiar hotel staff uniform standing there with a large, flat box under one arm.

Cautiously, she opened the door just enough to peer between it and the frame and said, "Yes?"

"Miss Dunbar?"

Again, "Yes?"

"Delivery for you. Courtesy of Mr. Lundi."

"What is it?"

He shrugged. "I just deliver, ma'am. I don't ask questions."

"Well, thank you." She took the package from him, though he kept his hand extended long after she'd taken possession. "Oh, of course." Her purse still sat on the table just by the door; the dime she fetched from it looked a bit forlorn in the pristine white glove.

"Thank you, ma'am," he said with heroic grace.

Once again alone, Dorothy Lynn ran back to the bed and tossed the package onto the rich, blue velvet cover. The box was tied with a thick, pink ribbon, which she tugged at with cautious curiosity. Once the ribbon was removed, she lifted the lid off the box to find a puddle of soft, rustling tissue paper and a note.

For today. We're going to church.

—*R*

She pushed the tissue paper aside and lifted out a dress made of soft knit jersey. Its color so reminded her of the piney trees back home that she held the fabric to her nose and inhaled, half-expecting to breathe in the scent of them. She held it out to notice the style—straight and narrow with a band that would fall well below her waist. The skirt below was pleated and would probably hit right at her knees. A row of bright-yellow wooden buttons ran down the length of the bodice, with one enormous, exaggerated disc that seemed designed to sit right on her hip. In the box, too, was a beautiful, ornate head scarf that incorporated both colors of the dress, as well as a pair of nylon stockings.

Dorothy Lynn laid everything out on the bed, trying to ignore that nagging bit of shame. It certainly wasn't the first time for Roland to give her a dress, but those were for the stage. More precisely, for the character she played on that stage. They oozed innocence to the point of being childish. This, clearly, was a sophisticated dress meant for a modern, sophisticated woman. This, in fact, could be worn by any woman she'd seen in the lobby last night. For good measure, she turned it over, just to make sure the garment had a fully covered back.

Something shiny peeked through the tissue at the corner of the box, where she found a pair of black patent-leather shoes—high-heeled with an ankle strap. Tucked inside the toe of one shoe was a tin of face powder; in the other, a bright-red lipstick and a kohl pencil.

"Well, won't I look smart having lunch at the Hotel Alexandria?"

Speaking the words out loud gave Dorothy Lynn a boost to the courage she lacked. She took off her housecoat and strode into the bathroom, yanking the ribbon used to tie back her hair as she did so. A flip of the switch flooded the room with light—almost blinding as it bounced off the white porcelain tub and sink. She'd left her hairbrush on the marble pedestal between the two, and she grabbed it, pulling it through her long, chestnut hair which, she had to admit, would be beautifully complemented by the green of the dress.

She turned on the tap and held the bristles of her brush under the running water before going over her hair one more time, leaving it smooth and damp. After braiding it, she rolled and pinned the plaits at the nape of her neck in the style that looked much more fashionable under the guidance of Agnes, or even Darlene. She washed her face with the cake of scented soap in the crystal dish on the sink's edge and patted it dry with the thick, soft towel hanging from a brass hook on the wall. With inexperienced hands, she powdered her face and lightly kohled her eyes, leaving the deep-red lipstick for last. Some instinct told her to touch a finger to her lips, then to her cheeks, where she rubbed the stuff into orbs of a paler shade.

"Oh my."

The mirror's ornate, gilded frame held a new face for her this morning, and a confusing one at that. But then, she was still wearing her nightgown. Minutes later, even with the new dress clinging perfectly to her body, something seemed amiss, like a mesh of different fashions had come to roost upon her—the makeup not suited to her face, the dress too revealing of her shape, her hair clinging to a world that had disappeared with the Great War. Something was missing.

And then she remembered the scarf.

It was silk, she knew, but heavier than any silk she could remember, and the colors within its pattern were as rich as those in the woods back home. A good yard long and eight inches wide, she held it at arm's length, trying to decide exactly what to do. She sat down on the edge of the bed, dislodging Roland's note, sending it fluttering to the floor. When she bent to pick it up, she noticed for the first time a drawing on the back of it—a simple sketch, really, of a woman who looked remarkably like Dorothy Lynn, her head wrapped in a scarf remarkably like this one, creating a cap that tied in a knot under one ear, left long over the disappearing shoulder.

He knew.

Using the picture as a guide, she created the same look on her real, live self.

Now, what to do for the intervening hour before she was to meet Roland downstairs? She glanced over to the upholstered wingback chair by the window, where her guitar sat upright, as if waiting. It had been days since she touched it—quite possibly the longest time she'd ever gone without at least strumming a few notes. She crossed over to it, but instead of opening the case, she pulled open the curtains, filling the room with sun. Then, not quite satisfied, she opened the window and leaned out, breathing in the air tinged with the unmistakable scent of the nearby ocean. Below her was a bustling street—automobiles and people vying to see who could create the most noise. It had been just that way last night, and she imagined it was possible that Los Angeles never did experience the natural cycle of sleep and restoration.

She closed her eyes and listened for a song, drumming her fingers on the sill in search of a rhythm, but none came. She leaned farther out, imagining the crowd below to be nothing more than an audience unleashed, hoping something worthy would come from her voice. Instead, she was met with a sharp whistle down below and opened her eyes to see a middle-aged man looking straight up at her.

"Hey, doll!" His voice easily carried up the four stories. "G'head and jump. I'll catch ya!"

He held his arms wide open in anticipation of an embrace, and she pulled herself quickly back inside, slamming the window shut.

Dorothy Lynn moved as far away from the window as she could and sat on the unrumpled side of the bed next to the ticking clock. Still nearly an hour before she was supposed to meet Roland. Having spent so many nights in hotels while traveling with Sister Aimee, she knew what she would find upon opening the bedside table, and there it was. The Holy Bible, with the familiar Gideons' light.

She took the Bible from the drawer and opened the front pages, seeking the list of Scripture references intended to guide the reader to passages that would provide comfort and instruction in times of need.

The Way of Salvation.
Comfort in Time of Loneliness.
Courage in Time of Fear.
Strength in Time of Temptation.

And more . . .
At this moment, so many applied, but given the encounter

at the window and the uncertain days ahead, she ran her finger down the page, registering the verses meant to give "Courage in Time of Fear." Though the chapter and verse were instantly familiar, she turned to the passage, the sixth chapter of Ephesians.

> Finally, my brethren, be strong in the Lord, and in the
> power of his might. Put on the whole armour of God,
> that ye may be able to stand against the wiles of the
> devil. For we wrestle not against flesh and blood, but
> against principalities, against powers, against the rulers
> of the darkness of this world, against spiritual wickedness
> in high places.

Dorothy Lynn closed the book and went once again to study her reflection. Respectable, modest, and—even in her limited estimation—fashionable. How proud Darlene would be at the transformation, not only in her outer appearance, but her inner appreciation. The dresses she'd brought from Heron's Nest lay forgotten at the bottom of her trunk, and the thought of wearing them seemed as foreign as wearing something like this had once been. In this outfit, she could belong with any other stylish woman on the streets, in the lobby, even in the magazines.

And what had that gotten her when she ventured a peek out the window?

"'Wherefore,'" she said, quoting from memory, "'take unto you the whole armour of God, that ye may be able to withstand in the evil day, and having done all, to stand.'"

Still early, and feeling fully armed against wickedness, she walked out of the room, locking the door behind her, and dropped the room key into her purse. There was one panic-ridden second when she couldn't remember which way to turn to find the elevator, but a ding from around the nearest corner guided her steps.

The operator gave her an appreciative look, as did more than one patron in the lobby when she emerged on the first floor. The women, she assumed, admired her dress, but she wouldn't let herself think about what might lie behind the men's glances.

The lobby, he'd said. At noon. Perhaps he'd forgotten just how vast the lobby was. Did he mean near the entrance? At the desk? Dead center under the stained-glass skylight? Whatever confidence her appearance had given began to fade as she noticed everyone around her was moving—men walking brisk and tall, women with a perfect slow, slouching slink. She, once again, stood frozen.

"You look lost." The voice was thick and unpleasant, much like the man behind it.

"Just waiting," she said. "For a friend."

"I should be so lucky to be your friend."

She recognized immediately that there'd been no harm in his conversation and worked up a smile that she hoped would convey both disinterest and warmth as he touched stubby fingers to his hat and backed away.

The encounter, brief as it was, renewed her confidence. She took a deep breath and moved her body in a stroll of nonchalance. Strains of music underscored her sliding steps, rising above the conversations echoing in the marbled room. A single piano, played in a way that brought the notes dancing through the air. The only piano she'd ever known was the weathered instrument in her father's church. It had three missing keys, and those that remained battled valiantly to pound out the Sunday hymns under the unrelenting fingers of Mrs. Rusty Keyes.

She found herself being pulled by the music, enticed by

its sheer prettiness, and followed it to the source—a gleaming white grand piano near the window looking out into the street. The pianist was a thin gentleman with even thinner blond hair that showed gaps of pale pink scalp between the comb marks. He largely played unnoticed in the midst of so much milling, save for a modest audience gathered directly around the piano. Dorothy Lynn moved closer behind him, wanting to get a glimpse of his long, agile fingers that moved like ten pale ribbons in a breeze.

His milky tenor voice gave life to lyrics about somebody's sweet jazz baby. He finished the tune with a fanciful run on the keys followed by a final jaunty chord. The sparse crowd rewarded him with polite applause, and Dorothy Lynn joined them in their praise.

The pianist took up a soft, rambling tune and asked, "Any requests?"

"Yeah," said a man in a garish red plaid suit. "Beethoven's Fifth."

"Sorry, fella," said the pianist without missing a beat. "I haven't learned the first four yet."

The crowd laughed, and once again Dorothy Lynn joined them.

"'Apple Blossom Time'!"

Dorothy Lynn couldn't tell which woman had shouted it, but everyone in the crowd sighed their approval.

"No way, Betty," the pianist said, letting his fingers continue their ambling up and down the keyboard. "Songs about weddings give me the heebie-jeebies." He shuddered and struck an ominous minor chord, much to the crowd's amusement.

"'Alice Blue Gown'!"

It was the same woman's voice, and this time the mere

mention of the song title provided the comedy. Everybody laughed and echoed the request.

"Hey, c'mon! Bad enough I was too thin to fight, you gotta get me singin' about my favorite dress? What are ya doing to me?"

But the crowd would not be deterred, its single voice taking on a lighthearted jeer.

"Well, I can play it," he said finally, the first measures of the tune already beginning to take form, "but one of you ladies is gonna have to sing it. Any volunteers?"

All demurred at the prospect, and those who attempted the first note or two were roared down by the others.

"Hey there, sister."

Dorothy Lynn looked over her shoulder to make sure he was talking to her.

"Me?"

"Yeah. You're looking mighty coy. Wanna give it a whirl?"

She knew the song, of course. It was the same tune she and Darlene were dancing to when Roland came to the house that afternoon. The memory was sweet, and she could still hear her sister's voice singing along with the record.

She listened. "Is that the only key you know it in?"

Apparently the crowd found her a good-natured ally, one not afraid to stand up to the uncooperative entertainer.

"This better for you?" He immediately transposed the tune to a lower key, of which, after testing it out just under her breath, Dorothy Lynn approved.

Once again the introductory notes, and then she sang.

I once had a gown, it was almost new,
Oh, the daintiest thing, it was sweet Alice blue,

With little forget-me-nots placed here and there,
When I had it on, oh, I walked on the air!

By now this was nothing new to her, singing in front of a crowd, but the intimacy of this setting elicited none of the anxiety of being on a stage. Nor did it ignite any sense of power. She could walk away at this moment, midverse, before the chorus, and no consequences would follow. But here, though her voice rose in well-received solo, she felt like nothing more than one of the crowd, and when the next line came, she opened her arms wide, beckoning the others to join her.

And it wore, and it wore, and it wore,
'Til it went, and it wasn't no more.

When they launched into the chorus, men and women alike were singing of their cherished Alice blue gown, leaning on each other in exaggerated sentimentality. Each verse, though, was hers alone. When the final note died away, applause five times what the pianist himself had received filled the cavernous hotel lobby, and the elegant musician stood from his bench only to bow to Dorothy Lynn.

"Baby, baby, baby." He came to her, wrapped his long arms around her, and—this stranger—planted a crushing kiss on her cheek. "You could make me a star."

She was too surprised to respond with anything but a laugh, and before she knew it, he was back at the keyboard with the first notes of "Second Hand Rose," and she enthusiastically joined him.

Singing had never felt like this before. At times it had given her peace, at other times joy, but she couldn't recall a time when she had fun. This seemed more like a long, lyrical laugh, a musical game. She looked like a new woman and sang like one too, scooping some of the notes with a jokey growl to the delight of her playmates just an arm's length away, quick to supply lyrics when her memory faltered.

She was midway through the final chorus when Roland Lundi joined the crowd. The hat and suit were familiar, but the expression on his face was as alien as his new tie—not angry, but clearly not amused. When the song ended, his applause was polite; in fact, were he the only one clapping, there might not have been any sound at all. As he approached the piano, Dorothy Lynn didn't know if she should be prepared to gloat or apologize, but it turned out neither would be necessary. He strolled right past her, hand outstretched to the man at the keyboard.

"Look at you, Bernie. Trying to steal my girl?"

"Roly-poly," the pianist—Bernie—said, pumping Roland's hand with an enthusiasm that dislodged a few strands of his thin hair. "Back in town, are ya? She's yours? She's fabulous." Then, to Dorothy Lynn, "Ditch this bum and run away with me. New York, baby. Broadway."

"I'm not his girl and I'm not goin' to New York," Dorothy Lynn said. "I don't think I'd last an hour with either him or the city before going crazy."

Then Roland was beside her in a way he'd never been before, his hand in the curve of her waist, tucking her close.

"Don't be cruel, sweetheart," he said, giving her a proprietary squeeze, "making poor Bernie here think he stands a chance."

Bernie shrugged in comic defeat. "What is it about you dames always going for the Valentino type? What's wrong with being tall and pale with the physique of a wet noodle?"

It all had the humor of a rehearsed comedy routine, and

Dorothy Lynn joined the spectators in laughter, even offering a good-bye wave worthy of a stage-left exit. Once they were away, however, with Bernie's next serenade a distant melody, she wrenched herself from Roland's grip. "I'm not your girl."

"You look beautiful."

"Thank you," she said, instantly deflated. "For the compliment and the clothes. I feel—"

"Chic? Stunning?"

"Different. I guess I got rather carried away back there."

"Don't sweat it, sweetie. You looked like you were having fun, but Bernie's kind of a cad-about-town."

"Well, then, that's one more thing for me to thank you for."

He steered her out of the hotel and onto the street, where her eyes automatically scanned for the car they'd driven in the night before.

"Today we walk," Roland said. "Fresh air and exercise—at least as far as the streetcar. Then lunch, then church."

"Church? It's Thursday, isn't it?" So many days' travel, she'd lost track.

"Friday, actually. But who's counting?" Another of his answers that answered nothing.

⋘§⋙

"This is our stop." Roland reached up to ring the bell, then cleared a way to the back of the car, descending first so he could stand on the sidewalk and hand Dorothy Lynn down.

"I'm telling you, six months from today, you're going to see people lined up around the block here. Saturday, Sunday, Tuesday—it won't matter. Remember that last night in Kansas City? People scrambling to get through the door? That's what we're going to have here, only there won't be any panic, because

207

there won't be any final nights. It'll be Sister Aimee Semple McPherson every day, every night. Bringing the Word of God to a dying world."

Dorothy Lynn paid no attention to the sights around them, focusing only on Roland's face as he spoke, his hands as they gestured toward an imaginary marquee. "Because we all told her, 'You're only one woman. You can't be everywhere at one time, so be in one place all the time.'"

"But why not in the middle of the country? Why out here?"

He laughed. "'Out here'? Sweetheart, give it time, and Los Angeles, California, is going to be the center of the world. And here's why." He stopped and, putting his hands on her shoulders, turned her around to see what would have been impossible to miss.

A temple.

There was simply no other word to describe it. Too big for a church, too sacred for a theater. The rounded building rested below a huge, domed roof. Columns were interspersed along the facade, its surface awash in blinding white. She'd seen pictures of the Roman Colosseum in her history textbook in school—grand even in its state of ruin. Here, on the other side of the world, stood its rival. Not its equal, of course, and certainly not created with such pagan intent, but truly colossal, even behind the scaffolds of construction.

"Look at that," Dorothy Lynn said, as if it would be possible to do anything else.

"Angelus Temple," Roland said. "The Church of the Foursquare Gospel."

"It's enormous!"

"Want to see inside?"

"Can we? It's not open, is it?"

Roland reached into his pocket and retrieved a ring of keys. "Remember this from here on out: stick with me, and you can go anywhere you want."

She punched his arm playfully but followed him behind the tall, wooden fence, past wheelbarrows full of concrete and bricks. Men of all shapes and sizes touched their caps in greeting as they walked by, and a few even took off their leather work gloves to shake his hand, welcoming him back.

"Is there anybody you don't know?" she asked as they made their way through a maze of garden beds. "Are we havin' dinner with the mayor?"

"Not tonight. He's otherwise engaged."

"But you know him?" she asked, surprised at his response to what she'd meant as a joke.

"I've met him once or twice. Sometimes, since her divorce, Aimee needs an escort to social functions."

"And you're happy to oblige?"

"She changed my life. What wouldn't I do?"

They arrived at a nondescript door set in the middle of a looming white wall. It took three tries for Roland to find the right key for the lock, and when he did, the door opened like a great, gaping maw.

"Goodness, Mr. Lundi. How much time have I spent with you in dark hallways?" Still, she walked over the threshold and gasped when the closing of the door plunged them into complete and utter darkness.

His familiar touch steadied her.

"There's nothing in here. Just walk."

The place smelled of concrete, lumber, and paint—not unpleasant, but raw. She kept her hand firmly in the crook of Roland's arm.

"Can't you light a match or something?"

"Hold on."

She had just a second to wonder if "holding on" wasn't his intent when the soft sound of a switch brought forth light.

"Nothing special here. This is the hall for deliveries and such. But it'll take us clear through to backstage."

One corridor led to another, one corner to the next, until they came upon a familiar gray world.

"It *is* a theater."

"It's not. A theater is a place of entertainment; this is a hall of worship. Sister Aimee's an evangelist for a new age—it's a new church."

"But—" She held back her protest, recognizing that Roland had no interest in conversation and even less in debate. Instead, at his invitation, she followed him through a mass of wire and rope to a thick black curtain, which he pulled aside.

"Now, look out there."

It took more than a few steps for her to emerge on the stage, and when she did, she wished he'd come out with her so she'd have something to steady her legs. The theater—for at this moment, no other word applied—was massive. Dimly lit by domes recessed in the ceiling, the deep-red seating stretched farther than her eye could see. Ornate wood carvings decorated the walls, and even though rolls of carpeting lay in the aisles, the grandeur of this place rose above anything she'd ever imagined.

"So what do you think?" He spoke from his familiar place—stage left, behind the curtain.

"Beautiful." The word had never been so inadequate.

"Can't you just see her out here?"

She could, in a long white dress, her signature flowing sleeves.

In fact, after just these few minutes, Dorothy Lynn couldn't picture her anyplace else.

"Try it out."

"What?"

"Even without a microphone, you need to hear your voice. Sing something."

She'd walked to the center of the stage, and he remained behind the curtain. Anyone out in the audience might think she was speaking to some unseen phantom. "Don't be silly."

"I'm not being silly. You deserve to hear yourself on a stage like this."

She turned to the strip of darkness emitting his voice. "I don't have my guitar. I can't sing without my guitar."

"I heard you this morning, sounding quite good."

"I hardly think this is the place for 'Second Hand Rose,'" she said, hoping to quench the tiny, nagging desire within her to hear her voice in this place.

"Sing my favorite."

"But there's nobody here."

He emerged from behind the curtain. "I'm here, and you're here. And the Lord is here. What could possibly be wrong about singing a song to him in a place of worship?"

"Nothin', of course."

"Do you know what kind of show opened in Kansas City the night after you sang in the theater there?"

"No."

"Neither do I. And it doesn't matter. But it won't be Aimee, and all those people who were touched by God? What happens to them? We'll never know. All those people in all those cities. Thousands. Here, we'll see five thousand in a single afternoon. And another five thousand the next day, the next week. Or the same ones—they can come back, again and again. Like I did when she changed my life. Now close your eyes."

She did, and all the splendor disappeared. He was right behind her, humming a few notes in her ear, as if she could ever forget the song that was his favorite. It moved him to tears at nearly every service. She took a deep breath.

I can hear my Savior calling,
I can hear my Savior calling,
I can hear my Savior calling,
"Take thy cross and follow, follow me."

Had she been singing only to fulfill Roland's desire, she might have stopped there. But from the very first word, echoed in this magnificent place, she'd longed to hear more.

Where he leads me I will follow,
Where he leads me I will follow,
Where he leads me I will follow;
I'll go with him, with him, all the way.

This was the first place she'd ever been that came close to the sumptuousness of her own forest back home, but while the canopy of trees there held her voice close within God's creation, the vast auditorium seemed to lift it up to heaven.

By the end she realized Roland was singing softly with her in an uncertain, though not unpleasant, harmony.

"Do you feel like the Lord has led you here, Dorothy?"

His question precluded another verse, and she was almost relieved at the release from the intimacy. "No. I think *you* brought me here."

"You don't think God is capable of working through people?"

"Of course he is, but I see this more as an indulgence on his part. His plans for me are back at home."

"How can you know that for sure?"

"Because my heart is there."

"Ah, you're a follower of the heart. A luxury reserved for the young."

She wanted to banter back that he, too, was such a follower, but the hint of sadness in his voice kept her from doing so. Sometimes when they talked like this, she felt like their ages had been turned upside down, she the sage and he the dreamer. "How old are you, Mr. Lundi?"

"Old enough," he said. "Thirty, if you must know."

"That's not old at all. Can I ask you another question?" At his blessing, she spoke quietly, knowing a mouse's whisper would echo in this place. "Are you in love with her?"

His eyes widened. "With Aimee?"

"Who else?" A lifetime ago she would have said, *Your wife.*

"A little, I guess," he said, surprising her with his candor. "But who isn't?"

"It all seems so complicated, this life. And it scares me to think how much—"

"You'd love it?" he finished.

"I never would have sought it if it hadn't been revealed. Maybe if I'd seen it first . . ." She didn't dare go on.

"Which is why Lundi ought to get you home directly."

The voice, unmistakable, came from the backstage shadows, and the purposeful steps of Sister Aimee brought her to join them on the stage.

"Aimee," Roland greeted with a steady, casual air. "What are you doing here?"

"I could ask you the same thing, I suppose."

"We had some time," Roland said, "so I thought I would give our Dorothy a tour of the temple. Let her see how she likes the stage."

"And how does she?"

The phrasing of the question left Dorothy Lynn unsure as to whether she should answer on her own behalf, bringing her back to that feeling of uncertainty she experienced at their first meeting.

"Ask her," Roland said.

Sister Aimee did not repeat herself but turned to fully face Dorothy Lynn.

"It's beautiful," Dorothy Lynn said. "Really, the most magnificent thing I've ever seen."

"Do you know who built this temple?"

"From donations, I suppose. All those offerin's you took up at the services."

"Is that really what you think?"

Roland appeared ready to jump to her aid, but Sister Aimee held up a hand to stop him.

"God built this temple. He gave me the vision when I was but a child, and I have invested my time and my flesh in his Kingdom. I have taken the gifts he has given me to bring the gospel to the length and breadth of this country. And with every soul I touched, he gave me a brick. With every man saved from damnation, a scrap of cloth. With every woman rescued from the squalor of sin, a beam, a light, a floor, a roof. And every day, when I hear of its progress, when our needs have been met as I meet the spiritual needs of others, I say, 'Thank you, Jesus, for giving me a home.'"

She'd separated from them and strode across the stage, and Dorothy Lynn knew she envisioned the empty seats filled with the lost come seeking.

"The Gospel of Matthew," she continued, hitting a stride, "in chapter 8, verse 20, says, 'The foxes have holes, and the birds of the air have nests; but the Son of man hath not where to lay his head.' And yet—" she stood at the edge of the stage, the toes of her shoes peeping out over the orchestra pit—"he has given me this. Me, his humble, lowly servant. How much less do I deserve?"

She spread her arms wide, and Dorothy Lynn held her breath, not with enthusiasm for this temple, but fear that Sister Aimee was about to dive off the stage and die within it.

"It's a miracle," Roland said. "Nothing less."

Sister Aimee dropped her pose and stepped back but did not turn around. "It is no miracle, Lundi. It is the result of many years of praying, thousands of hours of labor, and a singular vision. Mine."

"Of course."

For the first time Dorothy Lynn saw Roland truly flustered, and her heart ached.

"So I apologize," she said, addressing Dorothy Lynn, "if Lundi has given you the impression that you will share this with me."

"He hasn't."

"Then why are you here?"

"An oversight on my part," Roland said, regaining a shadow of his familiar swagger. "I didn't think to book her passage separately from the rest of the company. Something I intend to rectify at once. I simply thought, given her contribution, she might want to see what it is we're building."

"And where is she staying during this time of oversight? At the Alexandria?"

"In our second room."

"It is not *our* room. They are *my* rooms. To be used at my discretion and leisure. And given that this will now be a permanent home, I expect to have more visitors—investors, I should say—who will be better served as my guests there. Am I clear?"

"Rarely are you anything but."

He took a cigarette from his pocket and lit it, blowing a narrow ribbon of smoke out of the corner of his mouth, daring Sister Aimee to demand its extinction.

Instead, she flashed an indulgent smile that didn't quite reach her eyes. "I'm glad. And seeing as my travels will be far less frequent, I'm sure I'll find myself less in need of your services. We are in a time of great transition, after all. I'm sure you will be able to find another mode of employment."

"I'll leave a forwarding address at the front desk."

It was like watching two butting rams with locked horns.

"Perfect," Sister Aimee said with an air of decisive victory, though Roland showed no outward sign of defeat. She turned to Dorothy Lynn and shook her hand. "God bless you, my girl. You do have a lovely voice."

"Thank you," Dorothy Lynn said, though she'd never heard a compliment so empty.

"And be sure Lundi takes you to see the ocean before you leave. It's magnificent."

She had no parting words for Roland, nor did he say anything as she left. When she disappeared, he lifted his foot and stubbed the cigarette out with the bottom of his shoe.

"You heard the lady." He tossed the butt into the orchestra pit. "Let's go to the beach."

❧❧❧

"Seems a waste for one day," Dorothy Lynn said, refusing Roland's offer to buy her a new bathing costume. "There's not much call for such things in Heron's Nest."

At Roland's insistence, she'd left her shoes and stockings in the car, as had he. The sight of his pale, bare ankles and feet—both dotted with black hair—made him seem all the more vulnerable.

With one arm he carried a blanket pulled from the trunk; she held the other arm as they walked down the embankment, the sand beneath her toes feeling nothing short of wonderful. The sky was hazy—a perfect match to their mood.

"There it is," Roland said, presenting her this gift. "The Pacific Ocean."

"It looks like it could be the end of the world."

"But it can't. Because the world doesn't end. It just circles on itself and starts all over. Nothing but opportunity." Coming from any other man, those words might have sounded wistful, but Roland spoke them with reassuring certainty. "Let me get a picture. Just one, to finish up the roll."

She knew better than to protest. His reason, always, was "to finish up the roll," and he'd been snapping her picture with his Brownie box camera at every station and theater since she'd arrived breathless at the eight o'clock train in St. Louis. "Trust me," he'd said, "you'll be glad for the memories."

He had intended to take a picture outside the Angelus Temple, but this would be a happier shot. He directed her to take the scarf off her head, to let the wind loosen that hair. To free herself up.

She did as she was told, standing with the eternity of opportunity behind her. It was just a trick of the ear, she supposed, that each wave sounded closer. Surely he would tell her if she was in danger of being swallowed up and swept away.

At his instruction, she smiled, and she and Roland remained motionless while the wind whirled all about, the sound of snapping silk joining the chorus of the surf. It was the first picture he'd taken in which her feet were bare.

After Roland returned the camera to the car—not wanting to

risk the danger that a single grain of sand could do—they began to stroll along the water's edge. The waves sometimes lapping over their toes, sometimes not. Dorothy Lynn listened for a rhythm in the waves, and just as one appeared, a disrupting rush came in.

"It's jazz," Roland said.

"What is?"

"The waves. Syncopated, you know? Unpredictable."

"I was just thinkin' about that," she marveled. "How did you know?"

"Baby, I might not know a lot of things, but I know people."

"So, what do you think you'll do? For work, I mean."

"Oh, I don't know. Lay low for a few months until Aimee cools off. Like I did the last time she fired me."

"But do you know where we're goin' to go?"

"We aren't going anywhere."

"But Sister Aimee said—"

"Sister Aimee hasn't been cultivating a friendship with the manager for the past five years. She's never sent his kids a birthday present or given a five-dollar New Year's bonus to every single bellman, maid, and porter in the place. We'll leave when I say we leave."

The finality in his voice ruled out further argument, making her feel at once reckless and wild, yet protected and safe. Just a month ago, if anyone had asked her what it meant to feel excited, she would have blushed, recalling the moments spent alone with Brent—in his car, on the front porch swing, off the side of the path that led from his church to her home. Sweet, powerful embraces, the two of them wrapped together. Always, with Brent, there'd been a sense of inevitable security. Nothing at risk, no doubt of reward. There'd been no question she could ask that wouldn't have an answer waiting.

But here, with her bare feet perched on the edge of the world, her future stretched beyond the horizon. Cocooned by the sound of the crashing waves, she could easily imagine herself completely alone—alone with Roland, anyway. This was different from the solitude of the forest. From here, God's plans seemed much, much bigger, crafted from people and places she never knew existed. Strange how, a world away from anything familiar, she could still feel utterly and completely safe—like curling up in her father's lap, or resting in Brent's embrace. Simply being in Roland's presence brought back memories of both.

"It is magnificent," she said after a time. "Makes you think you might be able to go on livin' forever. Like lookin' at eternity."

"But it's not." He stopped and turned to look out to where the ocean touched the sky. "Even it has its limits. Its beginning and end." He held up a hand. "'Who shut up the sea with doors, when it brake forth, as if it had issued out of the womb? When I made the cloud the garment thereof, and thick darkness a swaddlingband for it, and brake up for it my decreed place, and set bars and doors, and said, Hitherto shalt thou come, but no further: and here shall thy proud waves be stayed?'"

She watched him, mesmerized. Never mind that the world encompassed the two of them. At that moment only Roland stood between her and the horizon. He recited the words from the book of Job—no, he *spoke* the words of God, making her feel as if they had been recorded in ancient time for the sole purpose of resurrection in this moment. No pulpit had ever made Brent sound so powerful; never had the sound of Scripture ever stolen her breath.

When Roland finally broke free of his soliloquy, he turned to her and winked. "See? She's not the only one who knows her Scriptures."

"You could be an actor."

He cocked a brow. "Not a minister?"

"You're too handsome." The words were out before she could stop them, and she couldn't hide her embarrassment.

"Isn't your minister handsome?"

"He is." Dorothy Lynn wasn't quite ready, yet, to bring Brent into the conversation. She took the initiative and set them strolling again. "In a more quiet, understated way."

"And you're crazy about him."

"I am."

"Crazy enough to forget about all of this?"

A burst of laughter came from a distance as a group of people—all young and vibrant in the sun—tumbled across each other, running toward the water. The men looked so healthy, lean, and strong. The women, too, the hems of their dark suits cut to reveal the entire length of their legs. Some without stockings. All bare-armed and bare-shouldered. Dorothy Lynn wore more fabric *under* her clothes.

For just a moment, they stole her answer. Imagine life here— one carefree day after another, just like this. Sea and sand and salt. Waking up and deciding where to go, what to do, how to fill a day. The sound of the waves took on the cadence of a cheering crowd that both tempted and taunted, and she forced a reply. "Yes."

"I'm not convinced."

"You don't need to be."

They moved away from the shoreline up onto the beach, where Roland spread the blanket out in a flourish and gestured for her to sit. It seemed such an intimate invitation, and her discomfort must have shown, because he took pains to stretch the blanket even wider before perching on the outmost corner.

"Trust me when I tell you, sweetheart, you're not my type. I prefer my ladies legal."

"I'm goin' to be nineteen in two weeks."

"You're going to be another man's wife in two weeks too. Or had you forgotten?"

She sat at the top corner of the blanket and stretched her legs out in front of her, trying not to feel shock when Roland laid himself flat on his back, his head a mere arm's length from her hip, his hat resting atop his face.

"Just twenty minutes or so," he said, his voice muffled. "You use this time to contemplate all of God and nature. Then we'll go home."

Home. For as long as they were welcome, anyway. For the moment, home was Roland, wherever he might be.

She watched the couples frolicking down the way. Certainly they must be nearly her age, but she felt so much older. Would Brent ever engage in such activity? She tried to picture him in one of those suits, his broad shoulders intersected by the straps of the top, his legs . . . She'd never seen his legs. In fact, she'd never seen as much of any man before today.

To keep her thoughts pure, she turned her gaze to the ocean, though her attention and eyes often glanced down at the man who snoozed beside her. She would miss him once she got home. He'd shared with her moments of passionate worship and quiet contemplation.

And she could never tell a soul. Not Darlene, not Ma, and certainly not Brent. How could she explain friendship with such a dashing, worldly gentleman? And those new stirrings, suggesting that it could be something more? Blame the warmth of the sun, the surging of the waves, the scenery of half-naked bodies engaged in such provocative—yet innocent—physicality.

Small snoring sounds were coming from under his hat. That, combined with the lapping waves and drowsy light, began to tug on Dorothy Lynn's strength. She scooted halfway down the blanket and, maintaining the distance between them, mimicked Roland's position. She brought the scarf lofting down over her face and closed her eyes. Hands folded over her chest, she envisioned herself as a narrow plank.

"Dorothy?" His voice seemed a continent away, even though he was close enough to touch.

"Mm-hmm?"

"Later, when we're driving back? Remind me that I've just had a brilliant idea."

She made a soft sound of promise before succumbing to the darkness of salt and sand and silk.

❧ CHAPTER FOURTEEN ❧

AS IT TURNED OUT, Roland kept his idea to himself on the ride back to the Alexandria, where they shared an early supper in the dining room before parting company for the night. At his instruction, Dorothy Lynn arrived at the same table the next morning to find a plate of scrambled eggs and a pot of coffee awaiting.

"Today, my girl, I'm taking you shopping for a dress."

"I have a dress, Mr. Lundi. A dozen of them. You've already done so much—"

"I guarantee you don't have a dress for where we're going tonight." He looked mischievous, completely reinvigorated, and recovered from yesterday's blow.

"Is this your big idea, then?"

He took a swig of orange juice. "I'm taking you to a premiere tonight. New Buster Keaton film. Aimee loves that guy. I had to shake a lot of hands to get these tickets, and they were waiting for me at the front desk when we got back yesterday afternoon."

"Are you sure? After yesterday, I don't know how comfortable I'd feel seein' her again."

He winked. "She doesn't know. These were left for me, and I just got fired."

"Why take me?"

"Because the movie world is smaller than the smallest town, and if we talk to enough people, somebody will know somebody who knows somebody who knows your brother."

Instantly, she brightened. "Do you really think so?"

"It's worth a shot. I've made arrangements at a boutique where Aimee has an account. They're expecting us later this afternoon. And after that, your hair. How do you feel about cutting it?"

She touched a tuft self-consciously. "Oh, Mr. Lundi. I couldn't—"

"Just remember, time was you thought you couldn't sing in front of a crowd, either."

The shop was called Les Femmes en Vogue—something Dorothy Lynn flatly refused to say aloud after Roland ridiculed her first attempts during their fifteen-minute walk from the Alexandria.

"I've called ahead," Roland said by way of assuaging her feelings, "with all your details. Celine's the best."

She couldn't imagine what details he could be talking about. Her size? Maybe, and the event, which she understood to be nothing less than a fancy party filled with movie stars. The thought of going to such a thing tumbled her breakfast, and she willed herself not to think on it anymore, especially when she walked into the pink-and-white foyer of Les Femmes en Vogue.

"Roland!" The woman's voice was deep and throaty, befitting its accent that made *Roland* sound like some foreign delicacy.

"Celine."

The two exchanged brief kisses to each other's cheeks, for which the slender woman had to bend. Then, to Dorothy Lynn's surprise, Celine offered her the same greeting.

"This is she?"

"This is."

"And she is lovely?"

Dorothy Lynn wasn't sure if the phrase sounded like a question because of the woman's accent or her surprise at Roland's judgment.

"She's in your hands," he said, heading toward the door. "I'll be back in an hour."

Celine's veneer of charm cracked only slightly once she was alone with Dorothy Lynn. "You sit," she said, using her long cigarette holder to point to a damask-covered chair in the corner. She went to a curtained doorway and hissed something in French. Soon after, a young woman dressed head to toe in shimmering green silk appeared.

"This one?" Celine said.

It took a moment for Dorothy Lynn to realize the woman was talking to her. "It's beautiful," she said at last.

Celine looked at the model, then Dorothy Lynn, then the model again; she took a drag on her cigarette and said, *"Non."*

With absolutely no change of expression, the model left, and at Celine's command, another—identical, as far as Dorothy Lynn could tell—stood in her place. She wore a gown of diagonal black and silver stripes and a jeweled cap.

"This one?"

"Looks like a zebra," Dorothy Lynn said.

Celine's wrinkled look of disdain was clearly meant for Dorothy Lynn's commentary, not the dress. *"Non."*

This time, the model gave Dorothy Lynn a withering glare clear up to the moment she disappeared behind the curtain.

"I'm sorry," Dorothy Lynn said. "I didn't mean—"

It took only one raised eyebrow to stanch her apology, at which point, never taking her eyes off Dorothy Lynn, Celine bared her teeth and said, *"La rouge."*

This time, when the girl came out, Dorothy Lynn sat up straighter in the chair and shook her head. "No."

"Oui."

She attempted the accent. *"Non."*

Celine strode across the room—a frightening vision—and placed a single thin, lacquer-tipped nail in the center of Dorothy Lynn's forehead. "Monsieur Lundi? He say I decide. I choose *la rouge*."

"But I couldn't—"

"Up."

Dorothy Lynn stood, feeling very much like prize livestock at a county fair.

"Tournez."

She turned, slowly.

Again, Celine looked at the model, then Dorothy Lynn, then the model again. This time, when she bared her teeth, it was in a triumphant grin. *"La rouge. C'est parfait.* We will deliver by six o'clock."

Dorothy Lynn knew she would win no argument with Celine, so she simply said, "Thank you," and planned to wage war with Roland later in the day. She had no reason to go to a movie premiere and no business going *anywhere* in that dress.

Well aware that protest would be futile, she allowed herself to be handed over to a woman in a pale-blue smock who appeared at Celine's calling.

"Les cheveux," she said, bringing Dorothy Lynn to full understanding as she tugged at her hair. *"Terrible."*

That she understood too.

❧❦❧

The woman in the mirror was more familiar than not. She'd fought valiantly in at least three languages to keep her hair free from the snapping scissors. The resulting style—a product of countless hot irons and pins—looked miraculously like a bob, especially tucked underneath the jeweled headband. Her eyes were heavily kohled and shadowed, her lips and cheeks rouged. When they'd finished, the gaggle of women assigned to her transformation insisted on walking her back to the hotel, declaring that it would be a disaster if Roland were to see her before she was complete.

Meaning, *la rouge.*

Now, at quarter to eight, she stood in her room at the Alexandria, waiting, while a few blocks away at Les Femmes en Vogue, Celine could rest in triumph: Dorothy Lynn was wearing the dress. It was red—what there was of it—made of alternating panels of silk and chiffon, sleeveless, and cut with a deep V in the front and the back. She'd known the minute it dropped over her shoulders that it was perfect. Her fears of being exposed disappeared behind the flashes of her own flesh. If anything, she was hidden. Disguised. Alone in this room, Dorothy Lynn Dunbar had disappeared, not to be found again until she heard the familiar knock on the door.

"Baby," Roland said, as punctuation to a long, wolfish whistle. "I'm not always right about everything, but when I am . . ."

"Enough," Dorothy Lynn said, suddenly feeling as bare and red as the dress. "I can't go out like this."

"Au contraire, sweetheart." He walked right past her, carrying

a box with *Les Femmes en Vogue* etched in gold on the lid, which he dropped unceremoniously on the bed. "I think it would be a crime for you *not* to go out like this. Fair warning, though. You stick right with me."

"You're not helping your case, Mr. Lundi." But already, after just a few minutes under his gaze, she felt her heart settle into a normal rhythm and her skin thicken around her.

"Stop with the 'Mr. Lundi' nonsense. Makes me feel old, and makes you sound like a little girl, which you're not."

"Not in this dress. It's scandalous. What would my mother say?"

"Your mother isn't here."

"Brent wouldn't approve."

"He would if he could see you."

She went back to the mirror, trying to see herself through Brent's eyes. More so, to imagine him standing behind her. Instead, Roland appeared. He wore an impeccably cut black tuxedo, set off by crisp white collar and cuffs. His hair was parted far to one side and slicked back, accentuating the angles of his dark, handsome face; his eyes sparkled like the topaz stones in his cuff links. She leaned back because he smelled good too—clean and spicy, nothing like his everyday scent of travel and tobacco.

"That color?" His breath warmed her neck. "That red against your skin looks like a rose in the snow."

"Roses don't belong in snow. They'd die."

"They die anyway, don't they? I suppose you'd think it a better fate to be pressed away in some book, dried and flat forever. Wouldn't it be better to have one moment of stunning beauty?"

Her heart pounded as every nerve in her body reached to

tickle the underside of her skin. "Just what are you suggestin',
Mr. Lundi?" Far too dangerous to call him anything else.

"Relax, *ma petite* rose. It's going to be a big movie crowd there
tonight. Lots of opportunities to shake hands and rub shoulders
and ask if any of them have a guy working on their set named
Donny Dunbar. It's a catchy-enough name, but if I have his
beautiful, sad sister in tow, it might jog a few more memories."

Still not completely convinced of his motives, she none-
theless allowed herself the space of a long, deep breath as she
weighed the danger of going out against the missed opportunity
if she were to stay here alone.

"Do you really think we might find him?"

"I don't know, sweetheart, but we'll sure have a blast trying."

"And you're not worried about what Sister Aimee will say
when she finds out?"

They'd been speaking to each other through their reflections.
He stepped away from her, out of the frame. "As of this minute,"
he said, patting his pockets in the familiar routine of searching
for a cigarette, "I am my own man. Cut loose and free."

"Please don't smoke in here," Dorothy Lynn said. The odor-
ous film left by previous tenants was horrible enough.

"Well," he said, smiling, "perhaps not totally free. Shall we?"

This, then, was her time to decide, and she did. "Lead on."

"Wait a minute." He stopped to open the box and produced
a black fringed shawl embellished with roses embroidered in a
silk that perfectly matched the shade of her dress. "Something to
throw over your shoulders to keep the chill—and the dogs—at
bay."

"Thank you," she said, though she felt much less gratitude
than her tone might suggest. "Where do you come up with these
things?"

"I'm a resourceful man," he said, and she knew he'd elaborate no further. "By the way, how do I look?"

"Handsome as always." Here, she underplayed her enthusiasm to avoid gushing, for he looked almost nothing like always.

He offered her his arm, and before she could register any other protest, she took it, holding herself close to him as they walked down the hall.

"Will the car be waiting out front?" she asked once they were in the elevator, not because she needed to know, but because the space felt too heavy with silence.

"I'll call for it from the lobby. I didn't know how much of a fight you were going to put up."

This comment brought a snicker from the boy working the elevator and prompted Dorothy Lynn to pinch the inside of Roland's arm, though she didn't let go of her grip.

Like never before, the lush lobby of the Alexandria Hotel welcomed her as she stepped across the lift's threshold. Eyes turned, as she knew they would; a few whispered comments identified her as the woman who had been singing at the piano the previous morning. She buried her face in Roland's shoulder, taking care not to smudge her makeup.

"Don't bother hiding," he whispered. "They know a star when they see one."

"I'm not a star," she said with a smile tugging at every word.

"Not yet. But I tell you, sweetheart, give me a month, and you'd be on magazines."

For reasons far different from those of her first day in the place, Dorothy Lynn dreaded being left alone for even a single minute among the potted palms and marbled columns. Already, the few scraps of silk she wore felt like they were melting away.

"I don't think this is a good idea," she said, not sure if he was listening, as his eyes roamed the room behind her, occasionally lighting up in greeting.

"To take the car?"

"To go."

He made a sound of impatience, took her arm, and steered her away from the desk. "Well, then, we need to come to a decision."

"I just . . . I'm not myself. This isn't me."

"All the more reason, don't you think?"

"I don't know of a single person who would approve, including myself."

"I don't believe you. About the others, of course. But you? If there wasn't some tiny, important part of you that didn't think this was a gas, then you wouldn't be here. Not in this lobby, not in this state. Look, I'm no kidnapper. I'm not going to throw you over my shoulder and carry you out the door. In ten minutes my car will be outside, and I'll be behind the wheel. If you want to join me, fine. If not, go upstairs, order up some supper, and go to bed. Your company is not so delightful that I'll grovel for it."

And he left.

A slap would have stung less. In the wake of his exit, she couldn't be sure if he was hurt by her lack of trust or frustrated by her indecision. Either way, she remained rooted to the floor, desiring with half her heart to follow him, if only the other half would give its permission. But then, the other half of her heart wasn't here. It was back home enjoying a peaceful, quiet Saturday night.

She had ten minutes. Long enough to obtain a blessing.

With quick, measured steps, she headed toward the row of phone booths across the lobby, but soon realized she'd forgotten to grab her purse when she left the room. Quicker steps brought her back to the concierge's desk, where the thick man with a thin moustache seemed quite eager to help.

"I'm afraid I'm locked out of my room," she said, having a clear memory of Roland locking her door behind them. He must have his own key.

"And I'm afraid I can't help you," the concierge said with one side of his moustache twitched up in a smirk. "The room is in Mr. Lundi's name, after all."

Some deep, primal instinct guided her movements, and with one coquettish shrug, the black silk shawl dropped off her bare shoulders, and his moustache twitched the other way.

"You see," she continued, leaning forward, "I need to make a phone call, and I left my purse in the room."

"You have a telephone in your purse?" He was so obviously pleased with the joke, she pretended to be too.

"No, but I have a bunch of nickels."

He used one chubby finger to trace his moustache, perhaps trying to settle it back into place, and with the other hand pushed a gilded candlestick telephone to the front of the desk.

"You're welcome to use mine." He trilled the final word.

"It's long distance."

"My darling girl, look around you. Do you think we are concerned about the cost of a phone call?"

Dorothy Lynn was more concerned about the fact that this man would be listening in on her conversation, but time was of the essence. She thanked him with a broad smile and edged as far away as the cord would allow. At the sound of the operator's voice, she almost asked for long distance, St. Louis, to speak with her sister, but Darlene was not the one to provide absolution. For that, only one voice would do, and within a minute, she heard a very familiar greeting on the line.

"Hello, Jessup? It's Dorothy Lynn Dunbar."

She waited to hear the click on the line indicating that Mrs. Tully, the operator, had hung up, but heard nothing until Jessup himself said, "Get off the line, Mary Lou."

At least it would take some time before the town gossips heard about the conversation.

"Well, girl," Jessup said, "you're just the voice for empty ears."

The smile she continued to flash at the nosy concierge turned into something genuine at the familiar greeting. "You, too. I'm sorry, but I don't have a lot of time. Is there anyone there who can fetch Brent—Pastor Logan—to the phone?"

"Well, not exactly . . ." He stretched his words long enough to reach through the lines, and she felt herself entangled in their grip. Jessup's place was never empty.

"I really can't leave a message. I need to talk to him, and I haven't much time."

"Is everything all right, Miss Dorothy?"

"It's fine." Only the thinly veiled curiosity of the concierge kept her tears at bay. Bad enough he could hear every word; she wouldn't let him see her cry, too. "I—I just haven't spoken with him in a while. You know, empty ears and all. . . ."

Jessup cleared his throat, and when he spoke again, he made an obvious attempt to keep his voice low.

"You have to tell me right now, Miss Dorothy. Are you hurt? Are you in danger?"

"Well, of course not," she said, masking her trepidation in cheer. "Why would you ask such a thing?"

"I don't know why you young people can't leave an old man out of your business."

She couldn't be sure, but something about the way he said the last sentence made her feel like he wasn't talking to her at all.

"Jessup?"

Then, muffled, "Seems to me you could tell her that yourself."

"Jessup?" She spoke loudly enough that even those coolly try-ing to ignore her stared openly. "Jessup, is Brent there? Can you put him on?"

But there was no conversation coming from the other end, just barely audible masculine murmuring followed by silence.

"Hello?" She toggled the receiver. "Operator? Hello?" The concierge was looking at her with nothing less than pity as he eased the phone out of her grip. "We seem to have been discon-nected," Dorothy Lynn said, fighting for her composure.

"Indeed," he said, obviously unconvinced. "Would you like to try again?"

He'd been there. Brent had been sitting *right there*, and he wouldn't talk to her. True, she'd promised not to speak to him until she returned home, and he was only trying to help her stay true to her word. To keep her from being even the least bit dis-honest, because how could she lie to a man who wouldn't speak to her? But while his silence bought him honesty, it denied her pardon.

Perhaps her own heart was enough after all.

"No," she told the concierge, "I don't need to try again tonight."

She clutched the shawl around her shoulders and, feeling confident even in the unfamiliar shoes, ran across the lobby and through the front door, just in time to call out Roland's name before he drove away.

❧ CHAPTER FIFTEEN ❧

THEY DROVE THROUGH HILLS so far away from the lights of the city that Dorothy Lynn began to wonder if the whole idea of a party wasn't really just a ruse to get her away from the hotel.

"You're sure you know where we're going?"

"Relax, sweetheart. I know this place like the back of my hand."

He'd been gracious enough to put up the top on the car, which she appreciated on behalf of not only her hair but also her body, which was given scant protection against the autumn chill. Still, the confines made her restless; she twisted and turned in her seat, trying to get a feel for the landscape. "It's so dark."

"Is it?" he said, and directed her attention out the passenger window. Two beams of light lit up the sky, moving and crossing one another in pillars that touched the stars.

"Back home we just put a candle in the window," Dorothy Lynn said, not quite sure herself if the wistfulness in her voice was due to nostalgia or awe.

"What's the use of having an exclusive party if you can't tell the whole world about it?"

At that point those searching lights were beckoning *her*, and she leaned forward in the car seat as if doing so would speed their arrival. "Whose house is it we're going to?"

Roland laid a finger to his lips. "You're not in the circle yet, sweetheart. You're a pretty girl on the arm of a quasi-invited guest. It's my job to know the details. You just need to show up and smile, smile, smile."

"That's all I've ever been, isn't it?"

"What are you saying?"

"Instead of 'smile, smile, smile' it was 'sing, sing, sing.' You used me."

"And here you are, unless you somehow think you got yourself out here."

His smile stopped just short of smugness, and she dropped back against the seat, pouting. She gave a sidelong glance at the first of what would be a dozen mansions filling the view through her window and chewed the inside of her cheek to keep herself from making any other ill-fated retort. He was right, of course. She'd used him, jumping on the opportunity to find her brother, selling her dignity for this slim chance of finding a man who didn't want to be found in a city full of people living a facade. Maybe Brent was right to step away. Hadn't she made her priorities clear?

She laid her head against the cool glass. "I need to go home."

He mumbled an exasperated something, turning the car not-so-smoothly down a wide, tree-lined street. "Tell you what, sweetheart. When we get to the party, I'll hop out, hand you the keys, and if you can find your way, you can drive yourself back."

"I mean *home*. To Heron's Nest."

"Well, if you think you know your way, just keep driving. I don't know what was going on inside your pretty head when you signed on, but you're not going to make me feel like I'm some sort of matinee villain throwing you over my shoulder. As a matter of fact—ah, what's all this?"

At some point, she'd started crying, silent tears that ran unchecked down her face. "I can't," she said with a hitch in her voice. "I've never driven a car, and I don't know where to go. I can't do anything. I've ruined absolutely everything, and now I'm trapped."

"What, ruined? Nothing's ruined."

"I telephoned, when you went to get the car."

"Your sister?"

She shook her head. "I wanted to talk to him. To tell him— everything. And where I was going tonight."

"The fiancé. Let me guess. He didn't approve."

"Worse. He wouldn't talk to me. Not a word. It's over, I suppose."

"Well, then," Roland said, bringing the car to a stop behind a long line of others, "at least it's one less thing for you to worry about."

She twisted in her seat. "How can you be so heartless?"

"Heartless? No. Glib, perhaps. You just don't see things the way I do."

"I'm glad I don't." Dorothy Lynn wiped her tears with the back of her hand, horrified at the black smudges left on her wrist. "Why would I want to? Why would I want to risk becoming what you are? Pathetic and alone. I've let you do this to me, bring me here where I don't belong."

"You don't know where you belong." He spoke calmly, facing forward, as he inched the car along. "You think you belong in some godforsaken forest because it's the only place you've ever known, and you think you belong to that preacher because he's the only man you've ever known. Can't you consider, for even one minute, that God has had other plans for you all along and you're just finding the strength to see what they are?"

"Was it God's plan for you to leave your wife?"

"I couldn't follow him with her."

"No, you couldn't follow Sister Aimee with her. They aren't one and the same, you know."

He tightened his jaw and took one hand off the wheel to pat his breast pocket. She reached out and stilled his fidgeting with a hand on his sleeve. "Don't you want that? Someone to share your life?"

"Sure, someday. Maybe. But tonight—"

They'd come to a full stop, and somehow the narrow road they'd been inching along had become a broad, circular drive in front of a structure that was bigger than the county courthouse back home. Roland fiddled with the car, setting the brake, and stepped out. The next thing she knew, a strange man in a short wool jacket and pillbox hat had taken his place behind the wheel, and her door was opening behind her.

"Miss?"

A young man in an identical uniform stood with his hand outstretched, giving Dorothy Lynn no option but to take it. She stepped into the cool night air and immediately pulled the silk shawl around her shoulders, grateful for Roland's foresight.

Dozens of people, bathed in the golden light pouring from countless windows, littered the lawn. They were beautiful, every last one of them—the women like a multitude of birds, dressed in bright silks and feathers and jewels. Dorothy Lynn could see herself fitting in among them, easing up to any little klatch and, in her dress, at least, fitting right in. What she would say, of course, she hadn't a clue. But her job wasn't to speak. What had Roland said? *Smile, smile, smile.*

With lingering tears growing cold on her cheeks, such a feat seemed impossible.

"Let me see." At her hesitancy, Roland took her by the shoulders and turned her around. The house, the people, the lawn, the lights—all disappeared. "Now, stick out your tongue."

"What?"

But she obeyed, as he must have known she would. Roland brought a corner of the shawl up, touched it to her tongue, then, with a firm grip on her chin, went to work wiping the tearstained makeup from around her eyes.

"Perfect," he said, giving her chin a tug. "You've got nothing to worry about."

"I've got everything to worry about."

"No." He drew her closer. "You've got nothing. Not a single soul here knows about your past, and nobody's got a hand on your future. Tonight—for the first time in your life, maybe—you've got no one to answer to. No one but God, and I think we'll both find a day when we're clinging to his mercy. Seems he has a lot more of it than your boyfriend."

"Don't talk about him," she said. All that independence he was talking about made her dizzy, like she was standing on a beam, alone, above a pit filled with her family, and she clutched at him for support. "I can't think about him, not here."

He kissed the tip of her nose and tucked her under his arm. "Best idea you've had tonight."

Roland handed the gilded, engraved invitation over to a beefy, disinterested man in a brown suit who guarded the front door. Doors, actually—massive and double. On the other side was a room equal in elegance and size to any castle of Dorothy Lynn's imagination, not that she'd spent much time imagining castles. The floor was made of marble, and the whole space echoed with conversation and laughter. The ceiling was at least two stories high, and as they moved through the room, she saw that a staircase carpeted in red velvet spiraled up to a balcony that spanned the entire length of the wall.

Dorothy Lynn tugged for Roland's attention. "Who lives here? A movie star?"

"Stars don't make this kind of green," he said. "This place belongs to the head of a studio."

"And you know him?"

Roland gave an enigmatic smile and patted her hand. He appeared to be on intimate, friendly terms with many of the party's population, shaking hands with men, blowing kisses to women, and returning shouts of "How are you, fella?" from one end of the room to the other.

It didn't take long to notice that many of the guests carried champagne glasses filled with golden, sparkling liquid, and others meandered holding short, squat ones filled with ice and amber. They walked with ambling gaits and spoke with animated, flushed faces. After a few silent conversations involving pointing fingers and jerking thumbs, Roland brought her into a more private, paneled room, where a gentleman in a white jacket presided behind a black lacquered bar.

"What'll it be, sir?" he asked. "Bubbly, or the house stock?"

"Ginger ale," Roland said, and when the man behind the bar looked confused, Roland leaned forward, smiled, and repeated himself. "The real stuff, like what you'd give your kid sister."

"You don't know my sister," the barman said, smirking, before producing a dark-green bottle and dispensing its contents into two short, squat glasses.

Dorothy Lynn thanked both of them as she brought the

fizzing drink up to take a sip, wrinkling her nose as the bubbles jumped up to touch it.

"They're serving alcohol?" she said, keeping her mouth fixed in a smile as she spoke. "Isn't that illegal?"

"Only as far as the law is concerned," Roland said. "And when you have money, the law doesn't go very far past your front door."

"What next? Will we get to meet Buster Keaton? Where do we see the movie?"

Roland took a sip of his drink and looked at it wistfully before taking another. "That's the thing about a premiere. It's more about the schmooze and the booze than the film. See? Sure, somewhere in this place there's a big room—a couple dozen seats and a projector. But did you come here to sit in the dark with me? Or have we got other plans?"

He started to move away, so she gripped her drink and tucked her free hand in the crook of his arm. "I'll do whatever you say, Mr. Lundi."

He pulled her close. "Don't say that to anyone but me if you're wearing a dress like that. Come on, sweetheart, let's mingle."

As they worked their way from room to room, Dorothy Lynn recalled an ancient conversation with her sister. Dorothy Lynn had been certain she'd never attend a smart party. But look at her now. In her wildest dreams, Darlene wouldn't believe the excess of fashion, wealth, and intoxication; she could hardly believe it herself. Some of the women's dresses trailed behind them, sweeping the floor with silk, while others barely came to their wearers' knees. There were gowns cut deep and low both in the back, where sharp spines jutted out of pale skin, and in the front, where rib cages poked between sequins and fringe. In comparison, she could see that her own dress hit the perfect note of fashion and modesty, and she made a silent promise to thank Celine for both her taste and her stubborn nature. She would tell Roland as much, but for now conversation was out of the question, as a twenty-piece band struck up a jazzy tune. A collective cheer went up among the guests, and the entire room erupted into dance. Roland lifted his eyebrows in quizzical invitation, but Dorothy Lynn shook her head.

"I don't know how," she shouted and was amused at his obvious relief.

He was steering her through pockets of people and sound when a voice rang out. "Lundi!"

A big, red-faced man with thinning hair and a rumpled tuxedo held a drink in one hand and extended the other, greeting Roland with a vigor that looked strong enough to catapult him across the room.

"H. C. Bendemann," Roland said, "how did you get in here?"

"Same as you, I suppose. Swiped an invite."

Roland laughed.

"And who is this?" the man wanted to know.

Roland made the introductions, explaining that Bendemann was the owner of this mansion and host of the party, and referring to Dorothy Lynn as a sweet songbird from the mountains, causing Bendemann's eyes to widen beyond the rims of his narrow spectacles.

"Here I was thinking you were attached to the *goyeh*."

"Not at all," Roland said. "I'm finding myself less and less attached every day, so if you've got word of any new opportunities for an enterprising man, I'd appreciate your handing my name around."

"Will do." He continued to eye Dorothy Lynn, who grew increasingly uncomfortable under his gaze.

She stepped closer to Roland, tugged on his sleeve, and whispered, "Ask him about Donny."

"Not yet." Roland spoke out of the corner of his mouth, barely moving his lips.

"But you said—"

"Later."

"Have I stepped up to a lovers' quarrel?" Bendemann interjected. "Come around with me, *pitzl*, and let's see what we can do."

The next thing Dorothy Lynn knew, her arm was captured in his moist, clammy hand, and she was being pulled away from Roland, who seemed unable—or unwilling—to do anything to keep her.

"It's my brother," she said, bending her arm in an effort to keep the man's body as far away from hers as possible. "I'm trying to find him."

His grip went slack. "Is he in some sort of trouble?"

"No, not at all. At least, I don't think so."

Bendemann dropped her altogether and took a sweeping look around the crowded room before moving menacingly toward Roland.

"What's this, Lundi? Bringing this *mazik* to a party you're barely invited to yourself. What's she hiding?"

"Relax," Roland said, lighting a cigarette with a nonchalance Dorothy Lynn especially appreciated. "Kid's working construction at one of the studios. She wants to pay him a surprise visit from back home. That's all."

"At Metro?"

Roland shrugged. "I don't know. Neither does she. Out in the sticks, Hollywood is Hollywood." He gathered her back to his side, gently, like some sort of mother duck. "I said if she'd dress up and be a good girl, I'd do what I could for her. That a problem?"

"Look around. Does this look like the party for a carpenter?"

"I didn't think it would do any harm to ask around."

"Just be careful how you ask—and careful who you ask. Some people don't like to be bothered with minutiae." He looked at Dorothy Lynn. "No offense, sweetie."

"Of course not," Roland spoke for her.

"What's the kid's name?"

"Donny." She spoke up before Roland got the chance. "Donny Dunbar."

"Donny Dunbar, eh?" Bendemann rocked back on his heels and spoke to the vaulted ceiling. "Got a nice ring to it. You sure he doesn't want to be on the screen? If he looks anything like you, he's got to be one handsome fellow."

She supposed she should have felt flattered. Instead, she imagined what little there was of her dress was losing the battle between her skin and Bendemann's lascivious gaze. Still, she knew Roland would expect her to smile, and she did, just slightly, hoping her disgust might somehow pass for an attempt at being coy.

"Not that I know of, Mr. Bendemann." She stretched her words into an exaggerated, honey-sweet drawl. "But all the girls back home in Heron's Nest sure loved him."

"Heron's Nest." He looked once again at Roland. "Is she for real?"

"As real as they get," Roland said, and she warmed at the pride in his voice. "Like the way people used to be, before the war took us all to hell and back."

The trio fell into silence—a sober island in the midst of so much festivity.

"My brother fought in the war," Dorothy Lynn said, soft enough that the older man had to lean down to hear. Real tears pooled in her eyes. "He's never come home. I just want to see him again, to tell him about my—" Something beyond Roland's subtle jab kept her from saying *wedding*, and she didn't dare mention her father in this place. Not that she believed the ghost of him would come barreling out of heaven to strike her down, but she'd taken enough foolish chances for one day. In the end, it didn't matter what she was going to say, because H. C. Bendemann had once more snatched her away from Roland's side, though this time in a slightly more paternal embrace.

"Well, then," he said, raising the hand that still held his cocktail to summon someone from across the room, "what's the use of having sway in this place if you can't use it to help a sweet kid like you?"

He downed the rest of his drink and handed the empty glass to a passing waiter, instructing Dorothy Lynn to hand hers to Roland, which she did unquestioningly. From the crowd at large had emerged a man in a cheap tweed jacket and rumpled hat, wearing a large camera on a thick strap around his neck.

"You and the lady, sir?" he asked, chomping a piece of chewing gum in the corner of his mouth.

"Indeed," Bendemann said, immediately releasing any fatherly tension from his embrace. "On three."

The photographer counted, and on "Three!" a flash exploded, adding to the cloud of cigarette smoke in the room.

"In the dailies tomorrow," Bendemann said, artfully slipping the photographer a folded bill. At least, that's what Dorothy Lynn assumed he was giving him, as the light from the flash lingered in the corners of her sight. "*Movie Weekly* and *Variety* next week. Got it?"

"Yes, sir." He reached into the breast pocket of his coat and pulled out a notebook and a stub of pencil. "Caption?" he said, before placing the notebook along the side of his mouth. "Or are we wanting to remain anonymous?"

"My name, of course, and Miss—it is *Miss*, isn't it?"

"It is," Roland said. "Miss Dorothy Lynn Dunbar," and he spelled it, keeping a careful eye over the photographer's shoulder.

"That should get some attention," Bendemann said, taking a new, filled glass from the same waiter who had carted his empty one away just a minute before.

"Indeed it should." Roland handed Dorothy Lynn her drink, and she numbly participated as the three touched their glasses together. "You're a powerful man."

"We'll see how powerful I am once my wife sees that picture. *Oy, gevalt!* You'll explain to her, won't you? God forbid she kick me to the street." He took a long, appreciative swallow of his drink before shaking Roland's hand and giving Dorothy Lynn a kiss on her cheek. Then he disappeared into the crowd.

"Can we go home now?" Dorothy Lynn asked, wiping the lingering alcohol from her face with the back of her hand.

Roland deposited their glasses on the tray of a passing waiter and picked up two others filled with champagne. "One drink."

She refused to even touch the glass.

"One drink," he insisted, "and one dance—not with me, but with some young sheik worthy of your company—and then straight home. Come on, my sweet rose. Enjoy your night in the snow."

Tiny, enticing bubbles frolicked above the rim. She'd asked Brent if they could have a bottle of champagne at their wedding, just as Darlene and Roy had. Enough for all the guests to join in a single toast. He'd said she was out of her mind. Prohibition aside, it was a fool who got drunk with wine. And now . . .

"It's too late," she said.

"It's not even eleven o'clock."

Distracted by Roland's misunderstanding, she reached for the glass. "Ma always said it was cheating to stay out past midnight. It keeps your feet in both days."

"What's wrong with that?"

"Our days are numbered by the Lord. If we live two at a time, we're getting more than our share."

"If that's the case, baby," he said, touching his glass to hers, "then we're staying out 'til dawn."

It tickled and burned at one time, leaving her unsure of both its delight and its danger. Roland, however, had no misgivings—no sooner were their glasses empty than two more arrived, and by the third, everything around the room was deliciously fuzzy.

Once, when Roland was off getting drinks, a woman in a dress made entirely of sheer gauze and strategic ribbons came up to her, leaned close, and in a booze-laden voice asked, "Who's your daddy?"

"Pastor Dunbar," Dorothy Lynn said, surprised at how thick the words were when she wasn't simply flipping out a joke. "But he's dead."

Ribbons rolled her eyes. "Not your *father*. Your *daddy*." She inclined her head toward Roland, who had a familiar champagne glass in one hand and one of the far more dangerous-looking dark liquid in the other.

Before he arrived, Dorothy Lynn cupped her hands around her mouth and bent straight to Ribbons's ear. "That's Roland Lundi. I think he may have ruined my life."

I have seen all the works that are done under the sun;
and, behold, all is vanity and vexation of spirit.

ECCLESIASTES 1:14

BREATH OF ANGELS
2:07 P.M.

They call this the "celebration room," even though most days it is indistin-
guishable from any other. The carpet is the same industrial mauve weave
as is found throughout the facility, and the tables are the same sturdy dining
sets that furnish the dining hall downstairs. One thing it does have is a generous window and sliding glass door opening to a narrow, walled-in patio
in case a family's celebration is given to moving outside.

Lynnie sits outside the celebration room, having dutifully taken a nap
after her tour of the grounds courtesy of Charlotte Hill. Had her caretakers
known the extent of her fitfulness during the prescribed nap, however, they
might not have credited her with compliance. A body as old as hers did not
expend its energy on tossing and turning, but her mind had never ceased
its questioning as she lay, eyes closed against the gray light of the drawn
drapes.

Now, freshly primped and propped in her wheelchair, she waits, staring
at the black sign with white plastic letters wedged in its creases.

RESERVED
October 14
2–3 p.m.

249

The clock on the wall indicates that her party should have started more than five minutes ago, and she wonders if, behind the large double door, last-minute preparations are under way. Balloons, maybe—those large, floating, colorful, silver-backed ones—or bright paper streamers looped from one industrial ceiling tile to the next. She strains to listen for music, or even conversation, but hears nothing.

She longs, suddenly, for Charlotte, who—in her mind, at least—would have an answer for all of this. But Charlotte, chastised for keeping Lynnie out too long, had turned the wheelchair over to the capable hands of Kaleena and disappeared among the covered walkways. She might have whispered a promise to return, but that could be nothing more than a trick of an old woman's mind that has lived with too many wishes.

With a gnarled hand she plucks at the pilling on the sleeve of her favorite blue sweater. Kaleena had asked if she wouldn't rather wear something slightly more festive? Pink, maybe, or the white cardigan with the golden thread and soft fur running along the buttons? But this is warm and familiar, though she can't help but think how it diminishes with every tiny, discarded ball of thread. Long ago, someone—or some machine, more likely—knit this sweater one stitch at a time, and here it binds itself in tiny balls to be pinched off by useless fingers and tossed onto the floor next to a wheelchair parked outside an empty celebration room. And to think, it's not half as old as Lynnie herself.

These are the thoughts that plague her as she waits. And waits. In her youth this might have become a song, and her feet, snug against the soft soles of her slippers, twitch against the imagined cool forest floor where she'd escape to write it. Her mind grows drowsy looking for a rhyme.

Sweater . . . Better?

Silly.

As always, she hears them long before she sees them. What used to be overlapping, clattering footsteps have become purposeful, careful sounds of nonskid soles assisted by rhythmic, tapping canes. They're arguing about gas prices, of all things, and the financial insanity of driving two extra blocks to save a nickel, at best. They've not even rounded the corner yet, and already she is exhausted.

"Aunt Dottie!"

She's not sure if it is RJ or Darren who first shouts out the greeting. The difference in age that so defined them as boys disappeared shortly after high school. Today, as both enjoy rare, hearty health for men in their nineties, a stranger would be hard-pressed to know which was older. Indeed, Lynnie hardly knows which is which. It's not until one of them bends to kiss her and she notices the scar on his bald, spotted pate—the testament of a collision between his head and a can of peas—that identifies him as Darren, the oft-wounded younger brother.

RJ patiently waits his turn before planting a dry kiss on her other cheek.

"Happy birthday, Aunt Dottie." He twists his hat in his hands and looks around. "Nobody else here?"

"Does it look like anyone else is here?" Darren asks, forever seeking argument.

"I thought they might already be inside the room."

"Then why would she be outside?"

"Maybe they got here before she did."

"Then why would they close the door?"

Shut up! Shut up! Shut up!

When they were little boys, Lynnie wouldn't have dared shout them down in such a way, for fear of incurring their mother's wrath. Now, in their old age, they've reverted to the same childish behavior, and she is again powerless to make them stop. She furrows her brow and looks from one to the other, but they are too entrenched in their argument to notice her displeasure. The round-faced clock ticks down another minute of her designated birthday party time, and the possibility that she'll spend every moment of it trapped in this hallway listening to two old men bicker is starting to seem very real when the sound of squeaking shoes and short, panting breath comes up from behind.

"Daddy! Uncle RJ! We can hear you clear down the hallway."

It's Penny, Darren's oldest daughter, looking so much like her grandmother it takes Lynnie's breath away. True, she's fatter than Darlene would have ever allowed herself to be, but they share an identical chin and nose and slightly lifted left eye.

Penny is all business this afternoon, hefting a bakery cake box, a canvas grocery bag, and an assortment of gift bags, each with its own tufted tissue paper spilling from the top.

"Is anybody else here?"

"Does it look like anyone else is here?" her father repeats.

Fearing a descent into the same argument, Lynnie forces a grunt from the back of her throat to bring the attention back to her.

"Of course, happy birthday, Great-Aunt Dottie. If I can get one of these two to open the door, we'll get things set up."

Grumbling, RJ complies. Darren wheels Lynnie, who stares at Penny's bustling behind, made even more entertaining as it wriggles beneath a pair of dark-blue stretch pants.

"Well, isn't this nice?" Penny says with enough enthusiasm to make it so. In truth, the celebration room is modest in its glory. It's warm in here—as always—and the tables have been covered with colored cloths that look like so much confetti. In the center of each is a glass vase with one or two plastic flowers—standard centerpieces for all occasions.

It turns out the answer to the question "Is anybody else here?" is yes. Seven people, actually, representing three generations: RJ's son—another Roy—his daughter Kathleen and her husband, Patrick, and their four children, whose names Lynnie has never bothered to learn. They all start with K, a practice she has always found maddening, and as far as she can remember, she's never had a single conversation with them beyond the obligatory thank-you and good-bye. Right now all of them—children, parents, and grandparents—are engrossed in their individual electronic gadgets, which accounts for the silence on the other side of the door.

"There you are," Kathleen says, rising from her chair. She is every bit as portly as Penny, though she dresses more fashionably to accommodate the extra weight. "You said two o'clock. We've been waiting in here for fifteen minutes."

"Well, I had to pick everything up, and the cake wasn't ready, and then I couldn't find a parking place . . ."

Penny's litany of complaints goes on, without the slightest attempt to hide her frustration.

"Next time let me know and I'll help out."

"Oh, next time? For the hundred-and-eighth?"

They find resolution in laughter, never acknowledging that Lynnie is there, waiting, listening. Instead, Penny forges on, dropping the cake on one of the tables and unpacking the grocery bag with boxes of crackers and plastic packages of cheese cubes.

"Kids," Kathleen says as she counts out a stack of paper plates, "go say happy birthday to your great-aunt Dottie."

"Great-great-great-aunt Dottie," Penny says, delighted. "Isn't that something?"

None of the children move until their father nudges one with his elbow. Then, with eyes rolled to the ceiling, the oldest—a surly-looking teen—takes to his feet and shuffles over to where Lynnie has been parked near the window.

"Hapbirthdaygrauntdottie," he mutters, not bothering to look away from the screen in his hands. It's a wonder he can see anything through the shock of hair in front of his eyes. One by one they follow suit, looking either at their electronic games, at the floor, or at something slightly behind her. Only the youngest—a five-year-old surprise—stares at her with unabashed terror, forgetting completely what she has been sent over to say. A helpful older brother slugs her in the arm hard enough to knock her off balance.

"Say 'happy birthday,' stupid!"

Her round little mouth struggles for the words, but ultimately tears win out and she runs back to the safety of her father, who absently gathers her into his lap.

"What a doofus," the slugger says as he rejoins his family at the table.

It seems only fitting that Darlene's descendants are as unpleasant as her own children, though were she still alive and in this very room, she would deny any hint of rudeness.

Lynnie raises her eyes. *You're the lucky one, dear sister.*

Oh, that she might be spared another repeat of this day.

The men congregate in muttering uselessness while the women putter about. Kathleen bops her finger, counting, and says, "Are we it?"

"I think so," Penny says. "Aunt Margaret simply couldn't make the trip. And really, at her age, what's the point?"

Aunt Margaret, of course, is Darlene's youngest child—the daughter she so hoped for—who married promptly at the age of eighteen and lived all over the world as an officer's wife before retiring in Orlando, Florida. She and all of her family had flown in to celebrate when Lynnie had lived a mere century. That party was not held in the celebration room. Rather, they had rented nearly an entire floor of the new Hampton Inn, and the party lasted most of a day with a catered dinner, a four-tiered cake, and champagne. A full hour was taken by each family member's heartfelt good-bye, each sure this would be the last they would see her this side of Glory.

Most were right. Today, only the St. Louis remnant has assembled— those living in the shadow of Finest Automobiles, Roy's car dealership, which RJ and Darren took over upon his retirement. It was a family joke that Finest Automobiles was a crucial third party in Patrick and Kathleen's courtship, and to think—someday Roy's legacy would be handed down to the sullen teen with nickel-size holes in his earlobes.

"We'll still be finished by three, right?" Patrick says, readjusting the daughter on his lap to better see his phone. "I have two clients to see."

"Yes," Kathleen says, indulgently. "It's just cake and snacks."

Penny looks disgusted. "Would it kill you to put work aside and enjoy one hour of family time?"

A smile tugs at Lynnie's mouth as she envisions him setting down his phone and keeling over. The kid might take a tumble, but children are resilient. Most of them, anyway.

"Besides," Penny continues, pouring punch into red plastic cups, "how many more opportunities like this do you think we're going to have? Maybe Christmas—"

"We're going to have to come back here for Christmas?" the slugger whines. Kathleen shoots him a warning look and sends a long-distance jab with the sharp cake knife.

"We'd give anything to have one more celebration with our mother,"

RJ or Darren says, and everyone in the room has the decency to look sad, though half never had the opportunity to meet her.

Suddenly, she is moving, being pushed by Penny, who—as always—smells like cake.

"Here we go," she says in that singsong voice that lets Lynnie know she's being addressed. "Let's get you up to the table and get you a snack."

Kathleen, the soul of efficiency, slides a plate of cheese and crackers onto the table.

"Can she eat those?" Penny asks above her head, whispering. "You don't think she might choke?"

"I hadn't thought of that," Kathleen says, and the food is whisked away. "Will she be able to eat the cake?"

"I think so. We'll have to watch and see if she needs any help."

"Maybe we should do the candles now, so we can all eat whatever, whenever."

"Sounds good," Penny says, and once again Lynnie is in motion, coming to a stop in front of a half sheet cake. The icing is white, with streams of colored frosting strewn down the sides. In the center, the words *Happy Birthday, Dothy* are piped in red.

"I'm sorry they misspelled your name," Penny says. "I couldn't decide if I should put Dorothy or Lynnie or Dottie or what. . . . That's the last time I order a cake over the phone."

"It'll taste the same," Roy III says, contributing his first wisdom to the gathering.

"That it will," Penny says, obviously hoping her cheerfulness will energize the room and gather them all in its warmth. "Now, Great-Aunt Dottie, we wanted to put on all 107 candles, but we were afraid the fire marshal wouldn't approve." She allowed for the unenthusiastic, obligatory laughter before continuing. "So I thought we'd each put a candle in the cake and take turns giving you a birthday blessing."

While Penny speaks, Kathleen is dutifully handing a tiny candle to each person—young and old—all of whom look bewildered to be in possession of such a thing.

"Uncle RJ? You're the oldest, so why don't you start."

The birthday candle looks silly in the old man's hand—undignified, somehow. He stares at it, as if seeking inspiration, then says to Penny, "I don't know what you want me to do."

"Just say something nice about your aunt Dottie. Something she's meant to you."

Her answer seems unhelpful, and he shifts his gaze to Lynnie, studying her.

"What's your favorite memory?" Penny prompts.

"She taught me to sing 'Glow-Worm,'" he says finally. "She played it on her guitar and taught me the words."

Lynnie remembers that day and can almost see the young boy behind the old man's carefully groomed face. She taps a rhythm on her lap and hums the tune, pleased to find the occasional note escaping to her audience.

"That's it," RJ says, then clears his throat. "'Shine, little glow-worm, glimmer, glimmer . . .'"

The two of them—he aloud, she in silence—sing the song through its first jaunty verse. For a moment, it's a summer's day and she can smell his sweaty head tucked against her arm, fascinated as her fingers find the chords. Her eyes rim with tears at the memory, and in the midst of the smattering of family applause, RJ takes her hand in his and brings it to his lips.

"You were as wonderful a mother as our own," he says, and it's the first moment she has ever truly loved him.

"Now, put the candle in the cake, Uncle RJ," Penny says, her own voice choked with emotion. "Daddy? You're next."

RJ, however, does not put the candle on the cake. Rather, he hands it to Penny and takes himself back to his table to wait.

"Our mother loved you very much," Darren says. He places a dry kiss on the top of her head, hands his candle to Penny, and joins his brother.

"You're not doing it right," Penny says, exasperated as she wedges the candles into the cake. "Roy?"

RJ's son looks lost and uncomfortable. Finally, he says, "I wish I'd

ALLISON PITTMAN

known you better," before handing his candle to his cousin and joining the other men.

"Well, this is not what I had in mind at all," Penny says. "This sounds more like a funeral than a birthday party. I mean, look at this woman. One hundred and seven years old! That's more than a century! Imagine the things she has seen, how the world has changed." She kneels beside the wheelchair. "I'd give anything to hear the stories locked up inside that head of yours."

"You had fifty years to hear them," Roy says. "You should have asked her back then."

"When I was a kid," she says, directing her comments to the children, who appear to have no intentions of listening, "I didn't care about the exploits of some old woman. And now it's too late."

"Wouldn't have mattered," RJ says. "Mom wouldn't let her tell them. Neither would Grandma. I remember hearing them up late at night right after Margaret was born saying what happened in California wasn't anybody's business."

"What happened in California?" Kathleen says. She has a Ritz cracker piled high with cheese cubes and pops the whole thing into her generous mouth.

RJ shrugs. "Never asked. All I remember is that she ran off right before her wedding."

"But she came back, didn't she?" Penny is still holding her candle aloft, not quite finished with her birthday blessing.

Lynnie listens to all of this with her heart full of unspoken secrets. No wonder she is a stranger to these people. How harmless it all seems now, hardly worth a lifetime of supposed scandal. Flesh and blood they may be, but Kaleena could have wheeled any old woman down the hall and parked her in the celebration room, and no one would have been the wiser. Not one person has mentioned seeing her on the *Today* show, and nobody has even a single picture to pass around and share memories. They could take a lesson from that Charlotte Hill. Her and her gadget with its pictures and songs.

The celebration room has a window that looks out onto the hallway,

257

and, seized with a longing for someone familiar, Lynnie cranes her neck around Penny's frothy mass in response to the feeling that someone on the other side is looking in.

There she is, the familiar pointy face and unnaturally black hair. She stands against the wall, arms folded, watching. Lynnie lifts one shaking hand, intending to beckon Charlotte inside. She, after all, holds the answers to all their questions. Her slouchy satchel holds the evidence of that secret time. Charlotte can clear her name and free her conscience, deflating whatever infamy Darlene's progeny have imagined.

But her hand is captured between Penny's soft, frosting-smudged ones.

"My birthday wish for you," she says, her mouth wide in a clownish smile, "is that we can all gather here together just like this next year. And that God will somehow touch your mind so you can realize just how much we all care."

There's no escaping the embrace to come. Lynnie's face is impaled on a hard bit of plastic—part of the autumn-themed embellishment on Penny's sweatshirt.

"Somebody take my picture," she says, her voice loud in Lynnie's ear. "Use my camera." Then Penny twists around, making the two of them cheek-to-cheek. She can smell the woman's face powder and imagines a smudge of makeup will be left behind when this ordeal is over.

Kathleen stands ready and says, "Say cheese," which one of the children thinks to protest as being cruel, given that the old lady can't talk.

"Penny can talk enough for both of them," Roy says, and the flash erupts in a moment of genuine laughter.

"Ah, that's nice," Kathleen says, walking over. She shows the image to Penny, who furrows her brow and claims to look fat before bending to show the picture to Lynnie.

She doesn't want to look, not while the young woman in the red dress is still so fresh in her mind. Penny, though, ever forceful, brings the camera around to invade her line of sight, and there they are—the essence of Darlene and the old woman she wouldn't live to become.

❧ CHAPTER SIXTEEN ❧

HER HAIR REEKED of cigarette smoke; her pillowcase was smeared with black. The red dress lay in a heap on the floor in a silk puddle around her shoes, with stockings, garters, and underthings strewn nearby.

She paused briefly, staring at this evidence while her sluggish mind began to knit together the memories of the woman she'd been the night before.

Champagne—that much she remembered, three glasses to start with. And something called shrimp cocktail, and other lovely foreign nibbles that Roland continuously foisted upon her, saying, "Eat something, sweetheart."

Dancing—her feet and her body fully engaged in frantic, unfamiliar steps. Soft-shaven cheeks pressed against hers, masculine hands touching the bare skin of her back—and lower, sometimes—before Roland-the-gentleman offered rescue.

Slurring tirades against Brent, and Sister Aimee, and boorish, repressive moral regimen.

Finally, fresh, cool air, downright icy as they drove. Where was the shawl? Telling Roland, "We have to go back. I'm freezing. Take me back," but still he drove on and on, his words lost in the roar of air between them.

A lopsided walk through the Alexandria lobby. A single foot trailing in the carpeted hall. The rough texture of the wall—more reliable than her spine. A key opening the lock.

Roland saying, "Okay, baby. I think you're done," before his lips were silenced by her own. Her fingers in his hair, her feet off the floor, her body encased in his arms. His protests as she reached for him.

And then, the protests silenced.

His touch behind the damp cloth that soothed her fevered face. His final words landing on her pillow as he tucked her away, soft and safe, long hidden from the mercies of a new day already on the cusp of dawn.

Oh, God. What have I done?

She made slow, unsteady progress to the bathroom, where she knelt with her cheek against the tub, aware of the porcelain changing from cool to warm as it filled with steaming hot water. When it was full, she climbed in and immediately submerged herself. She ran her fingers through the long hair floating loose. Then a panic set in as she felt a familiar bile rise within her. Heedless of the lakelike puddle she was making on the floor, Dorothy Lynn hurled herself out of the tub and was once again kneeling—this time at the commode as she heaved and retched, cleansing that much, at least, from within.

She scooped water from the tub and rinsed her mouth, then got back in and scrubbed her hair, her face, and every inch, working furiously at first, as if doing so would bring back her innocence. Then, slowly. She closed her eyes, the lapping of the bath's water reminiscent of the ocean's tide and Roland's voice reciting, *Hitherto, but no further*—sounding more like, "That's far enough, sweetheart"—before leaving her stranded on the shores of sleep.

Later, dried and dressed with her wet hair combed, braided,

and pinned, she spied a folded sheet of hotel stationery just under her door. Whether or not it had been there before her bath she couldn't say—she'd been in no shape to read it.

D—
> *Don't know how you'll be feeling this morning.*
> *I'm having sandwiches sent up at noon.*
>
> *Grins.*
> *—R*

Grins, indeed.

As if the note itself were a summons, a knock sounded at her door and a fresh-faced boy stood on the other side with a rolling cart. She was digging in her purse for a dime when he lifted his hand and said, "Already taken care of, ma'am," with such earnestness that she insisted, pressing the coin into his soft, cool flesh.

"For an ice cream," she said.

Once again alone, she lifted the silver dome to reveal a tray filled with triangle-shaped sandwiches of all sorts. There was also a pitcher of cold water and a pot of hot coffee—both of which seemed far more appealing. Still, she nibbled as much as her stomach allowed, pacing the length and breadth of her room, stepping around the dress at each pass. Had she taken it off herself? Had he? She kicked it halfway under the bed and gulped down a glass of water.

The note said nothing about when Roland would call on her today, but as surely as she knew that he would, she knew she couldn't face him. Not here, at least. Not at the scene of the transgression.

It was Sunday morning—well, Sunday afternoon. She should be in church. Not a theater, not a concert hall, but church. A place where she could meet with God, fellowship with him, praise and worship his name in the wake of grace.

No. Not church. What she needed was air. Fresh and clear, and grass under her feet. She'd been away from home for more than a month, and it had been that long since she'd had an opportunity for either.

The park, Pershing Square. She wrapped her sandwiches in some of the tissue paper from the lost shawl's box and put them in the velvet drawstring bag that had held her shoes. After swallowing the last of the coffee in three big gulps, she stuffed her battered journal into the sack with the sandwiches, grabbed her guitar, and headed for the elevator.

She stopped briefly at the front desk to leave a note of her own, lest Roland come looking for her later in the afternoon.

Will be back before dark.

—D

Once that was complete, she took no notice of the people and heeded no conversations or comments as she walked straight through the lobby to the street. Working from memory of previous outings, she turned left, fully confident that she would find her way.

It was a strange bit of forest to be growing in the midst of the city, as nothing about it seemed to have a direct connection to God's creative hand. The grass was green—maybe too green?—spread out in a perfect, clipped carpet stretched between paved walking paths. There were palm trees and oak trees and budding shrubs throughout. Clearly, some had to have been transplanted from far off, but given the newness and vitality of the city, who could say which was at home and which was a guest in the California soil?

Men and women in simple working clothes had shared Dorothy Lynn's inspiration and sat on benches along the paths, taking wax-paper-wrapped food from buckets and boxes. The sight of them—such good, honest people—made her stomach pinch in guilt. She'd done nothing to earn the meal she carried.

Unless she wanted to count her actions last night, which she didn't.

The farther she walked toward the center of the park, the fainter the sounds of traffic from the surrounding streets. Soon she could hear the soft crunch of her own footsteps, and she longed to abandon the path, take off her shoes, and feel the soft grass between her toes. She kept her eyes open to see if anybody else would set such an example, but no one here seemed to carry the same compulsion. Instead, she forgot her feet and lifted her face to breathe deep, filling her lungs with air, soft in its canopy of green.

A few more steps, a few more breaths, and her body fell into line. The pain that had been concentrated in her head began to dissolve, breaking up like the sugar cube in her coffee, infusing her muscles and bones with sweet welcome at its release. Her stomach came alive with hunger, gurgling so loud she feared she might disturb the young couple spooning on a bench as she walked by. It was time to find her own spot to sit and take in not only this surrounding bit of beauty, but also the collection of underappreciated sandwiches.

As her path prepared to cross another, she saw a man in a white coat pushing a cart that advertised ice-cold lemonade for a nickel. Thankful that she'd thought to toss a few coins into her skirt pocket, she bought some, drank it down, and immediately bought another, this time vowing to keep it in its waxed cup to wash down the sandwiches. It was a precarious business, trying to keep her nickel's purchase from sloshing over the sides while gripping the guitar case with her other hand and with the drawstring bag looped over her wrist, but she continued walking until, to her delight, her path opened up to a large, paved square with a fountain at its center. A wide, open spot seemed to be waiting just for her, and she headed straight for it.

The sun shone warm upon her as she took a sip of the lemonade before opening the pack of sandwiches, which had held up well during their journey. One after another she stuffed the little triangles into her mouth, dissolving the last bite with the lemonade. She wiped her mouth with the back of her hand and unsuccessfully attempted to suppress a satisfying belch.

She pulled her battered journal out of the sack and began to flip through the pages. So many verses, poems, songs—some she hadn't thought about in months. Maybe years. Her familiar, messy handwriting filled some pages, while others were left with only a few sparse lines floating, unfinished. Bringing the notebook close to her face, she inhaled, catching the faintest whiff of her beloved woods surrounding Heron's Nest. If she held it close, she could almost imagine herself there now, the constant running of the fountain providing a more sophisticated substitution for the babbling creek that ran along the path between her clearing and home.

How many hours were in this book? How much time spent feeling truly in the presence of God? And, more recently, in the company of Brent, his head in her lap as she ran her fingers absently through his sun-warmed hair, reading to him from these pages.

The words blurred behind her sudden tears, and she pushed the memory aside.

She set the book beside her and lifted her guitar from its case, strumming with one hand while the other turned the pages of her songs. Many of the tunes were lost to her memory, as she hadn't known, or hadn't bothered, to note the key or chords. Only the last song, the one performed on Sister Aimee's stage, had been carefully recorded during one stretch of travel while she played, stopped, jotted, and sang for three solid, painstaking hours.

She strummed the familiar chords and, with the assurance that the sound of the fountain would absorb her voice, began to sing the song that so many thousands of people had welcomed into their worship.

Jesus is coming!
Are you ready
to meet your Savior in the sky?

She closed her eyes and settled into herself, seeing not the vast audiences or white-lit stage, but one simple girl, here. Her heart lurched at every question sprung from her own lyrics.

Are you proud of the way that you're living?
Is he welcome in the life you lead today?

Questions she hadn't considered last night as she donned *la rouge*, drank champagne, danced, and . . .

So much of it a blur, which might be a matter of God's mercy so as not to be tormented with shame.

To combat the half-formed memories, she strummed louder, sang stronger, replacing silly melodies and profane jokes with her own reminder.

No man knows the hour,
and no man knows the day.
But when he gathers up the righteous,
will you be swept away?

The sound of the fountain strengthened her, reminding her of Jesus, the Living Water, and the assurance that his grace cleansed her more than any bath ever could. Stray drops touched her face, blocking the way for any tears to descend, like God himself touching her with his forgiveness for her sin. For a while she heard nothing but the water and her guitar and her voice, until a sound, faint and unfamiliar, interrupted.

She opened her eyes to see the lemonade cup wobbling on its base. Leaning forward, she saw the reason for the disturbance in the form of a nickel and two shiny pennies sitting among the final drops of the drink. She had no way of knowing who was responsible for such a gift, as people seemed to be walking away from her in all directions. So, midlyric, she said, "Thank you! May God bless you!" and continued to sing.

When she finished the song, one or two people within earshot offered indulgent applause, and she touched the brim of her hat in acknowledgment before picking up the cup and digging the coins from the bottom.

"I know this is an empty gesture that has no meaning," she said aloud, softly, "but I can't keep this gift no matter how small."

She closed her eyes and offered up a prayer.

"Oh, Lord, restore my soul. Restore my family and take me home. Do not let this journey be in vain."

She dropped the coins into the fountain, dipped her hand in the water to wash off the stickiness, and dried it on her dress.

Another song came to her heart, and her fingers readily found the chord.

Have you been to Jesus for the cleansing pow'r?
Are you washed in the blood of the Lamb?

She sang with the confidence of such cleansing, keeping her eyes open to connect with those who passed by, asking them in earnest if they were assured of their salvation. Many looked away, but she would not be discouraged. Others stopped and listened. Still others sang along with her, clapping softly, sharing her spirit through the familiar song.

The lemonade cup was closed inside her guitar case, leaving no means or invitation for money. Soon the fountain in Pershing Square became a place of worship worthy of the temple being constructed a few blocks away. When one song ended, she began another, and she felt pure, worshipful joy, singing for her own pleasure and, she hoped, her Lord's, for as much as the crowd gathered, she sang to him.

The songs scribbled in her notebook grew more and more forgotten as she drew from those she'd learned sitting in the front pew of her father's church, legs dangling, waiting for him to preach. During the third verse of "Rock of Ages," a high-tenor harmony emerged from the crowd, and she imagined her mother and sister beside her, on one of the few occasions when Pa allowed them to sing as a trio in front of the congregation.

She played on, ignoring the wave of homesickness washing over her, stronger than the nausea that had plagued her this morning. Only the cramping in her hands and the growing dryness of her throat bore witness to the passing of time. But she would not stop, even though she felt blisters forming on the tips of her fingers, even though she felt the corners of her lips clinging to each other with every syllable.

Until she knew she could sing just one more. Pulled from the depths came her own song once again, only now, for the first time, she sang in weakness, struggling for every note and lyric. The gathering grew silent, naturally, as none of them there could have heard it before, unless they'd been there when she first picked up her guitar.

There was only her voice, cushioned by the crowd, the trees lifting it up and out of the city, and by the time she got to the end of it, she had nothing left. Her back ached from sitting on the concrete step; her arms burned. She was begging for release—from her sin, from her song, from the responsibility of making any more decisions in this life. She closed her eyes at the final note.

"Thank you, Jesus," she whispered, her gratitude lifted up on the cloud of soft applause.

From the midst of this, one specific rhythm pierced through. Odd how she could be so familiar with a person to actually recognize the sound of his hands clapping, but she felt no surprise when she looked up to see Roland emerging from the crowd. He walked right to her and gently took the guitar from her aching arms, placing it as lovingly in its case as she herself would. He took her face in his hands and kissed her forehead, her temples, and finally, gently, her lips.

"Sister Aimee's a fool." She knew his words didn't carry any farther than the two of them, and, truthfully, given how close they were to each other, some part of her wondered if he'd actually said them at all.

"You found me," she said, not sure if she felt relief or disappointment.

"Better than that." He held one hand out to help her to her feet. When she was standing, he took his hat off to salute the crowd, saying, "This, people, is Miss Dorothy Lynn Dunbar. We hope you've had a blessing today."

Shielding herself behind him, she arched her back, hoping to twist a more pleasant sensation into the base of her spine.

Still, she kept a pleasant smile until the last of the listeners had dispersed.

"That," he said, once they were somewhat alone, "is what I call magic. People were talking about you up and down Fifth Street. I followed your voice all the way here. You never sounded like that before. I tell ya, if we could just get that on a stage—"

"I don't want to be on a stage."

"—or better yet, a record." He snapped his fingers and began walking. "That's the ticket there. We might be bringing the world to Sister Aimee, but you? Lay that voice on a gramophone recording, and we'll send it all over the country."

She listened, mute, as he wove a plan in the air between them, spun from nothing but his desire and her voice. He gestured as if he'd never touched her, gazed past her as if he'd never laid eyes on her softest, most hidden parts. His rapid-fire words skimmed just past her—nothing like the sweet syllables whispered against her skin. Had he forgotten? It wouldn't be an impossible conclusion, because he seemed to have disregarded her presence, not noticing that she hadn't followed him. In fact, she didn't know if she would ever follow him again.

"I just want to go home," she said. "Did you hear me, Mr. Lundi? I want to go home. This was a mistake. All of it."

He turned and cocked his head, looking at her as if studying a not-quite-finished work of art.

"*Mr. Lundi?* Sweetheart, after all we've been through?" He took a few steps closer and lowered his voice. "After last night?"

One by one, the paving stones surrounding the fountain dissolved, leaving the ground she stood on perilously unstable. She crossed her arms in front of her, holding on to herself as there was nothing else to hold on to, while every memory of every sin she'd tried so hard to forget snaked through the crumbling space between them and worked its way up to her unwilling mind.

She must have looked ill, because his expression changed to one of concern as he walked toward her.

"Don't touch me," she warned, backing away, willing to throw herself in the water if that's what it would take to escape.

"Baby . . ."

"Don't call me that. I'm not your *baby*. You're not my *daddy*. Whatever any of that even means."

He stopped at a respectful, though reachable, distance. "Of course not."

"I trusted you."

"As well you should. Lucky for you I didn't let you out of my sight, or you might have been one sad, lost little girl this morning."

"You kissed me."

"I could make the same accusation."

She clenched her jaw as if to keep from ever repeating the mistake. "And you took me to bed."

"Where I left you," he said authoritatively, "comfortable and intact."

"Not soon enough."

"You're still eligible to be the virginal bride by all biblical standards. As far as I know, at least."

She slapped him, a satisfying, palm-stinging slap, like something right out of the movies. But in the movies, you'd never see the red shadow of a palm print on Rudy Valentino's face.

"Careful, baby," he said, once they both recovered from the shock of her action. "That's your guitar-playing hand."

She sat back down on the edge of the fountain and he followed suit, putting them side by side with her guitar between them.

"I'm sorry," he said finally, twirling his hat in his hands. "I should have known better than to give in to any of that kind of temptation. But I am a man, and you're a beautiful girl."

"I was drunk." It was the first time she'd ever said such a thing, and the concept sounded completely foreign on her tongue.

"We both were."

She wasn't sure if Roland meant to bring them to an equal plane of victimization or blame, but even if theirs was a shared sin, nothing would bring him to her level of shame. In the clear light of day, facing him with her veil of innocence reduced to nothing more than the thinnest, palest gauze, she wrapped her arms around herself, more protective than she'd been the night before. "I hate myself."

"Don't." He looked like he very much wanted to reach for her, but he didn't. "If you're going to hate anyone, hate me."

"I can't. You're all I've got here."

"Well, lucky me for that, I guess. But I need to talk to Bendemann about slipping the cheap stuff to the guests. If that was champagne, then so's this." He gestured with his thumb to the fountain water in an obvious attempt at lightening the mood. Despite it all, she felt a smile tugging at her lips.

"I think you're lonely," she said. "Otherwise why would you ever pay so much attention to me?"

"I happen to think you could be something great," he said, but his bent posture, the hat twirling listlessly in his hand—all worked against his swagger.

"I'm all I ever want to be, Roland. I was before I came here, before I even met you. I just didn't realize it. I don't want a stage, or an audience, or a record. I just . . . I want to go home. I need to go home, because I never want to have another night like last night."

"In that, at least, we are in total agreement. And you have my promise as a gentleman, if you'll take it. But I am happy to report it was a worthwhile sacrifice of time and dignity."

She looked sidelong at him only to find him grinning at her. "What's that supposed to mean?"

"You know how I told you I'd found something better? Well, I've been on the phone all morning, and I believe I've found your brother."

❧ CHAPTER SEVENTEEN ❧

HE EXPLAINED THE CHAIN of events on their walk back to the Alexandria. It *had* been the photograph, published prominently on the society page of that morning's edition of the *Examiner* with the caption "Songbird Dorothy Lynn Dunbar cozies up to H. C. Bendemann in hopes of finding her long-lost brother."

Dorothy Lynn might have objected to the inaccuracy of the term "cozies up," but that exact phrase had spurred Mrs. Bendemann to action. Motivated by nothing less than to prove her husband's fidelity, phone calls were made to the heads of every major studio, who in turn called their heads of accounting, and by noon Roland had a phone call informing him that one Donald Dunbar appeared on the payroll for Silverlight Studios.

"Just like that?" Dorothy Lynn said. They'd walked out of the park and were once again surrounded by concrete buildings as far and as high as the eye could see—and this was just one tiny block.

"Just like that," he said. "This isn't the Wild West anymore. Everybody's got to be somewhere."

He walked her straight to her room, and the pain in her head resurfaced with half images of the night before. Stumbling steps, strong arms, slurred words in half-sung melodies. How she'd kissed him, full on his mouth, drawing him across the threshold when he opened the door.

And here they were again.

"Relax, sweetheart," he said, taking the key from her hand. "If making a little tipsy love turns out to be the stupidest thing you've ever done, you'll have live a charmed life."

"It's humiliating. And wrong. I don't love you. Not like I love Brent. Not that Brent and I have ever . . ." A new wave of nausea threatened.

"Look at it this way," Roland said, swinging her door open wide before taking one giant step away. "You've simply confirmed my assumption that I'm irresistible, which is far more comforting than the fear that I was merely delusional."

She risked a smile, and he rewarded her with a kiss to her burning cheek.

"I had a telephone sent up to your room," he said. "In case you want to call anyone."

"Thank you." She thought about the usual crowd gathered at Jessup's for the Sunday afternoon calls. They must be cleared out by this hour, and she was suddenly seized with a longing for her mother's voice.

"And an early supper? Say, six? I thought we'd try—"

"If you don't mind, I think I'd rather be on my own tonight. There's so much to think about."

"Of course." She managed to catch a hint of disappointment before he donned a cool mask of understanding. "Well, you have the telephone. Ask the operator to connect you to the kitchen whenever you're hungry and have something sent up."

"But I'll see you tomorrow?"

He tipped his hat in confirmation. "I have a few things to arrange before we get to this surprise reunion."

"Like what?"

"Like surprises."

She called out, "What surprises?" but he was already halfway down the hall and acknowledged her question only with a quick skip to his step. Just like that, he slipped from man to boy again, like some ageless being from a fairy tale.

Daddy. The flappers had it right.

Inside her room, a narrow table had been set up next to the bureau. On it sat a candlestick telephone, a pad of hotel stationery, and three sharpened pencils. She dropped her guitar case on the bed along with her hat and the drawstring bag. The moment she kicked off her shoes, she regretted not dangling her feet in the fountain's water or taking a few bare steps in the clipped green grass. Then again, it might be fitting that the next time she'd feel the earth beneath her feet would be at home. The city was a place for shoes.

She went to the bathroom and splashed cold water on her face to chase away the lingering blush brought on by memories of the night before, knowing full well her mother—miles away though she may be—would hear the shame in her voice. Then to the telephone for the increasingly familiar routine: outside operator, long distance, Missouri, Heron's Nest, number 005. The clock at the bedside gave the time as a little after two, so it would be after four at home—meaning the town would be deserted, with people still dozing after their Sunday naps, not yet roused again to make their way to church for the evening service.

Please be there, she thought, in both prayer and silent plea. And then, an answer.

"Hello." Jessup never answered the phone with a questioning tone, but with confidence that a task had been completed.

"Jessup? It's Dorothy Lynn Dunbar."

"Is it? Well, I must say it's about time."

"Excuse me?"

"Just that there's someone been spendin' most of this afternoon hopin' for one of these phones to ring with your voice on the other end of the line."

"Really?" *Brent?*

She allowed herself just a moment to hope he'd had a change of heart. If he'd only taken her call last night, then nothing . . . She glanced over at the bed, swallowed bile, and looked away. He'd forgive her; he'd have to. If he could sacrifice his pride to wait for her voice, then surely she could sacrifice her own to confess.

". . . and it's been quite an honor to spend this time with her, waiting."

Dorothy Lynn slumped in her chair. *Her.*

"Oh, it's my mother."

"Indeed it is. Didn't know if you'd be callin' or not."

Disappointment mingled with surprising relief. "I wasn't so sure myself until a few minutes ago. Can you put her on, please?"

Dorothy Lynn hadn't heard Ma's voice since she left Heron's Nest to visit Darlene, except for the imagined chastisement of just about every choice she'd made since embarking on that fateful trip. She stretched a single breath over the intervening seconds, placing the mouthpiece to her forehead as she exhaled, ridding herself of everything too dangerous to say. The earpiece, however, she kept in place, which proved an unfortunate decision as the brief, silent interlude was broken by her name, shouted, from a miraculous two thousand miles away.

"Honey-cub!"

"Hello, Ma."

"Are you there?"

"I'm here, Ma. And you don't need to shout."

"You can hear me? I hear you just fine!"

"Yes, Ma. We can hear each other. Isn't that wonderful?"

"Jessup says you're in California. Is that right?"

"Yes, Los Angeles. And, Ma—I have wonderful news."

"Your sister had the baby! A little girl!"

"I know—" she started before thinking that her mother might have been delighted at the opportunity to break the news. "She must be so excited to have a girl at last. What did they name her?"

"Margaret!"

"Two boys and a girl. The opposite of us."

"What's that?"

"Nothing, Ma. Never mind. I have good news too. Donny's here."

She heard her mother gasp and could picture the work-worn hand pressing up against her mouth. She'd never been a woman to express any extreme emotion, be it joy or sorrow; rather, she'd "hold her words" until the right ones came. So with the crackling on the line to hold them together, Dorothy Lynn waited.

"Is he—" Ma started, then lowered her voice. "Is he there with you now?"

"No," Dorothy Lynn said, immediately wishing she hadn't made this call. Geography aside, she wasn't any closer to Donny today than she'd been before she left home.

"Oh," Ma said, her disappointment making a sad, slow journey across the country.

Dorothy Lynn stumbled over her words, trying to make

amends. "I just today found out where he works, and we're planning to visit him tomorrow. I wanted to call you and tell you, and see if you had a message for me to give to him."

"'We'?"

How to explain Roland Lundi? "He's an older gentleman, Ma. Here at the hotel where I'm staying." She walked through the story like tiptoeing through thistles. "I told him everything I knew, and, well, he's been a tremendous help."

"I'm sure he has," Ma said, her suspicions unmistakable.

"He's an older man." True enough, but Dorothy Lynn had no desire to defend him. "What matters is I'll be seeing Donny tomorrow, and I hope he'll be coming home with me for the wedding."

"God willing." The edge around Ma's prayer seemed to encompass more than her wayward brother, and Dorothy Lynn gripped the phone tighter.

"There's going to be a wedding, Ma."

"Well, I hope so. Lord knows you need someone to keep you in line."

A dozen retorts rested on the edge of her tongue, but Dorothy Lynn held them inside, lest her mother learn just how far from the line she'd strayed. Instead, she said no man short of Pa would be able to do that, but Brent was about the best they could hope for.

"How is he, by the way?" she asked, hoping she sounded more confident than she felt.

"He preached this mornin', powerful sermon, but I can tell his heart's hurtin'. It's him you should be talkin' to, not me."

"He wants to see me face-to-face."

"And when's that gonna be?"

"Soon, Ma. I promise."

"It's two weeks away, honey-cub."

"I'll be there."

The vow settled between them. Vague as it was, it brought new, hopeful vigor to Ma's voice. "I got a package from your sister the other day. Great big box."

"What was it?" Dorothy Lynn tried to match her mother's enthusiasm.

"Why, your dress, of course."

For a single, honest second, Dorothy Lynn wondered, *What dress?* before she realized—her wedding dress. And then she couldn't speak at all.

"It's beautiful," Ma said, rushing to the rescue with conversation. "So modern, not like anythin' I've ever seen before."

Dorothy Lynn's eyes came to rest on the red silk dress hanging from a hook on the closet door. She'd left it in a pile on the floor this morning. The housekeeper had taken pity and shown it more respect.

"But I don't think your pa would approve."

Illogically, Dorothy Lynn repositioned herself, blocking the view of the dress from the phone.

"It's too modern," Ma continued. "He would've wanted you to wear my dress. Maybe that's what we shoulda done."

"I still can, if you'd rather."

"I'd be fine if you wore a flour sack. I just hope there'll be a weddin'."

"Ma—please. Aren't you excited about seeing Donny?"

"Haven't seen him yet. And I worry you've set yourself on a fool's errand."

"How can you say that? He's your son—my brother! I'm just trying to bring our family together."

"By tearin' your new family apart." Suddenly, the plush hotel room became the kitchen of Dorothy Lynn's childhood. She could almost smell the aroma of fresh biscuits and bacon as her mother toiled at the stove, chastising over her shoulder. "Stuff and nonsense, this fetchin' your brother. You've been lookin' for an excuse to get yourself away ever since that young man asked you to marry him. First runnin' off to St. Louis, then this mess I don't even know what to call."

"Ma—"

"You just better hope that Brent's the forgivin' sort, and I'm prayin' that you're gettin' this wanderlust knocked out of your system."

"I'll be home by the end of the week," Dorothy Lynn said, affixing a deadline without a clue as to its feasibility. Still, she followed with a promise.

"Don't you promise nothin'. Your brother was all for promises. Sayin' he'd be home by Christmas, then my birthday, then next summer. And never showed."

"He didn't have anything to come home to," Dorothy Lynn said, instantly regretting having done so. She might as well have slapped her mother in the face.

"I'm just sayin'," Ma said, clearly hurt, "that I don't want to hear promises. I don't want to hang my heart on a day, then be disappointed when it blows by."

"Then as soon as I can, Ma. As soon as I can fix it with Donny, we'll be home."

"Well, then. That'll be fine."

"One more thing? The sermon this morning? Since I wasn't there . . . what was the text?"

"Well, now, honey-cub, you haven't been here in a while."

"Please, it'll make me feel like home."

She could hear Ma's sigh from two thousand miles away.

"He's been talkin' on the vanity of vanities. Would do you well to read it."

Ecclesiastes. Her eyes searched out the Gideon Bible on the other side of the room. "I will."

"Today it was the rivers all runnin' into the ocean, and the ocean never fillin' up. All that runnin'. Useless. He was talkin' about you, honey-cub, wearin' his heart right there on the pulpit. There was weepin' in the pews."

She could picture him, standing before the church family who—no matter their flaws—made up the only family he could claim. Except, of course, for the Dunbars. And of them, only her mother remained.

"Will you tell him? That I called? Or do you think . . . Ma, do you think he'll still want me?"

Another bout of silence. "The announcement's still hangin' in the entry. But the Lord knows people are talkin'."

"I can't imagine they have anything useful to say."

"They have enough, girl. You get yourself home."

❧ CHAPTER EIGHTEEN ❦

IN A NOTE delivered the night before by a bellboy, Roland had written *early* as his only detail as to when they would be leaving, so she was grateful to have woken so fully rested long before the jangling alarm clock was due to rouse her. She splashed cold water on her face to wash away the memory of Ma's foreboding tone and forced a smile onto the smooth, pink reflection.

"We get to see Donny today."

The words brought out the dryness of her mouth, and she quickly drank two full glasses of water while standing at the sink. Refreshed without and within, she took another look in the mirror. "You were a child the last time he saw you. Just fourteen years old."

In that moment, she knew she couldn't face Donny with eyes lined with kohl and cheeks covered with rouge. Instead, she plaited her hair into one long braid, which she wound around her head in the style she'd worn before he went away to war. Folded neatly at the bottom of her trunk was the dress she'd worn when she left Heron's Nest. The soft cotton was faded, muting the calico print into nothing more than smudges of color.

She held it close, inhaling the familiar scent, suddenly longing for its comfort. This was a dress that had leaned up against trees as she sat on the forest floor, scribbling messy songs in her notebook. It had been washed in the tub on her own front porch. Brent had touched her in this dress—his broad, warm hand splayed against her back as he held her. What would he have thought of the red dress, where he could have put his hand in the same place and touched her skin?

"God, forgive me," she said aloud. Each thought of that night seemed to uncover a new sin.

She put the dress on, along with dark stockings and her familiar, sturdy shoes, thinking Donny would probably recognize her bare feet long before her face.

Now, not knowing exactly what Roland's definition of *early* meant, she settled in to wait.

❧❦❧

"I thought you'd be ready," Roland said thirty minutes later, holding himself back from his customary rush across her threshold.

"I am ready."

His eyes, an even richer brown in complementing his houndstooth jacket, traveled every inch of her, and he made no attempt to hide his disappointment in the journey. "What is that?"

"This is my dress. From home."

"You look like you should be in one of those cowboy movies. Like your landlord is going to defile you for the rent money or tie you to the railroad tracks."

"Stop it." She ran her hands along the front of the dress, wishing she'd at least had an opportunity to press it. "I want Donny to recognize me. I thought if I wore something familiar—"

"He'd think someone conked him on the head and he woke up back on the farm?"

"I'm not a flapper, Roland."

284

"Sweetheart, in that dress you're hardly even a woman. Aw, there you go. . . ."

Every moment she'd lived from the first taste of champagne to this very one erupted, and tears flowed once again—this time into the comforting, coarse material of Roland's lapel. "Ma said this was a fool's errand. That I was just trying to run—run away like Donny—and that Brent might not even want to m-marry me because everybody back home is talking. And I—I don't even know who I am anymore."

This last word came out more like a wail, but if she'd been seeking any sympathy from Roland, she found it wanting as he abruptly pushed her away, back to her own side of the threshold.

"Wrong. You know exactly who you are, and you're more than some backwoods preacher's daughter. You've got talent and potential and—when you work at it—style. You're just too terrified to enjoy it. And now you think that if you put on some dishrag of a dress and do your hair up like some milkmaid you can snuff out all those inconvenient desires."

"I don't have any desires except to go home."

"I believe you, sweetheart. And who knows? Maybe it's the best thing. But not like this. Not in the same dress you wore when you left."

"You're right," she said, feeling every fiber of the dress recoil from the task of covering her sin. "I'm not the same girl."

"No, you're not. You've sung in front of twenty thousand people. Plus dozens in the park. You were part of something that changed lives, a voice for Jesus in a way Sister Aimee could never be. This—" he captured her in a single, dismissive gesture— "throws all of that away."

"No." She stormed to the wardrobe, grabbed the red dress, and threw it in a heap at his feet. "*This* threw it all away."

Roland bent down and picked it up, turning the dress into nothing more than a silk scrap in his hand. "This is a dress. It isn't you, and I was hoping you'd forgiven me for . . . well, for everything."

"I have." She wanted to reach out for him but thought better. "Not that there's anything for me to forgive. I can't very well ask God to forgive me if I'm placing my sin on you."

"So instead you're punishing yourself. You can't erase what happened, so you're trying to bury the evidence."

"I told you I just wanted Donny to recognize me."

"He's not the same kid that ran away from the forest, and neither are you. You want to start your reunion with a lie?"

"It's not a lie."

"Isn't it?" He took a cigarette from his breast pocket, held it—unlit—between his first two fingers, and pointed at her with it. "How do you feel in that getup?"

"Comfortable," she said too quickly for it to be anything other than defensive. "Familiar."

His continued scrutiny, however, even behind the eventual cloud of smoke, brought her to truth. Even apart from the fact that the sleeves landed just above her wrists, she knew she'd outgrown the dress. The shoes felt heavy, the stockings itchy in their woolliness.

"You see?" Roland said, without the lash of condescension. "Now, put on something nice, fix your hair, and meet me at the car in thirty minutes. And bring the guitar."

"My guitar?" Her head reeled at how quickly he could change his tack between puffs on a cigarette.

He tossed the red dress inside, where it landed on the corner of the foot of the bed. "I'm hoping to wrangle one more favor out of you before you disappear."

❧❀❧

She found him waiting in the car with a white paper bag and a large round box. The bag held an array of sugar-dusted dough-nuts—still warm—from the bakery around the corner. The box, a stylish crushed-velvet hat—a perfect complement to the peach-colored chiffon blouse and modest brown skirt she'd opted to wear.

"Wonderful!" she said, settling into her seat. "How did you know?"

"That you'd be hungry?"

"About the hat." She pulled it down on her head before div-ing eagerly into the bag.

"I'm always a step ahead of you, baby. Thought you'd know that by this time."

The city had a crisp, clean feel this morning—like it had been scrubbed with the salt on the breeze. They drove in silence, hers fueled by nerves and pastry; his nothing more than his usual unflappable demeanor. Finally, as he brought the car to a stop at a square brick building on a street with only two other structures in view, she asked, "Where are we?"

He was already out of the car, lifting her guitar from the backseat. "I told you I had one more favor to ask."

"And yet you haven't asked me anything." She intended to stay in her seat, but he was opening the short iron gate at the front of the property, ready to disappear with her single prized possession. Frustrated, she followed.

"Is this the studio? Is this where Donny works?"

"Yes. And no."

"What does that mean?"

"Yes, it's a studio. And no, it isn't your brother's."

They'd arrived at a tall, arched door with a sign instructing all who stood there not to knock or ring the bell if the light above it was on. Their heads moved in unison to look at the red bulb, and upon finding it dark, Roland bypassed any knocking or ringing entirely, grabbed the handle, and walked inside, saying, "You'll see."

They were in a small room, bare save for a few photographs and wooden benches along three of the walls, and a desk where a telephone stood in a sea of scattered papers.

"It's not much," he said with a modest swoop of his arms, "but it's ours for the next couple of hours."

"For what, exactly?"

"To make a record, like we talked about."

She folded her arms and risked leaning against the wall, despite its dubious film. "When did we talk about this?"

"Okay, I've talked about it. Sometimes with you, sometimes not. But after looking around, I wish we could do this in Chicago. With all that jazz, they've got great studios in that town."

"Roland, I don't want to make a record."

"Why not?"

She wasn't expecting that question, and she didn't have an answer. "Why should I?"

"Leave me something, Dorothy." He said it like she owed him, like she bore some responsibility for bringing him to this sad, dingy place. But if she allowed herself to look beyond his carefully crafted edges, she saw something more than an obligation. Like he was asking for a memento of what they'd built together.

"What would you do with it?"

"You mean besides listen to it every night, dreaming of what you could have been?"

She made a playful grab for her guitar, but he snatched it away, holding the case at the neck like a hostage.

"I don't want to make a record, Mr. Lundi." She aimed for more insistence.

"Listen. Sister Aimee's going into radio. Her own license. Sure, mostly to broadcast her own sermons, but who's to say? People loved your song."

"So get someone else to sing it."

"Nobody sings it like you, sweetheart. Just come take a look." He opened a door next to a large curtain-covered window and, after a quick peek inside, motioned for Dorothy Lynn to follow.

"Is anyone else here?" she called before budging. Not that she was worried about being alone with Roland, but it seemed like there ought to be somebody in charge.

"Not yet." His voice sounded both distant and muffled. "I thought you might need some convincing, so I told Freddy to give us a few minutes. Come in here."

The longer she waited, the less choice she seemed to have, and she took a few tentative steps that quickened at his encouragement.

The dark, colorless room they'd first entered had done nothing to prepare her for what was on the other side. Her steps slowed again out of sheer awe. Here the ceiling was twice as high as in the outer office, and everything was painted a perfect, pristine white. Half of the floor was a series of three wide steps, the top one filled with neatly stacked chairs. Music stands were scattered about, and a massive piano—not as beautiful as the one in the Alexandria lobby, but somehow more authoritative—seemed to be holding court over all.

"Don't let any of this intimidate you." At some point, as she'd turned in a slow circle, taking everything in, Roland had come up behind her, and his whisper seemed little more than spoken breath in this big room. Her fingers were folded around the handle of her guitar case as he relinquished it to her, saying, "This is all you need."

He procured a high-backed stool and brought it to a place where a long, horn-shaped object protruded from an ominous-looking black curtain.

"Like you've always done, Dorothy. You just sit down, close your eyes, and sing. Right in here. The magic happens in the office back there."

"I sing for Jesus, whether I'm alone or in front of people who want to sing with me. I can't sing into a tube."

"You write your songs down, don't you? In that ratty little notebook."

"Yes." In fact, it was nestled in with the guitar at that very moment.

"This is nothing more than another way to write them down. To capture the words and the music all at once."

"I know what a record *is*. But I'd feel silly singing here, like this."

"I remember a time when you couldn't imagine yourself singing in front of an audience. And you managed to overcome that all right."

She smiled, warm with the memory of the lights and the voices raised in song alongside hers. "I felt the Lord with me then." The Lord, and Roland waiting in the wings.

"And he can't be with you here?"

At that moment the curtain covering the window on the office side slid open, startling both of them with the appearance of a lean, tired-looking man with a cigar the width of a lumberjack's thumb wedged into the corner of his mouth.

"Ah," Dorothy Lynn said. "Now *that's* inspiring."

"That's Freddy," Roland said. "Wait right here."

Left alone, she wandered over to the piano and, feeling bold, took a seat on the well-worn wooden bench. Sheets of music stood on the upraised rack. She ran her fingers across the pages. Mozart, then something called "Oh, How He Done Me Wrong," then something else that was nothing more than a few notes scribbled on the staffs in pencil, titled "Blooms in the Spring." More music graced the stand beside her, large sheets with covers featuring droopy women or couples engaged in desperate embrace. She browsed through lyrics, finding some that wrapped her up in longing for home and all it offered—her mother, soft forest floors, Brent's strong embrace and all that it promised. Others were silly or tragic, but all of them once had been a tune in somebody's head, notes scribbled down. They'd all been brought here and committed to a recording. They could last forever, while hers would disappear.

Looking through the window in the wall, she saw the men engaged in conversation. Good-natured, it seemed, with a few glances thrown her way. Roland's eyes wrapped her in affection, while Freddy seemed unimpressed. Finally, Roland took his wallet from his pocket and extracted a few bills, which Freddy pocketed without counting. Apparently, she'd been bought.

Roland walked back in, rubbing his hands together. "What do you think, sweetheart?"

She tapped her finger on the piano key, making a tiny, unintentional sound. "Looks like you've already decided."

"I need to pay for the time, no matter what we do. If you don't want to record your songs, maybe I'll just recite 'Mary Had a Little Lamb' for an hour. Send it to my kids."

"I'm sure they miss your voice."

He held up a warning finger. "I don't talk about them, remember?"

"You brought them up."

"I forget sometimes." He blinked, twice. "Now, what do you say?"

She twisted on the bench. "I owe you so much, Roland."

He took her hands in his and lifted her to her feet. "You don't owe me anything."

"Really? All the clothes? And the hotel? And finding Donny?"

"And to think. All for a song."

He still held her hands, and her gaze, and her brother, and though his eyes and smile were warm, she had the sense that none would be released without ransom.

"What do I have to do?" She could tell he was pleased, though he offered only the slightest squeeze of her hands to show it.

"Just what I told you." He released her to reposition the stool, scooting it here and there according to Freddy's silent direction from the other side of the window. "Sit here—" he patted the seat—"take up your guitar, and sing for me."

The next sound was the click of the latches on her guitar case. She took the instrument out and put the new hat in its place. Because the seat was higher than she anticipated, Roland offered his shoulder to steady her ascent, leaving her feeling a bit marooned when he stepped away.

"No hurry," he said. "One hour, one song. Take your time."

Freddy seemed engaged in whatever role he played in this process, and with minimal jostling, Roland turned the chair to take him out of her line of sight.

New, unfamiliar fears gathered within her. Perhaps not entirely unfamiliar. She'd felt the same way when she sang for Roland in the Strawn Brothers Music Store. And when she sang for Sister Aimee in her dressing room. And when she first faced an audience in that darkness beyond the light. Every time, at every turn, there was Roland. The last voice she heard before her own, the first face she saw upon opening her eyes. Why, then, should this be any different?

She hummed a few bars of the song she'd sung hundreds of times since that first afternoon when it was nothing more than a rattling nuisance, then brought her guitar in tune. "How does that sound?" She trusted his ear more than her own.

For an answer, Roland looked past her to Freddy and nodded.

She stared into the mouth of the horn, thinking it looked somewhat like a big telephone. She could imagine she was singing to Brent, though he'd refused to talk to her, or to her mother, despite how strongly she would disapprove of the whole process.

But when she thought about who she was at this moment, what she'd become—and what Christ had forgiven—she knew what she'd said to Roland moments before was true. She'd sing for Jesus, recording on wax the message he'd given her the way so many men had recorded such in books and paper and scrolls. "When do I start?"

Another silent consultation through the window, and then a simple, short nod of Roland's head.

She closed her eyes as her fingers found the opening chords, filling the biggest silence she'd ever known. The room was big enough to be a forest and a stage all at once.

Jesus is coming!
Are you ready
to meet your Savior in the sky?

As she sang, the lyrics grew in meaning. She *was* ready. She'd seen what the world had to offer, had a taste of sin and redemption. There was nothing here that she couldn't leave behind.

Brent and her mother, even. She'd left them both once before, after all, and they'd be joining her. Purified, cleansed, and only nineteen, she could list accomplishments she'd never known to dream about in her childhood. Were Jesus to take her this very minute, she could stand before him unashamed.

Tears stung the back of her throat, but she'd never finish the song if she gave in, so she closed her mouth and strummed until she knew she had control, then launched into the next verse.

When she opened her eyes at the final note, she found Roland standing closer than she imagined, with one finger to his lips and his other hand poised in a gesture meant to hold her still and silent. His eyes darted between hers and over her shoulder to Freddy, who must have been satisfied.

"Sweetheart," Roland said, breaking the silence, "that was perfect."

"I'm never going to sing it again." The revelation came to her as she spoke it.

"Nonsense. You have a church back home waiting for you."

She shook her head. "It's yours. Do what you want with it."

Dorothy Lynn held her guitar as Roland helped her down from the seat. "We have time," he said. "You don't want to record any others?"

"You said I could have it all for a song." She traded the guitar for the hat, settling one inside the velvet lining and tugging the other down to her ears. "I gave you a song. Fair?"

"Fair."

❧ CHAPTER NINETEEN ❧

THE GATES WERE MASSIVE works of scrolled iron with the words *Silverlight Studios* fashioned across the top.

"You seem nervous," Dorothy Lynn said as Roland began to slow the car.

"Not going to fool you, kid. I'm a little out of my element here."

"Ma always says the only person you can ever really fool is yourself."

"I need to meet this ma of yours someday."

Dorothy Lynn laughed, envisioning Roland Lundi with his linen suits, pinkie ring, and pre-rolled cigarettes strolling the twisted paths of Heron's Nest. "I don't think you'd quite fit in."

He clutched at his chest as if she'd shot an arrow through his heart, and she laughed some more.

A narrow shack stood at the gate's entrance, and as they approached, a man in a blue broadcloth uniform stepped out of it, signaling for them to stop. "Business here?" he said, placing two meaty hands on top of the car door.

"Yes." All traces of insecurity erased, Roland reached into his breast pocket and took out a sheet of paper. From her seat, she could see it was high quality, and both the watermark and the heading at the top looked quite official and impressive. What was actually typed in its center, however, was lost, though the message was as short as the signature.

The guard knit his brows and moved his lips in silent reading before he looked at Roland with a new respect. "Lot seven, sir. You're going to go through these gates and take a left. Three studios down on the right."

"Thank you, Sarge." Roland tipped his hat before taking back the letter.

Neither spoke before they'd driven through the gates, at which point Dorothy Lynn asked just what the paper said.

"Long story there," Roland said, taking the first left turn. "But when you get back home and people ask if you got to meet Rudy Valentino while you were in Hollywood, you tell them no, but you did get a chance to take a drive with his far more attractive cousin."

She gave his arm a playful slap. "You didn't."

He laughed. "The letter simply says that I am escorting the singer Dorothy Lynn Dunbar to film stage seven at H. C. Bendemann's request."

"Well, that's closer to the truth, anyway. Although I'm hardly famous."

"No, but you are a singer, and most of the people in this town aren't half as famous as they claim to be."

The property was a maze of plain square buildings, each with a number displayed in bold black paint. If the buildings themselves were plain, however, the people walking in and out of them were not. Dorothy Lynn tried not to gawk, for fear of alerting everyone around that she and Roland were impostors, but she could not take her eyes away from the array of costumed men and women

roaming around. Some, naturally, were dressed in everyday cloth-
ing, and others in formal attire that put to shame the finest she'd
seen at the Alexandria Hotel. But then, ambling alongside a man
in a tuxedo was another dressed as a Roman centurion. Women,
too, were in ball gowns and furs or long calico dresses and sun-
bonnets. At one point Roland let out a low, slow whistle and said,
"What would Ma say about that?" calling her attention to a group
of six young women dressed in what appeared to be nothing but
clear balloons held together by some miracle of stitchery.

He brought the car to a roped-off area where automobiles
were parked in short, neat rows.

"This looks nothing like the postcard," Dorothy Lynn said,
recalling it with a niggling fear that one of the links in Roland's
chain of information had been deceptive.

"Nothing here looks like what it is."

Dorothy Lynn found herself shaking long after the car's
engine went still. For the first time Roland didn't seem to have a
plan. Always before, he'd be telling her to get in, get out, follow
him, stay there, wait, hurry. Now she sat beside him, quiet, until
the knotting of nerves worked its way loose enough for her to
ask, "What do I do?"

"I'll go in with you, if you like. Make the introduction—well,
not an *introduction* exactly. But you know, smooth things over."

She made no attempt to hide her relief. "I'd like that."

He came around to open her door and handed her out, where
she straightened her hat and smoothed her skirt, silently grateful that he'd forced her to change out of her old, shapeless dress.
"Should I take my guitar?"

"Why would you?"

She hesitated, looking at the case lying in the backseat. "It's
his."

"You'll see him again."

While Dorothy Lynn had only seen a few films in her lifetime, she always imagined the making of them to be glamorous—silks and temples and gold brocade. Instead, she saw shoddy buildings, some nothing more than a facade supported by beams along the back side, and then the enormous box they were about to enter. The door was massive, more like a barn than anything else, and the unknown behind it loomed, suddenly terrifying. She grabbed Roland's sleeve. "I can't."

"Can't what, sweetheart?"

"I can't go in there. What if this is all a lie, or a joke? Or what if Donny got wind that I was coming and didn't show up? What if he's stayed away all these years because of some terrible secret, or because he was horribly wounded in the war? What if he's burned, or missing a leg, or—"

Roland took her by the shoulders and gave her enough of a shake to knock the hat nearly over her eyes. "What if any of it? Or all of it? What is staying out here going to change?"

"Nothing, I suppose."

"How about a compromise? You stay here, and I'll go get him. Bring him right out to you."

"But how will you even know who he is?"

He spread his arms wide. "Baby, when have I ever let you down?"

She granted him that point with a smile.

"You don't talk to anybody, understand?"

"Understand."

"And I'll go get what you came here for."

He disappeared behind the door with the air of somebody who deserved such an entrance, and Dorothy Lynn leaned up against the wall beside it. A man in a Civil War uniform led a team of horses, followed by a group of women in flowing white robes.

Imagine working in such a place, seeing such things every day. Her mind stirred with the strangeness of it all, unable to form any single coherent opinion. What series of paths led Donny here? In a way, she supposed, it wasn't much different from Heron's Nest—goodness knew there were more than a few eccentrics living back home, but they all mostly looked the same on the outside. But this? How strange to see Napoleon Bonaparte from her history textbook walking alongside a man in some sort of velvet cape, both of them smoking cigarettes and arguing about President Harding's return to normalcy.

"Dorothy?" Roland's voice pulled her immediately out of her reverie. She twisted her head to find it—to finally find him. *Donny.*

Not so very changed from the day he left for war. His hair on the sides was shorn as it had been then, but that on top had been allowed to grow long, and it hung over his forehead—curlier than she'd ever known it to be. The jaw was stronger and shaded with a day's beard, but the eyes were the same dark-rimmed gray. Same as her own.

He said nothing, simply stared at her with his mouth open slightly—just enough to confirm his identity with the one jagged bottom tooth he'd chipped when he'd tried to entertain her by impersonating a squirrel with an acorn.

"Donny." So long since she'd seen him, so long since the name had been anything more than a part of wistful conversation. Here he was, in the flesh, and without giving a thought to waiting for an invitation, she threw her arms around him.

When she'd last hugged him before he boarded the bus, her arms—scrawny as she was—wrapped clean around. But he'd grown broader over the years, his chest and shoulders expanded nearly twofold, though his waist was nearly as trim.

"Dottie." His voice was deeper too, bringing with it the intervening years during which he'd grown from the older brother of her memories to the man of her mythology. It was a hero's voice, an adventurer's voice, yet every moment of their childhood rang clear in his utterance of her name.

She held him tighter, for fear he'd turn and walk away the minute she let go, as he made no move to return her embrace. Theirs might be a bond of blood, but they seemed joined only by her relentless grip.

"How did you find me?" It was the same question he'd ask when they were children playing hide-'n'-hunt in the woods around their home. Then, as now, Darlene had been the key, scouting him out and sending Dorothy Lynn in to make the kill.

She stepped away, feeling self-conscious and shy and silly. "You sent that postcard to Darlene, and I . . . God gave me a chance to come find you."

"This is where I bow out," Roland said, though his eyes were questioning, asking Dorothy Lynn's permission.

"Thank you, Mr. Lundi," she said, not knowing if her gratitude was either warranted or sufficient.

"You two catch up. Take as long as you need. I'll meet you at the car."

He kissed her cheek, and she almost ran after him. Instead, she took a deep breath and faced the fear she hadn't thought possible. "Are you not happy at all to see me, Donny?"

He scratched at his beard. "No one's called me Donny in years. I go by Don. And I guess I'm just in shock. How've you been?"

"Fine," she said, as if chatting with a church friend on a

Sunday afternoon. "But I have so much to tell you. Is there some-place where we can go and talk?"

"I'm working, Dottie." He'd buried his hands in his pockets, so he used his shoulders to gesture toward the door behind him. That's when she noticed that every inch of him seemed jittery.

"Later, then. Tonight? We can have dinner at the hotel, or Roland—Mr. Lundi—would take me just about anywhere to meet you."

"Come inside," he said, as if whisking her away secretively. "I get a dinner break at noon. We can go to the canteen together and talk there."

"That sounds fun." The words came out too quickly to sound convincing, but she hoped her bright smile would fill the deficit.

Donny—Don—led her into an echoing, cavernous space with a comforting smell of lumber and dust. Dozens of people milled around, each seemingly with his own purpose. Enormous lights hung from beams crisscrossing high on the wall. At the front, a complete, perfect miniature house was in midconstruction. Not a house, exactly, but a series of rooms, as if the fourth wall of a family home had been carefully shorn away, exposing the family's secrets. It was suspended at least four feet off the ground, and after a deafening metallic squeal that brought Dorothy Lynn's hands to her ears, the entire structure began to tilt to one side.

"Fella's making a movie about a boy who dreams a giant picks up his house and carries it away," Don explained once the sound mercifully stopped. "So the house has to move. When we put the furniture in, it'll scoot around—pictures falling, kids rolling out of bed . . ."

"And you built this?"

"Not the machine, but I studied how the guy did it. I worked on the house. Whole layout was my idea."

She bubbled with pride. "What's the name of the picture?"

"Don't know yet. The kid's the real star, I guess. I don't keep up much with all of that stuff. I just build what they tell me."

Here, talking about his work, he almost seemed relaxed, and she wished she'd first met him in the shadow of his labor. He even took her elbow in a tentative grip, undoubtedly to steer her to a place where she'd be out of the way. Before he could, though, a group of men dressed just like him in plain working clothes arrived, one of them holding a copy of the *Examiner*.

"Hey, Dunbar," the tallest of the three said, "I see she found you."

Don looked at her, then them, then her again, confused until he was shown the folded paper. She watched the expression on his face change, and when he looked at her again, it was with unabashed embarrassment and accusation.

"I can explain." She reached for the paper, but any explanation that might have taken place was swallowed up by the sound of the house once again being lifted and tilted, accompanied by the rousing cheer of all who watched.

"I'm taking my break," Don shouted, and she heard him only because his grip had tightened, wrenching her closer to him. Next thing she knew, her patent-leather shoes were barely skimming the concrete floor as her big brother took her away.

"What were you thinking?" he said when they'd once again met the sunlight.

"I'm sorry. I didn't know they would write—"

"I mean what were you thinking coming here at all? What happened to the little sister I left back home?"

Now *she* was angry, and she ripped her arm away. "That was five years ago, Donny. What did you expect?"

"Not this." He folded the paper and shoved it deep into his

pocket. "This town isn't the place for a nice girl like you—or at least like you're supposed to be."

"Fine time for you to become protective."

"Let me ask you again. Why are you here? Who was that man with you?"

"Please," she begged. "There's so much. Can't we sit down somewhere? And talk?"

"Explain on the way."

He shifted directions and she began to tell him about her journey, beginning with the visit to Darlene in St. Louis. The Rudy Valentino movie, seeing Sister Aimee, the Chinese restaurant, her song, the theaters and trains, and finally, here. She let the photograph speak for itself. Throughout the story, Don remained silent by her side as they walked, playing the role of both brother and confessor.

"Then Roland—Mr. Lundi—made some phone calls, and we found you. And, well, here we are."

The story seemed so insignificant when reduced to such a timeline.

"Sister Aimee," he said, as if testing the name. "I've heard of her."

"She's wonderful," Dorothy Lynn said.

"And you were onstage with her?"

"Briefly." Already it seemed more like a dream than a memory.

They'd come to a place where twenty or so long wooden tables were lined up under a blue canvas tarp.

"The talent eats inside," Don said, pointing to a nondescript building to the left. "I guess a week ago, you'd be in there. But today, with me . . . well, this is us."

The two wove through the aisles between the tables to where a sort of wagon was parked at the front. A wide shelf extended from it, on which metal trays were stacked. Don took a tray and set it on the counter.

"What is it today?" he asked of the man behind it.

"Corn chowder." The stain on the front of his formerly white apron looked like he'd survived a tumble into the impressive pot.

"Two," Don said. "And biscuits." He turned to Dorothy Lynn. "Don't be fooled; the food's good. Are you hungry?"

"Yes." She wasn't, but if eating a steaming bowl of corn chowder was the price for sitting with her brother, then she'd gladly pay it.

Don dropped two nickels in a jar and took the tray laden with two bowls of soup, a plate of biscuits, and two glasses of water. The long tables and benches were designed so they couldn't expect to have their own table, but he set the tray down at a spot where a buffer of space afforded some privacy. She sat across from him, and when he'd set their places, he reached for her hand. "Bless, O Father, this meal. Amen."

It wasn't until he said *amen* that Dorothy Lynn was fully aware a prayer was being said at all. She was closing her eyes as he opened his, and the guilt of it made her smile.

"You always did forget to say grace," Don said with a hint of his familiar twinkle. "Does it still give you the tummyaches like Pa said it would?" He scooped a heaping spoonful of chowder, but the mention of their father made it impossible for Dorothy Lynn to follow suit.

"About Pa . . ." It was all she needed to say before the welcome bit of humor died. His knowing look spared her from speaking the final, fateful words.

"When?"

"Last winter. Doctor said he must have been sick for a long time, but none of us knew—not until close to the end. When he got sick, we wrote to you at the last address—the one in Seattle, I think—but didn't hear back."

"I was already here."

"Well, that explains it. Darlene wrote a letter here, too, to general delivery, but it's one of the reasons I wanted to find you, to tell you in person. He would have loved to have seen you—"

"It's not my fault he died."

"Of course not." She'd been stirring her soup listlessly and dropped her spoon, surprised at both his bitterness and his accusation.

"I have enough blood on my hands; I won't take his."

"Donny . . ." She reached to reclaim the companionable touch they'd shared as he blessed their uneaten food, but he recoiled as if she'd burned him.

"I'm sorry." He took a drink of his water, his hand visibly shaking, and seemed calmer as he wiped his chin with the back of his sleeve. "What was the other?"

"The other what?"

"The other reason you came. You said one was to tell me about Pa." He'd become still again, almost cold.

"Well, maybe there's three." She decided to dole out the news as slowly as she could to extend their visit. Surely some bit of it would usher her back into his affections. "Darlene just had another baby. A girl. Her third." She added this last detail not knowing exactly how many of Darlene's children he knew about at all.

His reaction was that of a distant relative—a cousin, maybe, in town for a long-postponed reunion—dipping his spoon into the chowder three times before saying, "That's nice. And what about you?"

"Well," she said, disappointed that he seemed so intent on rushing through her list, "I'm going to get married."

"To that guy?" He gestured vaguely with a biscuit.

"Mr. Lundi? Of course not. He's, well, more of a chaperone, I guess."

"Looked to me like you need a chaperone between you and *him*."

"I'm marrying a man named Brent Logan. Back in Heron's Nest. He took over the pulpit after Pa died."

"You're marrying a preacher?" Again a hint of humor—light edging out the deadness in his eyes.

"Why shouldn't I?" She took a defensive spoonful of chowder, finding it quite delicious.

"Grow up the preacher's daughter only to become the preacher's wife. No wonder you ran off."

"I didn't run off!"

"Then why are you here?"

"I came to find you, to tell you about Pa and ask you to come back."

"I'm not going back."

Their heated exchange had captured the attention of several of their fellow diners, particularly a group of young women who alternately sneered at Dorothy Lynn and cast longing, fluttering glances at her brother.

"Script girls." He inclined his head their way after flashing them the same crooked smile that had always turned the young ladies of Heron's Nest into twittering fools.

"What do they do?"

"They carry the scripts."

"I see."

"How's Ma?"

"She's good. Happy about the wedding, of course. And the baby. But she misses Pa. And you."

"I can't go home."

"Of course not—not to stay. But since Pa can't be there to give me away, I thought . . . I hoped you would."

His face took on a look of pain more pure than she'd ever witnessed, strong enough that she could feel it pierce beneath her own skin.

"It's your home, Donny."

"No, this is my home."

"Just for a visit? Is it the money? Because I have a little—"

"It's not the money."

"Then what?"

"I've already been back."

The script girls were staring, but she didn't care. She tossed her spoon into her bowl and shoved the whole mess onto the metal tray, causing a racket impressive enough to make them snicker into their Coca-Cola bottles. "When?"

"Right after the war."

"Nobody's ever told me."

"Nobody knew. I was on the bus—or that horrible hay wagon with a motor they use for a bus. I was the only one, and it was late at night. Or dark, anyway. And the driver stopped right at Jessup's road. You know the one? Leads right into town?"

She nodded. Neither the hay wagon nor the road had changed.

"So the driver said, 'Welcome home, son,' and up until then, I couldn't wait to get back, to see everybody and taste Ma's cooking and hear Pa preach, and even tussle with you."

"We were waiting," she said. "I remember we got a telegram, and for days and days Ma made your favorite supper."

"Baked ham and grits."

"Every night, in case you came home. Then one night she didn't, and we haven't had it since. What happened?"

He clouded. "You wouldn't believe, Sis, the things we saw over there. Or what I did—what I had to do."

She moved once again to touch him, and he didn't flinch away. "It was war, Donny. But it's over."

"It's never really over. Not in here." He touched his head, and she noticed for the first time a small scar, previously hidden by his long hair. Was that the result of a war wound? Or something less traumatizing? Or even a remnant from childhood that she'd never given any mind to before?

"I couldn't get out. I couldn't bring all the ugliness and horror of those memories into home. I didn't want to taint it. I didn't want to frighten you, so I stayed away."

"But staying away frightened us."

"It's what I had to do to stay sane. I had to get away from my old life, reinvent myself. I didn't want to answer questions or tell stories. I couldn't watch Pete Williams hobble around with that one leg or look Mr. Stubbins in the eye, knowing his son was shot to bits in France. I couldn't get off that bus and pretend I was the same kid I used to be, so I stayed on it and became somebody else."

"You can't really become a different person."

She could see him fighting for control. "Of course you can."

"Not in your heart."

"Do you know how much it hurts to even sit here with you? For me to know that you're this close to me?" His lips barely moved as he spoke, and he held her hand so tightly she feared her bones would turn to dust in his grip, giving her a taste of the battle raging within him.

"You don't think it will hurt me to get up and walk away? To go back home without you? What'll I tell Ma?"

He released her hand and took a wide, sweeping glance

around, much to the delight of the script girls, one of whom shifted on her bench, crossing one leg over the other with a brazen shift of her skirt.

"You know what I love about this place?" His gaze was locked on the girls.

"I can probably guess."

He turned back to her. "Not just the studio, although that, too, but California. Los Angeles. Nobody cares who I am or where I've been or what I've done. I don't have to tell them anything. They don't ask questions. And if they do, they don't expect the truth."

"You don't think I'll have to answer some questions when I get home?"

"You'll have to deal with your own demons however you want."

"I don't have demons. I gave that all over to God. And maybe . . ." Her heart softened. All those nights watching audiences melt under the weight of grace. So many had been young men just like him, soldiers with wounds both visible and invisible, and she'd seen them weep with healing. "Ah, Donny. You need Jesus. Whatever horrible things you think you've done, confess them to him."

He smiled—genuine, indulgent, and warm. "I'm at peace with God, for all that I've done. Every decision. Every choice. Running to California doesn't mean I've run away from him. It's . . . it was just what I had to do. I don't expect you to understand."

"Well, I don't. I don't know why you thought you had to run away from us." She sounded petulant, but she didn't care. Part of her envied his escape from the prying ears of Heron's Nest, but then she remembered Ma at the window, Ma too scared to ask if there'd been a letter. How could he turn his back on her? "Can I at least tell Ma that you'll write?"

"You can, but I can't promise I will, and I don't want to keep disappointing her over and over again."

"So we're supposed to just live with this hole in our family? Pa's gone; there's nothing to be done about that. But you're here, alive. We deserve to know that much at least."

"And now you know," he pointed out. "But what difference does it make? Look how life has gone on without me. Pa died, Darlene has a new baby. You're getting married. . . ."

"And you?"

"I'm . . . happy. Content, anyway."

She believed him, thinking he had been—at least until this visit, when she'd dug up every buried anguish to lay at his feet. Might as well heap on one more. "Just a letter, Don. Please? To set her heart at peace."

"You can speak for me. I've told you everything."

At that point there seemed nothing left to say, and it was by tacit agreement that Don gathered their uneaten food on the tray and pushed it to the end of the table, where a young man in an apron cleaner than the chef's carted it away.

"Will you walk me back? I don't think I quite know my way around."

He extended his arm. "I'd be honored."

It was the final blow to the script girls. They rolled their kohl-lined eyes and turned up their noses in an oddly comical, somewhat beautiful choreographed motion. Still, Don stopped at their table. "Good afternoon, ladies."

They mumbled something that passed for a greeting.

"I was wondering if you could settle a bet. You see, my sister here swears she saw one of you in *Orphans of the Storm*, but I'm not so sure. Can you help us settle up? There's two bits riding on it."

At the word *sister*, all four had instantly brightened. One, sporting a helmet of sleek black hair and lips close to purple in their redness, spoke for the quartet. "If we was actresses, we sure wouldn't be lunching out here, would we?"

She had an accent that made *here* sound like *he-yah*, the same pattern Roland fell into when he wasn't conscious of his speech.

He turned to Dorothy Lynn. "My point exactly."

He then held out his hand, seeming determined to leave it there, open, until she dug into her purse and produced a dime. "It's all I have."

He thanked her, thanked the girls, and took her arm again.

"So I haven't completely ruined your day."

He granted gentle agreement. "Not completely."

"I'm sorry."

"You couldn't have known."

Their conversation strolled as slowly as their steps, as Dorothy Lynn determined to make this afternoon last as long as possible. If nothing else, her brother seemed agreeable to the pace. They passed one building after another, each identical to the last, but she knew fantastical differences lurked within. In their silences, she tried to imagine what they concealed. Other miniature houses? Or castles, maybe, based on the number of women she saw walking around in long velvet gowns.

"So this is it?" she said, turning quickly away from the copper-toned man dressed in leather breeches. "You're staying here forever?"

"For now, anyway. If I ever leave, I'll tell you."

"Don't make us wait, Donny." She'd use these final minutes for one last plea. "Write to Ma and explain. She just wants to know that you're alive and well."

"I can't promise."

311

"Good. Ma says you can only promise or do, but not both."

They arrived at the car, where Roland was deep in conversation with the most striking woman Dorothy Lynn had ever seen. She had dark, bobbed hair, red lips, and a way of looking regal even with her short stature and dancer's pants. He was in the process of handing her his card and saying, "I'm at the Hotel Alexandria. Meet me there for lunch later in the week, and I'll have some news for you."

"Thank you, Mr. Lundi." Her voice was throaty and cultured, and she offered only a passing glance at Don and Dorothy Lynn as she left.

"She's a dancer," Roland said, as if the woman's legs weren't sufficient identification, "but she wants to be an actress. And I tell you, I have an eye. You remember that name—Lucille LeSueur. I'm going to make her a star."

Don kissed Dorothy Lynn on the cheek and reached out to shake Roland's hand. "Thank you for taking such good care of my baby sister. Can you see that she gets home safe?"

Roland looked from one to the other. "This the end of the road for you two?"

"We had a good sit-down visit," Dorothy Lynn said, controlling the threatening tears.

"How about I get a picture?" Roland reached into the car for his Brownie. "I'll have a copy delivered to you here, sport."

Don agreed and looped his arm over Dorothy Lynn's shoulder. "Let's get the car in it. I'll pretend it's mine."

Roland took another step back and looked down through the viewer. They smiled on his command, and while Dorothy Lynn knew she should be looking at the camera, she instead turned her gaze on Don, studying her brother's strong profile.

"I got one more left," Roland said when he released them from their pose.

"Let me get the two of you." Don took the camera and the two men traded places. This time she stared straight at the photographer, knowing how small and square and upside-down she must look in his eyes.

"That's it." Don bent to put the Brownie back in the car and reached out to run a finger along the guitar case.

"Your guitar's in there," Dorothy Lynn said with a quaver to her voice. "You can have it back if you like."

"It's yours," he said. "Keep it." She found herself awash in relief.

He hugged her then, and she held tight, so grateful for the warmth that had been absent from their first embrace. She wanted to remind him one more time to write to Ma, or to her, or to Darlene, but the truce they'd called seemed so fragile, she dared not disrupt it. Instead she said, "I love you, Donny. We all do."

"Give my love to Ma."

"The wedding's Saturday after next," she ventured, "in case you change your mind."

He lifted the hat off her head and kissed her at her temple. "I'll be thinking of you."

And she knew, if she walked down an aisle at all, she'd walk down alone.

※

She'd insisted he bring her to the beach, hoping the sound of the waves would clear her head. This was the last place she'd truly felt at peace, and she searched for that feeling again as she stood at the edge of the sea. How terrifying it must have been for early man to see such a sight, to think that the world simply dropped off and ended where the ocean's water poured over the side into some unknown abyss. Then, too, how enticing to see it stretch, seemingly forever. An endless future. No wonder they climbed into vessels and set sail to parts unknown. Mountains could be climbed, roads traveled, but the sea presented itself as infinite and unforgiving. It drew and it drew. Large, crashing waves, so impressive in the distance, reduced themselves to deceptively harmless lapping. She looked down to see them covering her feet, then receding, then covering again. A matter of a few steps, and she'd be drawn in, drawn under, swept away.

She dug her heels in deeper, burying herself up to her ankles. The endless unknown was Donny's choice, and with her hands held high, she sent him silent blessing, asking the Creator of this miracle to do the same. Her brother's life was in her Heavenly Father's hands, and he'd kept him safe thus far.

"This far and forever," she said, and her words disappeared in the sound of the surf.

Not long, and the sun would dip under the horizon, ending this day, but for Dorothy Lynn it would end so much more. Her future stretched behind her, in the east where the sun would rise in the morning. Back home, by whatever means would get her there. Back to Brent if he would have her. And even if he wouldn't.

She lifted her foot from where she'd covered it with cool, wet sand, and balanced the solid mass before shaking it, sifting the clumps between her toes into the shallow space below.

A high-pitched whistle pierced the wind, and she turned to see Roland returning from his errand to buy them each a cold drink from a vendor farther up the beach. He held the bottle of Coca-Cola high, beckoning. Back at the car, Dorothy Lynn did what she could to knock the excess sand from her feet before climbing in to join him, perched atop the backseat. Using a small, metal opener, he pried the top off each bottle, sending a fizzy hiss to join the pounding surf. They took a first, long drink together—she welcoming the sweet scratch of the liquid to a throat that had spent the better part of the day sore with unshed tears.

"What can I tell you, sweetheart?" Roland wiped his lips with his sleeve. "War changes people."

"Ma was right. A fool's errand." It occurred to her for the first time that Ma must have suspected Donny's state of mind all along.

"No such thing," Roland said. "A dead end, maybe. It's the fool who takes that same road again."

"You can be very wise when you want to be, Mr. Lundi."

"So I keep trying to convince the world."

"You've convinced me. And I guess Donny would agree with you. That's why he never came back. Says he's changed too much. Maybe I have too. He makes it seem so easy, starting over."

"You wouldn't be the first kid to want a bigger life than what was waiting on the farm."

"There's no farm."

"You wouldn't be the first girl to leave a guy hanging, either." His voice made it impossible to know whether he spoke of Brent or himself, and his eyes kept the answer hidden in an ocean-long gaze.

She nudged her shoulder against his and took a guess. "You've already moved on, Mr. Lundi. With Miss Lucille, the dancer? I'm surprised you remember my name."

"Dancers," he said dismissively. He drained the last of the dark drops before tossing the green glass onto the beach, leaving Dorothy Lynn with no clearer understanding.

"I don't know if Brent will be waiting for me when I get

home. If he'll still want me. And it's almost certain he won't after I tell him—if I tell him . . ."

"So don't."

"If he's my husband, he'll have a right to know."

"But he's not. See that fellow down the beach?" He pointed to a young man in rolled pants and shirtsleeves walking along the water's edge. "Your guy has about as much a claim on you as that one. Who's to say he can't come over here with a line that'll make you forget me and the reverend both? You're about as obligated to that preacher of yours as you are to him. Or to me."

"There's one difference," she said, running her finger along the cold, curved shape of the bottle. "I don't love that fellow on the beach."

The silent possibility that she might love him mixed with the salted air, and she drank the last of the caramel-sweet drink to keep from saying so out loud. When she finished, he took the bottle from her and tossed it to where it made a satisfying clink against his. Then, while the effervescence of it lingered, he kissed her. This was not one of the fatherly kisses she'd come to expect or anything like the drunken collision at the edge of her memory. This was a man kissing a woman, a mutual giving and taking of taste and touch.

"Oh, Roland," she said when he released her for breath, but then his palms were cool against her pulse, and she let him kiss her again. Not out of fear or twisted obligation, as she had when she launched herself on him the night of the party, and not out of the physically-charged desire she'd felt from the first time she kissed Brent. This was the first kiss born from the woman she'd become. A kiss for this moment, for its own sake, given and received without gratitude or promise.

Her hat tumbled to her feet as he pulled her closer. She could feel the faint roughness of the afternoon's whiskers as he trailed kisses the length of her neck; it was how she imagined the warm sand would feel beneath her bare skin.

This could be home. No fear, no questions. No expectation of truth. What was it Donny had said? *"Nobody cares who I am or where I've been or what I've done. I don't have to tell them anything. They don't ask questions. And if they do, they don't expect the truth."*

And yet—

"Stop," she said, not sure if she was talking to her mind or her body. Whatever the case, Roland obeyed, at least as far as his kisses were concerned. He still held her close, her cheek resting against his temple as the horizon beckoned. "There's a part of me, I think, that will always wonder what would have happened if I'd stayed. Just like Donny. Become a whole new person, maybe even a famous one. But I don't think that's a person I'd ever want to be."

He pulled away and looked at her. The dark fringe of his lashes framed an indulgent, almost humorous smolder. "So? Stay."

"You don't mean that."

He offered what was probably meant to be a noncommittal shrug, but she sensed something deeper, something she never would have expected if she'd been the same girl who had stumbled into his solitary Chinese lunch such a short time before.

"Do you love me, Roland? And don't say no, because I won't believe it. A girl knows—a woman knows."

"Of course I love you." Even the vastness of the sea and sky left no room for doubt. "About as much as you love me."

"And how much is that?"

Her fingers were entwined in his, and he raised them up to kiss them. "Enough."

It should have been the perfect answer, complete in its simplicity, but for one last time she relied on the wisdom he'd gained from living so much more of a life than she'd ever dreamed possible. So she, too, kissed their interlacing and looked up, searching for one final answer.

"Enough," he repeated, "for me to put you on the next train home, because you should never give up a guy you want to marry for one who doesn't want to marry you."

She rested in the pool of his affection. "It's more than that, you know. It's my whole life—Brent just happens to be at the center of everything. Or at least he should have been. And he will be, just as soon as I get home."

"And that, sweetheart, is when I hope you'll love me enough to let me remain a fond, distant memory."

"Always."

It seemed the perfect time to wrest her hand away from his, and she smoothed her skirt, wishing she could smooth away the awkward moments certain to follow.

"Just promise me one thing," he said, and she waited silently, watching his jaw tense in preparation for the words to follow. "Quit beating yourself up, understand? And promise me something else, too. When you go back home, don't you fall on your knees asking that preacher to forgive you. You walk into that place with your head up high. You did something noble for your family. You did something beautiful for God, and don't you ever let anybody take that away from you. You understand?"

She nodded and wiped her nose with the sleeve of her blouse.

"Look at you," he said, "already halfway back to the country life."

This time when he took her hand, it was only to help her step gingerly from the backseat to the front, where she stuffed her stockings into her purse and slid her shoes on her bare, sandy feet. Roland emitted some halfhearted grumbling about his fond memory being nothing less than half the beach tracked into his car, but by the time he'd tugged his hat down low, lit a smoke, and brought the engine to its powerful purr, she knew she'd been forgiven.

The car bumped over sand and rushes before finding the smooth surface that would take them back into the city. Dorothy Lynn closed her eyes and let the salted air rush over her, almost rough against her skin. At the edge of this cleansing darkness, she heard Roland's voice.

"For the last time—you love this fellow?"

She lolled her head in his direction. "Yes."

"Really, truly, like the movies, love him?"

"Yes!"

He took a final drag on his cigarette and tossed it over the side. "Well then, baby. That's enough."

Enticed and emboldened, she ripped her hat from her head and held it in a clenched fist as she stood, steadying herself with a grip on the windshield. Never before had she felt this free; never before had she moved this fast. The wind freed her hair from its pins, and it whipped about her head and face, turning her into what her mother certainly would have dubbed a "wild, wood-born child." She might have sand between her toes rather than bits of hard-packed forest floor, but she'd finally become that child again. If she took the time, she might just hear the whisper of a new song, but the roaring wind took it away. It would whirl and twirl and wind its way to reunite with her in the clearing.

BREATH OF ANGELS
6:00 P.M.

Supper is a quiet affair, but the solitude is a welcome relief from the tedious company of the afternoon. They've brought her a cup of warm beef broth and a plate of buttered bread.

"After all that rich cake this afternoon," Nurse Betten said as she set the tray on Lynnie's bedside table, "you want something easy on your stomach."

Now Lynnie sips the broth and nibbles the bread, wishing it were melba toast.

It's only six o'clock, but the room is already autumn-dark. It's the best part about getting old, being able to put a day behind you as soon as the sun sets. She'll take her last sip of broth during the final, feel-good story on NBC News with Brian Williams, waiting for Nurse Betten—or somebody—to assist her in one last trip to the bathroom, then doze until ten, when she'll wake up to watch the local broadcast and see what has been happening in the world just outside the walls of Breath of Angels.

Another day. One of the many the Lord has given her.

There is a soft rap and a sliver of light slices across her darkened room, revealing the thin, irregular silhouette of Charlotte Hill.

"Can I come in?" she asks, and waits as if Lynnie can give her an answer before slipping through the narrow opening.

On the TV, a nine-year-old girl hauls a little red wagon along the sidewalk in some bighearted adventure. Charlotte watches the television, and Lynnie watches Charlotte, and that's what happens until Brian Williams wishes them all a good night. Lynnie reaches for the remote, which is never far away, and pushes the big button at the top, plunging the room into deep shadow until Charlotte snaps on the lamp.

"Looked like a nice party this afternoon."

Lynnie lets out a beef-broth-tinged breath and rolls her eyes.

Charlotte laughs. "All right, it looked terrible."

Why didn't you come in?

"They don't know me, or that I'm family. Grandpa Jimmy—he's your nephew too—always said we had family here, but Great-Grandpa . . ."

Never wrote more than a few letters until Ma died, and then . . . nothing.

"He lived a long time too, you know. He died about twelve years ago. He was almost a hundred. I guess longevity runs in our family, huh?"

Not Darlene. Just sixty-seven when her heart gave out.

"I remember him, though. Even though I was a kid, I loved to hear his stories about the movies. I can watch them with my friends and say, 'See that? My great-grandfather built that.' And my grandmother still talks about the day she fetched Lon Chaney's makeup case and when she made Joan Crawford scream because she was hiding in one of the cabinets of a set her daddy was working on."

Joan Crawford. Lucille LeSueur. She'd never forgotten the name.

"I told them that I was going to come find you as soon as I turned eighteen."

Of course you did. It's the age of adventure.

"It took me a while, though. I'm about to turn twenty. When I knew I was coming here, I looked for everything I could find about you. I didn't bring the record, because I was afraid it would break, and Grandpa only had one copy. I've looked for it on eBay, but no luck so far." She is speaking incredibly fast, taking what was left of Lynnie's dinner and moving it to the table by the door. "But I thought you might want to see these." She drops her leather backpack on the bed near Lynnie's feet and takes out an old cigar box wrapped with twine. "These were with Great-Grandpa's things. I snuck them out of Mom's antique closet."

She's working the twine with her short, dark fingernails, finally untying it as the door flies open and Nurse Betten pokes her head through.

"Happy birthday again, Miss Lynnie," she says before her eyes light on Charlotte. "What are you still doing here?"

"Just visiting," Charlotte says. "A little longer. I'm kind of a fan."

"A fan?"

"She was a singer. Back in the twenties? Gospel music, like bluegrass."

"Is that a fact?"

"You know that song . . . ?" Charlotte sings a few lines and, hearing it live—not with that device—Lynnie could swear she is hearing her own voice transported through time. Roland Lundi would love this girl.

"I love that song!" Nurse Betten says. "And you've got a real nice voice. You should go on one of those shows."

"Maybe," Charlotte says. "If I could ever get the courage to go onstage. People scare me."

Lynnie wants to say, *Just close your eyes, and they disappear,* but Nurse Betten beats her to it before waving a chastising finger in Charlotte's direction.

"And not much longer. Miss Lynnie's had a long day, haven't you, Miss Lynnie?"

She shouts this last part, a habit Lynnie despises, and starts to duck out the door when Charlotte calls her back in. "Can I tell you something?"

"Of course, sweetie." Nurse Betten comes inside. "What do you need?"

Charlotte takes a deep breath. "I'm not a CSV. I'm not a volunteer at all. See? No badge."

Nurse Betten claps her hands and shoots Lynnie a smile. "So you're just a fan? How exciting. But you didn't need to sneak in. We would have let you come visit."

"No," Charlotte says. "I'm family. Distant, long-lost, whatever. My great-grandfather was her brother."

"Oh." Nurse Betten draws out the sound as if giving them a clue to the time it takes for her to come to a full understanding. "How was the party? Was it nice? I wish I could have been there, but—"

"I didn't go to the party. They don't know me; we're not, you know, close."

"Oh, that's too bad. Life is so short."

Charlotte laughs, and Lynnie loves her for it. "Not always."

Nurse Betten looks confused for just a second before a chuckle ripples along her scrubs. "Well, I'm glad the two of you had a chance to visit today. But not too late, if you don't mind. They get so tired at this age."

"I understand."

"Can I get you anything? Coffee, maybe? Or there's cake from her party. The family left it for the nurses."

"That sounds awesome," Charlotte says. "Thank you."

"How 'bout you, Miss Lynnie?" Nurse Betten shouts. "Would you like another piece of your cake?"

Lynnie holds up her hand. *A small one.*

"Well, fine, then. Why don't you follow me to the nurses' station and I'll let you get just what you want."

"Be right back," Charlotte says over her shoulder before leaving Lynnie alone with the cigar box.

She should wait. Charlotte, after all, has no doubt brought whatever is in it to share with her. But she brings one finger to the lid, runs it along the edge. With the right amount of effort, the lid lifts and falls backward, exposing the contents within. She sits up, reaches inside, and finds the first item. It's a folded, faded bit of newspaper, and she need not unfold it to know exactly what she will see. When she closes her eyes, she can hear the music—jazz, meant for dancing, and her feet twitch beneath the sheet in memory. She tastes champagne on her tongue and feels the bubbles misting beneath her nose.

And that dress—nothing she's worn since ever made her feel the way that dress did. Even as the decades played on, when she wore perfectly modest sundresses or even—on much rarer occasions—shorts, she never felt that perfect combination of exposed and beautiful. She could feel the red silk brushing her legs, the touch of Roland's hand on her back.

Roland.

Lynnie thought of him now and then, more often in those first days when, out of the clear blue, her voice would come spilling through the family radio. "It's nothing," she'd explained at Sunday dinner. "They let anybody make records in Los Angeles."

And after a few months, she'd never been heard on those airwaves again. In fact, she'd never heard that *song* again—not from her mouth or any other—until today.

She reaches into the cigar box again and brings out an envelope. Once white, it has come to something that looks yellow in the lamplight. In the top left-hand corner is the address for the Hotel Alexandria. She brings the envelope to her face and inhales, expecting to smell the perfumes of the elegant women who strolled its lobby.

It is addressed to Don Dunbar, care of Silverlight Studios, written in block, irregular-size letters. Much as Roland had worked to define his appearance and his speech, he still had the penmanship of a modest upbringing.

"You're peeking." Charlotte is back, proving why the shoes she wears are called sneakers. "But that's okay—I was going to share with you anyway."

She carries two plates of cake and a Styrofoam cup of coffee with the confidence of an experienced waitress.

"Eat now? Or after? I don't want to get frosting on the pictures."

Lynnie reaches her hand for the cake, eager for a moment of celebration.

"Do you want to hear about my family? Well, yours too, I guess."

Lynnie nods, eager.

"It's one of the reasons I wanted to meet you. One of my earliest memories is listening to Great-Grandpa and Great-Grandma tell about the day they met. She was jealous because he was talking to a pretty girl, but then he said it was his sister, and they had a bet. . . ."

The script girl!

Suddenly, the bite of cake on her tongue is the sweetest taste she's ever known, and she can see hints of a sleek Louise Brooks bob in the irregular, pointed tufts of Charlotte's black hair.

"And look at this." Charlotte leans forward and reaches inside the cigar box, bringing forth a thin, silver coin. "He called it his lucky dime."

My dime. But she wouldn't take it back.

"This is their wedding picture," Charlotte says, producing a photograph that confirms Lynnie's assumptions. "My family says I look like her, and I was thinking about getting my hair cut like that. Everybody's wearing bangs these days."

Lynnie nods and hands over her half-eaten cake, eager to see the contents of the envelope, but Charlotte continues talking, listing names and events of people she's never heard of and doesn't particularly care about.

"Anyway, I didn't know if you'd gotten married or changed your name, and I didn't know your sister's family name, so I talked my mom into doing one of those genealogy sites, you know? Then, you know, just a bunch of Google and stuff, and here we are."

Lynnie goes so far as to put her twisted fingers on the envelope and nudge it across the table.

"Oh, yeah." Charlotte speaks through the last bite of cake, leaving Lynnie mesmerized by the bit of frosting smudged on the ring piercing through her lip. It disappears briefly within her mouth and comes out clean.

Fascinating.

"These pictures are why I had to come find you." She took out the first. "It says this is in St. Louis."

Lynnie takes it from her, holding it close and as still as she can in her shaking hand. Roland had said, "You'll be glad to have the memories." But she'd refused his offer to have them mailed to her at Heron's Nest. She'd stored every moment of those days within the infinite folds of her mind. What power could a scrap of paper, void of movement and voice and color, possibly have?

The image is tiny, but she remembers the moment vividly. It was the day they left, and the two women stand side by side. The old Brownie had captured them laughing, as if they'd been friends, or even sisters.

"That's Aimee Semple McPherson."

It is.

"She was an amazing woman. And you knew her?"

Lynnie nods.

"And this one—just says, *sisters.*"

It's Darlene. Somehow, she's always remembered Darlene as being ungainly, huge in her pregnancy. But those must have been her inexperienced eyes, because she looks beautiful. Radiant, but sad. Her smile is forced for the camera, as is Lynnie's own. There's a blur at the margin of the image where one of the boys—who remembers which one—had just been unceremoniously chased away.

Lynnie holds out her hand, making a writing gesture, and Charlotte digs through her bag, producing a pen. When she first came out of the last stroke, once she'd resigned herself to a life without speech, she often had a pad and pencil, ready to communicate as she could. But words often dissolved between her mind and the paper, and her life had become so simple, there'd been little need.

Now, as she takes the pen from Charlotte's hand, the entire act seems unfamiliar. Charlotte turns the picture over and Lynnie writes, *Darlene and me. Aug. 1922.*

She's horrified at the trail of letters left behind. They are disjointed and half-formed, more like the product of a seven-year-old than one who's lived a century beyond that. But Charlotte brightens and says, "Oh, of course," before picking another picture from the pile.

"I love this one. It's you, I guess, playing your guitar?"

This is Kansas City, at a park just a few blocks from their hotel. That much she remembers, but the picture itself is a surprise. In it, she is hunched over her guitar, eyes closed—mouth, too. There's a posture of prayer, but instead of having hands clasped, one holds the strings to a chord, and the other is a blur of motion.

"You look so beautiful . . . and peaceful. There aren't a lot of candid shots from that era. I think the photographer was a little bit in love with you."

Enough.

Lynnie drops the photograph and shakes her head, still fearful of the thought of it, even with Roland long in Glory and she not far. Had he loved her? Sometimes, when she thought back to that final afternoon on the beach, she knew for certain that he did. Not with the innocence that drove her own affections, but with enough compassion to set her free and send her home.

"This is the guy, right? Here with you next to this old car? This cracks me up because it says, *Remember, my car!* on the back."

Lynnie would laugh if she had the strength, but a familiar, draining feeling hovers as the day takes its toll.

"You're getting tired. I'm sorry, but just one more? I recognize the station, but I'm not sure if this is when you first arrived in Los Angeles or when you left."

Lynnie doesn't need to see the picture to know. There'd been no pictures when she arrived—not of her, anyway. Sister Aimee had been the subject of reporters' and photographers' interest that day. This picture was yet another that Roland called his "last one—just to finish off the roll, sweetheart."

The girl in the picture is wearing a brocade skirt and peach-colored blouse that the woman in the bed can feel on her skin. It had been cleaned and pressed and was forever one of her favorites. He'd told her to take off her hat, as the shadow hid her face, and she's clutching it in one hand while the other holds her ever-present guitar. A modest pile of bags is at her feet, and as soon as the picture is snapped, the tears that are invisible to the unsophisticated lens will pour down her face.

"So it's the day you left?"

Yes.

"And you never saw him again?"

Surely Charlotte speaks of Donny, but the answer is the same for Roland.

Never.

When she remembers a last embrace, a final soft kiss, it is Roland, not Donny. Roland had bent to her, touched his lips to hers, merged forever the scent and taste of tobacco. She'd never smoke herself, for fear of tainting the memory.

Charlotte takes the picture and examines it closely. "You were even younger than me, weren't you? You could have been a star. Would have made it much easier to find you."

Suddenly it's clear what must be done. This minute, before the rushing tide of sleep steals her away. Lynnie presses Nurse Betten's call button on the side of her bed, then fumbles through the pictures, separating out the unposed image of her playing the guitar. She flips it over and drums her fingers, waiting.

"Is something wrong?" Charlotte asks. "Can I get you anything?"

Lynnie trains her eyes on the door.

"I'm sorry. If you want me to leave, I'll go."

A burst of strength surges through Lynnie as she grasps Charlotte's arm. It's the first time in her life that she's touched a tattoo, and some part of her wonders if the intricate Celtic cross is somewhat responsible for the exigency she feels.

"What you need, Miss Lynnie?" Nurse Betten is amply cheerful as she walks through the door.

"I think something might be wrong," Charlotte says, covering Lynnie's hand with her own. "She just, I don't know . . . changed."

Lynnie beckons Nurse Betten over, and when she arrives at her side, taps the photograph.

"Is that you? My goodness, how beautiful." She looks up at Charlotte. "She still has that guitar, you know."

"Seriously?" Charlotte's voice is full of awe.

Nodding, Lynnie takes the photograph and forces it into Charlotte's hand, disregarding any folds or crinkles the transfer might inflict.

"You want the girl to keep the picture?"

Lynnie shakes her head.

"It is my picture."

Lynnie presses it into her flesh and forces two grunts from her throat. *Guitar.*

Nurse Betten claps as if she's solved a game show puzzle. "She wants you to have her guitar."

Lynnie nods and points to the closet, but Nurse Betten, caught up in the enthusiasm of the moment, is already there, lifting the case from the top shelf.

Already Lynnie can smell it, feel the warm, worn handle in the curve of her fingers.

"It's heavier than I thought," Nurse Betten says, and Lynnie can feel the ache of it in her shoulder as she carried it on the train, and the surprising ghost of regret that would sneak up every now and then since the day she carried it off.

She moves her legs, making room for the case on the foot of the bed. Nurse Betten steps aside to give Charlotte the honor of opening the latches.

It's not the first time Lynnie has heard this sound over the years. There had been other guitars—one given to her as a wedding gift by her husband, another on her fiftieth birthday. She'd played in countless Sunday services and every county fair, but never *that* song, and not with Donny's guitar. Not since that morning in the recording studio. Often, when she'd find herself alone, and then later, when solitude loomed as a constant state of being, she'd flipped those latches, sometimes even opening the lid to tuck a treasure inside that space between the curve of the instrument and the softness of the velvet.

Charlotte looks into the case as if discovering a relic. "Can I lift it out?"

Lynnie pleads with her to do just that.

"It's a Martin."

1912.

She lifts it out the way one would lift a baby, with gentle support at the neck and an arm cradling the body. Lynnie longs to take it from her, but she knows it wouldn't be the same. The silken sheen has turned to dry, parched wood, and the strings are little more than a layer of dust along the frets. Junk to anyone else—especially any of those who'd gathered today in the celebration room. Charlotte, though, holds it in all its priceless glory.

"They used to string them with actual catgut," Charlotte says, whispering. "They've disintegrated." She looks at Lynnie. "You haven't played in a long time, have you?"

A lifetime.

"Is it ruined?" Nurse Betten asks.

"It's in good shape," Charlotte says, turning it over in her hands. "I know a guy in Santa Fe who does amazing work. He can restore it." She looks to Lynnie. "If that's okay with you."

Lynnie gestures a blessing.

"And I'll bring it back? It might be a couple of months, though."

Lynnie waves her off.

"I think she wants you to keep it," Nurse Betten says.

For a couple of months. From this point and forever.

"I couldn't. This thing could be worth a fortune, and the rest of her family doesn't even know I exist."

Nurse Betten cups her hand around her mouth and whispers, "The rest of her family barely knows *she* exists. They'd just trash it."

Lynnie looks away, embarrassed for both her family and the place she holds in it. She knows nothing of what has become of most of her material possessions—not those from her home, or her first apartment at Breath of Angels. She's thought, always, that it didn't matter. Once she's with Jesus, in Glory, none of it will matter. They were the stuff of dust, like the catgut strings on her guitar. But now, seeing new life possible for the only object she's ever treasured—a life that will take it to someplace as exotic as Santa Fe—that truth takes hold. Before her eyes, she sees both an inheritance and an heir, something she never felt she deserved.

"And who's this?"

She can see that Charlotte is holding yet another snapshot, but the shadows are crowding too quickly to answer.

⇜ CHAPTER TWENTY ⇝

FOR THE LAST HUNDRED MILES or so, Dorothy Lynn had the bus to herself, and she wondered if that was always the case when a Heron's Nest resident came back to the roost. Not that many ever came back. People left; people stayed. She didn't know anybody who had ever done both.

"Normally I'd just drop you right here at the main road." Her driver, Alvin DuBose, was a Heron's Nest regular, but not a resident. Nobody knew exactly where he lived, and given the basket of snacks he kept beside his seat, it wasn't too far-fetched to believe the legend that he actually lived on the bus. "But seeing you're a lady and all alone, I'll take you right up to the door of your choosing."

"Thank you," Dorothy Lynn said, "but I'm worried the road up to my house might be a bit narrow."

"Oh, I've hauled this old girl up and down roads you wouldn't believe. Always an adventure, you know what I mean?"

"I'm sure."

"Yep. You just never know where one road is going to lead you. Or how many switchbacks and pathways you're gonna have to take to make your way home again."

"No, you don't."

He'd been at this for over an hour, trying to wheedle a story out of her. When she got on the bus, she'd been one of a dozen passengers. Some, like her, were sleepy from spending days and nights on the train; others were awake and eager, with the early morning bringing adventure. All gathered together in the narrow seats, facing one another with unspoken stories.

Unspoken, that is, until Alvin DuBose loosened their tongues, asking questions and telling tales of his own. Then conversation smothered her, making her want to scream for silence. Town after town, passengers and luggage dropped away, leaving her alone, exposed, as Alvin's final, uncracked nut.

"And I tell ya," he said in continued, valiant effort, "there's nothin' I like more about my job than having the opportunity to bring people home. There's adventure aplenty out there, but nothing compares to home. What's that the song says? About all the nests? 'Better than a palace with a gilded dome is the love nest you can call home.'" He sang this last part, creating a close facsimile of a popular tune.

"I like that song."

"Yeah? Sing me a few bars."

"Oh, I don't think so."

"I see that guitar there. You gotta be some sort of singer."

"It's my brother's," Dorothy Lynn said.

"Aw, that's nice."

He didn't go on to explain just why he thought it was nice, perhaps because he was hoping she would fill in the details. But her head was too full of what she would say to her mother, how she would explain that her only son never intended to come home. Or to Brent, as she faced him with no evidence of her good intentions.

Alvin was humming about the love nest they called home,

and Dorothy Lynn perched on the edge of her seat in anticipation of returning to her own. The canopy of forest, her own room in the house she shared with Ma. And Brent. Would she still have a place in his heart after she ran away from the promise of their future?

They all twisted together, these feelings of place and belonging and love, like the very streets of Heron's Nest. No wonder the town didn't have the straight, orderly blocks and streets she'd seen in the cities. People wandered from home to home, wearing footpaths to one another. It was confusing and unwelcoming to a stranger—that's what Brent had said when he first arrived, that the town was laid out like some sort of secret language.

She'd laughed and said, "Isn't that the way with every family?"

Alvin DuBose brought the bus to a sputtering halt in front of Jessup's, which served as a bus station along with all its other responsibilities.

"Wish I coulda gotten you home before dark," Alvin said, consulting his watch.

"What time is it?"

"Just after seven o'clock."

"That's fine," Dorothy Lynn said. "It's early."

Alvin creaked open the door and stepped out, standing ready to hand Dorothy Lynn down.

"Got someone coming to meet you?"

"Not that I know of," she said. At Roland's insistence, she had sent a telegram home before boarding the train in Los Angeles, but her exact time of arrival had been impossible to determine.

"Where do you suppose Jessup is?"

"Church," she said simply. "Sunday night service."

"What about your bags? I have to make time to Houston tonight."

"Someone will fetch them later. Tomorrow, I suppose. Jessup will let them keep here tonight. You go on."

"All right—" he sounded dubious—"but I don't like the idea of leaving you alone in the dark."

"I'll be fine," she said. "I'll meet up with my family at the church."

By family, she meant Brent. Ma had taken to staying home on Sunday nights once Pa became too sick to go. After he passed, she stayed there, claiming her own fatigue, but Dorothy Lynn had known even then it was a ruse to give Brent a chance to walk her home with only darkness as chaperone. Always, Ma would be on the porch, waiting—even if the temperature had dropped near to freezing—ignorant of the final bend in the road that would allow them to kiss with abandon outside of her view. Then again, few things ever really escaped Ma's perception, and Dorothy Lynn knew the hour was coming when she would face her mother as confessor—an hour fraught with equal eagerness and dread.

When he'd stacked her bags and guitar on Jessup's well-seasoned porch, she met him at the front of the bus and handed over a generous stack of bills.

"Oh, no, miss," he said, not looking the least bit tempted, "you paid your full fare in Springfield."

"It's a tip." She held them closer.

"That's too much."

"No, please. It's yours."

Actually, it was Roland's, the last of the money he'd given her to finance her trip home. She couldn't imagine his money would be a good fit for any future expense.

"Well, then, I thank you. But I'm not movin' an inch until I see you safely to the church."

"Very well," she said, and started off in the direction that would lead her home.

❦

Music and light poured through the windows, signaling that the service was coming to an end. Sometimes, on Sunday nights, there'd be no sermon at all, unless the congregation seemed in need of some urgent teaching. They would sing and pray and give testimony of God's work instead.

"Who has a word?" Pa would say before relinquishing his pulpit to the parishioner who had witnessed a miracle in the days past. Or to someone newly humbled by the Holy Spirit. Sometimes there'd be a sister or brother, repentant of a rash of recent sin, tearfully confessing all to God and family, and the church would weep in embrace, and Deacon Keyes would erupt in song.

> *Coming home, coming home,*
> *Nevermore to roam.*
> *Open wide thine arms of love.*
> *Lord, I'm coming home.*

Perhaps if she'd arrived an hour earlier, she could have been that repentant one, looking for all to take her back as the sweet girl, the late pastor's daughter, who'd turned her back on pursuing a life of sin and wanted only the promises God held for her at home. But then she remembered Roland's admonition to hold her head up high and not to grovel for grace. With that thought, she quickened her step.

As she drew closer to the church, she heard them singing "Jesus Is All the World to Me." It was one of Brent's least favorites, though Deacon Keyes loved to hold his hand extended, taking the congregation to the end of their breath with the final "He's my friiiiieeeeeennnnnndddd." Thus they sang, and Dorothy Lynn knew she would have ample time to slip in, with the thunderous note to camouflage the sound of the opening and closing door.

She waved a small, silent good-bye to Alvin DuBose and slipped into the coatroom. There, hanging where it had since the first of summer, was the pale-green parchment with decorated scrolls at each corner.

The Church Family Is Invited
to the Joining of Two Lives
Pastor Brent Logan
and
Miss Dorothy Lynn Dunbar
Saturday, October 14
10:00 a.m.
Reception to Follow

She took it off the wall and held it close. *It can't be too late.*

Inside, the song had come to an end. Soon the door between the coatroom and the sanctuary would open. Like the thief that she was, Dorothy Lynn tucked herself into a corner, between the wall and the tall cabinet where the extra hymnals, communion plates, and lost-and-found Bibles were stored.

"Still not a word?" The voice belonged to Mrs. Philbin, mother of the worthless bootlegger in Virginia.

"Not a call since last Sunday." Even away from her switchboard, Mrs. Tully's voice was unmistakable.

"Thought I heard there was a telegram."

"You women ought to be ashamed." It was Jessup come to squelch the gossip. "Bad enough askin' for prayer for some poor, wandering child, as if we all don't know who that child is."

"We are merely concerned," Mrs. Tully said. Of the two, she was far more believable in making that claim. "There's to be a wedding on Saturday, and still no bride."

"Are you sure there's going to be a wedding?" Mrs. Philbin sounded downright victorious at the prospect of having someone in town bring about a humiliation equal to her son's.

From her hiding place, Dorothy Lynn clutched the framed invitation. They must have noticed the blank space on the wall amidst the other announcements of Sunday school pancake suppers and the blanket drive for the poor.

As more and more congregants poured into the cloakroom, the missing invitation became the sole topic of conversation.

When had it been taken down?

Who had taken it?

Surely it was here earlier, as several people made it their daily mission to check.

Did Pastor Logan know?

Did he take it down?

Or was it that Mrs. Dunbar, poor soul, who might have done better to show her face in Sunday evening service?

When the hush fell, she knew Brent had entered the room. And then, for the first time in what seemed like forever, she heard his voice. "What is all this?"

Dorothy Lynn wanted to leap from her hiding place right then, climb over the crowd and into his arms. But something in the way he spoke, a barely contained tension, gave her little reassurance that she would be any more welcome than she had been when she came out of nowhere to embrace her brother.

"Sorry about that, Brent," Jessup said, asking absolution for the crowd. "Couldn't herd them out fast enough."

She ventured a peep around the cabinet to see the congregation part like a sea as Brent—nearly a head taller than most of them—walked the path they provided.

"So," said Mrs. Philbin, ever eager to seek a scandal, "is the wedding off?"

A few kind souls hushed her, if for no other reason than to hear his reply.

"Who did this?" Brent asked, edging close to sounding angry. When nobody replied, he repeated the question, louder this time, exposing everyone in the room to the potential of his temper.

A kind of shudder went through the crowd, a blood-lusting thrill, and heads turned from one to another in anticipatory accusation. Soon the silence was broken and indictments began to fly. Names and motives accompanied by pointed fingers and denial. A boisterous crescendo of blame, untouched by the call for silence by Brent, Jessup, and even Rusty Keyes, who simply couldn't abide the discordance.

Finally, to protect the flock of the man she loved, Dorothy Lynn stepped out from her place of hiding and held the evidence in question high above her head. "I took it."

Anybody walking past the church outside might have thought a ghost had appeared from behind the Christian flag, such was the collective gasp that went out. From his spot within the midst of his people, Brent turned to see what had garnered such shocked attention.

"Lynnie. You're home."

No joy, no anger, no adulation or disdain. Just the statement of a simple fact.

Those who had recently been so vocal were struck dumb,

and no one could have thought that their presence would be welcome a minute longer. One by one they left, holding their silence at least as far as the steps, before they would disappear into the night. Or, more likely, to Ma's house, under the guise of bringing good tidings.

Jessup, largely responsible for their swift exit, was the last to leave. In a gesture of unprecedented tenderness, he offered Dorothy Lynn a kiss to her cheek. "Your bags at my place?"

She nodded, not wanting to say another word until it would be for Brent's ears alone.

"I'll see that they get to your ma's."

Then they were alone. Rather, she was, because Brent wordlessly took himself back into the sanctuary.

Dorothy Lynn waited for a moment, not knowing what to do until the words of Roland's favorite hymn came to her heart: *Where he leads me I will follow.*

She stood at the back of the church, inhaling the familiar scent of well-worn wood and soft-paged hymnals. At the front, the blackboard registered fifty-three in attendance last Sunday with an offering of $89.75. Below it, in the family pew, Brent sat with his back to her, his head bowed.

Her footsteps echoed as she walked up the aisle. There should be music playing and a bouquet in her hand. Instead, there was silence and a thin sheet of paper bearing an uncertain promise.

She stopped at the front, having nowhere to go but to the pulpit, or to him. If she sat in the opposite pew, with just the aisle between them, she would feel a thousand miles away. "May I sit with you?"

He said nothing.

Fear, greater than any she experienced on a stage, churned

within, more sour than the taste of H. C. Bendemann's liquor. "Brent—"

Without saying a word, without looking up, he held out his hand and she took it, touching him at last. She brought his hand to her lips and kissed it, going down to her knees where he'd be forced to look in her eyes. "I promised I would come back."

He looked at her, sat up straight, and brought her to sit beside him. "I've been a fool, Lynnie."

"No," she said, finding the idea impossible. Then, knowing that he was never one to utter idle words, she ceased her protest.

"You wouldn't believe the horrors I've allowed myself to imagine."

She could, in fact, while offering realities to trump them. "You told me not to call," she said.

"I know."

"And when I *did* call, you wouldn't talk to me."

"I guess I didn't expect it to last so long."

"But you told me—"

"I know."

She longed for him to say her name again. No one else ever called her Lynnie. "Is it—am I too late, Brent?"

"I could ask you the same thing."

There had been so many moments when his fears might have become reality. When she first took the stage, when she first stepped on the train. The enticing allure of California, the beach, Roland. She'd had one opportunity after another to replace a life spent with him.

"I'm here," she said, having turned her back on all of it.

"And that's supposed to be enough?"

"It's all I have."

His eyes swam with questions, and she felt the tug of

confession in her throat. But every transgression she knew to be a sin had been laid at the feet of Jesus, and his grace enabled her to breathe within Brent's scrutiny.

"Then you've nothing to tell me."

"Oh, no. I have a *world* to tell you."

"Starting with this?" He reached out and touched a finger to her lips, still colored with rouge.

"I think it's pretty," she said, prepared to defend its innocence as she witnessed the battle within him.

In lieu of a response, he cupped the back of her head and brought her to him, touching his lips to hers in a way that granted forgiveness and promise. For all she knew, their last kiss had been yesterday. For this moment, anyway, life in between was reduced to rubble. There would be time enough later—a lifetime of such kisses—to sweep it away and silence any accusing memories.

He drew back, looking at her with curiosity.

"You've changed."

"I have." Of that she was certain.

"And will you tell me now? Everything?"

She touched his face. Already he felt more real than any part of the story she was about to tell.

"I will, but not here. Will you walk me home? You know someone's gone to Ma, and she'll be frantic."

"Of course. But first, I have something for you."

She stayed no more than a step apart from him as he turned off the lights throughout the church and locked the doors. The little parsonage was just a few steps away, and she'd only been inside a handful of times since Brent began to court her—both of them keenly aware of the scrutiny of Heron's Nest. Still, there were no surprises when he struck a match and lit an ancient lamp, illuminating the poor, shabby room that she longed to call home.

"Wait here," he said, before disappearing into the bedroom. Seconds later he appeared, carrying a guitar case made of rich, chestnut-colored leather. Of course, he didn't know about the one she'd acquired at Strawn Brothers, but this was far more beautiful and luxurious.

"Oh, Brent—it's just what I needed."

He grinned, obviously pleased. "Your mother told me you'd seen Donny. And I thought you might have returned his, but even before I knew, I wanted you to have something of your own. So . . . have a seat."

His words were confusing at first; then, as understanding came, she backed to the worn sofa and sat down, allowing Brent to place the leather case in her lap. With trembling fingers, she opened the latches to reveal a beautiful new instrument—wood like silk, the color of honey, and the initials *DLL* burned within the curve. Dorothy Lynn Logan. Her new name.

"Oh, darling," she said, her heart too full to say anything else. She lifted the instrument from its case and strummed a chord, wincing at the discordant sound. They laughed at the noise.

"That's not what I imagined," Brent said, sitting beside her.

"I can tune it. Not this minute, because my pipe—" she stopped herself, redirecting her comment away from what would forever be Donny's guitar—"is with my luggage. But later? You'll see." She kissed his cheek. "It'll be perfect."

The night had turned cold when they stepped outside, and she gravitated instantly to his warmth. With his arm wrapped around her, they walked the twisting aisles of Heron's Nest and the dark, familiar path through the forest to her mother's home.

At first, she did not burden him with anything for which she'd sought redemption. But the rest—all the sweet, untarnished memories, all the soul-searching moments of self-reflection—all these she told with unbridled enthusiasm. Tales that—here, so close to the ground—seemed more like the stuff of fantasy. She tried to capture the sound of thousands of voices raised in worship; she sang a few phrases of her song; she imitated the snooty concierge at the Hotel Alexandria and racked her brain trying to recall all the costumes at Silverlight Studios. She wept for the brother who would not come home.

They'd come to that point in the road that had afforded them their first opportunity to share their secrets, and Brent pulled her close just as he had when their love was new.

"There's more," she said, wondering how she could ever fit her confession between them.

"I know." His words puffed in steam between them, so much sweeter than the smoke of a cigarette. "This man—"

"He saved me, my darling. From a life of wondering. He showed me everything I could have, if only I would walk away from you. From everything that's real. From everything I've ever really wanted."

She wished her presence could speak for her, that she could crawl inside his skin somehow and let him feel her love and be assured to a depth no words could ever reach. There remained a bridge to be crossed between the last man who had held her and the one who shared her breath this night.

"I did some stupid, stupid things, Brent. Things that I regret so deeply. . . ."

"Is coming home one of them?"

She looked up and rested her palm against his face, which felt warm despite the chill of the evening.

"Never. But you should know—"

"I will. Someday. But for tonight, what was lost has been

found." Then he cupped her face in his hands and kissed her as deep as the trees grew high.

She would have willingly stayed there all night—for the rest of her life, really, were there some way to construct a dwelling around their embrace. In time, though, Brent pulled away, then stepped away, until only the touch of their hands kept them connected.

"You need to get home," he said, his breath ragged in a way she recognized from times before, a way that dragged her heartbeat with it.

"I am home."

He brought her hands to his lips. "I mean, to your mother's. Before the whole town shows up."

Still holding her hand, he guided her back onto the path, and they walked together as they had so many nights in the life they'd shared so far. Then, as always, they came into the clearing and Dorothy Lynn saw the familiar silhouette in the lamplight.

"Ma!"

Her feet leapt to new life, and she started to run up the path, but stopped short at the tug of Brent's hand.

"Run with me," she said, glancing back.

"Go on. You two have a wedding to plan. I'll catch up."

He kissed her again and held her so tightly she feared she'd break. Then, delighted and whole, she walked halfway up the path to her home before turning on her heel and running back to jump into his waiting arms.

"Do you see, darling?" she whispered, loving the feel of being lifted off the ground. "I will always, and forever, choose you."

One generation passeth away, and another
generation cometh: but the earth abideth for ever.

ECCLESIASTES 1:4

BREATH OF ANGELS
11:22 P.M.

The room is never completely dark, so she can still see the image on the photograph. Charlotte Hill, she supposes, is long gone. The night staff is never comfortable with visitors, not even those waiting out a death vigil. Because really, given the circumstances of those who have "moved on," what night isn't?

The last thing she remembers before giving in to sleep is Charlotte's question.

"And who's this?"

She left the photograph on the bedside table along with a pen as some sort of hint, she supposes, for Lynnie to identify the young man and woman in the picture.

With hair newly bobbed, she is wearing her peach-colored chiffon blouse and brocade skirt, Brent a brown suit. Lynnie knows this not only because she clearly remembers the day the picture was taken, but also because they'd had the photographer tint the prints.

Little wonder that nobody ever realizes it is a wedding picture upon first glance. There are no flowers, no veil. There had been a dress painstakingly sewn by her sister, but as she discovered the night before the wedding, it proved too ill-fitting to be worn with any serious intention. She'd been

347

tempted to run to the parsonage in the wee morning hours, pound on the door, and tell Brent the dress was unsuitable and she was leaving for St. Louis to retrieve her mother's, but his trust—even as they joined their hands in matrimony—was still too fragile.

When she went to the market, she'd tell him, "I'll be back."

When she went to visit her newborn niece, she promised to return.

When she drove a car for the first time, went to the movies, succumbed to the twilight sleep of childbirth, she promised always and forever to choose him over any other. When she wandered into the darkness of mourning as she handed each one over to Jesus—two little girls, one little boy, and a grown hero in the Second World War—he alone gave her a reason to live.

And even when she stood bathed in the light of Glory, ready to meet her Savior, she followed the tide back to where Brent's gnarled hand clasped hers. She'd opened her eyes to find him watching, waiting for one more chance to say, "Lynnie. You're home."

Months later, when it was he who slipped away, she'd kissed his wrinkled cheek and made her final promise.

All of this she wants to write on the back of the picture, but the space is so small and the story so big. Still, she turns it over, and in the pale-blue night-light writes, *My life.*

And no more.

Her head fills with the words of a long-forgotten song. Not the one newly sprung to life, but one forever lost—tucked away in the pocket of a pretty pink dress—its words half-rubbed away for the shame of longing. It's never had a tune, until now, when a million voices rise up in melody.

> *My world is full of pleasant places,*
> *Surrounded by familiar faces,*
> *Yet sometimes I yearn for life beyond these lines.*

Finally she feels the Lord's blessing to have such a yearning, and the boundary line is broken.

She opens her mouth and sings, *Jesus is coming . . .* But it's Charlotte's voice she hears, which is just fine for Charlotte. Jesus will come for her, but is he coming for Lynnie? Or has she had it wrong all this time?

Late. Late. Late.

She feels both moss and mud caught up between her toes as she flies across the soft carpet of the forest floor, and somewhere far off the promise of a City beckons.

He's waiting.

He's *been* waiting.

And Lynnie runs.

DISCUSSION QUESTIONS

1. At the beginning of the story, we meet Dorothy Lynn on the night before her 107th birthday. What are your thoughts—or fears—about living for an entire century?

2. Dorothy Lynn worships God through her music—both in her secluded spot in the woods and on a stage in front of thousands of people. Is the worship at both venues equally valid? What are the pitfalls of each?

3. Do you think Dorothy Lynn's decision to join Roland on the jaunt to Los Angeles calls her love for Brent into question? Why do you think she wanted to go? Did you approve of her choice? Why or why not?

4. In Dorothy Lynn's sister, Darlene, we see a woman who has embraced many elements of modern womanhood while still exemplifying a very traditional role. In today's world, is it possible for women to be both forward-thinking and traditional? What are the challenges—then and now—to living that way?

5. The real-life Aimee Semple McPherson was one of the most powerful women of her day—a true pioneer in evangelism and one of the first women to hold a radio broadcasting license. She also owned a movie production studio and published several magazines. How important is it for

women to have key roles in the work of evangelism? What contributions can women make in spreading the gospel that are different from what men are able to do?

6. The story brings Dorothy Lynn together with Charlotte Hill—a young, heretofore unknown great-great-niece. What opportunities will Charlotte have in her life that Dorothy Lynn never had? What challenges?

7. Dorothy Lynn's brother, Donny, could not face returning to his prewar life after his return from war. Have you ever known anyone who had a similar reaction to returning from military service? Do you think Donny made the right choice? What do you think of Dorothy Lynn's decision to let him pursue a new path?

8. What were your reactions to Dorothy Lynn's assembled family—Roy and Darlene's descendants? How do their intergenerational dynamics compare to those in your own family? What are some ways extended families can stay close despite the passing of time and the challenges of keeping in touch—or is that even possible?

9. Do you think Dorothy Lynn is truly attracted to Roland Lundi, or is she more enthralled with everything he represents? What evidence do you have for your answer? How would her life have been different if she had chosen to stay in California with him?

10. Have you ever come to a fork in the road like the one Dorothy Lynn faces? How did—or would—you go about choosing which path to take? And what kinds of "little" choices do we make every day that contribute toward the larger path our lives end up taking?

11. Ecclesiastes 2:11 (NLT) says, "But as I looked at everything I had worked so hard to accomplish, it was all so meaningless—like chasing the wind. There was nothing really worthwhile anywhere." Is that an accurate assessment of Dorothy Lynn's life? Why or why not? How did the passages from Ecclesiastes used throughout this story influence the way you read it?

12. Why is worship an important part of the Christian life? What is your favorite worship song? Why?

A NOTE FROM THE AUTHOR

I KNEW I WANTED to write a series set in the 1920s, but I was having a hard time convincing anyone that it would be a good idea. I'm a Christian writer of Christian fiction, and—let's face it—the Jazz Age isn't exactly known for its piety.

We call these years the Roaring Twenties, and they were indeed a time of roaring change. Men returned from fighting the Great War on foreign soil with a new taste for sophistication and adventure. Women, having won the right to vote, stormed the walls of feminine convention, shedding their long hair and long skirts in a new zest for freedom. Thrust into a world where wild parties replaced church socials and cars with rumble seats stole the road from Sunday buggy rides, young girls saw the fair-skinned, long-legged flapper heralded as the new feminine ideal.

So how to incorporate all of that into a series exploring issues of faith? While I was pondering that, my agent extraordinaire, Bill Jensen, asked me, "Have you ever heard of Aimee Semple McPherson?" I was googling even before he finished speaking, and a whole new world opened up to me. Rising to her calling in a way that would have been impossible in any other decade, evangelist Aimee Semple McPherson brought her urgent plea for repentance to small towns with her traveling revivals, also launching a multimedia ministry through her magazine, *The Bridal Call*, as well as radio and film. Her bobbed hair and attention to fashion made her a towering figure of modern faith, bringing millions to worship at her Los Angeles church.

And there was my focus. Not just flappers, not just floozies, but godly Christian women who were afforded astonishing opportunities to explore their gifts in a world that was becoming increasingly accepting of their contributions.

The idea of beginning this book at the end of Dorothy Lynn's life turned out to be the jumping-off point for the whole story. I actually watch the *Today* show every morning; I see that spinning jam jar and the faces of those who have lived for a century or more and wonder about the things they have witnessed. Still, there was a crucial element missing, because not everybody would agree that the final years of Dorothy Lynn's life were resplendent with blessings. Then I went to a funeral for the mother of a dear friend, Matt. Years earlier she had suffered a stroke, during which she was given a glimpse of the life to come. She spent her final years on earth with a frustrated longing—grateful for the additional time with her family, but eager to return to the glory she knew awaited her. I went home that afternoon and wrote and wrote and wrote.

All for a Song is ultimately a story of longing, of searching for what you think you lack. If we are to yearn for anything, let it be for the return of Jesus Christ. In the meantime, let us love one another, giving gifts of grace.

ABOUT THE AUTHOR

AWARD-WINNING AUTHOR ALLISON PITTMAN left a seventeen-year teaching career in 2005 to follow the Lord's calling into the world of Christian fiction, and God continues to bless her step of faith. Her novels *For Time and Eternity* and *Forsaking All Others* were both finalists for the Christy Award for excellence in Christian fiction, and her novel *Stealing Home* won the American Christian Fiction Writers' Carol Award. She heads up a successful, thriving writers group in San Antonio, Texas, where she lives with her husband, Mike, their three sons, and the canine star of the family—Stella.

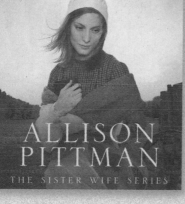

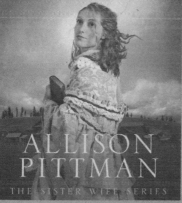